The Savannah Stories

Rotten To The Core

The Savannah Stories

Rotten To The Core

J.L. Lemon

Copyright © 2015 by J.L. Lemon. Printed by Lulu.com 2015. All rights reserved. No part of this book may be used or reproduced in any manner whatsoever without written permission, except in the case of brief quotations embodied in critical articles or reviews.

ISBN-13: 978-0-9909589-3-2

Published 2015

"What A Wonderful World" © David Weiss and Bob Thiele

For Dad and in memory of Mom

Seeing true love through you both proves some fairy tales are real and that love never dies, no matter what. Ever.

For Aunt Virginia

I am blessed to have you in my life as both an aunt and a close friend. You are an inspiration to all who know you.

Many a good hanging prevents a bad marriage

William Shakespeare

1

NOW

By noon he checked into Atlanta's Westin Peachtree hotel, his room a cool pleasant cocoon from the sweltering heat. Frankenmuth, Michigan, his hometown, rarely experienced such miserable weather. He preferred the milder clime where he and his brother could kick back and drink a beer while they watched the Pistons lose again.

Personal business brought him to the New York of the South. He owed a debt to a particular homicide detective. Once he settled in with his laptop, he clicked on a search engine and typed Savannah Prince Rutherford.

Several pages popped onto the screen, each one highlighting the name in bold black letters. Most referred to murders she investigated, the last, most notable being the Bob Davenport murder.

He scrolled down the results until an unusual sight appeared. Savannah and her sister Georgia competed on a cooking show called Family Throwdown. According to the website, the two sisters reigned as champions for five episodes until a husband/wife team defeated them. He skimmed the page in search of one piece of information. He clicked on Savannah's profile picture. There it was. Detective Savannah Prince resided in Dunwoody, a suburb of Atlanta, but he saw no specific address. Of course, he thought. Cops were always paranoid, afraid of retribution, so they never listed an address. One particular cop *should* be paranoid, he smiled at her image, because he was more resourceful than other people. He knew how to find her house. He'd simply let her lead him to it.

Years ago he drove the route a few times from Sandy Springs to the police station on Maple Drive. The drive from downtown was shorter, about eight miles. He climbed in his rented car, struck out for Buckhead. He merged onto I-75 North then onto I-85 until the exit for Piedmont Road appeared. A couple of more turns and there it was – the police station for Zone 2. It resembled a spacious house with patrol units and detective's personal cars parked in back.

He waited for her shift to end and was surprised when she exited the building twenty minutes after he arrived. She wore jeans, sneakers and a dark blue blouse. Not her standard work attire. Also atypical – the baby in the carrier she toted to the car. The baby, along with her marriage, surprised him the most about her. Rare as rocking horse shit, his brother always said. No one in their right mind said domesticated and Savannah Prince in the same breath, not unless they cracked a joke.

She secured the infant seat in the back of a newer blue Dodge Charger, got in then pulled out of the station lot. He used discretion when following her. She may have been a drunk but she was a cautious drunk. One who would notice the Honda traveling two cars behind her, mirroring her lane changes and turns.

He followed the Charger to Dunwoody. She hung a right on Tilly Mill Road. He stayed back, in case she pulled into an entrance. A minute later the Charger's brake lights lit up, the turn signal blinked on and she made a slow turn into a driveway. It was then he drove past, taking note of the address. 4886 Tilly Mill Road. That's all he needed...

O   O   O

The next day he ventured back, turning from Mt. Vernon Road onto Tilly Mill Road. The latter was a long street. He counted seventeen, no, eighteen intersections before finally arriving at the four thousand block.

Tilly Mill Road was a picturesque avenue with abundant tall, leafy trees crowding the front yards all the way to the street. There were so many oaks, pines and various trees one could not see from one house to another. Properties were lined with the beasts, leaving a mere slot of space for driveways. Mailboxes, both elegant and plain, stood beside the entry of each drive.

He let off the gas, coasting until the mailbox for 4886 came into view. He pulled to the curb of 4884, easing forward until a sliver of space between pines revealed the reason for this jaunt. Wearing jeans and a gray APD t-shirt, Savannah Rutherford stood outside, garden hose in hand, watering her hibiscus.

Her husband Ennis – another detective – still had four hours left to his shift. He'd met Ennis. The Texan seemed less volatile than Savannah, at least until provoked. The two moved from the little house he remembered to the larger abode in Dunwoody, away from the hustle and bustle and overcrowded highways and high crime.

The neighborhood was newer than her previous residence and the home larger, more elegant. A one story something-or-other-type house. He'd have called it a ranch house but his wife would have known the exact style. She bandied terms like French Colonial, Cape Cod, and Tudor around like common knowledge. His wife's depth of many things not only impressed but astounded him. She wouldn't approve of his watching this woman or of him following her. It was rude to track people like animals, she'd probably explain. But, he'd say, this wasn't just any person. This woman lived to destroy others.

Savannah's house was wide and deep – he guessed two thousand square feet, maybe less – with a traditional Southern porch that took up half the front of the house, complete with white painted balusters and a couple of white wicker chairs. She'd added a couple of potted flowers, one on each side of the front door, each plant a deep purple.

The lush lawn looked well cared for, the flower beds immaculate, and the two massive oak trees shaded their house from the searing afternoon sun. But it was the hedgerow beneath what appeared to be a bedroom window that sparked an idea. A possible hiding place for later.

Ah, the happy little family, he smiled to himself. Mama, Daddy and baby living in a nice house with two cars, her Charger and his Ram, and all was right with the world. For now.

He watched Savannah water the flowers with care. The bright red blooms reminded him of his wife's flower bed at home. She loved gardening and in spring, summer and fall, spent as much time outside as inside. To see Savannah tending a flower garden was foreign to him.

She'd changed over the years but he'd bet his life underneath the domestic shell lurked the same stubborn wiseass he remembered, the loudmouth drunk he loathed.

He wanted her on edge, to throw her off balance. His campaign began simply enough. Hang up calls. Nag her with an incessantly ringing phone and Savannah would probably blow her top. He started yesterday dialing the home phone, waiting for her to answer, waiting for her anger to engage and to slam the phone down. She kept her calm for now but it wouldn't last. He never said a word, didn't have to. On a few occasions, without uttering one curse, her inflection told the anonymous caller his fate if she caught him. The temper simmered beneath the surface, waiting to explode, he sensed it with each call. Every ring of her phone flustered Savannah more, increasing her anxiety, her anger, her questions.

He prided himself on being one of the few people capable of ruffling that composed woman sprinkling her cherished hibiscus. He'd driven her to near violence when she was a rookie cop. In fact, she *had* laid hands on him. Of course he had laid hands on her too so tit for tat, he figured. She chalked up a victory with their last meeting but this time would be different…

O O O

Riding the Weston Peachtree glass elevator to the fiftieth floor, he closed his eyes, running his plan through his mind again. First things first. Approach her then immobilize her. Speed and agility were essential.

Between the police training and her brother Seth's self defense tutelage, she'd strike back quick if he hesitated. Anyone foolish enough to misjudge her swiftness and strength deserved to get their asses kicked. Like that bastard Jeffrey Holland. If only he'd cut her throat then, it would have saved *him* the trouble of doing it *now*. But Holland, like so many others, assumed he controlled her, assumed he'd broken her spirit as well as her body but Savannah was tougher than most people realized.

The elevator chimed, the doors slid open. He opened his eyes to see an attractive brunette climb aboard. Being the gentleman, he nodded, said hello. She gave a terse nod, turned and waited for the doors to close again. Just like Savannah, he sneered. A snob who thought she was better than him. His wife wasn't like that. No, his wife was down-to-earth, courteous to anyone she met, whether friend or stranger. The bitch in front of him – and Savannah – could learn a lot from his beautiful wife.

The elevator stopped at the fiftieth floor and without looking back, stepped around the woman. He proceeded to his room, slipped in the key card, returned it to his pocket. He booked a spacious, elegant room to organize his thoughts and strategy. He angled past the king size bed covered in pristine white sheets and soft white blanket. He made his way to the window, pulled the floor length beige drapes open. His room overlooked the northeast side of Atlanta. Dunwoody was located there, snug between Sandy Springs and Norcross.

There was only one snag in his plan he had yet to solve. Savannah had that baby. The kid might enter into the equation when he made his move and he didn't need the extra hassle of a crying brat on his hands. Of course the kid provided hefty leverage for her to cooperate too. Perhaps he should catch her cradling her bundle of joy and instead of threatening the mighty detective, point the gun at the kid and see how mouthy and bold Mama was.

He pulled himself from the fantasy, strode to the closet, reached in his pocket for a small key. He retrieved a small black suitcase with a padlock on it. He unlocked the case. The supplies were still there, all undisturbed, all in order as he'd placed them. Always meticulous. Always in order. His wife appreciated his neatness and told him so on several occasions. No cleaning up after this man, no way. He washed and ironed his own clothes, putting them away according to his own preference. She hadn't understood his system but she respected it, left it alone.

He removed the spring assisted folding knife, flicked it open to its full ten inch length. The razor sharp five inch stainless steel hawkbill blade was sure to grab Savannah's attention, especially when nestled at her throat. Rummaging the rest of his supplies, he checked the .45 automatic and the extra ammunition. All there. Rolls of duct tape. Twenty feet of sturdy rope. Plastic drop cloths. Handcuffs. Oh yes. The handcuffs. They were more symbolic than functional for him. He couldn't wait to cinch the bracelets around her wrists. See how the bitch liked wearing them herself, he thought. Show her how it felt to struggle for freedom, knowing it was futile.

She'd underestimated him during their last meeting. And she'd soon find that out.

2

NOW

Cleaning the house was one thing. It required a vacuum, dusting cloth and a few other items that wiped away dirt, filth and germs. Cleaning out photos and sorting through them, on the other hand, entailed more than Savannah bargained for. It involved going back in time, recalling good or bad memories, reliving situations she either wished she could forget or wished she could relive.

At the current time, she wished for a match. Any open flame sufficed, anything to reduce the picture to ashes. For such a handsome guy Toby Jackson had been a mean son of a bitch. The picture, taken at Georgia's birthday party, showed Toby with his girlfriend – a newly minted rookie cop – both presenting mile wide smiles as his muscular arms enfolded her snug against his chest. The young woman in the picture sure looked happy for an idiot, Savannah reflected. Little did she know that in a few short weeks after that photo, she'd be sporting bruises on her kidneys from his ridiculous accusation of her sleeping with another guy – ironically another cop. Yes, she thought now, what a fool I was. Resisting the urge to crumple the photo, she sat it atop the trash pile.

The next photo showed her with Adam Rafferty, an academy classmate *and* the very cop Toby accused her of sleeping with. This picture she'd keep. Taken at a police charity function, the couple both dressed casual in t-shirts, jeans and sneakers for the event. By that time, she and Adam promoted their friendship to bona fide dating. Savannah felt safe and happy with Adam. During their days at the academy, when her energy flagged and the days ran long, she indulged in a daydream or two about Adam. After all, he wasn't exactly a dog in the looks department. Oh no. He had classic good looks, with a mixture of James Garner and Tony Curtis in their younger years. The guy belonged on a romance novel and with his brawny physique with the gun belt strapped across those lean, strong hips, he epitomized female fantasy to a tee.

Unlike Toby, her mother would have loved Adam. Kind, good manners and soft spoken. She and Mr. Rafferty made a handsome couple, according to Georgia who took an instant shine to him. That sentiment hadn't lasted when Adam broke off the relationship, devastating Savannah. Cupid aimed his arrow at a waitress who worked at their favorite café and got lucky with a twofor that time. His arrow ricocheted off the waitress and imbedded itself in Adam. Mr. Rafferty soon dumped Savannah to begin dating the waitress that looked ludicrously cute in the skimpy little skirt and apron. Painful as it was to lose him, Savannah wished them both well. Through the grapevine, she heard he'd married his waitress and had a kid or two. Glancing back to the photo, she found herself wondering what happened to her good friend. They lost touch after his marriage and hadn't crossed paths since.

She placed the picture in the keep pile. She'd dedicated the morning to cleaning out drawers and closets. Maternity leave afforded valuable time for Lily's care and in the meantime gave Mama the opportunity to clean the house and purge the past. Plus, the long overdue task of sorting photos was cathartic. Tossing old painful memories, keeping the good ones. She planned to organize them in albums for the future when Lily could appreciate the visual family history. For now though, their baby's biggest concerns remained simple. Food, sleep, clean diapers and lots of love. She slept soundly in her crib for thirty minutes so far, a blessing Savannah thanked God for since the baby kept her awake an extra hour the previous night.

The phone rang for the third time that morning. The last two had been hang-up calls. It rang a total of twenty-one times with hang-ups in less than thirty-six hours. All when Ennis was at work. The annoyance of such interruptions stoked her anger. Not only were they unnecessary but keeping Lily asleep proved harder than herding cats, as Ennis might say.

She picked up the phone with a succinct, "Hello." Silence ensued. She repeated the greeting. This time she heard a little cough that the man tried to disguise by covering the receiver.

She lowered her voice to avoid waking Lily, "Either say something or stop calling." Resisting the urge to slam the phone in the cradle, she dropped it into place, waiting for it to ring back. Her brain flipped through a mental Rolodex of people who might love driving her nuts. Toby Jackson rated in the top ten but he was safely behind bars for molesting his daughter. Then there was Cole Jordan who really loved to irritate her but he was busy trying not to drop the soap in his own prison showers to bother her. And her number one fan, Jeffrey Holland, also sat in prison for torturing and killing nearly two dozen women in two states. He'd had his turn with her and Georgia but they'd proven too strong and clever for him. Holland might have been the best suspect for the weird calls but Savannah knew him. Mr. Jeffrey did not play phone tag games. He came straight for whatever he wanted and that was her. Until he was released, she had no realistic fear of him. That's when her mind drew a blank. Sure she put away criminals of all sorts, some threatened her with violence but that went with being a cop.

Picking up the phone, she dialed her colleague Christine Clark. Past the hellos, she stated her request, "Would you check the incoming calls to our home phone? I've been getting hang-ups for two days now. And I mean a lot of them."

"Not your normal telemarketers?"

"No and it always rings when Ennis isn't here." She heard Christine pecking on a keyboard. Savannah prayed the answer came quick and with a name attached. She'd hunt down the nagging caller and beat him with the damn phone if she had to.

"I assume you don't want him to know," Christine said.

"Not until I have a name. It's a guy calling."

"No talking or obscene breathing like a teenage boy pulling a prank?"

"Teenagers usually don't schedule calls when the husband isn't around. I need to know how seriously to take this jerk. I've got Lily to worry about now." Just to be sure, "Would you run a check on Jeffrey and Cole, make sure they're still tucked away in their cozy prison cells?"

"Sure. Anything else?"

Although a long shot, something nettled her about Toby. Maybe it was due to the reminiscing she'd done that morning but running his name made sense too. His parting words from his jail cell rang in her mind. *The next time I see you, I'll kill you.* "Run the name Tobias Jerome Jackson too."

"Boy, his folks didn't like him, did they? *Tobias Jerome?* I'll get on it and call you back when I find something." Christine paused then, "Savannah, this guy could be dangerous and you're all alone with the baby. Sure you don't want to tell Ennis?"

"I'll tell him tonight. Thanks, Christine."

They concluded the conversation and Savannah resumed sorting pictures. One of Toby and her together. Another of Toby. Toby, Toby, Toby. She tossed them in the trash with complete gratification. She ran across photos of her academy graduation, a few of them with Georgia, Leah and Seth and more with Adam Rafferty.

A picture of her with her mother came next. Savannah needed no date on the back to tell her when it was taken. A year before Charlene's diagnosis. Her mother, dressed in her favorite Christmas sweater and slacks, looked so healthy and happy as she smiled with her husband and girls that holiday. R.J. stood behind his wife, a glass of scotch in his hand but still smiling at Seth who snapped the picture. Charlene had an arm around each daughter, pulling them close for the photo. Everyone grinned like fools, Savannah mentioned at the time. Now she wanted that moment back, to relive it just once more – and grin like a fool.

Her throat tightened as the urge to weep swelled in her chest. She placed the picture aside, turned it face down. The painful memories never faded, she winced. Never. Charlene's outer beauty was evident. She reminded all who saw her of Rita Hayworth. But her inner beauty flourished with a loving, generous soul. She made friends easily, always wanted to help, went to church, knew her Bible and believed the Lord's every word. Then she died, leaving the world one angel less and her family without their rock and stability.

"Okay," Savannah stated matter-of-factly. She sniffed back tears while gathering her mother's photo and the remaining ones, placed them all back in the shoebox from where they came. "Time for a break. A long break."

The phone rang and she braced herself. This time she wouldn't be so gentle to the bastard ruining her day. "Hello," she barked into the receiver.

"Yikes," Christine shivered. "Don't know about the perv, but you've convinced me to leave you alone."

She felt silly – and regretful – that she'd yelled at her friend, "Sorry, Christine. Figured it was him again."

"Got a number though it doesn't really help. It's coming from a burn phone. It pings off the cell towers around the Westin Peachtree. Of the names you mentioned, only Tobias Jackson was released from prison. Jeffrey and Cole are still at Norcross. From what I gathered, Jackson got out a month ago but is still on probation for child molestation."

Toby was free. Running around the city for weeks without her knowledge. Now what did she do?   Was it him on the phone or some other crazy she'd forgotten about?

"One more thing," Christine mentioned with unease. "Ennis caught me running Jackson's name. He wasn't happy, especially when I refused to tell him why."

"I'll explain everything tonight," she promised.

3

NOW

He hunkered behind the hedge that lined the Rutherford's open bedroom window. Savannah and Ennis left the blinds closed but raised the window a couple of inches, he assumed, for fresh air. Fresh, hot, humid summer air. Welcome to Atlanta. The travel guides failed to mention how damn blistering the city was in late spring and early summer. The stifling heat reminded him of a desert except for the clinging humidity he never acclimated to. He hated Atlanta because of the weather but his wife loved it. He'd do anything for her, even live in this miserable hellhole.

He'd tuned his hearing to the couple retiring to the bedroom at a late eleven thirty. He cocked his head this way and that until he could barely see through the slats in the blinds.

They argued for ten minutes over one name. Toby Jackson. Why was she checking on him, Ennis demanded to know. Her response: *Because Toby vowed to kill her when he got out of prison – and guess who's out of prison?*

Then Savannah broached the subject of the mysterious hang up calls.   Once Ennis heard about them, he recited a list of rules and regulations she should adhere to, to keep her and the baby safe. Predictably, Savannah balked at most, bursting into an indignant – yet subdued – argument about feeling like a prisoner in her own home.   A situation easily remedied with assertiveness and Smith & Wesson, she said, punctuating the statement by lifting her .38.

Through the blinds he caught sight of the .38 in her hand.   She planned to be armed at all times and that complicated matters.   He'd deal with that later, work it into his plans.   For now he chanced another glimpse inside.   He squinted through the slats to see Savannah shrug from her blouse.   She turned her back to the window and his gut twisted. Dozens of white shiny scars slashed across her back giving him pause. He'd read Jeffrey Holland brutally beat her but seeing the results warned him not to underestimate Savannah Rutherford either.   Anyone who survived a beating that horrendous was no weak-willed creature.   She possessed a strength he overlooked in the time they'd known each other.

She changed into a pair of pajamas the color of her blue eyes.   No matter his resentment toward her, Savannah did have beautiful eyes.   He remembered that.   Only problem was she used them for several things, not just seeing.   She cried, laughed, lashed out and judged with them but her specialty – ripping people apart with one look.

"How's your case going?" she tried changing the subject.

"Stalled," he replied.   "I can't get Roger Ferguson's son to contact me. Tried all day."

"Jimmy's his name, right?"

Ennis pulled his pajama bottoms over his hips.   He adopted a snooty tone, "He prefers James."

"He may be out of town. It is the weekend." She sat on the edge of the bed, stretching her back and rolling her shoulder, "Lord, babies are heavier than you think."

"Allow me," Ennis settled behind her, rubbing her shoulders, the fingers kneading slow and deep until she groaned a thank you.

"I'm taking flowers to Mama tomorrow," she said through a contented moan.

"Oh yeah," Ennis replied. "This week is her birthday."

He watched her head tip forward until her chin touched her chest. "M-hmm," she said. "I'll take flowers this week and Georgia will replace them next week with hers."

Ennis kept working on one spot in particular until she jerked, pulling away with a mild whimper. He drew her back to him, telling her to stay still, "You've got that knot again. It takes a while to work out." He waited for her to relax before beginning again, "Sure you feel up to going right now? You've been kinda down lately."

"I'm going. Mama depends on those flowers. I let her down when she was sick, I'm not letting her down now."

"You didn't let her down, sugar. You did the best you could."

She shrugged away from his touch, leveling an *are-you-insane* glare at him, "Were you there?"

Squinting between the blinds, he noticed Ennis learned quick. Her husband shook his head, lifting his hands in surrender, "No, I wasn't but it kills me to see you berate yourself about it all the time. In my opinion, your mama would have understood. She knew you, babe. She knew you did your best."

He expected Savannah to jump down Hubby's throat with a scathing lecture. That's how he remembered her. Lightning fast temper that burned red hot. Instead she sighed, resigned, "I'm going to bed." She leaned to her husband, kissed him then crawled beneath the covers.

He watched Ennis shake his head hopelessly, switch off the light. In the moonlight filtering through the blinds he saw Ennis snuggle behind her, draping his arm over her waist to hold her close. After a delicate kiss, her patient husband bid her goodnight.

So she felt guilty over her mother's illness. Who would have guessed? He only recalled an angry young woman pickled to the gills with bourbon, daring the world to step over some imaginary line which, in turn, declared an unseen imaginary war with her. He'd done that a few times, a few times were on purpose. She fought like a wildcat when provoked, whether physically or verbally. Either way, he'd held his own. Brought her down a notch or two back then too. He intended to bring her to her knees now. All that was required was a good, detailed plan to cage the wildcat.

4

NOW

Stately pines and mature oak and magnolia trees shaded the gently rolling hills of Westover Memorial Park Cemetery. An assortment of flowers contrasted against the sprawling eighty-three acre carpet of green grass. In the distance, pink azaleas and camellias accented the oriental meditation garden built back in nineteen seventy-four, sixty-two years after the cemetery's creation. From spring-like vibrant pinks and deep purples to autumn's copper, crimson and gold, Westover brought beauty and life to a place with so much sadness and death.

Ennis turned left off Wheeler Road into the cemetery, easing the Charger at a leisure pace down the narrow drive. Flower arrangements dotted the landscape, neatly assembled in their respective vases.

The car passed beneath an area of thick, established oaks, their limbs stretching overhead in graceful arms to provide shade along the way to her mother's grave.

The smell of freshly mowed grass hung heavy in the warm humid air. The staff maintained the grounds with attentive care, ensuring angel statues and various monuments looked their best, that the driveway was clean and clear of debris and that headstones received proper care.

Savannah noticed many vases burgeoned with flowers, real and silk. Others had a single stem protruding from the top, waving like a lonely hand in the breeze.

Ennis slowed at an intersecting road. Savannah pointed left. It was an unconscious habit since Ennis knew his way to the grave as well as she did. After the turn Savannah focused on Charlene's resting place. The sight forced her to look twice. Inside Charlene's brass vase sat six red roses. The sun wilted the once beautiful blooms, leaving their blackening heads bowing in symbolic remorse.

The car stopped. Ennis tended to Lily in the back seat while Savannah headed to the grave, her own floral contribution in hand. Setting her flowers aside, she bent down to see a handwritten note attached to one of the rose stems in the vase. "My Dearest" it read.

"Georgia put those out?" Ennis asked, trying not to disturb their sleeping daughter in the carrier he held. Evidently he hadn't seen the note, "She doesn't normally use real flowers."

The corners of her mouth lifted in a sad smile, "Daddy. Sometimes he brings flowers. Always red roses." She crouched to brush the dried leaves and grass from her mother's headstone until the brass and granite plates were both spotless. Without fail she placed a bouquet of flowers at Charlene's grave on her birthday. She and Georgia agreed to a system. Georgia had Christmas, Savannah had their mother's birthday and they both shared custody at Mother's Day. They allowed a week after each occasion then the other sister replaced the flowers with their own. As R.J. proved, he occasionally exercised his ability to surprise people and placed six roses in the vase. Savannah imagined him staggering his way up the narrow concrete walkway, flowers in one hand, a scotch bottle in the other. He probably spent more time at the grave than anyone realized. Savannah guessed their marriage was, like any other marriage, more than what people saw on the surface. No matter how tumultuous the argument or how drunk her father got, the two seemed to share a special bond and a love only they understood.

The name Charlene Lynette Prince shined through just as the sun broke free of the clouds overhead. It was as if God smiled on her mother's resting place. She still missed her mother, even after all the years she'd been gone. When she looked at her name, Savannah remembered her beautiful smile, soft voice, her bountiful joy and abiding faith in God. Most of all, she recalled the happy times they shared, the Christmases and Thanksgivings and birthdays. Then her mind inevitably sank to the darker moments toward the end of her mother's life. The pain she suffered as the cancer slowly stole her life away. Savannah remembered wanting to cherish each breath Charlene took but couldn't because it was an agonizing struggle for every one of them.

"Here's the flowers." Ennis extended the bouquet of lilies – her mother's favorite.

He'd seen Savannah slip into the gloomy reflective mood upon sight of the grave and, as always, tried to pull her from the terrible memories. Ennis retrieved his hanky, dabbed a falling tear from her cheek, "It's harder on you this year than before. Probably because of Lily."

Their newborn daughter did inspire thoughts and reflections of yesteryear when Savannah, Georgia and their mother all shared laughs, stories and hugs. Now Savannah was a mama and she wanted to be a good one, like her sweet mother. She nodded then glanced at their baby girl in the carrier, "I'll put these in the vase and we'll go. She'll get fussy soon."

"You mean hungry. That girl can put away a meal faster than me."

Savannah laughed through the tears that still threatened to fall. Leave it to Ennis. He always knew how to cheer her up. She placed the lilies in the vase above her mother's name and took a moment to arrange them, "Happy Birthday, Mama. Wish you were here with us. You'd love Lily. She's a much better baby than I was —"

Her phone vibrated on her hip and that downright irritated her. She had to shore up her courage to face her mother's headstone each time she visited, now someone invaded her sacred time with her. She glanced at Caller ID. Georgia. She sighed, halfway joking, "Well, Mama, nothing's changed. Georgia's still got rotten timing." She clicked on, "Hi, sis."

"Hi. Are you on the road?"

"We just got to the cemetery."

"Oh, I'll let you go then."

"What did you need?"

"Are you planning on seeing Daddy?"

"He's never in a good mood on Mama's birthday so no, not today." Savannah understood the darkness that enveloped her father on this day every year. Ennis was right. Charlene's absence took the knees from under her this year. To some extent, she attributed it to post partum depression, at least the speed of the mood swings and their intensity.

"That's a good idea," Georgia agreed. "His mood will make yours worse," she said, quickly following it with, "and I know you've been struggling lately."

She shifted her gaze to Ennis, "Common knowledge is it?"

"You're my sister, Savannah. I can tell when you're depressed. Don't blame Ennis, he didn't say a word."

A shiver raked down her back. She turned, surveying their surroundings. Someone watched them, she'd had the feeling all day. Even as they parked at the curb, the nagging sensation heightened. She scouted the cemetery but only saw two other people placing flowers at graves. No other visible vehicles. It appeared safe but something told her it wasn't and her number one reason for the feeling – Toby. Stalking wasn't new to Mr. Jackson. He'd stalked her before, when they dated, when she broke up with him.

"Have you heard from Dane?" Georgia asked. "He was supposed to call me when his plane landed in Amarillo this morning but he hasn't."

Savannah glanced at her watch. It read 4:06. "Dane hasn't called me." She referred to Ennis who shook his head, "Ennis hasn't heard from him either. Maybe he got distracted. He's got a lot on his mind with the wedding."

And that was no joke. Since Georgia and Dane announced plans to get hitched, the bride-to-be penned a mountain of "to do" lists, kept the phone hot with calls for bridesmaids gowns, her bridal attire, photographers, invitations, and a million other tasks and appointments. Savannah was glad her own nuptials rated on the tamer side. She and Ennis went for simplicity at the Rutherford Ranch in Texas. Georgia and Dane chose the same venue but with way more pomp and circumstance. Savannah had been measured a hundred times in as many ways just for her matron of honor dress. One more fitting and she'd call it good.

She tried to assure Georgia, "Call the ranch. He's probably in the middle of coordinating something with Mama." Mama being Ennis and Dane's mother. A lady with soft, pleasant features resembling Ellie Ewing and a heart of gold to match.

Georgia sighed, "You're probably right. I'll call later. He left here with a list a mile long. I'll tell you, this wedding is considerably more effort than my first one."

Savannah laughed, "You're first wedding was at the Justice of the Peace before Matthew deployed. Not much planning there."

Georgia joined with her own chuckle, "I guess you're right. The only experience I've had planning a wedding was helping with yours."

"And you did an excellent job so calm down. Give Dane a call later and see what he's been into."

"I will. Hey, how about supper tomorrow night?" Her sister offered, "I'll drag out the Omaha steaks."

"Sounds good. I'll bring a cake for dessert."

Georgia saved the Omaha steaks for special occasions. Savannah wondered if the supper invite had to do with cheering her up because of Charlene's birthday or keeping Georgia's own spirits buoyed because

Dane left town. Either way, they'd savor a delicious meal and enjoy each other's company. The sisters came a long way from a time when neither particularly liked the other...

5

THEN

Walton Way spanned across half of Augusta. Residences primarily populated the western end with a few fast food places and churches sprinkled in between while businesses and the Richmond County Sheriff's Department clustered on the east end.

Savannah's neighborhood was in an older, scenic area where large lush lawns insulated the homes from the hustle and bustle of traffic, and old, established trees lined the street. Some homes still had the original red brick driveways. The Prince property did not have a brick drive but a regular concrete one that led to a cream colored two story home trimmed in white, its porch stretching the length of the house with six evenly spaced pillars supporting it. That porch and its swing saw a lot over the years. As a child Savannah played with her dolls on the steps. Her first kiss came at the tender age of seven when a bashful Roy Carlson finally quit hemming and hawing long enough to plant a fleeting, klutzy kiss on her lips. Her bashful giggle prompted him to dive in for seconds.

Years later she, Georgia and their mother spent hours in the shade of her mother's prized magnolia tree, shelling black-eyed peas, shucking corn or just relaxing with a glass of sweet tea.

The sun's glow dimmed to a fiery orange, the last throes of heat waning for the evening when she pulled into the driveway. She looked toward the inviting porch, glad to be home from a long day of studies and golf practice.

So far Savannah's senior year had been superb. Her grades hovered in the A and B range and she rode high on her golf game's success. Her current achievements earned her regular recognition in the local paper The Augusta Chronicle, four more trophies (and the season wasn't over yet) and the honor of captain of the golf team.

Savannah hoisted the heavy golf bag onto her shoulder, slammed the trunk. She hated muggy spring days in Augusta. The sweltering humidity sank to the bones, especially in late afternoon. But this was her future if she played college then professional golf, she reminded herself, and a person made sacrifices to accomplish their dreams. By her junior year, schools around the region took note of her success and rewarded her with scholarship offers. She researched the schools, their golf programs and coaches. She ultimately signed a letter of intent with Georgia Tech. She chose the school for many reasons, one being the fact she could live with her sister and still attend college since Georgia generously offered her guest room. They would finally spend more time together like they wanted.

Lugging the bag to the front door, she wondered how her mother felt that day. Charlene's arthritis worsened over the last month or so, leaving her in tears more often than not so the impromptu shopping trip with Georgia surprised Savannah. It also inspired hope that the doctor's visit a week earlier proved beneficial despite the fact she saw no real improvement in their mother's condition.

She sat the golf bag down long enough to key the lock and open the front door. Back over her shoulder the bag went until she deposited it in the corner of the entry.

A delicious aroma drifted to her. Her mother's spicy fried chicken. Charlene hadn't prepared the meal in several months so that night's supper would be a most welcome treat. Savannah's discerning nose detected a hint of savory corn mingling with the frying chicken which, together, enticed an automatic hunger pain to rattle her stomach.

When she turned around, she noticed the living room sparkled and the parchment colored carpet had been freshly vacuumed. The cherry wood coffee table gleamed, as well as the built-in bookcases flanking sides of the stone fireplace. Either her mother felt much better or Georgia cleaned house because no one except a neat freak cleaned like her sister. "Mama," she called, wandering into the kitchen, "I'm home."

She heard the chicken sizzling in the cast iron skillet, saw potatoes boiling on the back burner and the savory corn up front where Charlene babied it to perfection. Her mother stood at the stove, tending it all, then lifted her left knee slightly to shake out the pain. Savannah grew up seeing her mother shake one calf then the other, hoping to relieve the stiffness and ache of her arthritis. She'd had bad knees and ankles since her teenage years. Lately however, Charlene repeated the motion with more frequency and intensity. Except for the troublesome arthritis, her mother looked and acted younger than forty-six. A picture of sheer elegance and beauty, she reminded those who met her of the movie star

Rita Hayworth, only with green eyes and wavy shoulder length chestnut hair. She stood Georgia's height at five feet six inches, her waist trim and shapely and her attitude eternally upbeat, no matter the situation.

Charlene turned from the stove, embraced her daughter, "You look tired, honey." She opened a cabinet for a glass, poured her daughter some orange juice, "Have some juice before supper."

Savannah thanked her. Looking around, even the kitchen looked wiped down and spruced up. Spotless white cabinets and the beige granite countertops shined like mirrors. "Mama, did you spend all day shopping and cleaning?"

"No, Georgia brought me home then stayed long enough to tidy the kitchen and living room. She's out running errands right now. She's staying for supper."

"She'd be foolish not to. Everything smells scrumptious." She watched her mother shake her left calf again then rub her knee.

Charlene noticed her staring and straightened with a pained grimace, "Daddy fixed your shelf. You can display your trophy now. How did practice go today?"

Savannah drank the orange juice, her vision sweeping from her mother's knees to her face, "Fine. Worked with my driver a while then my putter."

"You said the state championships are scheduled for May twenty-third?"

"M-hmm. Hope I do well."

"You'll do fine. If you win, it'll be a perfect birthday gift for me."

Savannah chuckled, "No pressure, right?" Her smile faded when her mother winced again. She nudged Charlene from the stove, "Mama, I'll finish supper. Rest your legs. I can tell you're hurting."

Charlene welcomed the offer, eased into a nearby dining chair with a wince, "Just a long day, sweetheart. Spent nearly all day in Atlanta."

Savannah turned the chicken in the skillet then poured her mother a glass of sweet tea and another of water. Without a word, she grabbed her mother's pain medication, shook a pill into her hand for her, "Maybe this will help."

"Thank you, honey," her mother smiled, her brow still furrowed. She rubbed her knees, her eyes squeezed tight against the pain.

The reaction worried Savannah. Charlene braved the arthritis until tears sprung to her eyes and it broke Savannah's heart to see her in such misery. She'd prayed to God that the new medication proved more effective but it clearly wasn't.

After swallowing the pill, Charlene's hand migrated back to her knee, "I wanted to surprise you girls with the fried chicken. It's your favorite." She shrugged with a sigh, "I'm sorry you have to finish supper."

"Mama, it's no problem. I can't believe you had the energy to tackle a meal this big after shopping all day."

Charlene looked away. Was that guilt Savannah detected in her eyes? But guilt over what?

The chicken finished cooking and she removed the pieces from the pan, sat them on the waiting platter lined with paper towels. She recognized the platter as Grandma Culberson's best china, the one with tiny pink roses in the middle – along with a few chips around the edge for character's sake. Savannah plated one wing as an appetizer for her mother then checked the potatoes and corn.

From the corner of her eye, she noticed her mother picked at the chicken instead of digging in. "Mama, are you okay?"

Charlene dabbed a tear from her eye, "I'm really tired. I think I'll lie down until Georgia arrives." She braced a hand on the table, the other on the chair and pushed to her feet with a groan. Savannah helped her to the couch, covered her with a quilt. Charlene closed her eyes, "Thank you, Flower."

It had been ages since her mother called her Flower. Savannah smiled at the nickname. Then the smile faded as her concern rooted deeper with questions about her mother's sudden frailty and why the doctor hadn't run tests. Arthritis shouldn't progress this fast, she thought. Maybe she'd call the doctor's office, ask about running tests. Any tests that could help her mother.

Charlene rested fitfully for twenty minutes then limped back to the kitchen to the dining chair. Ten minutes later, Savannah heard a key in the front door lock. She stalked through the living room, livid with her sister for keeping their mother out so long. When the door swung open, Georgia's apparel and appearance confused her, then made her own attire of shorts and Georgia Tech t-shirt (showing loyalty to her new school) seem substandard for the fried chicken supper. Georgia's perfect makeup and stylish navy blue pantsuit and heels said business meeting, not shopping, and if it weren't for her drawn, grim features, the older sister would have looked devastatingly beautiful as usual.

Georgia slid the key from the lock, "How's Mama?"

Savannah watched her drop the keys in her purse then place it on the entry table. "Just up from a nap," was the huffy reply. "She had to lie down because she stayed out too long." Yes, she was irritable and yes, she blamed her sister for their mother's misery that afternoon. And yes, she wanted Georgia to know it.

Georgia shrugged from the suit jacket, laid it carefully across the back of the couch, her words clipped and curt, "If that's your way of telling me her suffering is my fault, I had no choice." She stopped, sniffed the air, "Chicken?" Her shoulders slumped, "Tell me she didn't stand up and…"

"She did. She said she wanted to surprise us."

"She shouldn't be up cooking, not in her shape."

"She started supper, I finished it. I came home late from practice. I did what I could."

"Georgia," their mother called from the kitchen, "is that you?"

The older sister stepped past Savannah, "Yes, Mama, I'm here. Traffic was awful, that's what took so long."

"Hey," Savannah called, halting Georgia in her tracks. "You're kinda overdressed for shopping, aren't you?" Georgia's dress code consisted of skirts and dresses for church, pantsuits for business, and casual for shopping. Today said business, not pleasure and Savannah wanted to know why.

Georgia exhaled a weary breath, "Let's eat supper. I'll explain it then." She walked away, leaving her sister on the verge of seething.

Savannah joined the two in the kitchen, saw Georgia kiss

Charlene's cheek then whisper something to her. Their mother glanced briefly at Savannah then pursed her lips, tilted her head in a somber nod.

Savannah gathered the plates and silverware while they whispered among themselves. The old bitterness and jealousy reared up and she clenched her jaw, determined to keep it at bay. Since Georgia moved to Atlanta, Savannah and their mother grew closer than ever. Now, with the secret whispers and day long shopping trip, she felt left out.

"Savannah," Georgia's voice snapped her out of the haze of envy, "if you set the table, I'll bring the food over."

She nearly saluted. *Yes ma'am, anything you say, ma'am.* General Georgia, the leader of the family, arrived to take charge of anything and everything this side of war, pestilence and world hunger. Savannah loved her sister but the woman lived to commandeer situations. She volunteered for bake sales at the church, not just baking for them but organizing and planning them. She made charts, lists, reducing a simple fundraiser to a complex mathematical conundrum only she understood the calculations to. Georgia was a good person, but an exhausting one at times.

They sat down to eat, with Savannah having the heartiest appetite among the three. The lack of consumption across the table made her self-conscious. It unnerved her when, halfway through the meal, both her mother and sister focused on her. She placed the drumstick in the plate, wiped her hands on the napkin, pushed her plate back, "Do I look funny? Why are you both staring at me?"

"We need to talk to you about Mama's condition," Georgia stated matter-of-factly.

"I didn't go shopping today, sweetheart," Charlene said, reached across and took her daughter's hand, "Please forgive me for lying. I didn't want you to know until we were sure."

The mood of the room darkened. Savannah saw the sullen frowns return to both faces. Wild notions and suppositions toyed with her panic button. Arthritis shouldn't progress this fast, she remembered thinking only half an hour ago. But it *had* to be arthritis, she argued back, just a really bad case of it. Right? She held on to that hope until seeing her mother avert her eyes again.

Now Savannah wanted to pull away but her mother's hold tightened. Something was wrong, the foreboding feeling warned, and it was about to get much, much worse. "Sure about what?"

As if sensing Savannah's desire to flee, Charlene refused to surrender her youngest child's hand, "Georgia took me to the doctor today. Well, two doctors actually. I had a CT scan and an MRI last week."

"Why those tests? You went in for arthritis." *It has to be arthritis. It just has to be. Please, Lord, let it only be arthritis.* But in that brief time, her brain reasoned the facts. CT scans, MRI scans, her mother out all day, her mood sinking faster than the Titanic and the biggest tell of all – no eye contact. No, it wasn't arthritis.

Emotion gripped her throat like a talon. Her heart kicked in her chest making her lightheaded and shaky. Someone hadn't been honest with her last week. Hadn't told her the truth about the doctor's appointment and then lied about shopping that day. That someone was Georgia. She shot an accusing glance at her sister then shifted back to her mother, waiting.

Charlene broke eye contact, focused instead on her prized flower garden outside the kitchen window. Georgia took a deep breath, her voice calm as she explained, "Last week they found a lump in her breast. That's the reason for the tests – and a biopsy."

"And…" Savannah pressed. She wanted to slap the answer out of her sister. Georgia knew for at least a week something was wrong and she hadn't told her. Biopsy said one thing. Cancer. But she'd damn well make her sister say the word.

Instead of Georgia, Charlene assumed the responsibility of saying, "It's cancer."

The floor seemed to collapse under her, leaving her in a surreal free-fall, scrambling to contain the turmoil before it overwhelmed her. It was one thing to think the word but entirely different hearing it. The urge to cry, yell and hit something all converged in a mix of confusion that left her stunned, unable to do anything, even speak.

The delicious supper now crept up her throat in a gradual acidic tidal wave, the whole meal threatening a return trip. She swallowed it back, held a hand to her stomach. This couldn't be happening, she assured herself, not to her mother. The word had been spoken quietly, almost a whisper, but it shrieked in Savannah's mind, causing her to cringe. "They have treatments for it. They just have to find the right one for her," she said, hoping – praying – they agreed. People survived cancer every day, she told herself. With surgery or treatments, it was possible. "Chemo, radiation, they even do surgery to remove tumors. There are options."

No one said a word.   Charlene continued staring outside. Georgia made no effort to agree.   People survive cancer every day, she assured herself again, and our mother can too.   Savannah repeated, "There *are* options, right?"

Georgia's mouth pursed into a thin line, obviously attempting to restrain her emotions. When she regained sufficient control, she clarified, "Savannah, the scans show it has spread to her lung and bones.   It's terminal."

O   O   O

Savannah wondered how she'd managed to hold up in front of Charlene. Instead of the flood of tears fighting for freedom, she shed some while giving encouragement to her mother, vowing to help her, to be there for her. But Charlene's primary concern revolved around her family. She wanted her husband and children to be "okay" when she passed away. Savannah struggled for an answer. How did someone promise to be okay when nothing would ever be okay again?   Not her, not her daddy or siblings and certainly not her relationship with Georgia. The two had always been close. Besides their mother, Savannah considered her sister her best friend. That evening, however, she walked away when Georgia pleaded for a chance to explain.   No explanation, reason or excuse promised to lessen the sting of betrayal. Her sister lied to her by not informing her of the cancer. Forgiveness was unlikely anytime soon – if ever.

Instead of accepting her sister's efforts to console her, she called her boyfriend, big, burly Roy Carlson. She needed a man's strong, comforting embrace. The two sat on the front porch steps with her weeping in his arms, her composure crumbling like her life the past hour.

She swiped her cheeks with the back of her hand. Glancing behind her into the entry, she saw her mother standing near the door, Georgia by her side, watching Savannah cry a river. Georgia's features conveyed empathy, Charlene's sad concern. They headed to the stairs, Georgia's arm around their mother as she accompanied her to bed. Savannah hated herself for letting her mother see the tears. She needed a strong, supportive daughter, not a weepy wimp.

Strong. Supportive. Like Georgia. A hot arrow of anger and jealousy shot through Savannah. Who did Georgia think she was? Their parents had two daughters, not one. And until that night the baby had been left out of everything.

Dark hair, good looking and a killer smile, Roy posed quite a temptation to her over the years. That night, however, he presented her a different kind of temptation. A shiny silver flask he pulled from his hip pocket, "Here. This'll help you relax."

Since when did Roy Carlson start drinking anything stronger than beer, she wondered. "It's not scotch, is it?" Because she'd drink Drano before voluntarily ingesting scotch.

"Nope. It's my favorite uncle. Uncle Jack."

He unscrewed the lid, held it under her nose. Savannah drew back at the sharp biting smell. Whiskey. She'd smelled it plenty of times but never drank it. "Smells like turpentine."

He waved it in front of her, "But this turpentine makes you

forget your troubles. Just take one swallow. You'll feel better."

What a splendid idea, to feel better, she thought. Savannah took the flask, tipped it into her mouth. Immediately her stomach heaved – even before she swallowed. The stuff burned her tongue like liquid flames. And the taste? Ugh.

He laughed at her reaction, "It won't stop burning till you swallow."

She thought about that. It sure didn't feel safe to swallow. Tears of pain, not sorrow, stung her eyes now. She made a conscious effort to open her throat and let the amber acid slide into her already protesting stomach.

The instant she did, the whiskey blazed a fiery wake from her tongue, down her throat and hit her gut like napalm. She'd never felt anything so incendiary except jalapeno peppers – but she *liked* those. "Shee-yet," she hissed then elbowed Roy, "you better not have poisoned me."

He put his arm around her shoulders, pulled her closer, "Give it a minute."

It didn't take a minute. The burning faded to a pleasant heat inside her, threading through her veins, relaxing her. It wrapped her in a cloak of fuzzy warmth, dulling the sadness a shade. So she lifted the flask again, tipping it further this time, taking a few more swallows.

"You like my poison?" Roy joked.

If it eased the hell raging in her mind, she'd drink jet fuel – but decided there wasn't much difference between the two anyway. She nodded and downed two more swallows. He retrieved the flask, "Take it easy or you'll be swinging from the chandeliers."

"Indian giver," she griped with a hint of a smile.

"But I'm *your* Indian giver," he leaned in to kiss her.

Four heavy thuds on the glass screen door startled the two. Savannah jerked around to see Georgia standing with hands on hips, her brow sinking. She crooked her finger at her younger sister. General Georgia was pissed off. *Well, join the club, sis. There's room for us all.*

Savannah kissed Roy who slid the flask back in his pocket. She noticed Georgia eyed the silver container with contempt. Once on her feet, Savannah curled her hands into fists, "What do *you* want?"

"Ouch," Roy flinched. "Even I felt that one."

She used a gentler tone with her beau, "Unless you're leaving that flask, hush up."

He handed it over, "Take it. I'll let your sister take the brunt of your temper."

Oh, yes. She would brace Georgia and get some answers or Little Miss Perfect would regret it. Savannah promised Roy she'd return the flask minus the magic juice. He kissed her cheek, "Keep it. Looks like you're gonna need a refill soon." However he took a moment to caution, "No killing your sister. I don't want our wedding to be from a jailhouse."

She didn't reply. She stared daggers at Georgia, yanked the screen door open, and slipped past her sister who refused to move aside.

"Georgia," Roy called, "I'm sorry to hear about your mother–"

Georgia shut the door in his face, cutting him off mid-sentence while addressing Savannah, "I saw you knock back a healthy amount of whatever's in that thing. What is it?"

"None of your business," she jerked the flask from her sibling's reach.

Georgia crossed her arms, "So your answer to this situation is to drink?" She leaned toward Savannah, a knowing glare darkening her features, "Bourbon. I can smell it."

"So what? You drink brandy."

"Not often and certainly not from a flask."

How typically haughty, Savannah thought. "Pardon me for being common. I take what I can get."

A humorless laugh emerged, "You drink anymore of it and you'll get a whopper hangover, that's what. You're not used to drinking, Savannah. Mama would be so upset if she found out."

The alcohol emboldened her, darkened her mood to a dangerous level – one she'd never experienced before. One that dared her to punch her sister for her lies and treachery. Savannah advanced on her, backing her against the wall, "Then don't tell her. Like you didn't tell me about the lump in her breast."

Georgia's lack of fear ramped Savannah's anger to the threshold of violence. The older sister stood, visually challenging Savannah who stood three inches taller, "I had my reasons for not telling you."

Savannah's blue eyes flared, "Reasons for not informing me of our mother's condition?" She stepped closer, "There are no reasons, only stupid excuses. *And* the fact you think you're her only daughter. *She's my mother too, not just yours.*"

"Mama's resting so be quiet," Georgia lashed out. "You can be angry at me, Savannah. Call me names, drink that flask full of booze, hold a grudge until we die. None of it changes the fact Mama has terminal cancer."

"I should have been at the doctor with her." Her hand rolled to a fist. *Hit her*, Roy's Uncle Jack encouraged. *She deserves it. Hit her until she hurts as bad as you do.* "You denied me that. You want to take care of her yourself. You think you're the only one who can."

She scowled, "That's the booze talking. You'll have plenty of opportunities to help and you know it."

"Oh, is Princess Georgia going to allow it?"

Georgia struck hard and fast. Her palm landed squarely across her sister's face, hitting hard enough Savannah whimpered and left Georgia slinging the pain from her hand.

Savannah's hand raced to her stinging cheek, rubbing the heat and tenderness out.

Georgia's eyes narrowed, "Grow up, Savannah. I don't have time to babysit your hurt feelings and Mama surely doesn't."

Uncle Jack retreated like a kicked dog, taking his antagonistic attitude and bravado with him. A trace of common sense filtered past the alcohol, telling her that Georgia experienced the same mixed-up surplus of feelings – anger, confusion, heartache and more. Savannah realized the truth. Uncle Jack forced the issue by loosening her tongue and inhibitions.   She'd made an utter fool of herself and hated that she considered knocking Georgia sideways. Plus, her sister surprisingly knocked the shit out of *her* which considerably dampened her enthusiasm for payback.

Touching her sore cheek, Savannah regretted spurring her sister. The petite, mild-mannered woman before her packed a hell of a wallop. Her shoulders slumped with a sincere, "I'm sorry."

Georgia released a pent up breath, "And I'm sorry for hitting you. I shouldn't have done that."

Savannah kept her voice to a whisper so Charlene couldn't hear, "How long does she have?"

Georgia looked away.

"*How long*?" Savannah pushed.

Georgia finally met her gaze, "The doctor wants to do chemo, to see if he can shrink some of the tumors. Mama's leaning toward refusing treatment. If she declines chemo, the outlook isn't past four months. Otherwise it's around eight. If she's lucky, maybe a year."

Savannah's knees went weak. The numbers sliced through the haze of whiskey, bringing the harsh reality to light. She had less than a year to spend with her mother. Maybe only a few months. Savannah never considered her mother dying at such an early age. Forty-friggin'-six.

She harshly muttered the Savior's name under her breath. No, she envisioned her mama with a full head of gray hair, laugh lines at her eyes and mouth and exercising that infectious laughter while cradling her grandbabies in her arms. None of that would happen now. Fate or God or someone was robbing Charlene of that future, robbing her children of their mother, and R.J. of his wife.

Savannah backed away, allowing Georgia breathing room. The older sister stepped past, opting to sit in the wingback chair beside the fireplace, "She asked the doctor for a few days to think but it's already in her lung, her back and knees. That's why she can't stand a long time."

"Doesn't she need a second opinion?" She swayed a bit, wishing she hadn't tipped that flask so liberally. It was either the booze or the residual shock of the evening hadn't worn off…

"Today was the second opinion."

The crushing weight of the statement brought tears to her eyes. Tears and another resurgence of anger. Anger of feeling powerless, anger that *their* mother received this devastating news. She'd lost a week out of whatever time Charlene had left. "Why didn't you tell me?"

An empathetic frown spread on Georgia's face, "I wanted to. Mama asked me not to. You had your tournament and she knew you stood a good chance of winning. She wanted your schedule uninterrupted until we knew for sure about her condition."

"My tournament? She thinks I care more about golf than her?" When she turned, her vision locked on the trophy awaiting proper display. Oh, she'd display it alright. She clumsily jerked it off the mantle. Uncle Jack returned with a vengeance to fuel her rage, "Golf is just a sport–"

"Savannah," Georgia scolded, "be quiet. Mama's asleep."

Grief overwhelmed her. Hurt and betrayal ran hot and thick through her veins. Charlene chose to keep her uninformed because of a stupid golf tournament.

She stared at the heavy gold trophy. Its beauty and meaning filled her with pride, with hope for the future. Until now. Now it symbolized deception, lies of omission. She grasped it, hating it more with each passing second, "I don't care about golf! I care about Mama!" Her arm pulled back, aiming for the fireplace with full intentions of smashing the award to bits.

"Savannah!" a voice cried from the stairway.

Savannah froze, her arm still drawn back to throw the trophy. She glanced back to see their mother, her shaking hands gripping the railing, her burgundy nightgown hanging on her slender frame.

Charlene's voice softened, "Don't destroy that beautiful trophy. You worked hard for it." She flinched with pain, "Put it back, sweetheart."

Savannah eased it onto the mantle, ashamed that her mother witnessed her tantrum.

Charlene gifted her with a warm smile, "Thank you. Now you girls stop arguing. This is the time we need each other the most. Agreed?"

Both daughters nodded. Charlene turned to ascend the stairs but her leg buckled. Savannah watched as the moment progressed in slow motion. The wide-eyed terror contorting their mother's pretty face. Her gasp as she groped for a steady hold on the railing. Their mother was about to tumble down the stairs.

In that short time, panic overrode the whiskey's dizzying effects and Savannah launched into a dead run, bounding up the stairs with Georgia right behind her. Leaping the stairs in twos, Savannah stretched out her arms, catching and bracing her mother from behind before she fell. She wrapped Charlene in a secure, tender embrace, "It's okay, Mama. I've got you."

Her mother grasped her youngest girl's forearms for stability. Savannah heard the fear in her rapid breaths, felt it in her trembling hands. For the first time, Savannah realized the challenge ahead of her and her family. The cancer already affected her mother's balance, already robbed her surefootedness. Savannah dreaded to see what it took next before it stole the most important thing. Her mother's life. For now however, she was Charlene's legs, her strength, "Let's get you back to bed, Mama. Georgia and I will tuck *you* in for a change."

Once they settled her in, Charlene patted the bed, told Savannah to sit next to her. Georgia stood beside her, a hand on Savannah's shoulder. Savannah thought about shrugging away but didn't want to upset their mother.

Charlene smiled, touched Savannah's cheek, "You feel left out and I'm sorry about that. I never wanted you to feel that way. And don't be angry with your sister. She did what I asked, that's all."

She frowned, still wounded by the decision, "Why wouldn't you want me there with you?"

The soft warm hand slid down her arm to her hand, "You're my baby, my beautiful Flower. A mother's instinct is to protect her babies. I wish I could protect you all from this but I can't, not now. Starting today, I promise I'll tell you everything."

"What about Seth?"

"Since he's in Germany, it's hard for him to come home right now."

"But he deserves to know."

She nodded with a tender smile, "Georgia's calling him

tomorrow. Listen to me, sweetheart. I need something from you."

"Anything, Mama, you name it."

"I'm not going to lecture you but I will give my advice. Don't start drinking. You see what it's done to Daddy."

The same embarrassment engulfed her. Her cheeks burned with shame, "I'm sorry, Mama. I was so upset and –"

"Roy gave her the flask," Georgia tattled.

Savannah snapped around to give her sister a piece of her mind. Charlene drew her attention back to her with a gentle touch, "Roy's a sweet young man. He's been good to you and that's what I want. But now he's leading you in a dangerous direction with that flask and I don't appreciate it. If I hear Roy offered you another drink," her voice strengthened, "I'll horsewhip that boy within an inch of his life. Understand?"

She hung her head, "Yes, Mama."

Charlene took her hand, held it, "Everyone makes mistakes, baby. This situation is hard enough. Don't make it harder by drinking." She gave her hand a soft squeeze, "Now. I'm done giving advice for today. I do want you and Georgia to stop arguing. I know my girls and you'll both be there for me but I'm not the only one who needs support. Your sister is bearing a large burden with all this." She touched her cheek again, "She needs you and you need her. Be there for one another. During this difficult time of treatments, surgery or whatever happens, be there to hold Georgia too. And when I'm gone..."

Tears flowed so fast Savannah couldn't wipe them fast enough. Her composure disintegrated as the sheer finality of the situation hit full force. "Mama, don't talk like that," she cried.

"Savannah, this is important. When I'm gone, you will need each other more. Please promise me you will stay close."

"We will, Mama," Georgia confirmed with Savannah nodding in agreement. Arms suddenly wrapped around Savannah from behind as she wept uncontrollably in Georgia's embrace.

O   O   O

Savannah kept a keen eye to the driveway, hoping to park in her usual spot beside her mother's Caprice. Five houses away she saw that possibility disappear with Georgia's Grand Prix occupying the space.

She pulled behind the Caprice, leaving her sister plenty of room to leave when, and if, she chose to. Savannah wished Georgia would go back to Atlanta but for the last three months she'd brought suitcases loaded with clothes and she reclaimed the upstairs bathroom that Savannah used as her own for the last few years. In that time they'd reverted to the same family from years past, only more edgy. Fights erupted between her and Georgia over the simplest things. Supper. The bathroom. Unmade beds. The shiny flask Roy gave Savannah. That subject alone caused the fiercest arguments.

So, in preparation for another confrontation, Savannah shifted the Avenger into Park, killed the engine, and withdrew her pretty flask in a symbolic impertinence toward her sister but also because she needed fortification. A calming sense of relief washed through her at the first swallow. Her vision fell the crumpled letter in the passenger seat. The mighty Georgia Tech University put her on notice – improve your grades and your golf game and we won't jerk your scholarship away. She snorted. If the bigwigs at Georgia Tech didn't want her, who cared? Her golf game sucked and her grades slipped but her mother was dying so screw everyone who didn't understand. She tipped the flask again, shoved the letter in her pocket and decided to brave General Georgia.

Her watch read 5:35. That meant in ten minutes Charlene needed another dose of pain medication. Georgia graciously allowed her sister to tend to their ailing mother every night after golf practice, provided she had no homework. She *always* had homework – a detail Georgia damn well realized. Savannah suspected she used the stipulation as leverage to prevent her from caring for their mother. If it wasn't homework, the General harped on her drinking. Savannah wasn't an idiot. She needed a clear head to assist Charlene with tasks such as helping her to the bathroom, bathing her or dispensing medication. As emotionally draining and painful as it was to watch her mother deteriorate, Savannah kept her drinking to a bare minimum until Georgia resumed control – or the *responsibilities* as her sister so eloquently phrased it. Then Savannah retreated to her room for homework duties and indulged in enough bourbon to dull reality for the night.

Their father would be arriving home soon so she climbed from the car, retrieved the golf bag, slung it over her shoulder and trudged to the front door. She hesitated. With key in hand, she stopped, feeling the dread set in again. It happened each night upon arriving home. The sight of her mother physically hurt now. Savannah's heart ached deep in her chest. She cried herself to sleep at night. She drank a little more then a little more to dry the tears, to cloud her mind, to get through the dark, quiet hours wondering if that night was the night Charlene passed away. The once lively and joyful lady lay one bedroom away, listless, her eyes hollow, her body wasting away.

The key shook in Savannah's hand. If she could run away from it all she would – except running away meant abandoning her mother and she would never do that. Savannah gripped the key, shoved it in the lock, opened the door and crossed the threshold. It was time to get to work.

The golf bag hit the entry floor with a thud and muted metallic clang. She sneered at the traitorous clubs, wondering why she bothered to practice anymore. Her scores suffered the last few months, racking up embarrassing numbers at tournaments she should have won – and *would* have six months earlier if she hadn't developed the most abominable condition known to a golfer. The dreaded yips. The ball and her clubs defied her, leaving her swinging like an amateur at the little round bastard that refused to drop in the hole. Her driver, the singular club that earned her the title *The Augusta Bomber*, betrayed her by sometimes launching the ball into a hook or slice so far off the fairway she dropped a stroke or two just to find it again. The Augusta Chronicle's nickname for her, once feared by competitors, seemed like a joke lately. The Augusta Bomber was now dropping duds.

Georgia appeared at the kitchen entry, the worry lines smoothing at the sight of her sister, "I'm glad you're home. What was that noise?"

"My future circling the drain."

"What happened?"

"I've gone from hero to zero. I suck at golf."

Georgia's voice softened, "It's the stress, hon. You're distracted and tired. How are your grades?"

"Mediocre, as usual, but don't tell Daddy. I'm having a bad enough week." She tossed a baleful glare at her once cherished clubs, "Thanks to them." She neglected to tell Georgia just how bad the week had been. The fact the coach nagged her for reasons why her game took such a catastrophic nosedive. The fact he demoted her from team captain then rearranged the team, cutting her three spots to nearly last. The fact he, that afternoon, debated aloud whether to keep her on the team at all. No, Savannah locked the information in her mental vault and threw away the key. No one needed to know she was a loser, or taking the fast train to becoming one.

"I hope you're hungry," Georgia returned to the stove. "I fixed a meatloaf for us."

Savannah headed to the kitchen where the aromas of chicken soup and Georgia's meatloaf mingled in the air. Four days a week, Georgia prepared the homemade soup for their mother since it was her favorite. Small, frequent meals, the doctors reminded at every appointment. Small, frequent meals. They forgot to say those small frequent meals might not stay down. They forgot to explain how to maintain a cancer patient's strength and weight when their stomach rejected the simplest food or drink. The doctors forgot a lot but damn sure demanded their patient appear front and center for every single appointment whether she felt like it or not, whether on disease weakened legs or being wheeled in a wheelchair, and still fighting nausea without any food on her stomach.

Judging by the last week, Savannah knew there was little hope that Charlene might keep the chicken soup down. Their mother loved Georgia's meals but it didn't mean she'd hold it down any better than she could Savannah's sad attempt at cooking. Georgia's talent for culinary endeavors verged on genius. She took a basic recipe and added this or that or changed something but it always tasted delicious. Her meatloaf started with the usual ingredients then she tossed in a little Worcestershire, Dijon mustard and her secret ingredient: half a cup of heavy cream. On a normal day, Savannah indulged in second servings on Georgia's meatloaf but her appetite eluded her since their mother's diagnosis and adding salt to her wounds, her future in golf hung perilously in the balance.

She greeted Georgia with a hug then stiffened when she heard her sister draw a sharp breath. She smelled the booze, no doubt.

Scrumptious meatloaf or not, she was not in the mood to square off with the General, not after the day she'd had, "I'll grab a snack later. First I'll take Mama her pills."

"If you'll stir the soup, I'll take care of Mama. You need to eat a *meal*, Savannah. You're losing too much weight."

"Hello, Pot. Meet Kettle. You've trimmed down too." She reached in the fridge for a Yoo-Hoo, took a generous swallow. "I'm not hungry. I'll grab a snack when I am." She reached for Charlene's pain medication when Georgia snatched it from under her hand. Savannah rolled her eyes, "What are you doing?"

"You've been drinking. I can smell it on you."

Why did every conversation end in an argument these days, she wondered. And it all centered around drinking. She sat the Yoo-Hoo down hard, "I had one drink. That doesn't mean I'm incapable of helping."

"You are impaired enough I don't trust you with these meds. You could easily overdose her." She marched to the kitchen doorway. Savannah blocked her exit. They stared at each other, daring the other to step over the usual imaginary line.

"You think I'd do that to Mama?" Savannah clenched her teeth, both hands rolling to fists.

"Not intentionally, no." A light of fear registered in the older sister's eyes as she stepped back again. She opened her mouth to speak but Savannah cut her off, "I love Mama. I wouldn't hurt her. Period. Give me that bottle. Don't make me take it from you."

Georgia swallowed hard, stood her ground, "What's the dose? How much are you supposed to give her?"

"Two pills every four hours. If you haven't screwed up the schedule by being late with the last dose, her next one is now ten minutes late because you'd rather fight with me than help our mother. *Give me that damn bottle.*" Her fist opened to receive the medication, her narrowed vision never straying from her sister's.

"What the hell's going on here?" R.J. griped from behind Savannah. "You two at it again?"

She never looked away, "Georgia doesn't think I'm capable of helping Mama because I had one drink."

R.J. sighed, positioned himself between them. He asked

Savannah, "How many pills does your mother need?"

She started toward her sister, "Two every four hours – if I could only get them from Mein Führer over there."

R.J. braced his hands on her shoulders, stopping her. He spoke to his eldest girl, "Georgia, give your sister the pills."

"But Daddy," Georgia complained, "how do we know how much she's had to drink? She could overdose Mama–"

Savannah stepped around R.J., shoved Georgia against the wall hard enough she cringed. Savannah stabbed a finger at her older sister, "You say that again and I'll slug you."

R.J.'s hand clutched her arm, crushing it beneath its grasp. Savannah whimpered as he spun her to face him, "Want me to knock ya *through* that wall?"

She yanked at her arm that began throbbing. R.J. refused to let go, "Answer me, Savannah. I *will* hit ya hard enough ya sail through it. Do ya want me to do that?"

"No, Daddy."

He released her, "Push your sister again and I will." Then he rounded on Georgia, "And let her help Mama without bitching at her."

"But Daddy," Georgia complained.

"Just do it."

Savannah stabbed a finger at her, "And don't say I'll overdose Mama or I'll–"

R.J.'s hand seized her jaw, bore down until tears sprung to her eyes, "Only thing preventin' me from knocking sense into ya both is the fact your mama's dying. 'Stead of using your tongues to slice each other to bits, use 'em to make Mama smile in her last days. 'Cause if ya keep this shit up, I'll put ya both out of commission *then* where will Mama's help be?"

A tear slid down her cheek but she dare not wipe it away. He was livid enough to follow through on his threat. She stood, waiting for his temper to abate – praying it would – and waiting for him to let go. When he did, her teeth ached, the pain traveling through her neck into her shoulders. It convinced her that thumping Georgia held no appeal since their father packed way more punch in his swing than she did hers.

R.J. shook his head, "You two make me sick. Makes me wonder if you're really my kids." He went to the fridge and Georgia stepped away, giving him room to search inside. He stuck his head in, reached for a beer and a chicken salad sandwich Georgia prepared earlier for him. He stood up, closed the door and addressed his daughters, "Act like sisters, for God's sakes. Get along." He swiped the prescription bottle from Georgia, plunked it in Savannah's hand, "Hurry up with those pills. She needs 'em. When you're done, you and I need to talk. Your coach called me."

Chaste fear froze her in place. Coach Warren hadn't mentioned calling her daddy. Now she wondered what he'd said. Had he mentioned the letter from Georgia Tech? God knows Warren harped at her enough about it. Once they got wind of her titanic downward spiral (probably with the coach's help), the world went to hell.

Warren overstepped his bounds when he called her daddy. Savannah's anger fired hot at her nosy coach. If he didn't want her on the team, fine, just don't involve her father. If Warren understood how

R.J. *talked* to his children, the man would have decided against bothering him. She dreaded more than climbing the stairs now. She dreaded descending them as well. "Yessir," she replied, wincing as she left the kitchen, started up the stairs.

"All this stuff with Mama's caused it," he said, his voice calmer. "I tried to tell him to give ya a break."

"Thank you, Daddy." She meant it. He sounded downright sympathetic, not incensed with the phone call, which surprised her. And since he hadn't mentioned Georgia Tech, maybe Warren stopped short of telling R.J. about the letter. For now. It still irked her that Warren contacted him. She was a private person about her problems and if she'd wanted the coach to know about her mother, she'd have told him... "Wait," she stopped. "You *told* Warren about Mama?"

"Well, *you* wouldn't, would ya? He wanted to know why you were moody, why you've lost weight and why you can't hit the ball anymore. He thought you were on dope."

"No," Georgia graciously volunteered, "just bourbon."

Savannah barely curbed the urge to charge into the kitchen and belt her sister. Images of R.J. making good on his promise to knock her through the wall backed her down. She did, however, express a clipped, "Shut up, Georgia."

"*Both of ya* shut up. Once I told him about Mama, he understood and he's not tossing ya from the team."

She closed her eyes on a groan. Her well-meaning, albeit nosy coach managed to harass and humiliate her. Her shame reached abysmal depths when Georgia gasped upon hearing the announcement. She hadn't intended on telling her anything (at least not yet) and thanks to Coach Warren, Pandora's Box blew open. What a genuine humanitarian. Thanks, Coach, Savannah griped silently, thanks a lot. By week's end, the whole world would hear how she flushed a promising golf career and the scholarship along with it – or was about to.

"He was kicking her off the team?" Georgia repeated, mortified.

Yes, R.J. replied but it wasn't entirely true. Coach Warren said he'd considered it for the past two weeks and gave her forewarning of it – if her scores and efforts failed to show improvement. He accused her of slacking, not concentrating, not trying.

Georgia leaned out the kitchen doorway, glanced at Savannah standing halfway up the stairs, her hand gripping the railing hard enough to splinter the wood.

One look at her sister and guilt weighed Savannah down heavier than concrete. She hated disappointing Georgia and judging from her expression, she'd done that and more.

A regular at her tournaments until Charlene's diagnosis, Georgia cheered the loudest with every win and offered solace with each loss.

Georgia looked as if she'd been knifed in the heart, "I asked about your tournaments and you said they went fine. You said everything was fine. Why did you lie to me?"

The emphasis on the word *me* caused Savannah to cower, deflated with regret. She hung her head, unable to meet her sister's devastated gaze, "I was embarrassed and I knew you'd be upset. I'm sorry." She broke into a run, sprinting up the stairs to the bathroom where she fought back tears and felt the name *failure* sink to the bone.

Not only had she let down her teammates, her coach and herself but she'd probably destroyed her sister's trust, the one person besides their mother who stood by her in all times, in all ways.

She stared in the mirror, scowling at her reflection. *From hero to zero. That's me.*

Thumbing her tears away, she regrouped her composure and drew up a glass of water. She prayed she hadn't kept her mother waiting too long for the pain medication. With the arguing and delays, Charlene was surely hurting and it was all Savannah's fault.

Before entering the bedroom, she steeled herself. She tried to present a positive front with her mother but each day her spirits sank lower when she saw her so frail and withering away. Charlene's body failed but her mind stayed razor-sharp. At an early age Savannah learned her mother read expressions, tuned into voices. The woman ferreted out lies like a human lie detector. Those beautiful, acute green eyes assessed anyone walking into the bedroom – and did so with implacable precision.

Savannah walked in, sat the glass on the nightstand. Charlene's eyes eased open, revealing clear green pools. Pools that, as anticipated, searched for trouble in her daughter's features. "How's my Flower today?" She labored to sound strong, cheery.

Savannah held her mother's hand that felt warm and soft, "Flower is fine, Mama. How are you?"

"Fair to middlin', I'd say," she answered, attempting a smile.

Always the optimist, Savannah marveled. No matter what life dealt her, her mother approached it head-on with faith, prayers and hope. Charlene's little smile trembled, revealing that fact she'd been braving the pain, masking it with the upbeat gesture. It drove Savannah's self-reproach straight to her heart. Their mother suffered, her pain rooting deeper while her children bickered about stupid subjects such as golf, drinking and homegrown dictators.

"I've got your pills right here. I'm sorry I'm late with them." Savannah helped her sit up, her back braced against the headboard with a pillow behind her.

"I heard you and Daddy talking. What's wrong?"

"Just having some issues with my coach. I'll work them out, don't worry." She extended the pain medication to her mother whose hand quivered beneath hers. Savannah tried not to notice how the hands, always so steady, shook like leaves in a storm. She struggled to ignore those telltale signs of weakness, of her mama's decline, but they haunted her at night in her sleep, making nighttime as hellacious as her waking hours. "Here Mama," she held the pills to Charlene's mouth, "open." She placed the pills on her mama's tongue then helped her hold the glass.

Her mother's warm hands cupped around hers while she sipped. Charlene pulled away, swallowed with an awkward, "Never imagined I'd need help simply holding a glass."

The corners of Savannah's mouth lifted a degree, battling to hide her sadness, "Everyone needs help on occasion."

"You're beginning to sound like your sister."

She shrugged, teasing, "Eh, Georgia's right every so often, I'll give her that."

Charlene enjoyed the lighthearted comment. The little laugh still retained a hint of her mother's jubilance from years past. She patted her daughter's hand, "You two getting along yet?"

"It's touchy but we're getting there," she lied.

Her mother frowned. The human lie detector, she thought. Still finely tuned and hard at work. She'd heard the arguments, the heated exchanges that softened to whispered, sometimes unkind remarks between the sisters.

"It breaks my heart to see you both at odds. You idolized Georgia growing up. She loved that you did. You were happiest when you were together."

She remembered it with clarity. She adored her older sister, depended on her. They shared love and laughter, cried tears together. It seemed so long ago…

"Honey," Charlene said, "she means well and you do too. Your personalities are such that you clash over silly things."

"*We argue about you.* You're not a silly thing." Anger and hurt rose in her voice, "She doesn't trust me to help you…"

Charlene's unsteady touch pressed to Savannah's lips, shushing her, "I'll have a talk with her but, sweetheart, this is hard on her too. Remember that. You're both under such stress. I pray that you grow closer as time passes. I pray that someday you're as close as you were as children…"

O O O

Later that evening, Savannah hunkered over her desk, toiling with the mind-numbing subject of economics. Four pages of homework left and bedtime loomed forty minutes away. She'd never get to sleep at that rate. She'd never graduate either if she didn't concentrate. Heaving a sigh, she reread the same page in her textbook – for the third time.

Her mother's recollections trickled in between market economies and gross domestic product, drawing her into the past when Georgia sat beside her little sister, teaching her *numbers* as R.J. called them. No one except Georgia understood the method needed to teach her basic math. And when she saw six year-old Savannah swinging Grandpa Prince's sand wedge – which was far too long and unwieldy for the girl holding it – she hadn't complained or accused her of laziness. Instead of bawling her out for not helping gather apples in the orchard, Georgia propped a sturdy crate beneath the youngster to compensate for the club length. Years later Georgia wiped her tears the day Brian Wallace broke up with her in tenth grade. She also ran off Brian's much older brother when he made moves on her baby sister. She and Georgia shared a close knit relationship ever since Savannah could remember. She wanted it back, to feel her sister's love again, her arms around her, and be comforted in this exhaustive, traumatic time. She promised to try harder, to support Georgia and help her as she'd done countless times for her. She just wanted her sister back.

A soft knock on the door interrupted the meager progress on her homework. Fatigue set in from the whole arduous, frustrating day and the bed invited her to climb in and throw the covers over her head. She closed the textbook, giving up on homework for the night. She'd fit it in before class the next morning. "Come in," she said, figuring Georgia wanted to hash out their latest argument once and for all. The night would go on forever, she feared, and belted back a healthy amount of Uncle Jack to brace herself. The satisfying warm curtain descended past her throat to her stomach. By the time Georgia wound up for a lecture, Uncle Jack's magic glow would wrap Savannah in soft, quiet apathy. She was tired, she'd tell her sister. So tired of fighting...

Her sister stepped in, eased the door closed, "Got a minute?"

Savannah turned in the chair, facing her, then motioned to the bed – *have a seat* – which Georgia did.

In the muted light from the desk lamp, Georgia looked much older than twenty-four. Tiny lines between her brows were more pronounced that night than usual. Her face was drawn, her eyes red and puffy. She'd been crying and anyone who knew Georgia realized she almost always wept in silence. Savannah heard her dissolve into inconsolable weeping just twice in her life.

Georgia grasped an already wadded tissue in her hand, lifted it, dabbed her eyes, "What happened to us?"

Her nose sounded stuffy like she had a cold. She'd cried a long time, probably in her room, and Savannah hadn't heard one sniffle. Georgia stared at her, baffled, "We've always been close, you've always shared your problems with me and I've never minded your help. I mean, what *happened* to us?"

The conversation veered into unforeseen territory. Savannah expected a lecture about drinking, an edict shutting her out of Charlene's care, anything but that question. She pointed to the bedroom next door. Mama, her expression said. Mama's cancer happened.

Georgia blew her nose, wiped it with the remnants of her tissue. Savannah handed her the box from her desk. Georgia thanked her then began pouring her heart out, "This situation has brought us to our knees. It's so difficult to see her in this shape. So kind and beautiful." Her voice wavered, "She never hurt anyone in her life and look at her. All the misery and indignities of that damn disease and she doesn't deserve it, not one bit."

Savannah rose from the chair, seeing her sister battling her emotions and failing. Georgia shouldered the lion's share of responsibility while insisting Savannah keep a normal schedule if possible. The older sister cooked, cleaned, tended to doctor's appointments all while ensuring their mother stayed as comfortable as possible. She'd done it for months with few precious hours to herself and with no complaints. She'd had six brief months to enjoy her newlywed status to U.S.M.C. Lieutenant Matthew Carlisle before their mother's diagnosis. They got hitched at City Hall, had one week together and off he went, deployed overseas for the war. Now he called at absurd times – mostly during the night, cheating Georgia of a full night's sleep. The totality of Georgia's stress and strain began to show and she needed comfort. Savannah saw the chance to mend fences and took it.

She covered Georgia's hand with hers, gave it a squeeze. It opened a flood of tears from Georgia who wrapped her arms around her, clinging so tight it hurt. Savannah returned the embrace, held her while she cried. She had no words of wisdom and not many of encouragement either. Telling her everything would be okay was ludicrous because they both understood it would never be okay again. She hoped actions spoke louder than words because the latter's well ran dry.

That night constituted only the third time she'd heard Georgia weep non-stop. Savannah tried to console and calm her but nothing seemed to work.

Between heaving sobs, Georgia finally said, "I don't want to lose you too," then followed it with a squeeze a python would have appreciated.

The pressure sent sharp bolts of pain through her back and ribs but she didn't care. Her sister's declaration inspired pure relief and delight. It gave her hope Georgia still cared.

"I *can't* lose you too," Georgia pulled away to meet eye to eye, "We can't let this destroy our relationship. I love you and I need you."

The corners of Savannah's mouth lifted. Tears of her own spilled down her cheeks, "I love you and need you too. I always have and always will."

Georgia broke down once more, and again constricted her embrace to the point her sister grimaced. "You can help with Mama," Georgia cried. "I'm sorry for treating you like a drunk."

"And I'm sorry for pushing you earlier. I regret doing that and I regret not telling you about Coach Warren or my tournaments. I just felt like you had enough to deal with. I was embarrassed and now I feel like a chump for lying to you. I love you and you didn't deserve that."

The strength of Georgia's embrace stunned Savannah. She clung to her younger sister as hard as Savannah clung to her while they both apologized again. Perhaps, Savannah thought, they *both* finally awoke from their childish behavior to be what R.J. demanded that afternoon.

Sisters.

6

THEN

Savannah accelerated down Walton Way, speeding through red lights, ignoring honking horns and hoping no police officers lurked nearby. The Avenger roared up to fifty miles per hour along portions of the street and a speeding ticket would put her in hot water with her cousin Bobby Prince, the Richmond County Sheriff. Since graduation, he'd hired her onto the department for clerical work so her job might cease to exist if she got caught breaking the law. He took transgressions within his department seriously and worked hard maintaining a spotless reputation with the public so she was good and fired if she got cited for speeding *and* endangering his beloved citizens.

The car bounced through another intersection, launching her an inch off the seat, the rebound scraping the Dodge's undercarriage on the asphalt. Through her tears, she gauged every intersection for clear passage, snapping her head left, right then left again. She had to get to University Hospital. She barely understood Georgia when she'd called. Her sister battled an explosion of emotion, Savannah heard it in her restrained voice. Sorrowful sobs traveled the line into Savannah's ear.

Her sister sniffed back the emotion only to surrender to it again, leaving Savannah panicked, demanding answers. It was Seth who commandeered the phone with his usual blunt, military tone, "Get to University quick. Mama's dying."

The building loomed a few blocks away. This was it. The day she dreaded for months. Her mother's tender touch, her soft, encouraging voice, her beautiful carefree smile and laugh would all be memories after today. The sparkle in her eyes gone forever.

Tears blurred Savannah's vision, forcing her to blink them back. Her objective was simple: get to the hospital before her mother died. In her ride-alongs with Bobby over the years, Savannah learned the knack of driving like a cop. How to traverse intersections without killing herself or others, how to corner at a higher than normal rate of speed, how to get places in a big hurry. However they'd been in a sheriff's car with lights and siren heralding their approach. Today, she had nothing except her instinct and experience of riding shotgun in Bobby's patrol car to get her there safe.

She looked both ways then gunned the car through another intersection. Cars screeched to a halt, pedestrians jumped back to the curb. Another motorist blared their horn when she passed. University Hospital approached – the place she needed to be. One block separated her from her mother's bedside.

Savannah slowed for the turn into the emergency room parking lot, swung into a slot and killed the engine. The second her feet hit the parking lot, she embarked on another race with time. Charlene had been a patient at University many times since her diagnosis, giving Savannah plenty of opportunity to memorize the place from the emergency room to the upper floors. All she needed was her mother's room number and she could attempt to prepare for the most difficult task of her life. Saying goodbye to her mother.

She sprinted across the parking lot, charged through the emergency room doors. She fought to the front of the line, asking for Charlene's room number. The nurse clicked the keys on the computer. Seconds ticked away while Savannah waited. Her heart pounded in her chest and ears. Her lungs heaved for breath, to gain control of *something* in her life that day. Why was it taking the woman so long to find the number?

Another nurse, shuffled through a handful of folders, "Charlene Prince is in room 7." Then proceeded to direct the panicked teenager with a pointing finger, "Through the doors, down the hall then–"

Turn right, Savannah finished.   She burst through the double doors, rushed down the hall, threw on the brakes for the right turn and slipped. She barely managed to stay on her feet, regaining her balance with a hand on the wall then glanced up. The sight stopped her cold. Her body strangely disengaged from the fright of nearly falling, the noisy surroundings and the people staring at her.

Georgia, Matthew, Seth and Leah all stood at the end of the hall. An inconsolable Georgia sought refuge in her husband's arms. Seth held his wife as she wept, his expression grim.

Savannah ran toward them, intending to talk to her precious mother before she passed away. She wanted to say *I love you*. That's all she needed. For Charlene to know in those last moments that she loved her with every bit of love a child's heart could hold. She'd expressed those words a million times to her mother but this time was different. She *had* to tell her one last time. One last time.

The same surreal feeling swept over her. She pleaded for it to be a nightmare. Recovering from nightmares was easy. Burying her mother would devastate her. Watching her suffer those few months consumed Savannah little by little, eroding hope, replacing it with the vulnerability and loneliness of a scared, lost child. Her mother wasted away, refused to eat. Her cries of unbearable pain branded Savannah's memory, making her thankful for the morphine that dulled her mother's agony. But Charlene had been *alive*. Moving, breathing, talking. Death meant forever. No future. Only the past.

She squeezed between the two couples only for Seth to grab her arm, "Van, wait."

"I can't," she fought to pry herself loose. "I've got to tell her something before she passes."

"But –"

"Savannah," Georgia said between sobs, "she's gone."

She looked in the window to see R.J. sitting by their mother's side, holding and stroking her hand. He pressed it to his cheek, his shoulders shaking as he cried. The sight struck Savannah odd. She'd never seen her father cry. In her whole life she'd witnessed every emotion except grief. Now R.J. sat beside his wife, his weeping so mournful it hurt to hear him.

Savannah tried to move, to go inside but her legs felt leaden. Her mother hadn't moved, hadn't drawn breath in those few seconds. She lay peacefully in the bed, covered in a pink hospital blanket, her eyes closed in eternal slumber.

"I'm too late?" How could this happen, her mind reeled. How could fate be so unbelievably cruel? First the diagnosis, then the treatments failed and when time came for goodbyes, she was *late?* After racing the streets, breaking numerous traffic laws, risking life and limb to say goodbye to her mother, she was too late? Chaste anger flowed through her. Fate or God or whoever really hated her. To be cheated out of a last goodbye, something or someone truly despised her. She wanted to hit something, anything. The sincere desire to rip things apart, to curse life, destiny and God raged inside her. The only thing preventing her from the latter: her mother. Charlene trusted God, prayed to Him every day and night. She knew her Bible, went to church and worshipped Him with an ironclad faith not even cancer could break. Savannah held her tongue about God for her mother's sake. But the innate desire to destroy something as wholly as Charlene's death destroyed her still rumbled dangerously close to the surface.

The gravity of the moment abruptly hit her, stealing her stability and strength. Leaning against the wall, her knees weakened, threatening to buckle. She burst into tears, "I'm too late. I wanted two minutes with her. *Two minutes.* I needed to tell her I loved her."

Seeing her collapse, Seth wrapped his arms around her, embracing her tight to him. She held to her brother, a lifeline from drowning in misery and sorrow.

His tightly restrained voice choked up, "She knew you loved her, Van. She knew."

"It's not fair." She realized how childish it sounded. Nothing was fair in life but to lose one's mother was a blow no one could truly prepare for. No more Mother's Day presents or cards, no more serenading Mama with "Happy Birthday" then hearing Charlene sing the same song to her two weeks later. Cancer silenced the sweet melodic voice that lulled Savannah to sleep as a child, the soothing touch that dried tears and smiling eyes that inspired cheerfulness and laughter with one glance. All gone. Forever.

"No, it's not fair but she's not hurting anymore," Seth replied. "She suffered for so long."

"What about us?" she asked. "We're suffering too."

"Don't you mean *what about you?*" Matthew accused. "What excuse will you use to drink now? Charlene's gone. You can't use your mother as a reason anymore."

"Matthew, don't," Georgia pleaded. She looked to Savannah who was sure she looked as shell-shocked at his outburst as everyone else. Georgia held her hand out to her, "She misses Mama like we all do."

Savannah readily accepted the comforting hold. They needed each other right then, not some boorish clod hurling condemnation and judgment. Who the hell did he think he was, anyway? He hadn't lost *his* mother. He scarcely supported his wife in her time of grief and stress, blaming his lapse of contact on his military duties.

Matthew unexpectedly ignored his wife's request, "Georgia, she'll be drunk thirty minutes after leaving here, we all know it."

"Shut up, Matthew," Seth warned, holding his sister tighter as she cried.

Georgia pulled away from her husband to join her siblings in a group hug. She vowed, "We'll be okay, Savannah. We will stick together like Mama wanted and we'll be okay."

The cruel reality struck hard. She'd never speak to her mother again, or hug or kiss her. Her heart weighed heavy inside her. She couldn't catch her breath. Her heart squeezed inside her chest. For a fleeting moment she wondered if a person could die of a broken heart. She felt helpless *and* hopeless, the way she had for months as her mother continued to slip away. "Why Mama? Why her?"

Seth constricted his hold on his sisters as if to brace himself and curb his own tears, "No one knows, Van. It just happened."

Savannah clung to her siblings while she cried, silently reciting what she wanted to tell her mother…

I love you, Mama. I'm sorry for all the arguments and harsh words over the years. I'm sorry for any trouble I caused and for disappointing you. You mean the world to me and always will. You were always there for me no matter what. If you were busy or feeling bad, you still made time. You are my mother, my trusted confidant and my lifelong friend. Throughout your life you've given love freely and made your family feel so cherished that your absence will shatter our world the moment you're gone. You are one of a kind, a treasure given to one man and three children who would gladly take your place if we could relieve your pain and suffering and make you whole again. If there is a God, He's taking the best and leaving us hollow with your loss. I hope someday to see you again. I love you, my dear sweet mother. I will miss you.

7

NOW

Lily's cries rattled from the baby monitor on the bedside table. The raucous bawling drew Savannah from the dreadful memories. Every year Charlene's birthday affected her in a negative way. She tried focusing on the happier times, but inevitably the bad memories triumphed over her efforts. This year was worse and since returning from the cemetery, her mood sank to darker shades of depression that she couldn't explain or rebound from.

Death caused a unique anguish for those left behind. Adding to the helplessness of losing a cherished loved one, the pain of loss consisted of memories that slipped in during quiet moments. Memories that tore with jagged teeth, shredding a person's peace of mind with *what if's* and *whys* until reopening the wounds anew.

To her, ghosts from the past floated around cemeteries and headstones, waiting to surround a person, slip into their minds and stay long after the visitor climbed in their car and drove away. That night Savannah descended deep into the past until she tasted the bourbon, felt the soft, warmth of her mother's skin, and smelled the pungency of her own panic.

She thumbed away the wetness from her eyes, hearing her daughter's cries graduate to a needy wailing. She dragged herself to her feet, waiting to ensure Ennis stayed asleep then grudgingly reminded herself the man could sleep through a train wreck.

Savannah imagined her mother trudging down the hallway, bleary-eyed and tired to tend to the screaming infant neither she nor her husband ever expected. They planned on two kids but God had other plans, Charlene later told Savannah. How many trips had her mother made down that hallway to change little Savannah's diapers, to feed her or simply soothe the child back to sleep?

Savannah shrugged into her robe and, like Charlene thirty-something years ago, trudged down the hallway to ease her child's upset. She flipped on the light, revealing her angel's red, teary face. "Hush now, baby. Mama's here," she lifted Lily from the crib. "Let's be quiet so we don't wake Daddy." The likelihood seemed rather remote but there was always a first time for everything, she thought.

Lily continued to cry as her mother placed her on the changing table, stripped her of the wet diaper. Savannah began humming "Hush Little Baby", hoping to quiet the child from her crying fit. When that didn't work, she finished diaper duty and sat in the nearby rocking chair with Lily against her chest. "Every time you cry like this, you want a song," she noticed. "My singing voice will never measure up to Grandma's but here goes." She began softly singing "What a Wonderful World", her mother's favorite song.

Savannah could hear her mother's silken, melodious voice singing mellow and low. *I see trees of green, red roses too, I see them bloom for me and you, And I think to myself what a wonderful world...*

Savannah began the second verse, her throat tightening as she proceeded. An all-consuming sadness stopped her midway through, sending her mind tumbling into the past and tripping over visions that drove the anguish deeper. There were wounds so deep they did not bleed. Memories so vivid a person risked losing themselves in the pain if they touched or revisited them. For Savannah, her mother's loss left a hole so vast, she rarely dared to toe the edge. That night she dared once too often. The tears in her eyes began falling in earnest and wouldn't stop.

o   o   o

Ennis turned over in bed, his arm stretching for its favorite perch – Savannah's hip. Instead his hand dropped to the mattress, bringing him awake. Propping on his elbow, he saw a soft light glowing from the nursery. Lily must have been fussing again and he'd missed it. It irritated his wife that he could, as she phrased it, "sleep through a warzone". At one point she practically accused him of conspiring against her but he realized it was exhaustion talking. Or at least he hoped it was. Well, no time like the present to show her consciousness did kick in on occasion. He'd take over baby duty and give her a break. Since she'd been on maternity leave, she'd shouldered most of the responsibilities regarding Lily's care – with him pitching in when he could. The constant activity and lack of sleep showed on her too. Lately she'd been moody and depressed, especially regarding her mother. He attributed her mood swings to weariness and the fact Charlene's birthday fell mere weeks before Savannah's own yearly milestone. The combination did not mix well, he assumed, because his wife approached the thirty-something years, a time women dreaded because the road led to the big, ugly landmark of forty. Savannah was well-adjusted about her age for now, but he suspected the closer ol' forty approached, her devil-may-care attitude might fly the coop.

Ennis rolled out of bed, padded to the nursery. Two steps out of their bedroom, he heard his wife's sultry velvet voice softly singing *What A Wonderful World.* The sweet-flowing sound floated in the air. The song – any song – was a rare delight until Lily's birth. His eyes closed on a smile. He loved her voice, adored her singing.

He knew when she sang or hummed that particular song she thought of her mother. It was Charlene's favorite, and, according to Savannah, she rocked her youngest daughter to sleep singing it. The longer Savannah sang, he heard sadness creep into her voice. When he peeked in the doorway, he saw her cradling Lily against her chest, mother's eyes closed, her cheek nuzzled at the baby's wispy dark hair.

He committed the poignant moment to memory. His wife in her blue sleeping sheep jammies and his baby daughter dressed in a pink Minnie Mouse sleeper, a gift from her Aunt Georgia and Uncle Dane.

Savannah rocked the sleeping infant, the tune wavering against a battle of tears. The song abruptly halted and he watched her wipe a hand across both cheeks. "Mama, I wish you were here," she whispered on a quivering breath. "I miss you so much..." She began crying, rose from the rocker to place Lily in her crib before surrendering wholly to her tears.

Ennis considered approaching his wife to console her. He stepped forward then stopped, hearing her still speaking to her mother while she cried. Ennis turned around, realizing his presence wasn't needed. She wanted time by herself, to work through the sorrow alone.

Returning to the bedroom, he released a quiet sigh, made a note to call Georgia later that morning. This situation required a heavy hitter, someone who understood his wife better than he did. That person was her sister.

When he woke up at five, her side of the bed remained empty. She hadn't come back all night. He rolled out, headed to the nursery, thinking perhaps she'd fallen asleep in the rocking chair. Lily slept soundly in the crib but the chair sat empty. Ennis went to the kitchen where he found Savannah in her pajamas, sitting with her head in her hands. The brimming coffee cup beside her felt cold to the touch. She sat, either unaware of his presence or ignoring it. Something was desperately wrong and he needed to pry the problem from her. Savannah, for all her good traits, closed like Fort Knox about her troubles. It required a clever soul and luck to finesse answers from her. Unfortunately he struck out most times. His only hope: Georgia.

He bent down, swept her hair aside and kissed her nape, "Babe? You okay? You didn't come back to bed."

"Bad night." She sounded bone weary, spiritless.

"Had those pretty regular lately. What's wrong?"

"Just reliving my mother's diagnosis and death." She added

sarcastically, "Real fun times." She rubbed her face in frustration, as if trying to erase the night from her mind.

He gently pulled her to her feet. One arm curled around her back, holding her to him as his lips pressed to hers. He meant for the soft kiss to bolster her. Instead, she parted from the kiss, snuggled into his embrace, and held him close. She rested her cheek against his chest with a sigh. "Must have been a *really* bad night," he said.

She nodded. The fact she declined to clarify told him the extent of her nighttime hours. Even after years of marriage she still hadn't disclosed the details of her mother's cancer or death. The mere mention of Charlene's name sent her tumbling into a brooding darkness. The last couple of days sent her into an all-out tailspin.

"I'm taking the day off," he said, tightening the hug.

"Don't do it on my account. I'll be okay."

He wasn't so sure. Her spiraling mood over the last several days caused him plenty of concern. Once she hit rock bottom the first thing she craved was booze. He doubted she'd visit a package store with Lily in tow but his presence might help curb the urge.

"Mama couldn't speak the last few days she was alive. She just opened and closed her eyes." Her hands curled to fists against his bare back. "Seth couldn't stand it. Georgia said he wouldn't go in and see her after that."

The pain in her voice clawed to his soul, "Babe, don't do this to yourself."

"Georgia called me at work. I was working for Bobby at the sheriff's office. I sped all the way to the hospital."

Ennis held her tight. He knew what came next. He heard the tears in her words just before she broke down, "Ten minutes. By the time I climbed in the car Mama was gone and I had no clue."

○ ○ ○

Georgia arrived within half an hour of his call. The sight of Savannah's sister trekking up the porch stairs relieved him in a thousand ways. Help was finally here. She entered the house carrying a paper sack filled with groceries. They exchanged hellos then she shook her head, "I should have anticipated this." She raked herself over the coals, "Having Lily, the hormones and lack of sleep, and of course Mama's birthday. I should have seen it coming."

He hefted the grocery bag out of her arms, "All she did this morning was talk about what your mother went through. It was like cutting herself with razor blades. It's like she blames herself for everything."

"She blames herself. She blames me. She blames God. Believe me, Ennis, I've heard it all, especially when she drank. What's she doing now?"

"I had her take a warm bath before she laid down. She's still wide awake."

She reached in her purse, took out a small prescription bottle, "Not for long, she's not. Thank God she's not nursing or these wouldn't be an option." She went to the kitchen sink, drew up a glass of water. "I'm betting it's postpartum depression contributing to her usual May

Mood.   Leah said depression can hang on for weeks or months after giving birth." She marched to the master bedroom, closed the door.

He eased to the door, careful not to make a sound. Savannah was awake and now mildly quarreling with Georgia about the tranquilizer. Georgia's unyielding tone softened from the sternness Ennis just witnessed. She spoke quietly, tenderly to her sister. Then emotions so chaste and fierce poured out of his wife that he covered his ears to drown out her crying.

Since their marriage he'd heard this kind of inconsolable weeping two other times and both revolved around Charlene.

He chanced listening again. Georgia's words soothed her sister whose crying ebbed to occasional sniffling. Savannah's voice calmed considerably after several minutes. The two were closer than any sisters he'd ever met. When one had problems, the other instinctively sensed it. He supposed with Charlene passing when Savannah was still a teenager, Georgia took her baby sister under her wing. She moved Savannah in with her shortly after Charlene's funeral and the two had been inseparable ever since.

The bedroom door opened. Georgia stepped out, closed the door behind her then handed him the prescription bottle, "Starting tomorrow, give her one at night for the next few nights. She's agreed to take them. If she reneges, call me."

Ennis examined the bottle. He recognized it as a powerful tranquilizer. A fire engine red warning label wrapped around the bottom. *Do not drink alcohol with this medication.* So far so good on that front. Savannah hadn't mentioned booze yet and he counted himself fortunate.

Georgia headed to the kitchen cabinet where Ennis left the grocery sack. "She's better now. She'll sleep through the afternoon. I'll stay with her if you need to go to work."

"I took the day off."

Georgia nodded. She switched to Little General mode since he'd called. It sounded nicer than Savannah's *General Georgia*, at least to him. Hand her a problem and she applied whip and spur until getting it resolved.

She unloaded the bag, removing a package of diced ham, an onion, hash browns, bacon, sour cream and packages of different cheeses. She reached in again to retrieve a bag of fresh peaches. "I'm making a ham breakfast casserole and a peach pie. You like ham casserole, don't you?"

Ennis's mouth watered. Only fools and idiots declined her ham casserole but still, "Georgia, you don't have to do all this. I can make something for supper."

She finally cracked a genuine grin and chuckled, "Ennis, bless your heart. You are a good man but you both need a meal more substantial than scrambled eggs tonight. You're welcome to help me cook though. I need mixing bowls, a pie dish," she began opening cabinets, "and where are her baking dishes?"

"Cabinet furthest to the right." He helped her gather the items she mentioned then while she tied Savannah's apron around her waist, he asked, "What's going on with her?"

"As it turns out, is more than Mama's death bothering her. She's afraid Toby will come after her – actually Lily. He'll do anything to hurt her and despite her cavalier attitude, she *is* scared of Toby. She mentioned several hang-up calls and the fact she sensed someone following you during the trip to the cemetery. She feels vulnerable in several ways. She lost Mama and she's afraid she'll lose Lily. I don't know how to help with her concern over Toby. I wish I did."

He did too. He planned to call around that morning, find out what he could about Jackson's release and whereabouts. He didn't know the whole story behind Savannah and Toby's relationship (again the door to Fort Knox slammed tight) but he knew enough to understand her fear of him. The man's ego far outweighed his common sense and he was built like an Alabama linebacker. He was married last account Ennis had but that was before Toby went to prison for molesting his young daughter.

Georgia continued, "Toby is a valid threat but I believe this mostly stems from postpartum depression. Mama's birthday always depresses her, you know that, and it doesn't help that her birthday is shortly after Mama's. She goes through periods like this but if we catch it in time," she lowered her voice, "she won't want to drink." Her eyes widened as if the notion suddenly sprung to mind. She pointed to the cabinets, "There's no booze is there?"

"Only beer and she hates it."

"Not if she's desperate and she's reaching that point."

He shook his head, "It's just shocked me, the intensity of this, that's all."

Georgia nodded to the dining table, "Sit down a minute. I'll try to explain." They sat down, Georgia carefully considered her words before speaking, "I suppose part of it was her drinking back then. She can't forgive herself for it. She couldn't cope so she drank which made things worse for her." She shook her head, "She still harbors so much guilt for things she did or didn't do for Mama and things she said to me."

"To you?"

"When Mama and I broke the news of the cancer. That's when Savannah began drinking. She said some things that hurt me but I knew it was anger directed at the situation. I understood that but she can't forgive herself. She tried to help when Mama got so bad. She did a good job when she was sober. Helped bathe her, medicate her, keep her company, but she still feels her efforts were inadequate."

Anyone who knew her realized Savannah demanded perfection from herself and when a sick loved one was involved, no one measured up to their own expectations – but such deep-rooted self-condemnation?

Georgia continued, "She's also under the impression Mama never cried or questioned God, that she was so strong nothing shook her faith, not even cancer. I heard Mama cry herself to sleep dozens of times pleading with God to heal her, asking Him why He hadn't." Georgia rubbed her temple, heaved a long sigh, "Mama was human. She asked God the same questions Savannah did when *she* was diagnosed. She suffered depression, doubts and spent a river of tears on them both. I've tried to tell Savannah this but she remembers it her way. She still feels inferior, like she let everyone down, especially me and Mama. She's living with profound guilt that she doesn't deserve. I don't think she's dealt with her death at all." She looked at her watch, "When was Lily's last meal?"

"Savannah fed her before she took her bath. I'll go check on her." They got up, and Ennis hugged her, "Georgia, thanks for coming over."

She smiled, returned the embrace, "No problem, Ennis. She and I have been through this numerous times."   When the parted, she slanted him a sly glance, "How are you at peeling peaches?"

"I can peel 'em like a pro. Ma canned them, made preserves and used the extras for pies and cobblers so I've got plenty of practice. Let me at 'em." *Then I'm making some calls about Toby Jackson…*

8

THEN

ACADEMY GRADUATION DAY

After twenty-two weeks of grueling training and tedious studying, graduation day from the Herbert T. Jenkins Police Academy finally arrived. The weight of daily evaluations lifted, the dread of written and oral exams and rigorous physical training eased, leaving graduation the last official step to becoming a police officer. Why then, did simply getting dressed seem harder than any of the rest she'd endured? Because she'd face hundreds of people that evening, including fellow officers, their families and *her* family? Or because, for the first time, she'd stand in the presence of every high ranking police official in Atlanta, including the chief?

She stared at her reflection in the mirror, reminded herself to breathe. He was the chief of police, the man who'd hand her the coveted diploma she worked so hard to earn. All day she recited the motions for when they called her name: *descend the auditorium stairs without tripping and killing yourself, approach the stage, climb the steps, turn, salute the chief, shake his hand, receive diploma, smile for the picture, return to seat, collapse.*

"Savannah, are you okay?" Georgia called from downstairs.

"No, but I'll survive," she added a P.S. of a whispered, "I hope." She angled her head, checked her hair. Georgia's efforts on the perfect bobtail surpassed anything she herself could ever accomplish. Her sister possessed great talent in many areas, and Savannah added styling hair to the list. Though the bun felt tighter than Grandma's girdle, she admired the way Georgia put a feminine swirl on the hairdo, making her feel at least halfway womanly in the uniform.

She reached for the heavy duty belt then felt her back twinge. Inhaling a slow deep breath, she let the spasm ease then abandoned the belt temporarily. No need to strap in yet, she thought. Her back always ached and her hips sported bruises from the duty belt's constant wear and tear. Between the unwieldy belts and running and exercising *in* those unwieldy belts, she'd be surprised if any graduates walked right that night.

She was grateful she developed the habit of running while in high school. It came in handy for those one-and-a-half-mile marathons that took down many recruits the first week. Six quit the first three days, another four were injured and sent to an orthopedic clinic. If the running, push-ups, jumping jacks and leg lifts didn't cull down the class, the boxing, wrestling and obstacle course did. Her worst experience during training – running an obstacle course after being pepper sprayed. Once the spray hit her, she nearly accused the instructor of firing a blowtorch in her eyeballs but was too busy trying to breathe. Her face burned like fire, tears blinded her and her eyes swelled, preventing any clear image of where she was going on the course. She fought through the pain and tears, resisting the urge to wipe her face for doing so meant spreading the inferno everywhere and driving the pain deeper. Her lungs burned as though she inhaled a flamethrower. The choking, coughing and gagging became too much for a handful of recruits but she struggled through the course, dripping tears and snot, cursing under her breath, steeling herself with determination, and refusing to give in.

"We've got an hour before we go," Georgia reminded from the hallway.

"I'll be ready." She examined her shoes that she'd spent twenty minutes shining and buffing to a flawless sheen. Now she did her mental inventory. White dress gloves, *check.* Tie, *check.* Hair, *check.* Shoes, *check.* Hat, tie, badge… *check.* Duty belt. *Ugh.*

Savannah glanced in the mirror to see her sister standing in the doorway, grinning ear to ear. "Let me see you," her sister bubbled with delight.

She practiced the military precision turn she'd use that night to face the chief. *Check.* A self-conscious grin brightened her face when Georgia beamed again, this time with pride. Her sister *should* have felt proud. After all, she'd ironed the uniform to marine excellence and polished the uniform's nameplate inscribed "Prince" to shining perfection.

"It's finally here. Graduation." Tears glistened in Georgia's eyes when she adjusted the badge that needed no adjustment, checked every button on the blouse that was already buttoned, smoothed her hands down the sleeves.

It was disarming to see Georgia so strangely flustered. It was as if Savannah was leaving home to fight a war or join the circus. "Are *you* okay?" Savannah asked.

"I'm so proud of you. You made your dream come true. I'm just so happy."

She cocked a brow, "That why you're weeping?"

Georgia nodded, thumbed away her tears, "Now, let's complete the ensemble and go get your diploma." She reached for the duty belt, leaving Savannah to wince on her behalf. Georgia hefted the fully equipped leather belt into her grasp. Her eyes bugged, "You're kidding. How heavy is this thing?"

A less-than-humorous smile curved Savannah's mouth as she relieved her sister of the cumbersome contraption. She wrapped the leather belt around her hips and buckled it, grateful her back didn't protest yet. She'd equipped the belt with two sets of handcuffs, her brand spanking new .38 revolver, radio and transmitter, pepper spray, flashlight and ammo holders. "It weighs exactly fourteen pounds. With the whole uniform I magically gain twenty pounds and it's not funny so don't laugh. Right now I feel as heavy as a Buick."

Georgia shook her head in disbelief, "Honestly, I don't see how you lug that thing around, much less run with it. That thing would cripple me."

Savannah harrumphed while plugging in the radio transmitter to the mike clipped at the epaulet on her left shoulder, "Let's revisit this conversation in a week and see how I'm walking. I may be in traction."

"It's no wonder when you haul two sacks of taters around your waist all day. Your back's going to kill you so I'll have the Tylenol handy for when we get home."

She wanted to laugh but realized her sister was right. The damn belt would hurt like hell and that was even after she'd arranged the items on the belt so nothing buried into her back when she sat down. Clockwise from the buckle were the handcuffs, pepper spray, the .38, a folding knife then the open area for her back then another set of handcuffs, the flashlight, radio and ammo pouches. She made sure the ammo pouches stayed on her left for fast access *and* so she didn't have to release her grip on the .38 to reload.

She slipped her white dress gloves in her pocket for the ceremony later then realized her neck felt funny. Of course she'd never worn a tie before either. Or buttoned her collar all the way up to her ears. "My tie straight?" She rolled her eyes, "Can't believe I'm asking if my *tie* is straight. I'm sure you never thought your sister would wear a tie. Glamorous, right?"

Georgia fiddled with the tie until she was pleased. She stood back, appraising Savannah in the all black uniform. The joyful smile returned, "You are a beautiful sight."

"Yeah," she snorted with sarcasm, "wearing a hot uniform, a tie, and this concrete belt. I'm real beautiful."

Georgia touched Savannah's cheek, "Mama would be proud of you. She always knew you'd accomplish whatever you set your mind to."

O   O   O

While the families gathered in the City Hall auditorium, Savannah paced the floor where the graduates gathered before the ceremony. Her friend and fellow graduate Adam Rafferty watched, amused, "I've never seen you this nervous."

"I've never been this nervous. Not even at high school graduation." She threw him a playful sneer, "How are you so calm?"

"I'm dying inside, believe me," he took that opportunity to join her step for step as he mimicked their drill instructor, "Left, right, left. C'mon, Prince, pick it up. You're falling behind. If you're gonna pace, do it right. What're ya doin'? Sightseeing?"

Savannah stopped, broke into a relaxed smile and gently nudged him with her elbow, "You joker." She sure liked Adam and the feeling seemed to be mutual from what she could tell. He certainly wasn't hard on the eyes either. He stood two inches taller than her at a respectable five feet eleven inches. His thick black hair curled at the first sign of any length so he kept it cut short. And his features reminded her of a young James Garner with their warmth and kindness that put a person automatically at ease with him.

Their friendship started as a competitive one. Challenging each other for quicker times on the mile-and-a-half run or for "just one more" push-up. With each week at the academy, the closer they became as confidants and mutual support. The two ate together, complained of their aches and pains together and shared jokes and family stories over the twenty-two week period.

The graduates formed a single line and began their trek down the stairs to the front row seats. Rafferty glanced back at her and winked.

Nothing ever bothered him. Throughout the academy his casual demeanor and jovial sense of humor bolstered her. Today was no different. "We've made it this far. A few more steps and it's over," he said. Then teased, "Just don't trip."

They made their way to the stairs, waiting their turn to enter the auditorium. The theater style seating accommodated a few hundred people, with families seated on one side, the graduates on the other. The instant she caught sight of the enormous room, a knot formed in her gut. The place was packed. Families filled every available seat.

As she descended the stairs behind Rafferty, she searched for Georgia and her sister-in-law Leah. They sat adjacent to Savannah's seat on the second row. Both smiled, gave her a covert wave. Beside Leah sat the biggest surprise of all. Her brother Seth sat next to his wife, grinning at his little sister with a thumbs-up. Being on active duty in the army, her brother wasn't sure if he'd make the graduation but promised to try. It was a joy to see them all there for her graduation.

A podium stood at the front of the massive room and behind that a sprawling semicircle of desks that resembled the Supreme Court. Along the front of the desk were twenty names, including the chief of police, deputy chief, zone commanders, academy director, instructors and other department leaders.

She followed Adam whose seat was to her left, closest to the aisle. From the corner of her eye she saw her family. She finally made them proud. She wrecked her golfing future when their mother was diagnosed with terminal cancer so getting this shield and diploma not only meant an accomplished goal, it meant redemption.

After the color guard and Pledge of Allegiance, the invocation followed. Though Savannah hadn't been close to God since her mother's illness, she bowed her head anyway. She took the opportunity to review the sequence of events coming next. Because of that, she heard only pieces of the prayer.

The police chief stepped to the podium, told everyone to be seated. His speech lasted an agonizing ten minutes. She and Rafferty exchanged glances from the corners of their eyes while the chief proceeded, "To the families of our new officers. This ceremony concludes twenty-two weeks of rigorous training that included classroom courses in constitutional law, Atlanta Police Department policy and procedure, hands-on defensive tactics, arrest techniques and daily physical fitness..."

Physical fitness? Try outright torture, she thought. Such a benign term "physical fitness" when the one-in-a-half mile run increased to five. When the instructors drove the recruits to their very physical limitations (to her surprise they actually admitted this). When she struggled to subdue and handcuff a giant (an instructor wearing a padded suit) while that giant wrestled with her and pushed her down while groping for her weapon. She ultimately won that fight (and retained custody of her gun too). Nope, she didn't consider most of it fitness but it sure as hell was all physical. Savannah's brain cramped at the memory of it all. The absolute hardest twenty-two weeks of her life and she felt every ache, strain and blister.

"...new officers," the chief continued, "remember the core values – professionalism, integrity, commitment. Challenge yourselves to be dedicated to the profession. I hope in thirty years you can celebrate tremendous success in this department. Congratulations."

The deputy chief, academy director and others rose from their desks, headed down to join the chief. They stood in a line beside him in a procession of police brass that caused her to feel faint. Don't screw up, she told herself. Not now, not after everything you went through to get here, to this day.

An officer handed the chief a diploma while another announced a name. The graduate rose from his seat, made his way down the stairs to receive the coveted certificate.

Savannah agonizingly waited through two dozen more presentations when she heard, "Officer Savannah Prince."

Rafferty gently elbowed her, "Get going before they change their minds."

She smiled at him and he winked, "Congrats, Savannah."

"You too, Adam." She, like the others, descended the stairs – without stumbling. She approached the chief, turned and saluted him. He returned the salute and extended his hand, gave hers a solid shake along with his congratulations. In his hand he held a leather covered folder with the city's insignia on the front and inside – the piece of paper she worked so hard for. Once in her possession, she thanked the chief and they both turned to the photographer and smiled. Photo taken, she made her way down the line of police brass, shaking hands and accepting their best wishes.

At the conclusion of the ceremony she was exhausted. Georgia, Leah and Seth stood with the rest of the families, applauding and cheering their new police officers. Tears welled in Savannah's eyes at the sheer delight in their faces. They were proud of her and frankly she felt a generous swell of pride in herself too. She and Rafferty shared one last hug, wished each other good luck. They'd probably need it, she thought. No telling who they'd be partnered with and the one partner besides Officer Deanna Bradley she never wanted – Riley Murphy.

9

THEN

"Lucky me. I won the lottery," Riley Murphy sneered. The fat, grumpy, early thirties uniform officer left no question about his new rookie. Well, Savannah thought, his rookie wasn't too pleased either. Besides being gruff, Murphy looked like a guy who enjoyed walking the Florida beaches in a Hawaiian shirt and shorts, scaring all the sharks away.

Savannah knew what he really meant by his comment but being a rookie cop, she just stood and tried not to irritate her new partner any more than she already had.

Riley turned back to Lt. Josh Hunter, hooked his thumbs in his gun belt, "Thanks for drawing my number with this one, Lieutenant. It makes me tingly all over."

For the last fifteen minutes, Hunter spoke highly of rookie Savannah Prince which made her squirm with unease. No one normally praised her but this lieutenant seemed to like her, at least a little. Hunter was a nice guy, about six to eight years her senior, attractive but also getting a few wrinkles at his eyes. The job aged people fast, she'd heard, and according to Murphy's sour frown and Hunter's tired eyes, it was true. She'd seen his fiery temper when provoked and never wanted to inflame the man.

Hunter braced his hands on his desk, then braced his cranky officer, "Murph, it's not like I saddled you with a goldbrick. She graduated fourth out of thirty-seven in the academy. She qualified as an expert marksman. Hell, she surpassed the whole class at the shooting range."

Riley wasn't convinced. He tapped a finger to his temple, "Gotta have the brains to know *when* to shoot." He wheeled back to Savannah who tried not to recoil, "You got any brains, Prince?"

Her mouth worked, she was sure of it, but no sound came out. No reply, no squeak, nothing. Freakin' wonderful first impression, she griped to herself.

Vindicated, Riley said, "See? Not lookin' good, Lieutenant. Told you. Who else you got in the hopper 'cause I need a good one this time."

The lieutenant stared at her, silently urging to speak. However being faced with the one cop everyone feared caused her throat to go dry. No more than fifteen minutes ago, she chatted up a storm with the lieutenant but being faced with Riley Murphy, the hardass who demanded perfection from his rookies was too much.

"Officer Prince," Hunter's brow rose, "how about speaking on your own behalf?"

Riley put hands to hips, "She mute?" He leaned in to make eye contact with her, "Hey, kid. You even remember your name?"

Of course she did. "Savannah Prince, sir." She tried for clear and confident. It fell out weak and pathetic. Nice work, Savannah, she berated. Real nice.

"Savannah? What, are you some kind of debutante? Who names their kid Savannah? You look like a Natalie. I'll call you Natalie."

"My name is *Savannah*, sir," she corrected in a stronger tone. She'd heard jokes all through the academy about her name. They teased her about Savannah one day and Prince the next. Besides school, she'd never endured so many callous jokes about something she not only couldn't change but was actually proud of. Her name.

Riley regarded her expression now. He glanced at Hunter. She glanced at Hunter who winked at her. Riley finally shrugged, "Savannah it is." He waved her along, "Come on, pup. I'll do my best to train you. Hope you're better than my last rookie."

They headed for the station entrance. Murphy kicked his stride into high gear, leaving her behind. For a fat guy, he could really move. "What happened to him?" she asked, trying to catch up.

He stopped to face her, "*She* got knocked up by a fellow uniform halfway through her first year. You interested in being a mom right now?"

She vehemently shook her head, "No way. I'm not cut out to be a mother. I'm not having any babies."

Murphy laughed and that irritated her. Driving her aggravation deeper, he replied, "Every female cop says that, Prince. Then the rabbit dies and they quit the job and go to work for Piggly Wiggly while raising junior on minimum wage." He chuckled under his breath, "Not cut out for it. If I had a nickel for every time I heard that..."

o   o   o

"Riley Murphy's a bear," Savannah told her sister when she got to Georgia's house that night. "In fact, I think he might eat small children for supper."

Georgia brought a bowl of fresh baked biscuits to the dining table. She'd spent hours on the fried chicken, mashed potatoes, gravy, biscuits and cole slaw. Savannah couldn't hold a quarter of the food prepared but as a reward for withstanding the bear, she intended to eat until she couldn't hold another ounce. Her sister went all out for Savannah on her first day at work, probably realizing it would be a nightmare. Savannah also suspected Georgia wanted to keep her mouth busy doing something other than drinking. She hated to tell her sister but Riley Murphy could drive anyone to drink, including Mother Teresa.

Georgia eyed the flask of bourbon sitting on the table. Savannah slanted a warning glare at her, one that defied argument. Her older sister sat a glass of sweet tea in front of her, "I'm sure he doesn't do that. Is he a bear or is he trying to instruct you on the job?"

Ah, so her sister required an example of Murphy's charm. Savannah scooted the tea aside, took a swallow from the flask. Okay, here goes, "Did Mama and Daddy name me PITA?"

"Peeta? Of course not. Who called you Peeta?"

"Murphy."

"Why? What is Peeta?"

"It stands for Pain In The Ass. So no, I don't think he's

instructing me at all." She threw back another drink, "He's. A. Bear."

"Hon, drink the tea," Georgia hinted.

She took a swallow of tea to appease her sister then reached for the bourbon again. Georgia swiped the flask, replacing it with a dinner plate. Savannah just rolled her eyes.

Georgia wasn't exactly a saint. She imbibed with a good amount of brandy when the moment struck so judging Savannah's indulgence – because that's what she considered it – wasn't exactly smart. "You know what Murphy did after shift? He went to the lieutenant and asked if there was a return policy on rookies."

Now Georgia laughed but had the sense to stop it as soon as it started. Savannah found no humor in it, "It's not funny, Georgia. That's like your publisher wanting to cancel your contract. If my partner refuses to ride with me, I'll get a bad name in the department and there goes my career."

That sobered the older sister quickly. Realizing the seriousness of the subject, she offered, "Maybe he calls every rookie PITA, who knows? Don't read too much into his personality until you know him better. Give him time, hon. Surely he'll grow on you."

"Like mold, I suspect." She reached across the table, grabbed the flask again.

Georgia scowled, "Before you crawl too far into that flask, Royal called me today."

Great. As if her life didn't have enough drama. Their apple and pecan orchards probably developed a disease on some grand scale and Royal and her brother Vincent had no clue how to eradicate it. It wasn't as if they were alone in the management of the place. They'd kept the longtime manager on staff so why didn't Royal call him? "Called for what?"

"She said the pecans have bugs." Georgia sat the cole slaw on the table, placed a spoon beside it.

Savannah drew in a deep breath. The aromas of all the dishes mingled, bringing on a hunger pain. One thing about Georgia. She'd cater to a person when they'd had a horrible day – or she expected them to. An impromptu smile curved her lips, "And she needs congressional approval to spray? That's why Ray is there. He's the orchard manager. He can and will spray the trees."

"She's running the place alone right now. Vincent went to California for a month and she and Ray got at odds so he quit."

"She ran him off?" Savannah groaned. "Dear God she's a menace sometimes." For Ray Slocum to quit, Royal must have exercised the usual Prince charisma which meant there was none. Now their flighty cousin tried to supervise an enormous fruit and pecan orchard by herself? But to know Royal was to not understand Royal. Savannah massaged her right eyebrow with her thumb. The Princes were masters at causing trouble in varying ways, "What *exactly* is wrong with the nuts?"

"She said the tips are turning brown."

"It's the Nut Casebearer again. She should spray for them now and again in a couple of weeks. If she doesn't, the nuts will drop."

Georgia begged her to call Royal and explain it to her. Savannah reluctantly agreed but added she'd first call Ray and plead him back. "Maybe my diplomatic side will show with him."

"You'll do fine. You and Ray always get along. You know, maybe we should entertain getting more involved with the place."

The mention of getting "more involved" weighed Savannah down like a pile driver. All she needed was a pair of cement shoes to close the deal. She wondered when the idea might germinate with Georgia. Of R.J.'s kids only she and Georgia inherited from Grandpa Prince. Seth was left out for the simple reason he didn't live in Georgia at the time of Grandpa's death – and Seth never forgave Grandpa for the snub either.

Savannah grabbed a piece of chicken and spooned cole slaw onto her plate, "Why did Vince leave during the growing season? He realizes how important those orchards are, right?"

"I'm sure he does and don't call him Vince. He hates it."

Savannah understood why. His and Royal's father – R.J.'s younger brother – had a penchant for the strange anyway. He named his dogs Stick and Mud. For his children, he decided to name his son Vincent and his daughter Royal which left them the monikers Vince Prince and Royal Prince – and neither of them appreciated it. Both kids had their own quirks but they really didn't deserve names that said *Go ahead. Laugh.*

Savannah took a bite of chicken and felt the pressure of the day melt away. She groaned with pleasure, "This meal is delicious."

Her sister brightened, "Thank you. I thought you might enjoy a chicken supper tonight." She laid her spoon down, flattened her napkin in her lap. Not just flattened but smoothed, re-smoothed and basically ironed to her thighs.

Savannah recognized the move. Georgia mustered the courage to broach a subject.   It was either about Savannah's drinking or her boyfriend Toby Jackson.   Since she'd already needled her about the drinking, it more than likely revolved around Toby. She was right.

"Toby still at work?" Georgia asked.

Savannah glanced at her watch, "Should be here anytime." She scooped another spoonful of potatoes into her mouth to prevent herself from chewing out her sister.

"Shouldn't you relax tonight? You've had a long day."

In other words, Georgia didn't want him there. Ever. Not that night, not the next, but ever.

Savannah swallowed, dabbed her mouth with the napkin while trying to concoct a decent explanation as to why she *really* needed to see him. She needed a hug and kiss – from a man.

Mercifully the doorbell rang before Georgia could expound on the idea. The older sister made no move to answer the door. Instead she lifted her tea glass and sipped, her vision never straying from Savannah.

Savannah sighed, rose from her chair and tossed her napkin on the table, "I know you don't approve but he is my boyfriend."

"Just think you could do better is all. He can't stay long. You've got an early morning and so do I."

She waved it off, "Yes, Mama." The instant she opened the door, big strapping Toby Jackson stood grinning at her, the smell of Old Spice wafting past, his short dark hair still glistening from his shower. He drew her into his embrace and planted a long, deep kiss on her. Clinging to his broad shoulders, Savannah relaxed in his arms, gladly responding to his affection. At least someone cared about her. Okay, she knew Georgia did but Toby's "caring" meant long kisses and snuggling together under the covers.

Two years her senior, Toby Jackson had the tanned, muscular physique of his trade: a construction worker. He worked all day building houses, went home to shower then made the rounds to Georgia's house to see Savannah. Neither Georgia nor Seth approved of Toby. Toby was spirited and lost his temper a lot but so did she. It wasn't the best relationship but it was hers and her siblings could mind their own business.

Toby parted from the kiss but kept one arm securely around her waist, "Hiya, beautiful. How'd your first day go?"

"It's better now," she punctuated the statement with a peck on his lips.

Toby bobbed his brow, "I brought a gift for my pretty police officer." He lifted his free hand that held a bottle of bourbon. Not just any bourbon either. Nearly the most expensive brand on the market. Toby knew the way to her heart.

"God, I love you more and more each day," she breathed, taking the bottle from him.

He kept her in his hold, "Hey, where's my reward for being so thoughtful?"

Savannah felt a giant grin surface. Circling her arms around his neck, she drew his lips to hers and "rewarded" him with a long, passionate kiss.

Someone pointedly cleared their throat from the kitchen. Georgia. Toby pulled back, whispering, "When are you finding your own place?"

"Soon as the big paychecks start rolling in." She stepped from his embrace and started toward the dining room. She answered Georgia's hint, "Coming, Mother."

Toby chuckled, gave her a playful swat while following behind, "So who's your new partner?"

"The Grinch. Out of all the partners, they stuck me with Murphy."

They stepped inside the dining room where her older sister had, in that brief time, cleared the table and managed to sit down again with her tea. Savannah's jaw dropped. Then it hit her. Georgia didn't want to feed Toby. She'd try to avoid it but he'd drop a hint and guilt would force her to offer a plate. But first Georgia offered a dressing-down, "Toby Jackson, I told you how I feel about you bringing liquor to Savannah. It's the last thing she needs."

Toby drew Savannah closer by the hip, "C'mon, Georgia, it's her first day as a bona fide cop. Give her a break."

Georgia wagged the flask back and forth, "She's already *celebrated* this evening."

Toby sniffed the air, "Wow, something sure smells good. Chicken?"

"M-hmm," Georgia replied, not making a move to get up.

Savannah pursed her lips. Toby tried to be polite, unlike her older sister who seemed determined to let Toby go hungry. "I'll grab you a plate," Savannah volunteered.

"There aren't many potatoes left," Georgia said as they went to the kitchen, finishing with the hint, "because I only cooked for two."

Savannah heard the smile in her voice. At the moment, getting her own place sounded better and better. Of course she never expected Georgia to cook for Toby but since there would be copious amounts of leftovers, why not share?

But somehow Georgia managed another magic trick while Savannah and Toby had been greeting each other. The platter, once brimming with breasts, wings, thighs and drumsticks – two full chickens – now held the two scrawniest drumsticks of the lot. Weariness and frustration mounted even as she reminded herself that Georgia prepared the meal – a meal meant as a gift to Savannah, not Toby, but still Savannah felt obliged to apologize for the lack of food, "Guess I should have saved you a breast."

Toby sidled behind her, his erection pressing against her bottom. Sweeping her hair to the side, he kissed her nape and let his hands roam up her stomach until his palms closed over her breasts, "That's okay," he whispered in her ear. "Here are my favorite breasts and I'll snack on them later."

"Savannah, would you bring me the tea please?" Georgia called.

The sound of her sister's voice killed the moment. Of course that's exactly what Georgia intended. Savannah handed the plate to Toby while she grabbed the pitcher of sweet tea. Toby said, "I'll pour our celebration drinks before your sister kicks me out."

Savannah marched the pitcher into the dining room and gently sat it beside Georgia's elbow, "You know, it wouldn't kill you to be nice to him."

The older sibling shrugged while refilling her glass, "Wouldn't kill him to stop hitting you either."

Toby walked in, thankfully oblivious to her comment, and sat two shot glasses on the table along with the bourbon bottle. He went back for his plate then plopped down beside Savannah. He filled both shot glasses full then scooted one to her. He addressed Georgia, "I chose shot glasses just to satisfy you, Georgia. Coulda hauled out the tumblers but thought better of it."

Georgia's cheeks flared red. Savannah felt her sister's anger percolating beneath the surface, saw defensiveness flash in her eyes. It was Georgia's house, not hers, so she tried to abide by her rules. Fact was, it was fun living with Georgia when they weren't fussing over men or bourbon. Savannah hated that Toby goaded her sister. Feeling threatened wasn't a valid reason and if he knew Georgia's temper, he wouldn't have done it. Savannah pushed the shot glass aside. She refused to poke sticks at her sister.

Toby sank his teeth into the drumstick, "So is this Murphy young and good looking? Do I need to worry?"

Georgia crossed her arms then cast a frown Savannah's way. He's already jealous, the look said. Her intense gaze forced Savannah to look away while she replied, "No, because he's old, fat and grumpy."

"Good," he replied around the mouthful of food.

Georgia's lip curled at his lack of manners. Savannah agreed Toby's social skills lacked at times but the man just spent all day in the heat, pounding nails and sawing two by fours.

Toby noticed their stares and swallowed uneasily, "Sorry. I

meant good that he's old and fat, not grumpy." He nudged the shot glass toward Savannah, "C'mon, gorgeous. Drink up."

"In a minute," she said. By allowing Toby to consume her culinary efforts meant only for them, Georgia's kindness stretched to its limit. Blatantly swallowing the bourbon in front of her – when she'd insisted Savannah abstain – would likely have driven her sister past the point of common civility.

"Savannah's got an early shift in the morning, Toby. Could you make this quick tonight? She needs rest."

Toby stopped eating. His dark eyes volleyed between Georgia and Savannah, but settled on his girlfriend, "Do you want me to leave?"

His expression raked a shiver down her back. He pointedly ignored Georgia, instead choosing to lay the decision at Savannah's feet. "No, I don't want you to leave but Georgia's right. I have to get up early for my shift."

He dropped the drumstick into the plate, the bone striking the china with a sharp clang. He raked the napkin across his mouth and rose to his feet, "Bye."

"Toby," Savannah scolded good-naturedly, "no one's kicking you out. I'm just tired."

"Well, so am I." He griped, "I work too, you know." He headed to the front door, grumbling the whole way, "You'd better get outta here fast or me and Georgia are going ten rounds and I guarantee I'll win."

"I like living with Georgia," she defended.

"I *don't* like you living with her, does that count?" Toby's face suddenly brightened, "Hey, I got it. Move in with me."

"Savannah," Georgia called from the kitchen. "Help me with the dishes."

She chose to overlook her sister's obvious interruption, "Move in with you?"

He slid his arms around her, pulled her close, "Sure. You could move in this weekend. Won't take that long to pack your stuff."

"Savannah," Georgia became more insistent.

"I can't move in with you, Toby. I appreciate the offer but I want my own place."

She felt his embrace harden. The loving embrace turned restrictive, his eyes narrowing, "Rent money is all you need?" He released her, reached in his hip pocket for his wallet, thumbed through what looked like several twenties and a couple of fifties. "How much?"

"You're not paying my rent. I have to find a place first anyway."

"This weekend. I want you out of this prison before next week."

"Savannah," Georgia's voice now sounded closer. A glance over her shoulder revealed her sister standing at the living room door glaring at Toby and holding a dishtowel, the ends wrapped around her fists like she wanted to strangle him with it.

"She's coming, Georgia." Toby ground the words between clenched teeth. "Give us a second to kiss goodnight." He tipped Savannah's chin up, wrapped his arm around her and crushed her against him. His lips descended on hers in a possessive, fiery kiss that nearly scared her. Toby's fingers threaded in her hair and closed, holding her to the kiss. His lips parted and before she could react, he shoved his tongue in her mouth. From the corner of her eye, she saw her older sister eyeballing the blatant display of affection.

Savannah tried to pull away, uncomfortable with Toby's boldness and the fact her sister stared them down. Toby's hand eased down her hair and throat to her breast. Savannah earnestly fought to separate herself from his wandering hands and the kiss that now seemed more vulgar than romantic. She pushed at his shoulders, sending him back a step, "Goodnight, Toby."

He wanted more. She'd felt his erection against her belly during the kiss and now it stood front and center in his jeans, the outline of it unquestionable. He scrubbed a hand through his hair, glared at Georgia then turned it on Savannah. "Yeah," he said, his voice rough with passion – and a good deal of anger, "goodnight."

Georgia waited for him to exit the house before marching past her sister and slamming the door behind him. She wheeled to Savannah, "You realize how dangerous he is, right? That kiss didn't look amorous, it looked like an animal defending its territory. You're gonna get hurt, worse than you ever imagined. If you don't get rid of Tobias Jackson, you will end up in the hospital or dead."

Savannah hated lectures. She wanted to tell her sister to mind her own business but two things prevented her from it. One, Georgia graciously let her live rent free with her and two, she knew Georgia was probably right. But, "You could end up hurt too if you keep pecking at him with your attitude."

The caution failed to faze Georgia, "Toby should learn a few things about me. First, I'm a longstanding member of the NRA and I own a gun. Two, like my little sister, I was taught how to shoot shotguns, rifles and handguns by our grandpa. You and I are experts with firearms thanks to Grandpa Prince. So don't let Toby get the drop on you, Savannah. He tries anything, shoot him and save yourself."

10

THEN

For six days she'd ridden in virtual silence with Murphy. The man mimicked a wall very well, she thought. She'd bet a hundred bucks every officer on duty – except Riley Murphy – interacted with their partner. His only true effort of communication came when he addressed her as PITA. At that point, his original choice of Natalie didn't sound so bad after all.

The seventh day felt longer and harder than usual. A vicious fight with Toby occupied the previous evening. It ended with her severing the relationship and as a parting gift, he slammed his fist into her right kidney twice. The blows sent her to her knees with tears streaming down her cheeks. All because he convinced himself she'd slept with Adam Rafferty instead of just having drinks after her shift.

Savannah also never realized the depth of his hatred of Georgia, not until he lashed out with his true feelings and not until he insulted her older sister with the ultimate female slur. One only used by knuckle-draggers, Savannah called them. Enraged, she hauled off and slapped him hard enough his cheek bloomed crimson and her hand went numb.

She turned to leave, her parting words being, "We're done, Toby. It's over." And his reply: a debilitating punch in the back. Then another.

She'd eventually pushed to her feet, bracing her back as she rose, then withdrew from his house, not silly enough to turn her back to him again. Now she contended with a stiffness rivaling an oak plank.

"Stay with the car, monitor the radio," Murphy ordered. "I'm grabbing some lunch."

"I'm hungry too," she complained.

"Yeah? What's your point?"

She'd experienced a multitude of rude wake-up calls that week. First Toby, now Murphy's denying her lunch. Since partnering up with him, they'd picked up lunch at convenience stores. Rubbery hot dogs, limp salads, and semi-warm hamburgers with equally warm vegetables. Today put a giant crappy cherry on her giant crappy week. No sit down, eat-in lunch for her. Men, she groused. Who needed them? She'd planned on grabbing a bite then horsing down two aspirin to relieve her aching back but thanks to her caveman partner, she'd have to wait until end of shift, dodder home and take a hot bath.

Murphy wheeled the car around a corner, eased in front of a small restaurant. He parked behind another unit occupied by Deanna Bradley and Adam Rafferty. Finally, Savannah thought. A friend.

While the other three officers climbed from their vehicles, Savannah gnashed her teeth against the pain. The duty belt dug into her already throbbing kidney when she pulled herself out of the cruiser. Murphy and Bradley stopped long enough to order their rookies to stay with the cars. Savannah and Adam looked at each other then leaned against the cruisers, Savannah taking extreme care with the move. For the past three evenings, the two academy friends met at O'Malley's Bar after shift, had a few drinks, and exchanged plenty of stories about their day. The longer she spent with Adam Rafferty, the more she liked him. His personality verged on jokester and the way he told stories made her laugh until she nearly cried. Adam Rafferty epitomized the exact opposite of Toby Jackson. A gentle man with an easygoing demeanor.

The two stood outside the small restaurant, watching happy, contented patrons straggle out after their meals. The air filled with delicious, tempting aromas of tangy barbecue, and juicy burgers. Savannah glanced at Adam, held a hand to her stomach and rubbed, "I'd pay a fortune for one bite of barbecue right now." *And a handful of Tylenol.*

Adam looked longingly inside, "This sucks. I mean, is this even legal?"

"Are you going to tangle with Bradley? 'Cause I'm not bucking Murphy."

They sighed simultaneously with Adam nudging closer to his unit's trunk and Savannah to the hood of her patrol car. "Hell of a way to lose weight," Rafferty joked, put his hat back on to shield the sun.

The light glinted off a ring on his right hand. She'd never seen the large silver ring before. He angled it for her to see. It was beautiful, she said, admiring the silver dragon claw and black onyx in the center. A lot of cops declined to wear rings for different reasons. Most cited safety. No one wanted to lose a finger during a fight with an unruly suspect. She presumed Rafferty wore it more for a statement than anything. She was right.

Adam explained, "Bradley wears her wedding ring. Figured I could wear my dragon claw. She hates it."

Savannah chuckled, "Is that why she won't let you eat? You irritate her on purpose?"

He gave a good-natured shrug, "Probably. So what's your story with Murphy?"

"Simple as PITA."

He frowned, "Yeah, I heard about the nickname. At least it's unique. Know what Bradley calls me? She says, '*You. You*, get over here.' Like she's calling a bratty kid."

Even though it hurt like hell, she automatically stood straighter upon seeing Riley finish his lunch and bid Bradley goodbye. He wanted PITA ready to go when he finished eating, he said.

She saw Riley stop at the counter a minute then exit the place carrying a hot dog on a plate. He pushed the plate at Savannah, "Eat this fast. You got five minutes and we're on duty."

She dared not smile at his act of kindness lest he assume she actually liked him. She did thank him however, despite the dog having relish on it. She'd eat a brick to ease her grumbling gut.

She glanced at Rafferty who pined for the food in her hand. He resembled a starving puppy, longing for one meager scrap.

Rafferty's partner was a hard-ass. Besides Riley, Officer Deanna Bradley was the least sought after partner among rookies. Savannah felt worse for Adam than she did for herself.

She split the hot dog down the middle, handed half to Rafferty who graciously thanked her. He whispered, "Hope Murphy doesn't tie you to the side mirror and make you run alongside the car for this."

Me too 'cause I'd be roadkill in two seconds. "He won't," she assured. She bit into her lunch and savored the taste, even with the relish on board.

Riley honked, tapped his watch. His diplomatic way of hurrying her up.

Both rookies finished off their lunch in record time. Rafferty wiped his mouth with the back of his hand, "You seeing anyone?"

"Nope." Not anymore. "Are you?"

He shook his head, "You enjoy our evenings at O'Malley's?"

"Very much." Was he kidding? He was the only person who didn't hound her about drinking or how much she drank. He embodied the perfect drinking buddy.

"Me too. Wanna have dinner sometime this week?"

"Sure. You name the night."

"Maybe a movie afterward?"

"Adam, I'd love to go out with you. A movie sounds great."

"*You.*" The word dropped like a boulder. Deanna Bradley stood, hands clamped to her duty belt, in all her five foot seven, linebacker glory. "Who said you could eat?" She scowled at her rookie then shifted the withering expression at Savannah. "Don't you belong over there?" she pointed to Riley who appeared as delighted as Deanna.

Savannah nodded then winked at Rafferty who winked back, "I'll call you."

Bradley took a closer look at her rookie, "Is that relish on your tie?" She gave Savannah a look that could melt glass. Savannah ignored her, gingerly sank into the passenger seat of the cruiser and blew out a breath. After meeting Bradley, she was grateful Riley was her partner.

"You take in stray animals too?" Murphy's peeved voice inquired. "Don't feed the rookies, Prince. Their partners will feed them if they need it. You owe me two bucks for the hot dog too, since you went and ruined my good deed for the day."

O   O   O

Savannah realized patrolling the streets was difficult and dangerous. Not knowing what the day held, whether the public would cooperate with her or not. In her first two weeks, she'd chased two teenage boys during a traffic stop. She struggled to catch up to the suspects, her legs churning for speed as the duty belt chafed and dug into her hips. A Buick, she'd told Georgia. She felt as heavy as a Buick with the extra twenty pounds of gear. After the first week on patrol she amended the description. She felt as heavy as a Peterbilt complete with a fully loaded trailer.

Precious few listened to the police, she decided, and once her kidney healed she resumed her regimen of running laps at Piedmont Park for strength and stamina.

She'd not been attacked yet, at least not by a suspect. Her partner, however, introduced her to the fine art of senior officer terrorism. Grill 'em till they cry Uncle, Aunt, Grandma and Fido seemed to be Riley Murphy's mantra. For the last several days she climbed in the cruiser to face the gruff overweight man in his thirties, and once they hit the road, he threw her into the fray. He barked questions better than a drill sergeant bent on haranguing his recruit. If she delayed with answers, he shook his head, mumbling "rookies" in a not-so-flattering way. Most times her answers arrived in a timely manner and that calmed the savage beast beside her.

A day earlier he fired off dozens of true or false questions, fill in the blanks, and had her explain how she'd handle theoretical situations. Upon completion of the day's third degree, she told Murphy the academy lasted twenty-two weeks. Twenty-two weeks of the same grilling and she managed to graduate fourth in her class. *And no,* she finished, *there weren't just four recruits in the class either.* She *earned* her badge, she said, the police department hadn't just tossed guns and badges at passers-by and turned them loose on society.

She'd gone home physically and mentally exhausted that night and without meaning to, overindulged in drinking. She now suffered a constant dull headache that aspirin hadn't touched. As they drove along Lenox Road Northeast, she thanked God Murphy hadn't begun his daily inquisition, though the man possessed an uncanny knack for locating and driving over every bump and pothole in a four mile radius, jarring her already aching brain.

Murphy leaned back, propped an elbow on the open window while steering the cruiser with one hand, "Mental checklist on responding to a call. Name 'em."

She blew out a breath, "Plan ahead when responding, I use all my senses to evaluate my surroundings, anticipate the unexpected, know where I am at all times–"

"So where are you now?"

She rubbed her forehead, willing the pain away, "The intersection of Lenox Road Northeast and Phipps Boulevard."

"You make a traffic stop," he said, wheeling the cruiser around a corner, pulled to the curb and parked. "The guy hands you his license. You take it with which hand?"

"My left," was her snappish answer. *Like I told you yesterday.*

"Why your left?"

"Murphy, c'mon." They covered the same subject every... single... day. She knew what to do and why. She needed experience, not an oral exam. She trapped those words behind clenched teeth but according to his expression, she needn't have bothered.

He knew exactly what she thought – and it didn't matter. " *Why?*" he stressed.

"To keep my gun hand free and, before you ask, I stand so that my gun is away from civilians and suspects. Murphy, I graduated, remember? I actually took notes."

"Hey," he argued, "you stop learning or you get complacent out here, you could die or get me killed. We're a team. Remember *that.* What you do affects me too. So when we're dispatched to a domestic, you gonna take off like Super PITA and save the day?"

Savannah laughed. Super Pain In The Ass. Now that was funny. What wasn't: his scowl at her amusement so she lost the smile, "While we're responding, I'd get more information if it's available. Is the disturbance in progress? Are there weapons involved and if so what kind?"

The lines on Riley's ruddy complexion smoothed. Apparently her answer pleased him.

"Did I pass your test today?" she asked.

"These tests will save your life." He surveyed their surroundings, watching people pass by. They sat in the opulent Buckhead shopping district. High dollar businesses lined the streets, their male clientele dressed in Armani suits, the women dressed in Louis Vuitton, Gucci, and Versace. Tourists stuck out like sore thumbs in jeans, shorts and casual wear, leaving them perfect targets for robbery and theft. She and Riley patrolled Zone 2 of the city which included Lenox Park and Lenox Square Mall, Piedmont Heights and Buckhead. They all had pros and cons but Buckhead's rich residents and general eccentricity seemed to be most renowned. Even their Kroger grocery store sported a unique name – Disco Kroger – because of its location next to the Limelight Disco in the nineteen seventies. The mirror ball from the Limelight hung inside the lobby of the Kroger to commemorate its legacy and each night the ball lit up and rotated until sunrise. Flamboyant, indisputable charm. That was Buckhead.

She felt lucky to be assigned Zone 2 after graduation. The upscale area of town still had various crimes, mainly robbery, however it lacked one aspect of Zones 3, 4, and 5. Rampant gang activity.

No matter the part of town, Savannah noticed there were three types of people. Some ignored the cruiser altogether, others gave it a brief glimpse then moved on while a few hung back, their expressions questioning the police's presence.

Riley broke into a genuine smile, "You got promise, kid, and you just earned your lunch."

Oh goody. "That mean you're paying?"

He shifted the cruiser into drive, angled into traffic, "You ain't got *that* much promise."

She figured he'd drive to the usual haunt for lunch. He did except he traveled the most convoluted route to the eatery. Where a street intersected, Murphy turned to explore it, then returned to the main thoroughfare. Savannah figured he either set her up for yet another question about location or he just generally sought to annoy her.

He turned again then slowed for a red light, "Somethin' you wanna tell me?"

Only that you're tempting fate with my stomach. I've ridden Six Flags rides that weren't as nauseating. "Like what?"

He glared at the rearview mirror, "How 'bout telling me who's been tailing us the last fifteen minutes? I don't have any fans anxious for an autograph so that leaves you."

Savannah sat straighter in the seat, glanced in the side view mirror. Riley added, "Three cars back. Dark blue Chevy, late-nineties model."

The description told her everything she needed but make it look good, she watched until seeing Toby's Malibu veer into sight. Closing her eyes, she cringed. Now he was stalking her at work.

"Who's dumb enough to follow a cop car?" Riley demanded.

"My ex-boyfriend," she grumbled.

"Well, it's time Ex-Boyfriend got a lesson in how his civil servants work."

Savannah wasn't sure what he meant until Riley swung the patrol car to the curb and stopped. Keeping his vision trained behind them, he waited. So did Savannah, "Murphy, if you'll let me talk to him, he'll–"

"No offense but clowns like this never listen to the little woman, even the ex-little woman. It takes a real authority figure to pound sense into them. Back me up and keep your mouth shut."

She saw Toby pull the Malibu to the curb a few spaces behind the patrol car. Riley opened his door, pushed himself out. He hitched up his duty belt, began the walk to Toby's car.

Savannah climbed from the cruiser, resisted the urge to rub her temple. The duty belt weighed like iron around her sore hips, making her cringe when she readjusted it. She begrudgingly followed her partner. The encounter would be a historic disaster, she complained to herself. Riley and Toby butting heads with her in the middle.

As they neared his car, Toby locked vision with her and she lifted a brow. What did you expect, the look said. She sidled up to the passenger side while Riley approached the driver. Her partner motioned for Toby to roll down his window. Toby did.

Murphy put a hand to the butt of his .38, the other on the roof of the Malibu, "You lost?"

Toby looked to his right toward Savannah. Before he made eye contact, Riley thumped the roof with his fist, "Hey, *I'm* talking to you."

Savannah saw Toby's jaw tighten and clench much like his hands gripped the steering wheel. She was grateful not to face his wrath later that night. Nope, not her problem anymore. That single thought reinforced her confidence in facing him.

Tobias Jackson answered, "Not lost, *sir*."

"Then what's your problem? You been following us for fifteen minutes."

"No problem. Just driving to work."

"Where's that?"

Toby replied, "Highland Construction."

Riley flicked his vision at his rookie than back to the driver, "License and insurance."

"C'mon, I'm headed to work. Can't you cut me a break?" As he reached in his hip pocket for his license, Toby shifted his vision from Riley to Savannah, "I'm just a guy trying to make ends meet, you know what I mean," he squinted at the name on her uniform, "Officer Prince?"

"Why you talkin' to her? Talk to *me*." He plucked the documentation from Toby's hand, looked it over. "Long way from home, Mr. Jackson. You takin' the scenic route today?"

"Had to drop off something to a friend."

It was a lie and Savannah knew it. Toby had no friends besides drunks and those drunks stayed drunk. They never regained enough conscious thought to need anything short of another beer.

"I see." Riley handed the license and insurance over to his rookie, "Run 'em."

Savannah hated that Toby couldn't leave her be. If he hadn't followed them, he wouldn't be in that position – but he wouldn't exactly see it that way. She marched to the cruiser while Riley kept Toby engaged in conversation.

She punched in the license and waited. Yes, he had insurance, no outstanding warrants. He did, however, have two previous arrests for assault. Assault. No shit, her right kidney panged an unhappy reminder.

Savannah walked back with the information, told Murphy there were no outstanding warrants but two previous arrests for assault.

Riley pointed to the passenger side of Toby's car. Back in position, it said, so she followed orders. He leaned to the window, handed back Toby's license and insurance, "According to our records, you've had some problems with law enforcement. Two arrests for assault."

When Toby looked at Savannah, his piercing gaze held a subtle warning. What, did he think she blabbed to her partner about his knuckles tattooing her kidney? Fat chance. She still struggled to gain Murphy's *attention* at times, much less his respect.

"A long time ago, sir," Toby assured as if he'd received sainthood since then. "A long time ago and I'm sure your records will prove it."

"Mr. Jackson, I'm going to give you some advice. Don't go where you're not wanted or needed. Your mother, your sister, your aunt and your *ex*-girlfriend can get along just fine without you meddling. In other words, Mr. Jackson, you follow our patrol unit again and I'll find something to haul you in for. Understand?"

Savannah forced herself to make solid eye contact with Toby despite the uneasy feeling in her gut. He'd been possessive of her but not to this extent. But, she wondered, was it possessiveness or a prelude to revenge for dumping him?

"Understood," Toby said with more calm than his demeanor indicated.

Murphy slapped the roof of the Malibu with a tense smile, "Have a nice day, Mr. Jackson, and count yourself lucky." Riley pointed Savannah toward the cruiser. She started toward it, hearing Toby crank the Malibu's engine, revving it. She may have broken up with him but Toby wasn't finished with her. She swallowed hard, lifted her chin and pushed her shoulders back, trying to show she wasn't scared of Toby Jackson. If she hadn't had a gun strapped to her hip, she wouldn't have been scared, she'd have been terrified.

o o o

"I'm not nosing in your business, Prince," Murphy mentioned as they opened their lockers. End of shift came quicker than she expected, quicker than she hoped. The day long headache wasn't as debilitating as Toby's temper. Now she had to change clothes and drive home with hopes Toby was passed out drunk at home so he couldn't confront her about that morning. She'd bet money he would since he was more brawn than brains.

Murphy slipped out of his uniform blouse, revealing a white t-shirt beneath, "I just think you oughta reassess your social acquaintances. That boy is trouble, if you ask me, which you didn't but I'm warning you anyway."

Savannah temporarily hung her duty belt in her locker, glad the weight of it was off her hips for the day. "I broke up with him, Murphy."

Riley pulled on a dress shirt, buttoned it, "Well, Construction

Clown ain't getting the drift." He stepped around the corner to face her, "Show him who's boss. Show him you're not his victim."

"I broke up with him, Murphy," she repeated. "I don't know why he followed us today."

"I do." He circled his temple with his finger, "PITA found a nutjob who won't take no for an answer. Guys like that, better keep your gun close by. 'Cause I meant it. Next time he screws around with me, I'll haul his ass in just for pissing me off."

"Do what you gotta do. I'm not stopping you."

He closed his locker, "I can help him understand what *take a hike* means, if you need me to. Keep it in mind. You're a PITA but you're my PITA. Anyway, good work out there today, kid. See you tomorrow."

"Bye, Murphy. And thanks." She proceeded to change and decided to keep her weapon with her. She felt safer with it, even without wearing the uniform. She was grateful to her brother Seth who, besides their grandfather, taught her the finer points of shooting. She just prayed she never had to test her skill on – or off – the job.

O O O

After shift, she drove to Georgia's. Making the turn onto Georgia's street, she slowed the black Avenger upon seeing Toby's Malibu parked in front of the neighbor's house, safely out of Georgia's sight.

She groaned. She'd hoped he'd pickled himself and passed out since being cut down by Murphy. No such luck. For a moment, she entertained heading to Piedmont Park and staying an hour. Toby got frustrated if he waited, he always did. Her aching back killed the idea of the park. Why should she avoid a confrontation she knew was inevitable? No, she refused to cower from the bastard, especially after he nailed her kidney. She'd pull into the driveway and tell her personal Mike Tyson to get lost once and for all.

She climbed out of the car, seeing Toby exit his Malibu at the curb. She did a doubletake at the contents of his hands. He held a rather large bouquet of red roses and white Asiatic lilies. She rolled her eyes as he hotfooted to her like nothing ever happened, "Hey, babe."

She just stared at him while the aches and pains of the day threatened to emerge in her mood. The only bright spot: the impending date with Adam Rafferty. They planned dinner and a movie that weekend, and he'd given her carte blanche on choosing everything.

Toby offered her the bouquet, "I got you these. To apologize for today. I was out of line."

"Yes, you were." She took the flowers since his hand remained extended. "Thanks for the flowers." She rounded the front of the Avenger toward the corner of the garage. "You can go now."

Toby grabbed her arm a little too hard then immediately softened his grasp, "I'm sorry for everything. I felt threatened, you know, when your partner pulled me over and you didn't take up for me."

"I couldn't, Toby. That's not my job. You shouldn't have been following us." She saw his jaw clench then quickly release, trying to conceal his anger.

Instead of admitting she was right, he changed the subject –

another trick she'd learned over time. Toby loved to divert subjects. If that failed, he started arguing. If that didn't work, he resorted to hitting. "I had a reason though," he said. "I wanted to tell you I found your charm bracelet but never got the chance."

Her brow lifted. She thought she'd lost the bracelet months ago. Memories raced back of scouring Toby's bedroom top to bottom in a panic, searching for the precious bracelet her mother bought for her sixteenth birthday. It was a beautiful brilliant silver with charms that her mother and Georgia gave her as gifts. There were five total. Georgia bought a heart that read *Sisters Forever*, and their mother added another heart along with a cross, a golf ball and a charm reading *Hole In One* in honor of Savannah's first during a tournament. She prized the bracelet and it broke her heart when it went missing. Now it suddenly – and conveniently – reappeared. "Where did you find it?"

"Under the dresser. Guess it got kicked under there."

Funny. I remember looking under the dresser at the time. She held her hand out, waiting for him to return it, "Thanks for finding it."

He shook his head, "I forgot it. Can you come by tonight? I tried to clean it up for you. You had five charms, right?"

"Right. Why don't you bring it to the station on your way to work? I'm too tired to go anywhere tonight."

He frowned, "I can't, babe. Boss wants us at work early because of the weather. I'll be cutting it close if I eat breakfast. Just drop by before ten and I'll have it waiting. I also found a couple of books you left behind. I'll gather those up too."

She ran her fingers through her hair, noticing *it* even hurt after her long day. "Toby, I can wait a day or two for you to bring it to the station. Today was hell out there."

He caressed her cheek, "If you'd come over, I'd rub your shoulders and back. You used to love that."

Yeah, until you busted me in the kidney a couple of weeks back. It still ached on occasion, a jolly little reminder how stupid she'd been hooking up with Toby in the first place.

She leaned away from his hand, "I wouldn't stay if I came by."

His shoulders slumped in defeat, his expression crestfallen. "I'm really sorry for what I did and said, Savannah. I'll wait up for you tonight. Please come over. I know you want that bracelet back."

Her hips and back ached from lugging around the weighty gun belt. Her legs and feet felt swollen. Her shoulders tensed until her back developed spasms. Running after a suspect carrying an twenty extra pounds drained a person. Her main goal was to eat supper and relax in a hot bath – and dream about supper and a movie with Adam Rafferty, a normal guy.

She shook a cramp out of her foot, "Give me time to eat and soak in the tub a while. I'll be at your place around nine."

O   O   O

"You've lost your mind," Georgia stated as cold, hard fact. "Don't go see him. He's dangerous. You don't know what he'll do."

The euphoric news of Adam's date fell down the black abyss called Toby Jackson. Georgia went from giddy to homicidal in two seconds flat so Savannah went upstairs to bathe. She closed the bathroom door hoping to short circuit the rant. It didn't work. Georgia marched in while Savannah stripped down and started the bath water.

"The roses and lilies are beautiful but are they worth a trip to the hospital – or the morgue?" Georgia suddenly gasped, "*Look at your hips.*"

Yes, the bruises were ugly but at least they matched. She discovered that whether standing or sitting, the belt's lower edge dug into her hip bones, leaving a bluish black bruise on each that hurt like hell, "I live with them, Georgia. I don't need to see them."

Her sister's frustration mounted, "Besides Toby, that gun belt is the bane of your existence."

Savannah hadn't the heart to argue because Georgia was right about both. She grabbed her flask and downed a few more swallows. Her sister's lips pursed, a sign she trapped scathing words behind them. She shook her head, settling for, "This is insane. First you commit to seeing that bastard again and now you're drinking before you go. You can't drive in that condition."

"I'll be lucky to walk in the morning and it hasn't got anything to do with bourbon. Don't lecture me, Georgia. My whole body hurts. I'm not getting drunk, I'm trying to relax." She gingerly slid into the warm bath, grimacing when her bottom hit the tub. Even her tailbone felt sore. The warm water embraced her aching body, providing a generous degree of instant relief. She leaned back and sighed.

Georgia took the opportunity to swipe the flask from her hand much to Savannah's exasperation. She rolled her eyes but kept quiet.

"If you stay home tonight, I'd give you a neck and back rub to loosen those muscles."

Her offer sounded divine unlike Toby's. Nothing surpassed Georgia's massages, especially after a difficult day. Savannah wanted to stay home and let her sister work her aggravations out on the tense muscles. Unfortunately though, "I really want that bracelet back, Georgia. It means a lot to me and I was convinced it was gone forever."

She crossed her arms, "Convenient how he found it after you broke up with him, isn't it?"

"Yes, I agree it is, but he has it and I want it."

"What if he's lying and doesn't have it?"

"I'll leave. Can I beg a back rub tomorrow night?"

Georgia appraised the pain etched into her sister's features and nodded, "Tomorrow then." She turned to leave the bathroom, stopping to say, "Savannah, please reconsider going. Or let me go with you. There's safety in numbers."

"And have you and Toby go round and round? I don't have the strength to pull you off him nor do I have strength to fill out a report of why you beat him to death."

"I don't have a good feeling about this."

Savannah closed her eyes, soaking in the warmth. She grinned, bobbed her brow, "I have a good feeling about Adam Rafferty. You'll like him."

Georgia refused to be deterred from the subject, "You're still going, aren't you?"

Her tone held a note of somber acceptance but Savannah

couldn't worry about it. "I'm still going. Hey, did I tell you I called Ray the other day? He's back and he sprayed the nuts. No worries there, at least." When she opened her eyes, a cheerless half-smile curved her sister's mouth.

"I'm worried he might kill you, Savannah."

"Ray?"

Upset at the silly joke, Georgia's temper flared, "*Toby*. When you pick up the bracelet – if he really has it – he could attack you. Then what?"

She shrugged, "Georgia, stop worrying. I'm taking my gun."

The statement drove her to rub her temple, "Shoot him if he tries anything. I've said it before. Do what you have to, just save yourself."

After the bath, Savannah drove to Toby's. He answered the door in only jeans and a suggestive grin, "Hey, gorgeous. Come on in."

His smile promised a night of passion her body couldn't handle even if she wanted to which she didn't. In fact, she felt quite sure *that* activity – with anyone – was an unattainable fantasy until her body improved from total wreck to general mess. She ignored his ravenous expression, "Where's the bracelet?"

He stepped to the bar, tilted a bottle of Jack Daniel's into two lowball glasses. He offered one to her. She refused, "Bracelet, Toby."

He sighed, swallowed the contents of one glass then shrugged, knocked back the other. He sat the glasses down, pointed to the sofa, "I put it in a bag with the books. Go ahead, since you're in such a hurry."

Savannah went to the sofa, opened the paper sack sitting on the cushion. There it was, still bright and shiny, just like new. That, along with three paperback thrillers she'd left behind. "I looked under the dresser when I misplaced it," she mentioned. "It wasn't there."

"Had to be. That's where I found it."

Bag in hand, she turned to face him, "Did you? Because I left it on the nightstand, not the dresser. I always left it on the nightstand."

Toby's good humor faded fast. He stalked toward her, "Are you accusing me of stealing it?"

She didn't answer but didn't back down. The gun on her hip rested against her elbow, and somehow she felt her hand gradually moving back to the holster. The trusty .38 on her hip might be her saving grace yet.

"What if I *borrowed* it?" he asked. "As insurance? Your mother gave you the bracelet. You'd do anything to get it back and I'd do anything to get you back. I've seen you with that bastard at O'Malley's every night the past week. Cops stick with cops, I guess."

"Stop following me, Toby. It's just plain wrong. Adam and I are friends, nothing more."

His words sharpened to razors, "Yeah, right. I believe that like I believe Georgia isn't part of the reason you broke up with me. The bitch finally poisoned you against me."

He stepped over the line with that comment. Savannah advanced on him, "Watch what you say about my sister. She's trying to protect me."

Toby stepped forward, meeting her, "Protect you from who?"

"Myself, obviously. I've made poor choices in my life and she warned me about every one of them."

He leaned down, met her eye to eye, "And I'm number one on that list, aren't I?"

"Yes, you are." She wheeled to leave before she made another bad decision and stayed to argue. Arguments with Toby Jackson ended with his fists swinging and her bruised and crying. How could she have been so clueless and stupid? She'd met him at one of the worst times in her life – on the anniversary of her mother's death. Savannah never fell in love before, never understood what it was, what it meant or what a loving relationship really involved. She knew she liked Toby when he wasn't violent. She loved the way he touched her, held her and when his mood was just right, he beguiled and seduced her with amorous gestures and sentimental sweet-nothings. He reminded her of a damaged Prince Charming and when they met, she'd felt damaged beyond repair because of her mother's death. They belonged together, these two broken, turbulent souls. Or so she thought…

His hand on her shoulder spun her to face his enraged features. Instinctively stepping back, she reached for her .38 but his fist buried in her stomach, sending her to her knees. He punched so hard she swore his knuckles dented her spine. Fighting the urge to puke, she again attempted to retrieve the gun.

"You've had your say," his temper fired white-hot, "now it's my turn."

She saw it coming and couldn't avoid it. His fist crashed into her jaw, splaying her onto her back, her head swimming in an eddy of dizziness.

Georgia's parting words soared to mind. *Don't go. He's crazy.*

You don't know what he'll do... Well, I do now, she thought.

His fist hammered her jaw again. A fog of gray clouded her vision. For an instant, she forgot where she was and why she was there. Then two hands slammed on her chest, ripped her blouse open, sending buttons flying. Ragged nails scraped and ripped down her breasts and belly as he stripped off the bra, tossed it aside. She tried to fight but the world kept spinning, trying to fall away and leave her unconscious and completely unable to defend herself.

She felt him strip off her jeans and panties, the sharp sting of his nails clawing down her belly and thighs. The fog rolled in again when she tried unsuccessfully to prop on her elbows and she flopped back before she passed out.

Toby now loomed over her, his long, thick erection an ominous portent of his intentions. She had to get away from him but everything moved in slow motion and her sluggish, uncoordinated movements hindered her progress. She managed to turn on her side, her goal – crawl to the door that stood only feet away.

His foot on her shoulder rolled her to her back, his heel anchoring her by the hip. When her vision cleared, she stared down the barrel of her .38.

"This what you wanted to give me tonight?" He clicked the hammer back, "I thought you were picking up a bracelet, not shooting me full of holes." He thrust the gun beneath her chin, "You wanted to show me who's boss, didn't you? To be a big shot and tell me I'm going to jail for assault. If I'm going to jail, sweetheart, I'm making it worth my while."

He'd already forced her thighs apart, kneeled between them. A smile crossed his face as he forced her gaze to his, "I'm really gonna enjoy this."

Savannah felt his mouth and teeth on her breast. A scream tore from her depths when he sank his teeth into the tender flesh. Her fingers raked his face, gouging at his eyes but he bit harder, his hands prying hers away and pinning them to the floor.

Crying at the pain traversing every nerve in her chest, she fought his strong hold, to maneuver for leverage. She pleaded with him to stop, begged him to let her go but his jaw slammed on the tender flesh in a second vicious attack. For few precious seconds pain replaced all reason. Once the throbbing ebbed a degree, the reality sank in of what came next if she didn't escape this maniac.

Toby sat back, circled one finger around the bite mark then held his bloody fingertip for her to see, "You ain't seen nothin' yet, bitch."

Those few words stirred a storm inside her. The pain finally lessened enough for her to reference Seth's self defense training. Toby leaned forward and she braced her hands on his shoulders. Anger dissolved his ominous smile, anger that she still had the spirit to battle him. He pushed against her hands but she locked her elbows, preventing him from bracing his hands on the floor.

"You wanna fight?" he challenged between clenched teeth. "Go ahead. You'll lose and you know it."

Savannah dug her right heel into the carpet, swiveled her left hip to gain some space between them. Toby's hand closed on her throat as she planted her left foot at the juncture of his thigh and hip and shoved.

The move pushed him away far enough to jam her right foot on his other hip. She shoved again with all her strength, sending Toby back several inches, and jarring his hand free of her throat. She curled up, drawing her knees to her chest. While he drew back to throw a punch, she drove her right heel deep into his stomach, kicked her left into his sternum, knocking him off-balance. Then she launched her heel at his chin. Bone collided with bone, Toby's head snapped to the side and with a yelp, fell backward at her feet.

She groped for her gun, climbed to her feet while he groaned about his jaw. The .38 shook violently in her hand when she aimed it at him, her finger firmly on the trigger. Georgia's voice echoed in her mind. *Shoot him and save yourself.*

Toby ran his bloody tongue along his teeth, lisping, "You bitch. My teeth are loose." He reached in his mouth, testing one or two, his rage building, "If you want to live, you'd better shoot me."

Shoot him, Georgia had said. *Save yourself.* Her left hand joined her right to hold the gun steady. A twinge in her left breast drew her attention to the source of her misery. He'd clawed bloody stripes down her breasts, belly and thighs that not only hurt but now began stinging like a swarm of bees. Blood seeped from the bites on her breast that ached deep into her shoulder and back.

He levered to his knees, "Either shoot me or lie down and take it like the whore you are."

She tightened her grip on the .38. The temptation of following Georgia's advice seemed rather simple. Hell, he even begged her to shoot him. But she couldn't. When he tried pushing to his feet, she reared back, booting him up the chin once more. She grimaced when the impact jammed her toes, sending a sharp pang up her calf.

Toby fell back with another yelp, thrusting his hand out in a *stop* gesture, a rare sight in their relationship. Toby surrendering.

"You come near me or Georgia again and I will shoot you," she vowed. "I swear I'll empty my gun."

She threw on her blouse, buttoning the only two remaining buttons then pulled on her jeans and shoes, and shoved her bra and panties in her pocket. She kept her gun trained on him as she backed to the door. The bag containing the bracelet and books tucked snug beneath her arm. As she stepped past his wet bar, she swiped the half empty bottle of Jack Daniels then limped to her car, and drove three blocks to a nearby park where she broke down to cry.

Thank God for Seth, she thought. With his army buddy, they taught her and Georgia the self defense moves after Seth's female colleague suffered a brutal rape. By the end of their brother's leave, both she and Georgia knew the moves by heart. Had Seth not insisted on the lessons, the night would have turned out much different.

She threw back a healthy amount of Jack to quell the ache of her throbbing jaw and breast. When the tears receded, she shored up her nerve and headed to Georgia's. Her sister would be on high alert upon her arrival, demanding answers to what happened. Savannah hadn't the heart to tell her. First, surviving the attack was difficult and traumatic enough, but confessing it to the person who'd cautioned her not to go, well, it would absolutely finish her off. Georgia could never know. She might *suspect* but Savannah refused to admit her bad judgment and stupidity nearly got her raped.

Savannah thumbed the latch on the glass screen door then jumped back when the heavy wooden door yanked open, revealing her sister's panicked expression.

"My God," Georgia gasped, looking her up and down, "what did he do to you?"

She opted for the obvious, "He hit me. Repeatedly." She walked past, went to the dining table and placed the paper sack on top. "Here's the bracelet. Bastard stole it, kept it for leverage to lure me back to him."

To her credit, Georgia overlooked the bottle of Jack and .38 she held. Instead she concentrated on Savannah's chin, "He belted you good. It's swelling. Come in here." She towed her sister to the kitchen for an ice pack.

Savannah barely restrained more tears, "I just want a bath and to go to bed."

"But your jaw–" She stopped as her eyes widened at her sister's half buttoned blouse, "Dear Lord, no. Did he..." She closed her eyes, regrouped her thoughts, "Did Toby Jackson–"

"Georgia, please," her voice wavered. It took every ounce of fortitude not to lose her already unraveling composure. She turned, limping up the stairway then stopped to say, "Thanks anyway, sis."

Once in the bathroom, she closed and locked the door before dissolving into tears. She took two solid pulls off the bourbon, noticing her hands still trembled. She tried shaking out the tremors but it didn't work. She reached over, turned the bathwater to hot, and let it run.

She shed her clothes, wincing at the long, bloody scratch marks down her stomach and bite marks on her breast. The evening's events converged, overwhelming her as she crouched at the toilet to heave.

She disregarded Georgia's knock at the door. After two more swells of sickness, she leaned her bare back against the cold tile wall, trying to gather her dignity and poise. She was safe now, she assured. Safe at home.

Georgia knocked again, this time harder, "Savannah, I heard you throw up. Open the door, I can help."

"No," she wiped another tear, took another drink. *No one can help me with this. Sickness or no sickness, I brought it on myself and I have to deal with the aftermath myself. The puking, the shakes, the wounds, the memories. All of it. Alone.*

"I called Riley to tell him about Toby."

The bourbon caught in her throat. A coughing fit ensued. Once she regained control, she held a hand to her sore gut, barking, "You what? Why'd you call him?" Of all people, she wanted to say. Georgia called Murphy. Savannah figured tomorrow her new nickname (a truly deserved one) would be Super Stupid PITA. The mere idea of her next shift caused her to kneel at the toilet and hurl until she groaned.

"I was afraid for you. You've been gone two hours, I didn't know what to do so I called him. He's been looking for you."

"I'm fine." Said the idiot who resembled a tiger mauling victim, she mused darkly, and turned herself inside out from tossing her cookies. "I'm taking a bath and going to bed."

"Savannah, tell me what happened tonight." Georgia's voice held a trace of panic. She tried the door again, "Let me in, *please.*"

"No," she replied with renewed finality. She stared at the door then tilted the bourbon to her lips, praying this slug stayed down because she needed it to dull the pain, memories and humiliation of the night. One more swallow, then another. The warmth spread through her body, easing a trivial amount of aching.

She wiped the tears from her cheeks and closed her eyes only to see Toby looming over. His ruthless smile. His fist sinking into her stomach. His teeth sinking into her breast. His nails raking her flesh until bringing blood.

"Why won't you open the door?" Georgia asked.

She couldn't stand the thought of her sister seeing her. In her mind she imagined Georgia scouring every inch of her, felt her taking a silent inventory of every injury, bruise and scratch. And Savannah would cower from the invasive stare, unable to muster the courage to meet her gaze with the knowledge it was all her very own fault.

She'd endured enough that night. Her sister just needed to accept the word *no*. She tipped the bottle again, took a smaller sip. "Georgia, I'll be out later. I just want to be alone right now. Please understand."

Moments of silence passed then Georgia offered, "I'm here if you need me, hon."

Savannah thanked her, reached, turned the bathwater off. She checked the temperature and jerked her hand back, cursing under her breath. She turned on the cold water to moderate the heat. She intended to take the longest bath in history. Just her and her pal Jack Daniels.

11

THEN

Savannah crawled out of bed early the next morning, after a brief, restless two hours of sleep. Her head sat heavy on her neck, her brain grinding to life after the bender the night before.

Her head pounded a tribal beat of misery, her stomach sore from Toby's attacks and from heaving. Her left breast itched. The instant her hand touched it she gasped. She dreaded her shift. She'd feel awful, ache all over and walk funny. Not to mention spending her day with Mr. Personality and his own inquisition of the previous night's events.

She slipped on a pair of jeans, carefully cradled her boobs into a bra then shrugged into a navy blue button down blouse. *Now face the music.* She squared her shoulders which lasted three seconds before reality hit along with the muscle aches. She slumped, blew out a breath and vowed to provide her inquisitive, well-meaning sister with vague answers. Georgia didn't need details. She didn't deserve those images in her mind, especially after warning her fool sister not to go anyway.

Savannah descended the stairs, the aroma of fresh coffee drifting to her. Mugs clinked together (ever thoughtful Georgia always poured two cups) however that morning Savannah's gut promised a mutiny if she entertained ingesting anything. She walked into the dining room where Georgia sat, dressed in jeans and elegant jade green pullover.

Her sister traced the rim of her cup, silently waiting while Savannah eased into her chair. "Morning," she said.

At least she hadn't slapped a *good* in front of it, Savannah thought. "Morning."

Georgia nodded to the cup on the table, "Cream with a touch of sugar, the way you like it."

She thanked her sister, brought the cup closer, wishing her stomach felt strong enough to drink it. Her hands cradled the cup, soaking in the warmth. The bracelet laid at the table's center. Savannah stared at it for the longest. She felt Georgia watching her, unblinking. Unease forced her vision away from the bracelet, the bait Toby used to lure her into his trap.

"You had nightmares this morning," Georgia said. "Kicking, groaning, talking in your sleep."

She rubbed her face, pushed the coffee aside, "Sorry if I woke you."

The claw marks made her belly and side sore. Her breast protested the bra and she tried ignoring the low level throb it developed. Before going to bed, she rummaged the medicine cabinet to find the peroxide, antibiotic cream and a box of Band-Aids to doctor the wounds. Crawling between the sheets hadn't afforded respite with her body hurting and her mind reliving the horrific evening. When she finally drifted off, nightmares haunted her, jarring her awake through the night.

And now she discovered she talked in her sleep. Asking what she said in the depths of her private hell only opened herself up to more questions. Questions she never intended to answer.

Georgia sipped her coffee, her gaze steady on Savannah, "I cleaned up the bathroom after you went to bed."

"I'm sorry you had to clean up my mess."

"I'm not complaining. You're normally good to tidy up, that's why I was worried."

"It was a long night. I'll do better." Her stomach joined the chorus with a mixture of nausea and a sharp twinge from where Toby punched her.

Georgia sat the cup down. The boldness of her stare caused Savannah to squirm. No one stared a person down like Georgia. And no one nagged like her either, "I found a bloody washcloth in the bathtub. I saw blood on your ripped blouse too."

Savannah remained silent. She hadn't missed the emphasis on *blood* or *ripped*. In the midst of her turmoil, she'd forgotten about the bloodstained blouse. Only a few small splotches dotted the fabric but even a dummy could tell the wounds were located on her belly and breast.

"I also picked up your panties and torn bra after they fell from your pocket. In the kitchen."

Anxiety set in. Her heart pummeled her ribs, beating so hard it felt close to bursting from her chest. She readjusted in the seat, hating her sister's acute (and dauntingly accurate) ability to read her. Georgia merely waited for confirmation that Toby jumped her. Between her arched brow, piercing green eyes, and loaded hints, *she* should have been the cop, Savannah griped inwardly. Georgia lined up the evidence in such a way she'd backed her into a corner but no amount of pressure or haranguing would coerce a confession. "Sorry," was all she said.

Georgia sighed. Savannah detected impatience but her sister's tone remained gentle, "Savannah, are you going to tell me what happened?"

Bolts of pain shot across her forehead, adding a new level of misery to the constant dull ache rolling in waves through her entire brain. "I told you what happened."

"I think you told me part of it," she suggested. "When you left here, you were wearing that bra and those panties and you certainly were not bleeding anywhere."

Savannah reached to rub a twinge in her breast then thought better of it. "Georgia, I don't feel well this morning so I don't need an inquisition no matter how diplomatically you present it. I told you he hit me. My jaw, my stomach," she whimpered on the last word. Her body revolted at the show of exasperation. She needed to stay still and calm but Georgia's constant pecking riled her.

"Lift your blouse. Show me."

"No."

"Why not?"

The damn headache trenched deeper. Why couldn't Georgia leave it be? "Because there's no need. You've seen bruises before."

"Should you have gone to the hospital last night instead of taking that bath?"

And there it was. The question. Were you raped? Savannah grew up reading between the lines. Her sister perfected the art of asking a question without actually asking *the* question.

"If I'd needed a hospital, I would have gone," she replied, trying to restrain her temper.

"Then why all the secrecy?"

Savannah slowly stood, gauged her aches, tried not to let them show, "I gotta get ready for my shift."

As she passed by, Georgia clasped her hand, gave it a tender squeeze. A tide of emotion swelled. Savannah closed her eyes, willing it away.

"You need medical attention," the softness returned to her sister's voice. "At least get treated for the wounds. I'll call Leah, she can look at them."

Her eyes popped wide then narrowed, conveying her precise thoughts on that subject. If she refused to show them to her own sister, why the hell would she flash them to her sister-in-law, the woman married to their temperamental brother who happened to be an Army Ranger? If Seth found out, he'd break Toby's neck – which the bastard deserved – but Seth didn't deserve a dishonorable discharge and prison time because of Savannah's bad decision. Had she stayed home, none of it would have happened.

Georgia continued, her hold tightening on her sister's hand, "I hope some day you'll tell me everything. I'm here if you need me."

Tears welled against her best efforts to stop them. "Thanks, sis," her throat tightened. "I can always count on you." Her control unwound at an alarming rate and she hurried to the stairs before she collapsed in a sobbing heap.

"Savannah."

She stopped at the bottom stair, looked back at her sister through the brimming tears.

"None of this is your fault. He's the one to blame, not you."

O   O   O

"Your ex-betrothed give you those bruises?" Riley's inquiry rang with an I-told-you-so. "I had one rookie get knocked up. Now I got another getting knocked out by a reject from the Village People."

She faced Murphy fully aware that her jaw colored coordinated with her uniform. Before leaving Georgia's, she shored her courage and backbone for the long shift with Riley's wiseass remarks. But she hadn't prepared for his stare.

He concentrated on the discoloration, "Your sister told me you went to see the genius. I drove by his address but your car wasn't there."

"But she called to say I was home and okay."

He pointed to her jaw, "You think that's the definition of okay? She told me you made it home, not that you were okay."

"I'm not seeing him again. I've learned my lesson."

He stepped closer, whispering, "That lesson come with a bonus you didn't expect? I mean, you're my partner so I care what happens to you but your sister was really upset when she called back."

Now she wondered what Georgia said. How explicit were her

details to Murphy? Judging by his expression, she'd told him everything.

Murphy furthered his inquiry, "You do realize what I'm asking, right? Or do I have to draw you a picture?"

His probing gaze commanded an answer, one she planned never to reveal – to anyone. "I don't want to talk about what did or didn't happen. I took care of it," she mumbled.

"That mean he's dead?"

She swore he sounded downright fatherly, "If he is it's not because of me."

"Too bad. Creeps like that shouldn't draw breath. Your sister seems nice. Very protective of you."

"I love her too. Just wish she'd mind her own business sometimes."

Cops passed by, pausing to survey her jaw then proceeded on their way. She already felt like a sideshow but Detective John Mathis, a rotund, grouchy fellow in his early thirties, made it worse when he stopped to stare, "Hey, kid. Nobody taught you to duck?"

"Hard to duck a train, Detective," she said, keeping the exasperation from her voice.

He leaned in with a covert whisper, "Then derail that train," he referenced her name on her uniform, "Officer Prince."

Dear God, she griped to herself. Did Georgia buy a newspaper ad to inform the world? Did the whole station know about her and Toby? "I derailed it last night, Detective."

Mathis clapped her on the shoulder which sent an arrow of pain into her breast, "Good for you, kid." He pointed to her .38 and pepper spray, "Remember, those ain't there for decoration. Use 'em." He shuffled away, much to her relief.

Adam Rafferty breezed past then, as everyone had, stopped cold at the sight of her jaw, "Damn. You get mugged by a Mack truck?" He shot Murphy an accusing look.

Riley put hands to hips, "It didn't happen on my watch, Rafferty. It was her ex-boyfriend did it." He hitched a thumb at the door, "Okay, PITA. Work off your frustrations on our unit. Get it ready and I'll be out in a minute. And I'm driving."

"You always do," she grumbled, grateful for the dismissal. She'd rather inspect the back seat of a cop car for contraband and hidden weapons than endure the grilling, both visual and verbal.

"Hey," Riley called, "don't forget to check the–"

"Tire pressures. Got it." At least he hadn't quizzed her on preparing their patrol car for the shift.

She heard Murphy strike up a chatty conversation with Rafferty, "So, what're you doing after shift or does Bradley still have you on a leash?"

"Why?" she heard Rafferty's confusion.

"Geez, you rookies are all alike. I'll spell it for you. I thought we might go to O'Malley's for a beer, or don't you drink?"

O O O

The day dragged into long, painful hours. The ache in her back and legs returned full force. The sweat from heat and constant activity awoke the fiery ache in her breast and along her stomach. By lunchtime, Riley noticed her unease and invited her in their usual restaurant to eat. If he felt pity for her, he exercised good sense not saying it but she appreciated his consideration, especially when they stopped by Disco Kroger for aspirin.

After shift, she piled in her car, drove to the park where she indulged in an ample drink from her flask. Until she could beg a prescription painkiller from Georgia, the booze had to deaden the pain.

She waited ten minutes, curious what Murphy and Rafferty found to talk about since they didn't know each other that well. She prayed it wasn't her but assumed they shared opinions on that subject at least a little. Twenty minutes passed when she decided booze sucked as a pain reliever and headed to Georgia's, grateful the day drew to a close. The trip home was uneventful until she turned onto Georgia's street to find Toby's Malibu sitting at the curb. She pulled over, braked to a stop. She retrieved her .38, laid it in her lap. It ain't there for decoration, Mathis said earlier. And she fully intended to keep the promise of emptying her gun into Toby if he came close to her or Georgia again.

She eased up the street into the driveway, shifted the car into park while keeping a close eye on the Malibu's occupant. She kept a tight hold on the .38 when she exited the Dodge.

The Malibu's door swung open. Toby slowly stepped from his car, his movements guarded and deliberate. Savannah kept the gun at her side. She picked up the pace to the door, hoping to get inside before he caught her.

"Coward," he accused.

She stood at the door, key in hand. Coward? Because she ran to the door to get away? After the night before? Right... She turned, expecting him to charge toward her, fist drawn. Instead she watched him limp up the driveway. His gimp perplexed her since her attack the night before concentrated above the waist. And why, after suffering her wrath, had he labeled her a coward? "Excuse me?" she asked.

He hobbled closer, "You're a damn coward, Savannah."

A two inch cut slashed across his cheek. Bruises ringed his swollen eyes. A thin line of dried blood trailed from his hairline past his right ear. Someone went to town on her evil ex and in a big way.

He gritted his teeth. His busted lip began seeping blood, "Gotta have your buddies kick my ass? Can't fight your own battles? That's a coward."

Had she heard him correctly? "Who kicked your ass?"

His chin trembled with rage but his wounds prevented a physical show of temper, "Your academy pals. Oh, and that fat ass partner of yours. They beat me and told me how they'd dispose of my body if I touched you again. Your new screw is a charmer. Took a tire iron to my leg – after he sliced my cheek open with that fancy ring he wears. Found yourself a hero there. So you should feel good about yourself."

"Oh, I do," she smirked. "But I never told them to work you over. I did pretty well myself last night. If you recall I nearly kicked your jaw to the backyard. Twice." She reached to slide the key in the door but it automatically came open. Georgia stood with her .22 in hand and an impressive facial interpretation of Clint Eastwood's Make My Day. Her expression foretold Toby's future if he dared move closer. She waved

Savannah inside while keeping the .22 level with Toby's broad chest.

He grimaced, "Oh great. Beat to hell by you and your pals now I'm gonna get shot by your sister."

Savannah waggled her .38, "Could be worse. Could get shot by both of us."

"Get off my property, Toby," Georgia warned. "I've already called the police."

His swollen eyes widened a degree as if he realized what that might mean. "I'm leaving, I'm leaving." He looked at Savannah, "I'll see you again someday. It'll be a day when your friends aren't around to protect you."

She stepped inside, cautioning, "But I'll still have my gun."

12

NOW

Savannah opened the scrapbook Georgia created to document her career as a cop. Her sister loved making scrapbooks. She'd made one filled with newspaper clippings and pictures of Savannah's golfing triumphs. That book was stored in Savannah's closet with other keepsakes. This one, though, she flipped through on occasion usually when she felt low or a stubborn case tested her ability and sanity.

Today she just wanted to peruse her past. Georgia began the book with Savannah's portrait in uniform. God, what an ugly picture, she thought. *Not only that, I look so... naïve.* Every rookie did, she noticed over the years. A cop's expression along with their features changed over time when the job brought home the brutal reality. You can't save everyone. Some can't be saved, some don't want to be saved. Others want to hurt or kill you just because you wear the uniform or carry the badge.

She turned pages, one after another, passing over academy graduation pictures. She skipped over photos of her with Riley Murphy. The rookie and her partner stood beside their cruiser. Murphy's smile resembled a sneer. Only a select number of people knew Murphy well enough to recognize the difference. There were snapshots of her with Adam Rafferty both in uniform and in casual attire. In her quest for a thorough scrapbook, Georgia included brief excerpts from the Atlanta Journal Constitution regarding arrests Savannah made. No officer was mentioned by name but Georgia's goal of a complete history meant including tiny articles that simply read "APD officers".

Georgia added a section for commendations, placing photos of presentation ceremonies prominently on each page. Savannah lamented the fact no female stood a chance of looking attractive – or even *female* – in the hot clunky dress uniform. At the time no woman, including her, gave a crap because they were too proud to *be* there in that hot clunky uniform.

Every subsequent page highlighted years of hard work and dedication. It also emphasized the toll of long hours, stress, and disappointments. The job aged her mentally and physically. From academy graduation to present day, she noticed the gradual appearance of tiny lines at her eyes, the emergence of silver strands beginning to shine from her dark hair. But the biggest change – the naïveté in her features disappeared.

Savannah was proud of her sister's efforts. Even now Georgia clipped articles for the book. Thumbing through the pages, she stopped at one headline from the AJC. A smile curved her lips. Her first high-profile case. A few months after being promoted to detective, the biggest case of the year landed in her lap.

"Cop Killer Arrested" the newspaper headline read. Below was a mug shot of the killer and beside it, Savannah's introduction into the public spotlight. She stood with Will Bradshaw, her partner at the time, along with her captain, lieutenant, and the chief of police. Bradshaw looked impassive, she noticed, while she tried for pleased and confident.

Savannah recalled the pride of being trusted with such a prominent case. Captain Josh Hunter had faith in her, he'd said, but also cautioned, "I hope you've got thick skin, Savannah. Cops don't like being grilled about their partner's death..."

O   O   O

THEN

THE ROOKIE DETECTIVE

"Get up there," Savannah growled at the two uniform cops beside her. She pointed to the roof of a nearby building where she saw flashes from a camera. A man stood, snapping pictures with a high dollar camera and telephoto lens. "Get up there now and throw that camera to the ground, hear me? I want to see it fly."

The two wide-eyed uniforms took off like flames licked their heels. Without taking her eyes off the photographer, Savannah marched to the curb opposite him, waiting while the cops scaled the old creaky fire escape.

A minute elapsed when the cops grabbed him, surprising the man with their strength and determination. The uniforms stripped the expensive camera from his grasp with him yelling protests of police brutality.

You ain't seen nothin' yet, asshole, she glared.

One uniform dangled the camera over the building's edge. Savannah motioned for him to throw it, not drop it. The uniform followed orders, flinging it like a fastball toward the sidewalk below. The camera shattered into several pieces upon impact, scattering in all directions. Savannah crossed the street, stomped it until it was unrecognizable.

She looked up, shielding her eyes from the overhead sun then shouted at the cops, "Now throw *him*!"

The photographer screamed bloody murder, putting up a vicious fight against the two cops who hadn't yet made a move to toss him. She backed up a step, locking vision with the terrified young man in custody, "You wanna take pictures of a dead cop? You pay the price. Toss him!"

Savannah's partner Will Bradshaw sidled next to her, amused at her actions, "Can't do that, Prince. Looks bad on TV." Thirty-four year old Will stood six feet tall, well-groomed and dressed in a gray suit fresh from Men's Warehouse. He was happily married, so he said, but still indulged in a look-see at the ladies when they passed by. He was a nice guy with a decent reserve of patience and desire to teach the rookie detective but he possessed one big flaw. He thought he was funny.

"That looks bad on TV?" she asked, incredulous. "Well, so does a dead cop." Frustrated now, she yelled, "Airmail his ass down here now!"

Will shook his head, that same ridiculous smirk on his face, "Calm down. He'll get his in lockup. You *are* gonna pay for that camera though. And you'll get your ass chewed by the boss so get ready."

Crap, she griped. Less than two months as a detective and already in trouble. Maybe Captain Josh Hunter would understand the heat of the moment. She could hope so. Because he wasn't a man she enjoyed seeing angry. So far she'd stayed out of his aim. Today, well, not so much. "Where the hell was Ethridge's partner when this went down?" Savannah asked Will.

He shrugged, "Don't know but he's in a squad car over here. We can talk to him if you're done playing Gallagher for the day, that is."

She rolled her eyes at his comment. His reference to the fruit-tossing comic left her cold the way leaving a nosy photographer alone did.

Will led her to a patrol unit parked twenty feet away from the crime scene. Earlier that afternoon, an officer on foot patrol found rookie officer Alexa Ethridge's body in an alley. She'd been shot in the face and back of the head. If it weren't for her badge number and name on her uniform, identifying her would have been impossible. The young, trim twenty-two year-old had curled her five foot five frame in the fetal position, her hand reaching for what Savannah guessed was her gun that was now missing. Ethridge's handcuffs lay only a foot away, as if someone jumped her in the middle of an arrest.

In that span of time, no one knew where Ethridge's partner was. Savannah and Will heard the radio transmissions between Ethridge, her partner and central dispatch. It started at 1:00 p.m. with a robbery call at Pendleton's Jewelry in Ansley Mall. Being an outdoor mall, it provided quick access and quick escape to pickpockets and robbers. Ethridge and her partner Colin Spencer responded to the call. Radio silence ensued for fifteen minutes. Then Spencer began calling for his partner over the radio. He summoned with her last name three times, and heard nothing. Then a trace of concern laced his voice as he switched to using her badge number. Finally full blown fear as he called her by her first name numerous times. Still nothing. He radioed dispatch, "I can't reach my partner," so central dispatch began its own campaign that yielded the same results. An hour after the initial call, the foot patrol found her dead in the alley.

Rule number one. Never leave your partner. It was drummed into a recruit's head day after day. Stay together. Call for backup but always stay together. From what Savannah heard on the radio transmissions before she and Will arrived on scene, Colin Spencer and Alexa Ethridge split up to catch the robbery suspect. And now she was dead.

Savannah and Will approached the car. She remembered Colin Spencer being in his late twenties, average looking with short cropped black hair, a narrow face and squinty eyes and a razor sharp tongue. She dreaded the interaction anyway but the questions they had guaranteed venomous hostility from the uniform.

They looked in the squad car to see Colin Spencer holding a blood-soaked cloth to his mouth. "What happened to you?" she asked him.

Spencer slowly lifted his head to meet her gaze. His eyes narrowed at her, his posture closing down as if the two detectives were enemies, "Alexa's buddies reminded me you don't leave your partner. You got something to add to it or are you just here to crucify me?"

"Why?" She wanted to know, "Did you kill your partner? That why they beat the shit outta you?" Because cops never turned on cops unless they had a damn good reason. Even if he hadn't pulled the trigger himself, leaving the rookie alone helped get her killed.

"Prince, c'mon on," Will's tone suggested she was hormonal, not logical. He glanced at Spencer who didn't appear appreciative of Will's intervention. Will continued, "Tell us what happened, why you split up."

"Because we had conflicting reports of where the perp went. Some said south, others east. So I headed south on Flagler, and I told Ethridge to call for backup and head east toward Allen Road." He purposefully turned to Savannah, "I know I screwed up, okay?" He removed the bloody cloth, revealing a busted lip, "I've been told. But I did not kill my partner."

"It was common knowledge you hated being partnered with a female rookie," she prodded.

"Gimme a break, Detective. Who *wants* a rookie, male or female? No, I wasn't happy but I dealt with it."

"So two weeks after graduation, you send her on a foot chase alone. Twenty-two, five foot five, maybe weighing one ten, one twenty. According to the radio transmissions, the suspect was black, six feet, one eighty – and armed."

Spencer read her expression, huffed out an expletive, "And you women think *we're* sexist. I thought she'd report in once in a damn while. I told her from Day One to keep me apprised of her whereabouts if we ever got separated."

"You didn't follow your own instructions, according to the

transmissions. No one knew where either of you were."

"Did you look for her?" Will asked.

"I looked, yeah. I went everywhere I thought she might go."

Savannah took over again, "Did you check this area? Walk it through, drive it?"

"I never got to this block."

"So this whole incident took place within two or three blocks, right?" Will inquired.

"Right."

Savannah said, "Witnesses say they heard gunshots as far away as three blocks. Did you?"

"I heard *something* but I was busy running, you know, trying to find the bastard."

The witnesses she and Will interviewed specifically stated gunshots. One block away, two blocks away and even a few three blocks away. Unlike other areas of Atlanta, people in that area weren't used to gunshots so for them to identify them as such told Savannah Mr. Spencer's story wasn't exactly adding up. "Tell us your exact route, starting from the store," Savannah told him.

"Are you auditioning for Internal Affairs?"

Will now frowned, "Answer her, Spencer."

He gingerly touched his cheek and winced, "Yeah, okay. We both left the store and like I said, I headed south on Flagler and told Alexa to head east toward Allen Road. I ran one block, turned right onto Montgomery, went to Monroe then turned left to run that block. No one I asked saw the guy so I turned around, went back up the street. I searched the block then headed another block over and still nothing. It's like the guy disappeared into thin air."

"When did you hear the gunshots?" Will asked.

"I heard two pops when I was running up Monroe. Came from the east or northeast."

"And you didn't investigate it, knowing your partner was in that vicinity?" Savannah inquired, unable to keep the anger from her tone.

Spencer gnashed his teeth then grimaced, "Do I have to talk to *you?*"

She tried for a Southern Belle smile, "'Fraid so. When *did* you start searching for her?"

"I tried calling her on the radio. I don't know how long. Then I took off looking."

Witness accounts had Spencer and Ethridge running together at one point on Monroe, the last leg of his pursuit. Spencer never mentioned being with her except outside the store. It made her wonder if he'd conveniently forgotten or hoped the witnesses got lost before they were interviewed. "Did you ever meet up with Ethridge during your pursuit?"

"No."

She and Will looked at each other. Now her partner's expression conveyed the same skepticism she had. Will asked, "And you packed up and went back to the station, right?"

Spencer noticed the icy nature of the question and curbed his smart mouth, "They said a female officer was heading back. I figured she caught a ride with another cop. When I got back, the captain sent me back out, saying she never showed up. Then here we are now."

Savannah and Will spent another twenty minutes with him then drove back to the station. Dusk fell in that time so they ordered a perimeter set up around the field a block from the alley Ethridge was found. Maybe her gun was there. It was a long shot but the brass spent overtime on cop killings.

The next morning the two detectives met in Will's office. Uniforms began searching the field for Ethridge's gun at day break. The phone rang all night with media wanting information and higher-ups demanding status reports.

Captain Josh Hunter walked in, his eyes bleary, his body showing the stress of the previous day, "Any leads?"

"Only the kinds you don't want to hear," Savannah replied.

Will agreed, "Spencer ain't looking free and clear in this, boss. There are discrepancies in his statement and some seriously questionable behavior. Besides him leaving his partner alone, he said he told her to call for backup but there's no record from dispatch that she did. Witnesses have him and Ethridge together on Monroe shortly before she was killed but others say she was alone. Spencer thinks we're out for him."

Josh half-shrugged, "Well, he *did* get the crap beat out of him by other officers."

"Deserved it too," Will told Savannah under this breath.

"Hey," Hunter warned, his tone making Savannah sit up and take notice, "I don't need you two going rogue on this guy because he made a mistake. That's Internal Affairs, not you. You're finding the killer, right?"

"Yes, boss," she attempted to dial down the tension in the room. "But his actions led up to the killing. We'll do an honest, thorough job. We don't want to believe a cop killed another cop either."

Josh put hands to hips, "Then keep a leash on your partner's mouth and don't listen to everything he says. You're new and still learning. And I sure don't need another overly opinionated detective under my command. I've already got Mathis. By the way, no one goes home again tonight. The chief approved extra overtime. Let's get this solved quick. All our jobs depend on it, even mine. The mayor and the chief are breathing fire about this. Before I go, Adam Rafferty wants to talk to you. Let's hope he's got some information."

Savannah sweetly inquired, "Do we fit him in before or after the chief, the commander, six lieutenants, and a handful of majors and captains?"

"I'm the only one you worry about right now." His brow sank at her, "I think I liked you better as a shy rookie."

The two detectives spoke to Rafferty who patrolled the Piedmont Heights area. He gave them a tip, saying he brought in a perp nicknamed Law for mugging a pregnant woman. He was known for robberies in and around Ansley Mall. If the guy didn't do it, he knew who did, Rafferty said.

It was 9:45 a.m. when Savannah and Will went to lockup where Law currently resided. Law was a wiry black kid in his late teens, wearing a white tank top and shorts big enough to serve as a parachute. His sneakers looked worse for wear, probably from all the running he did after stealing from pregnant women and tourists.

She and Will asked a few questions and the Law immediately twisted the conversation to money. He wasn't about to turn snitch, he said, not unless there was serious payoff involved.

Will glanced at Savannah like *what-an-asshole.* She lifted a brow, silently replying *what did you expect?* She volunteered to Law, "If your information leads to an arrest, the Police Benevolent Association will be your slot machine. Tell us what you know."

He stretched, his arms reaching long and wide, "I don't know. You cops'll say anything to trap a guy like me."

"Like you," Will repeated between clenched teeth. "You mean an upstanding citizen?"

Before he lashed out, Savannah took over. "You are already behind bars, *Law,*" she emphasized in a mocking tone. "It's Friday so we'll just let you ride the weekend, come back Monday and see if you're tired of this cage." She waved at Will to follow her, "C'mon. He's useless."

They were three steps past the cell when they heard him scramble to the door, "Hey, lady. Wait."

She swiveled on one heel to see his face mashed against the bars, his arm thrust out, waving them toward him. "You serious about the money?"

The two sauntered back. Will let her answer, "The PBA is *serious* about cop killings so yeah, there's good money involved." She crossed her arms, "Do you have a name?"

Law hemmed and hawed, clearly debating his situation and her offer. After fifteen seconds, he blurted, "Reaper."

She shook her head, "What does his mama call him?"

"Demarcus. Demarcus Harrison."

"And he killed the cop?"

Law looked away. He debated again then evidently remembered the money, "Alls I know is he came to my girlfriend's apartment about 1:15 or 1:30 and she said he was sweating a river and amped up. He was looking for me, wouldn't tell her why.   She said he hung around long enough to take a leak then left."

"That's not enough information," she said. "We need more to go on than sweat and a pit stop to pee."

Deflated, Law leaned his forehead against the bars, "He called me that morning, wanted me to help him knock off Pendleton Jewelers at Ansley Mall. Said he needed the money."

O   O   O

Savannah and Will drove to an apartment in Piedmont Heights to bring in Demarcus Harrison. The door opened to a twenty year-old broad shouldered black man with braids to his shoulders. Harrison answered the door in his boxer shorts, leaving the TV across the room blaring with an ultimate fighting match.

The detectives played down their visit, saying they wanted to talk about anything he might have seen at Ansley Mall the day before. They needed a witness statement if he would be so kind.

Savannah expected a fight, an argument, a denial, anything but cooperation. But she soon discovered that the unexpected occasionally happened. Harrison slipped on his jeans and a new black t-shirt and headed to the station with them.

It was 12:30 when they arrived. Savannah and Will sequestered Harrison in an interview room then checked on the status of the gun search in Piedmont Heights. Ethridge's gun was not found.

They returned to the interview room, asked Harrison to reconstruct the previous day. He explained he slept until 10:00 a.m. then ate breakfast then went to pick up oil for his car. He came back, put oil in the car then around 12:00 or 1:00 went to Ansley Mall to shop for new shoes at Phidippides. They didn't have his size so he left. He saw the two cops running from Pendleton's, figured someone robbed the place so he turned around, headed for Piedmont Park. Around 3:00, he went back home to his sister's apartment. Thankfully she was out of town, he said, so he could spend the remainder if the evening watching ultimate fighting without her griping at him.

Will and Savannah had him repeat his story. Over and over. And over. He stated it verbatim, parroting every word without a misstep or departure from the initial telling. After an hour and a half, Will's patience ran on rims. He leaned back in the metal chair, his back against the wall, hands behind his head. He stared at Savannah who did not notice his staring since her chosen position prevented it. With elbows on the table, she leaned her chin into her hands, eyes closed, hoping Harrison screwed up just once before she lunged at him and strangled the bastard.

"And that's what happened," Harrison sighed. "Just like I said before and before and before and–"

"Again," Will ordered. "Tell us again."

Savannah opened her eyes, saw her partner drilling her with his dark eyes.

"Start from the beginning," he told Harrison.

The black man shifted his vision between them, "You two got hearing issues or you got that memory disease 'cause I told this story at least–"

"The beginning," Savannah reiterated, praying her sister kept a cabinet full of aspirin and Tylenol or even a regular old hammer to clobber herself unconscious. She hadn't dropped by Georgia's for supper in two days because of the all-hands-on-deck with Ethridge's murder. She hadn't seen her own home in as many either and the lack of rest was showing on her.

After Harrison's droning account, his brow dipped, "How come y'all ain't asked 'bout the lady cop?"

A subtle spark of hope shown in the detective's eyes when their vision met. They avoided mentioning or referencing Alexa Ethridge for fear he'd shut down and demand a lawyer. Now was not the time to send the case in the crapper with exuberance so Savannah kept her tone indifferent, "Okay, Demarcus, we're asking about the lady cop."

He glanced at the one way mirror to his right then leaned onto the table, closer to her, his voice secretive, "When I was on Allen Road, some big black dude ran out in front of me 'bout half a block up. The lady cop was right behind him. They ran down the sidewalk till he hooked a right into an alley. I kept walking then I heard a woman scream *no* then I heard a *pop!*" The last word burst from his lips loud enough Savannah jerked with surprise. He continued, "I turned around, man, I was leaving then I heard her say *please don't* then I heard another *pop!*"

This time Savannah didn't jump. Sickness roiled in her belly as she stared back at Demarcus Harrison as he finished, "I left quick, man, I wasn't about to be no witness to that shit."

She didn't trust herself to speak, at least not to Reaper. She rose from the seat, her back creaking from the constant sitting and inactivity. The rest of her, however, spoiled to beat the hell out of their suspect. Her knuckles itched to pound the fake innocence off the bastard's face. She'd heard plenty about detectives who went postal on suspects. Her goal was to steer clear of that behavior however after hearing and seeing the guy at the table coolly dismiss a person's life and blame it on a phantom killer, she realized how unattainable that goal might be. "I need some air," she told Will. And a baseball bat – or that regular old hammer would do too.

He stood up, joined her in the hallway. He saw the rage on her face now, tried to lower the temperature, "You're two months into your promotion. Your head'll explode or you'll die of a heart attack before your first year if you let all these idiots get to you. Take a breath, regroup."

She nodded, realizing he was correct. Getting crazy only hurt her but, "He was taunting us. Telling us he was smarter."

"And they all pretty much do that. It's no different than being in uniform. Punks have attitude with a cop. Savannah, these guys aren't

MENSA members. He knows he's lying and he's challenged us to prove it. Think how we can. That's how you keep your head – or your heart – from exploding."

She questioned if detective work was her cup of tea. Her record as a uniform cop was exemplary. Attitude on the street she could deal with. The ones in the interview room – not yet, at least. It was then a brainstorm hit her, "Let's talk to Law again. I just had an idea."

"They've got pills to cure *that* condition," Will laughed.

They went downstairs to find Law in a sour mood. He wanted to know where his money was. Savannah, hungry and tired, explained the facts to him again. Information and arrest meant money. No arrest, no money. "Your girlfriend said Harrison dropped by looking for you shortly after that robbery, right?"

Law nodded, rolled his eyes, "You need to take notes, lady."

She nearly suggested where he should stick that comment but realized progress on the case probably depended on cooler heads. "And he went to the bathroom then left."

He nodded again. This time with no smartass remark.

Savannah asked, "Will you give us permission to look in your bathroom?"

"I gotta give permission? I thought you guys went wherever the hell you wanted."

"Listen to me, Law," her temper shortened considerably. She held it by a single unraveling strand, "If you give your permission, that eliminates a search warrant. That, in turn, makes things go faster with us which means you might get your money quicker."

The light bulb in his brain clicked on nice and bright, "Oh, I get it. Sure. Look in my bathroom. Clean it if you want. Anything to get my money sooner."

O   O   O

Law's girlfriend was at work when they arrived. They brought along two uniforms to guard the door while they went to the back of the apartment. It was small with scant furniture. A broken down brown sofa and a worn out green recliner both faced a small thirteen inch TV sitting on a crate draped in a towel. A picture of Jesus hung above the TV.

She and Will traipsed back to the bathroom. They both stopped cold at the ripe odor wafting from the small room. Savannah saw the color drain from her partner's face and figured her pallid hue matched his perfectly.

"Well," Will Bradshaw sighed, "let's wade through this hazmat hell. We'll both want decontamination showers when we get back."

Savannah wasn't sure he was joking. They ventured in, her steering clear of the petri dish of a toilet. A three foot wide hole in the ceiling gaped above them, exposing pipes and sparse insulation. She hoped they didn't have to climb up there to search for evidence.

Off to the right stood the combination bathtub/shower with a torn curtain shoved accordion-like to the wall. A gray colored ring circled the tub's interior. The sink sat to the left of the toilet with a medicine cabinet mounted above the former. Adding to the cramped little room was a linen closet to the left next to the door. It had two drawers at the bottom and two narrow doors above them.

The detectives slipped on latex gloves if for nothing else than to protect themselves from germs. Will tackled the toilet tank, "I'll get the gross shit outta the way first." He lifted the tank top and found nothing.

Savannah opened the bottom drawer of the linen closet. Law's girlfriend stored her thongs and panties in the drawer. She removed it from the cabinet, searched through it with no success. She went to the drawer above it. Washcloths, hand towels and... She jerked her hand back. Will saw her, "What'd you find? A snake?"

She uneasily cleared her throat, "Not a snake. Apparently Law's girlfriend has a not-so-little buddy to keep her company when he's not around." She shoved the battery operated sex toy back in the drawer then dared to spelunk deeper into it. God, she really wanted that decontamination shower Will mentioned earlier.

Will snugged in behind her, their bottoms brushing each other. He apologized, "Thought I'd rummage the med cabinet while you find all her extracurricular hobbies."

She did not laugh because she found more toys tucked away further in the drawer, "It's like the sex Olympics in here."

He chuckled, "I'll bet they got another competitor's slot if you're interested. You might win a gold medal."

She held a hand to her stomach, "Leave me alone, Will." She busied herself opening the cabinet doors to two shelves full of bath towels, every one of them sky blue. Shoving a hand between each neatly folded towel recovered nothing. She did the same with the stack next to it. Again nothing. "I'm beginning to think we're on that proverbial wild goose chase."

"You too? There's nothing in my cabinet but shit you buy at Walgreens or Kroger."

She took out the stacks to see another pile at the back. She resumed shoving her hand between the linens. Her hand bumped something solid, "Will."

"What? Does Law have a little buddy too?"

Savannah eased her hand around the object stuffed between the towels. A handle, a barrel, a cylinder and finally her finger traced a trigger guard. Carefully she pulled the object free. In her hands sat a police issue Smith & Wesson revolver. If it turned out to be Ethridge's weapon, things would drastically change for someone currently sitting at their stationhouse. If Demarcus Harrison's prints were on the gun, it didn't matter how many times he rehearsed his story, he was getting the death penalty.

"Bingo," Will grinned. "Maybe we'll get to introduce Reaper to his new friend. The Grim Reaper."

O   O   O

They returned to the station with the gun, slipping in the back door, away from the teeming media out front. They left the gun for analysis, hoping that if it was Ethridge's gun, good old Reaper grabbed on good and tight, leaving clear fingerprints for them to find.

Forensics sidelined all other jobs to check the weapon. Savannah and Will barely got a cup of coffee and a breather before forensics handed them the results.

They headed to the interview room, the weapon safely sealed in an evidence bag. Savannah opened the door to see Reaper splayed back in the chair, a stance reminiscent of Will earlier, except Mr. Harrison propped his feet onto the table for extra comfort.

The mere sight of Demarcus so casual fired her anger. Will forewarned her to keep her cool, not to let Harrison get under her skin. She rounded the table, watching Demarcus yawn.

"Y'all lettin' me go?" he asked.

Savannah glanced at Will letting him know her temper was just fine, thank you, but this asshole was about to lose his cavalier attitude. She reached forward, shoved Harrison's feet off the table. His chair slammed forward, jarring him to an upright position. Before giving him time to gain his composure, she tossed the gun onto the table, "I don't want to hear anymore about the lady cop chasing a black guy onto Allen Road, Demarcus. Not unless that black guy is you."

"It wasn't me," he vehemently shook his head. "I told you the truth."

"The truth?" she scoffed. "Pardon me, but your street name supports the fact you kill people. You want me to believe you're harmless and innocent? Call yourself Pooh Bear, not Reaper."

Will followed with, "We found this gun in Law's apartment."

"Then Law musta killed her 'cause I didn't."

Will pointed, "Demarcus, see that gun?"

He nodded. With one finger, Will pushed it toward him. Reaper's posture and expression remained defensive. He bowed back in the chair as if the gun might go off and kill him.

"Want to know about that gun?" Will asked.

"Not really," was the honest answer.

"Detective Prince, tell Pooh Bear what forensics found."

Savannah's vision narrowed at the killer. Images flashed in her brain of Alexa Ethridge struggling against Demarcus Harrison for her own weapon. The realization she lost the battle as he overpowered her, pried the gun from her grasp. Her begging him not to shoot her. He probably smiled at that, Savannah figured. Smiled and laughed as he watched a police officer beg for her life then gleefully pulled the trigger. Ethridge didn't die right away. She retained enough consciousness to utter one last plea. *Please don't...* Then the gun fired again, this time with the kill shot.

Savannah leaned down to Demarcus, her voice hard, matter-of-fact, "Forensics found your fingerprints are all over the lady cop's weapon. Not Law's but yours. They found two empty chambers in that weapon. The two shots that you fired into Officer Ethridge's head."

He bolted to his feet and threw a punch. She ducked the attack and as he ran for the door she kicked him, her foot landing against the back of his knee, collapsing his leg and sending him to the floor.

Will pulled his handcuffs, braced a knee in Harrison's back, pinning him. He glanced at his partner, "See? Stupid people always screw up. Repeatedly."

Savannah stared at Demarcus, "You killed Officer Ethridge and now we can put you away until they strap you to a table and inject that special cocktail," she poked his forearm, "right there. Tell your story to

God, Reaper, because we're letting Him sort this out."

Will's brow lifted, "Not bad for a first homicide, rookie. Captain'll be impressed with you."

Well, it wasn't all me, she thought with a proud smile. It paid to have friends in certain places and Adam Rafferty proved to be a very valuable one in many ways...

13

NOW

This was the day he waited for. The day all his planning paid off. He parked his car beside the curb halfway between Savannah's house and the neighbor's. He reviewed his plan. Step one. Isolate Ennis. He dialed the police station. A man introducing himself as Sergeant Bailey answered. He cleared his throat then perfected his old Uncle Wally's snobbish tone, "This is James Ferguson. I understand Detective Rutherford is looking for me regarding his case. Please tell him I'll be at the police station in fifteen minutes. Please extend my apologies for not returning his calls sooner. I've been out of town. Thank you."

He had to smile. Snooping beneath the window the other night proved priceless. Savannah and Ennis provided enough information for him to impersonate Ferguson and delay Ennis coming home.

Climbing out of the car, he stayed in the shadows of the trees while creeping toward her Dodge Charger. Step two. He slid his knife from the sheath, jammed it into the left front tire. Soon driver's side of the car sloped at slightly awkward angle. Step three. Lure her out. He would use her sister as bait. He dialed the home phone, waiting. She answered on the second ring, uttering the usual *hello*, minus the warmth. Businesslike. Cold. Typical Savannah.

He changed the timbre of his voice slightly, "This is the manager at Kroger on Roswell Road. Your sister asked me to call you. Her Tahoe's had engine trouble and she'd like you to pick her up. She'd have called you herself but said she forgot her phone."

Her tone softened, "You said Kroger on Roswell Road?"

"Yes, ma'am."

"Tell her I'll be right there. Oh, and tell her to stay in the car until I arrive. It's too dark for her to be out alone."

"Yes, ma'am. I'll tell her. Thank you." He hung up then chuckled at the simplicity of it. One call and he had her. He crouched behind the Charger, waiting, preparing for the most important step of all. Step four.

A minute later, she opened the door holding the baby carrier. He grimaced. *The baby.* He'd forgotten the baby again, probably because Savannah didn't seem very maternal all those years ago.

She turned from the door then groaned at the sight of the flat tire. A sigh later, she toted the baby back inside, assuring her that Mama would be right back. Fat chance of that, he smiled behind the fender.

Savannah stepped off the porch, leaned down to examine the tire closer. He made his move. He darted around the hood, gave her a solid shove. She threw her hands forward in an attempt to cushion her landing.

He tackled her on the driveway, heard the air rush from her lungs. He straddled her back and sank his weight into her spine, anchoring her to the pavement. A quick gasp alerted him she was about to cut loose with a doozy of a scream so he clamped one hand over her mouth while the other went to her throat. He felt her pulse racing against his thumb and fingers as he gradually applied pressure to the carotid arteries.

She screamed against his palm, clawing at the hand gripping her throat, trying to pry it loose. When that failed, she braced her hands on the pavement. He felt her pushing against him, trying to pull her knees beneath her for leverage. God, he thought in amazement, even in her mid-thirties she was still strong as a bull. Her arms shook from the strain as she channeled enough strength to lift his two hundred twenty pounds a few inches off the concrete. Her left knee bent until he felt her hip tilt into him. Slowly but surely she gained her leverage.

Pain shot through his hand, traveled up his arm to his shoulder. Her teeth sank into his palm and like the bulldog she was, not only refused to let go but locked her jaw on it. He tried to retain his calm while warm, sticky blood surfaced on his palm.

His brain beseeched him to pull loose, to end the agony, but he held true, praying she succumbed soon to the blood choke. "Go down already," he growled through clenched teeth. He broke into a cold sweat from nerves and pain – and at the thought of someone seeing them, or worse, of her getting free. At the rate she fought, he feared it might actually happen.

He applied stronger pressure on the arteries. Almost immediately her body slackened, her jaw relaxed, the iron grip of her teeth eased. He sighed, wiped the growing sweat from his brow. The pain from her bite grew unbearable quickly. He appraised the wound, wincing. Damn those pearly whites could crush rocks, he cringed. He slung his hand, dotting the concrete with droplets of blood. He couldn't blame her though. If he'd been ambushed from behind by a stranger – or what he believed to be a stranger – he'd bite the shit out of them too.

He scooped her into his arms, carried her to his rental parked at the property line, laid her in the back seat. He locked her wrists in the handcuffs for precaution then pressed a strip of duct tape over her mouth. Now to tend to Ennis. He dialed the station again, "This is Detective Rutherford's neighbor. Something's happened to his wife. It's important he goes home right now."

He pulled the battery from the phone, pocketed both. He'd toss them in the trash later but first he needed to get the hell gone. He got in the car, cranked the engine and headed in the direction of his temporary abode. At the first stop sign, he wrapped a handkerchief around his bleeding hand. He scowled in the rearview mirror at her. He really owed her for that one. His hand would be sore for weeks.

It took ten minutes to arrive at his rent house. The place sat away from the quiet street surrounded by a large yard. That and a brick security fence kept prying eyes from seeing him carry his cargo from the back seat to the house. It was a convenient and nice little place. His wife would have loved it. A cozy candidate for remodeling, something she enjoyed doing besides cooking and gardening.

He unlocked the front door, leaving it ajar then fetched Savannah, carrying her the way he carried his gorgeous bride over the threshold on their wedding night.

Savannah looked harmless lying unconscious on the sofa but he knew the truth. She was smart, strong and unpredictable. *And* the most malicious bitch he ever encountered.

He momentarily unlocked the cuffs then proceeded to undress her. Let her lie naked, exposed to the world the way he felt for years. The buttons on her pale purple blouse opened with ease. His fingers worked with dexterity and speed. Next he removed her jeans and panties then he reached behind her back, the bare skin warming his cool forearm. He unfastened her bra and slid it down her arms then tossed it aside with her other clothes.

Locking her hands behind her, he stood back and waited for Savannah to wake up and realize who was now in charge.

14

NOW

A violent shiver jerked Savannah awake. Cold air wafted across her body making her wonder if Ennis stripped the covers off her. And why wasn't he snoring? Normally their bedroom became a one man train station when he fell asleep.

Without opening her eyes, she reached back to reclaim her portion of the blanket. Her hand did not move. It felt anchored behind her so she tugged at it again. Then she felt it. The bite of metal digging into her wrists. The fog clouding her brain parted enough for her to sense a difference in her surroundings and notice the distinct smell of a dusty, stale room.

She opened her eyes, recalling a knee in her back, a hand over her mouth, another rendering her unconscious with a blood choke. But why was she so cold? Glancing down she saw nothing but bare skin. Her hands were handcuffed tight behind her. A strip of tape covered her mouth. Her mind reeled with questions until one specific thought sent panic racing through her. Where was Lily? What had the abductor done with her precious girl? It had to be Toby. The whole crazy scenario sounded like him. He attacked her, stripped her (she really dreaded finding out why he'd undressed her too) and planned to make good on his threat to kill her. However frightening her current situation was, the ultimate payback would be if he hurt or killed Lily. Savannah felt sure he knew that too.

She struggled to sit up but the soft, bulky, *ugly* brown couch prevented it. Dim light filtered through floor length beige drapes behind her. They were drawn, obscuring the view outside. Across the way sat a newer TV on a metal framework entertainment center. A DVD player was its only companion. Black and white Ansel Adams tree prints hung on the walls. She had no clue where she was, who *exactly* abducted her and most importantly what happened to Lily.

Her hands tingled, her arms hurt from being handcuffed. Her throat ached from the attacker's blood choke. She'd fought as hard as she could, for herself, for Lily who had been in her carrier. The fact she couldn't protect her own child infuriated her but the man pinning her down stole her consciousness while sinking two hundred pounds of muscle and bone onto her back. Toby gained muscle and weight in prison, that much she attested to. Years ago, she could have thrown him with the right leverage. This time he caught her in a vulnerable position. On her belly, unable to reach back or defend herself.

Savannah unfolded her legs that were bound together tight at the ankles with duct tape. When she stretched, she groaned.

Movement behind her startled her. She snapped around to see a man she'd forgotten about. He towered over the sofa with a pleased grin. He was dressed in camouflage pants and a gray t-shirt that outlined a wide, muscular chest and set of tree trunk arms. She stared straight into the eyes of a man who, surprisingly, wasn't Toby Jackson. No, she thought, this could be much, much worse…

Matthew Carlisle, Georgia's ex-husband, reached down and ripped the tape from her mouth. He smiled at her wince, "Hello, Savannah."

Confusion reigned. He should be overseas right now, shouldn't he? A universe away from Atlanta. A universe away from her sister. Yet there he stood, grinning like a boy who caught a butterfly and wanted to tear its wings off.

She leaned away, pressing into the couch. Matthew's drastic change in appearance unnerved her. A week's worth of dark stubble shadowed his jaw and chin, his dark hair – always cut into a military flattop – now grew out curly and most unkempt. His attire, normally spit and shine in his perfectly ironed uniform, deteriorated to camo pants and a wrinkled t-shirt. For Matthew Carlisle, he resembled a transient.

"Don't look so shocked," his smile sent a shiver along her spine. "I promised I'd be back."

She didn't care about his promises. She only cared about her little girl, "Is my baby safe? Did you hurt her?"

Disgust passed across his features, "You think I'd hurt your child? It's *you* I have issues with, not your baby, not your husband, but *you.*"

"And this is how you deal with issues?" she blurted without thinking. She regretted it almost immediately.

His meaty fingers dug into her jaw until her teeth ached, "That's right, you smartass bitch. Get wise with me and I'll show you trouble."

In the past, *trouble* meant slapping her. But slapping didn't equate to abducting her, tying her up and... and... and that was the problem racing through her mind. What came next?

She heard a noise in the back of the house. A man's voice. Not words but angry grumbling. Her heart sank while memories of Jeffrey and Cole raced back. She was up against two men. Again.

Matthew glanced in the direction of the noise, "Let's make this a party, my dearest sister-in-law."

Ex-sister-in-law, if you please, Mr. Crazy. And keep your little buddy to yourself. One nutcase at a time is plenty, thank you.

Matthew released her, leaving a deep throb pulsing along her jaw and neck as she worked the former to realign it. Matthew disappeared down the hallway. Her eyes closed, praying she escaped this nightmare soon. Considering her time with the last two other psychopaths, she really dreaded another round of fighting two more.

A muffled complaint filled the hallway. Someone wasn't happy. Matthew demanded the person move faster. Another subdued objection followed. Matthew came into view, his hand gripping an arm, yanking the person along. One harsh jerk brought the mystery man stumbling into the room, nearly tripping and falling to his knees. Dressed in jeans and a blue western shirt, the man's hands were tied behind him, a strip of duct tape stretched across his mouth to mute his grumblings. Dane Rutherford fought to retain his balance just as Matthew shoved him into a chair beside the sofa. He fell in the seat with a grunt. Her eyes flared, "My God. Dane, are you alright?" Stupid, her mind inquired, does look alright to you?

He grunted his answer with a shrug, met her gaze then immediately averted his vision, away from her nakedness.

Her brain tried to calculate the amount of time he'd been there. Nearly two days, she assumed. Dane was scheduled to land in Amarillo early the day before but no one heard from him. Georgia worried herself sick over it too. She and Mama Rutherford kept in constant contact trying to locate him and he'd been here all along, a captive of a lunatic.

She shifted her gaze to Matthew, narrowing it into a glare, "He's been here for two days?"

Dane gave a nod since Matthew refused to answer. Ennis's brother lifted his head, his face drawn, eyes struggling to stay open.

"Dane, has he hurt you?" she asked.

Without facing her, he shook his head. He made a sound that sounded like a question.

"I'm okay," she replied. He nodded.

"You're okay *for now*," Matthew amended with an iciness that closed her mouth. He continued, "Remember when you and your girlfriend ran me out of town in March?"

Yes, she remembered her and her colleague Christine Clark having strong words with him about leaving. They hadn't *run him out of town* though.

"Remember that phone call you made to my superior officer, telling him about that quarrel Georgia and I had at her house?"

She nodded again, not correcting his choice of words. In reality the term "quarrel" meant he'd rampaged inside Georgia's home, breaking the door and several pieces of furniture, pictures and glassware. All while

Georgia ran for her life and stopped only when she claimed her prized .22 and threatened to use him for target practice.

Matthew bent closer, "I got a dishonorable discharge because of it. I owe you for that."

The news of the dishonorable discharge stunned her. She heard it was a reduction in rank – that's all. Something else happened after he left Atlanta in March. Something drastic caused the marines to boot him from their ranks. A prickly unease trickled in. He blamed her for everything, went to the trouble of abducting her and now she panicked over what he intended to do with her so why not ask? "What are you planning to do?"

Matthew maintained steady eye contact as he rounded the sofa, dragged her to a sitting position. "Let's say if you cooperate, things go easier on you."

"Cooperate how exactly?" She pointedly stared at her bare self then at him.

His lip curled, "I stripped you to keep you under control, not to force myself on you."

"Forgive me, Matthew." *You creep.* "I've been in this situation before. Tied up and naked with a crazy man in my face. Considering my position, it's a reasonable question." The back of Matthew's hand collided with her right cheek, firing pain across every nerve from her cheek to her temple. A whimper caught at the back of her throat.

Dane struggled to his feet, voicing a loud complaint that Savannah assumed revolved around the reprehensible act of hitting a woman. With one hand Matthew pushed him back in the chair, then headed to the kitchen area. He returned with more duct tape. Stripping off two lengths, he secured Dane's ankles, one to each chair leg.

He cautioned Savannah, "Watch your tongue with me. Georgia's not here to protect you. To answer your question, your cooperation involves staying right there until I get my wife back."

Did he forget about Rachel Gordon, his little nurse in Iraq that he bedded? Had he suffered a lapse that erased those divorce papers he sent *plus* the nasty letter he penned basically telling Georgia *see ya, wouldn't wanna be ya*? In case he had, Savannah sought to refresh his memory, "Georgia's not your wife anymore. You served her divorce papers after screwing Florence Nightingale, remember?" This time a knife of pain drove into her brain when he backhanded her. Shying away now, she tried to explain, "I was stating fact. Don't hit me for that."

He leaned closer until she saw the black flecks in his brown eyes, "I'll tell you the facts. You're interfering in our lives the way you always have. Georgia and I will be happier together when you're not around but I need you right now. As long as you're here, she'll do anything to keep you safe. Even come back to me."

Any other day the declaration would have inspired hysterics. With Matthew's deranged behavior, however, the humor evaporated. She blew out a breath, "Boy, you better hope she loves me *a lot* to do that."

"*You'd* better hope she does," he corrected. "Your life depends on it."

He returned to the kitchen, leaving her wondering when the man's sanity fled the space between his ears. Expecting Georgia to recommit herself to a two-timing loose cannon that kidnapped her sister, stripped her to her birthday suit and bound her with duct tape? *Not friggin' likely.*

From the day Georgia introduced them, Savannah suspected Matthew wasn't the sweet Prince Charming he presented himself to be. Later she discovered an ominous character lurked below the surface, one he cleverly concealed from Georgia. Back then, Savannah endured his darker side by either walking away or lashing out, depending on her mood or level of drunkenness. Alcohol accentuated her boldness or stupidity, however one looked at it. But age, wisdom and motherhood oiled the panic button, tuning the radar to the option of *flight* instead of her old buddy *fight*. Fleeing appealed to her more than fighting a deranged man however fleeing required arms and legs, all of which currently remained disabled.

Savannah summoned that old self, the one that opposed Matthew with reckless, reason-be-damned courage but the fearless woman in her early twenties disappeared. Replacing her was a worried mother who desired to go home to her husband and baby, praying neither spent one night without her or she without them.

Matthew tinkered around in the kitchen, opening and closing cabinet drawers. Utensils clanged and clattered against each other, the faucet ran a minute then abruptly stopped. It was as if she and Dane weren't there and Matthew lived alone, washing dishes, tidying up. How odd, she thought, that a man held two others against their will and obsessed over dirty dishes. But that described Matthew, at least in years past. Organization. Structure. *Perfection.*

She remembered Georgia met Matthew at a book signing for her second book. According to Georgia, Matthew Carlisle entered the small quaint bookstore in full uniform. Standing regal and handsome (this too according to Georgia), he scanned the immediate area until meeting her gaze. Without so much as a smile, he approached the display with her two books and laid them before her to sign. "The name's Matthew Carlisle," he held his hand palm up toward her. She placed hers in his, expecting a handshake. What she got was a gesture that sent a tingle down her spine, she'd said. He curled his fingers around hers in a tender grasp then pressed a lingering kiss to her hand. Georgia gushed over the marine's charm. Savannah found it difficult to imagine her gushing over anything. Not her mature, levelheaded sister. Georgia had introduced herself to which Mr. Carlisle responded, "I know who you are. You're going to be my wife."

He showered Georgia in flower bouquets, trinkets, and jewelry. Savannah's sister developed a girlish joy associated with teenagers. That coy blushing, the giddiness, and fun loving demeanor Savannah saw on rare occasion. Matthew poured on the attention and made it count. Georgia fell hard and fast for the lieutenant and that didn't set well with Savannah. Not because she was jealous but because the sensible sister she grew up with abandoned ship somewhere between *I met the sweetest man* and *I want you to be my bridesmaid.*

The day Savannah met him, she pegged him as a poster child for obsessive compulsive behavior when he nitpicked how she held her utensils at supper. "Haven't seen anyone eat that way since I was stationed in Europe," he said.

Annoyed, Georgia explained, "Savannah's always held her utensils Continental style. It's not improper, just different."

Matthew lifted a brow. Savannah sensed a hint of reproach for her "different" manner of eating.

He suggested, "Have you tried holding them American style?"

"No," she replied matter-of-factly. She understood the difference between Continental and American style dining etiquette. She held her utensils Continental but instead of lifting the fork to her mouth tines down, she flipped them over – American style. So technically, she'd tell him, she was a half-breed diner.

"Matthew," Georgia frowned, "leave her alone about it."

But Matthew never left her alone about anything. While he was home on leave, Savannah kept to herself – as much as he let her. She ignored his blatant criticizing, his nitpicking and "suggestions" that she move out. For Georgia's sake, she avoided arguing with him but she also noticed that Matthew never argued in front of his wife. He tucked his horns, tail and cloven hooves out of sight around Georgia and waited until she was gone to confront Savannah about little things. Leaving her coat in the wrong place (for one minute). Staying out too late (which was none of his business). Her drinking (again, none of his business). Not helping Georgia with household chores or cooking (which she did).

By the time she was a rookie cop, Matthew earned a promotion to captain, a title that seemed to inflate his already bloated ego. Every night after shift she went straight upstairs to her room to her bourbon – the one thing in her life that didn't judge or belittle her. She avoided getting stone drunk, no matter what her new brother-in-law thought.

She permitted herself only so much each night since hangovers and eight hour shifts didn't mix. She allowed herself enough to cloud her mind, drop off asleep and spend a few hours blissfully unaware of life and its problems. Enough to dull the confrontations, bad moods and hassles the public insisted on inflicting on law enforcement officers. And enough to forget Matthew Carlisle was married to her sister.

Their animosity escalated when she arrived home one evening after indulging in a few drinks after shift with Riley Murphy. She drank until a numbness set in that might allow her to tolerate Matthew that evening. She stepped inside, her uniform slung across her forearm and duty belt looped over her shoulder. With her nemesis nowhere in sight, she sighed with relief, hoping for a peaceful evening.

"Georgia's at the store," Matthew announced, startling her from her short-lived serenity.

"Thanks for the newsflash," she turned, seeing him zero in on the uniform.

He stepped from the kitchen, hands on hips, "Georgia's not ironing your uniforms anymore. Do it yourself."

Yes, Sergeant Major, she bit her tongue, forbidding it to slip. To reduce his rank whether in jest or anger might cause a riot. "My uniform is going to the cleaners, Captain. And for the record, I never asked her to do anything." *I should have had that other shot of Jack,* she lamented. Now she had to endure the Inquisition semi-sober.

She relieved herself of the duty belt, laying it across the arm of the sofa long enough to hang the uniform in the closet.

"Get that gun off the sofa. Put it where it belongs."

But it won't fit up your tight marine ass, she ached to reply then fantasized about giving it a try and pulling the trigger.

Matthew continued, this time barking over her shoulder, "Georgia and I like order in this house." He stepped around her, reached for the belt, "I'll move it for you since you won't do much to help around here."

The liquor buzz evaporated in an instant. Her hand shot to his wrist, her vision sharpening to a razor's edge. Without a word, she let her scowl and firm grasp serve as a warning not to touch her duty belt. Matthew stared at her hand then lifted his vision to hers, "Feeling cocky these days since you wear that gun, aren't you?"

"Secure is the word," she corrected, sliding the belt off the sofa and into her grasp.

"You're a danger to the public. Carrying a gun and badge and being a drunk. You're going to accidentally kill someone."

"Tell me, wise, almighty Yoda, where did you buy your crystal ball?" She marched to the stairs, intending to forego supper, grab a few drinks and a bath then hit the hay.

Matthew spun her to face him, the motion dropping the duty belt from her shoulder to her wrist where she caught it. Matthew's cheeks bloomed fiery red, "I'm done with you, Savannah." He reached in his pocket, removed a folded ad from the newspaper, shoved it in her hand, "Here's your new address. Get out before I do something I regret."

What should have infuriated her incited only a mild flare up, "Where is it? Kirkwood? The Bluff? Cabbage Town?" Three of the worst parts of town. Gangs, dope dealers, murders, rapes. Just where

Matthew probably wanted her.

"Bankhead."

Not to be confused with Buckhead, the *nice* part of town. "Oh, so I only have to sleep with my gun under my pillow, not on my hip."

His back straightened. She recognized this sign. It indicated he'd "reached his limit" with her. She predicted the next step perfectly. His hands bunched into fists. This was a caution for her to shut up and do what she was told. Matthew should have known her better. "Daddy was right," she said. "You should have stayed in Frankenstein, Michigan."

His jaw clenched, "I paid the first two months' rent for you. Be out of here by the weekend."

"Where's she going?"

Without either of them hearing her, Georgia arrived from the grocery store, a paper sack cradled in her arm, confusion ruling her features. Seeing the two squared off, she sat the bag down, expecting an answer. From Matthew.

"She's moving out," he magically brightened. "Didn't she tell you?"

Georgia's eyes sprung wide at her sister, "No, she didn't."

"That's because," Savannah replied, "*she* didn't know about it herself. Matthew graciously paid my first two months' rent. In Bankhead."

Now her sister's mouth dropped open with disbelief, "She can't move there. It's too dangerous. Matthew, she doesn't need to move."

Matthew hurled a vicious glare at Savannah – ensuring his wife didn't see it, "She needs her own place. It won't kill her, Georgia."

"She's not moving, especially to Bankhead. You don't know the bad parts of this city."

Oh, yes he does, Savannah sing-songed to herself. *He knows more than you think, sis.* She strutted to Georgia, slung her arm around her shoulders, "See, Matthew? We're like twins. You can't have one without the other." She squeezed her sister close, grateful that Georgia defended her and protected her from the brute across the way.

Georgia returned the embrace, clearly still confused by what she walked in on, "Let's drop this subject of moving. Matthew, you're going back in another week. If Savannah leaves, I'm alone and I'm not ready to live alone again." She picked up the grocery bag, marched into the kitchen, leaving the two behind.

Feeling relieved and plenty satisfied with the conversation's results, Savannah started up the stairs again, "Didn't work, did it?"

"Not this time but don't get too comfortable."

"With you around, how could I?"

15

NOW

Street lamps in the near distance provided minimal light inside the living room. Savannah estimated the time around nine-thirty or ten. Earlier that evening, Matthew left without a word but not before reinforcing his handiwork on his two captives. For Savannah he found a not-so-comfortable hardwood chair that rubbed her tailbone raw. Her hips and ankles hurt from the two rounds of duct tape he'd cinched around them. For Dane he gifted another strip around each ankle.

She glanced at Dane. His head drooped to his chest and besides his rapid breathing, he hadn't moved since Matthew walked out. She called Dane, hoping to rouse him, but he managed only a weak groan.

She strained to reach the tape on her hips with her cuffed hands, planning to begin the painful, arduous task of peeling enough away to rip the tape in half. It stuck like a second skin. Trying again, she grimaced as she pried one square inch loose. She sighed, opting to give her wrists and arms a temporary rest. "Dane," she called. "You awake?"

He barely nodded.

"I'm trying to get loose so I can call for help. Just hang on." If she managed to free her hips, she'd try sliding her wrists beneath her bottom to her ankles then peel the tape from them. If that worked, she'd loop the handcuffs under her feet, bringing her hands in front of her. Then she could finally free Dane.

The door lock snapped open. She immediately stilled when Matthew stepped in, closed the door behind him. In his hand he held a pizza and in his other, a paper sack. He seemed pleased his two prisoners remained as he'd left, stuck like flies to flypaper. "I'm impressed," he told Savannah. "I figured you'd be on the floor squirming your way to the door by now."

"You intend to share that pizza or will you starve us?" she inquired.

"Keep a civil tongue and I'll share." He rattled the paper sack, "If you're real good, I might share my beer with you."

"Keep the beer. I'd like pizza and water. Dane might like some beer with his."

"He gets nothing. He's trying to steal my wife."

"Matthew, come on. How about one piece and a glass of water?"

"I said no."

Shock registered, "Has he had anything to eat or drink since he's been here?"

"No and he won't."

She looked at Dane who managed a small, one-shouldered shrug. That explained his drooping posture and lethargic demeanor. Outraged, she demanded, "Matthew, for God's sake. At least give him food and water."

Heavy footfalls pounded the floor. Dane's eyes widened while they tracked Matthew around the sofa until he bent face to face with Savannah. The ex-marine shouted, "I make the decisions here, not you. I will not feed a man who is after my wife."

His tirade drew her back in the chair, her tone even and calm, "My point was if you want to keep us alive to hear Georgia's answer, food and water are required."

"I called her while I was out. She's considering my offer."

Her initial thought brought tremendous indignation with it, "What do you mean, she's *considering your offer?*" Not that she wanted Georgia hitched to the nutcase again but shit, didn't she love her sister and Dane enough to lie to the bastard and say yes? She took a moment to think it over. Maybe Georgia stalled with the answer, tried to buy time. What she didn't realize – Dane's time was running out.

Matthew evidently sensed her concern, "You won't be waiting long. I gave her twelve hours to decide. So once we're back together your troubles are over." He glared at Dane, "And so are his."

She and Dane exchanged glances. She cleared her throat uneasily, "Then may I request that Dane and I both be allowed a meal and a glass or two of water? Please?"

He mulled over the plea. Savannah waited, praying he'd say yes for Dane's sake. Matthew shifted his vision between the two then, "I might feed you but not him."

"What can I do to change your mind about Dane? He needs water, Matthew."

He shook his finger at her, "Your mouth is your biggest

detriment. You just talked yourself out of anything." He traipsed down the hall, leaving Savannah worrying about Dane. His chest rose and fell in shallow breaths. His head still bowed against his chest. She had to free herself because waiting was a death sentence for Ennis's brother and she could never live with herself if that happened. "Don't give up, Dane." She finished with more confidence than she felt, "I'm working on a plan." One that involved the excruciating task of peeling herself free from untold yards of duct tape. Past that, she'd wing it.

It was another hour before Matthew retired to the bedroom. He flipped the room switch, leaving only the street lamp's subdued glow seeping through the drapes. Savannah resumed removing the tape around her back. Over the hours the adhesive bonded to her warm skin and peeling the duct tape inch by painful inch equaled a scene from medieval times. Forget the Iron Maiden or the Rack. Wrap a person in duct tape and peel it off centimeter by centimeter. The hardiest soul would beg for mercy.

By the time she pulled free, tears blurred her vision, perspiration glistened on her skin. A careful, tremulous breath replaced the swallowed whimpers and groans. Savannah rose from the seat with slow, cautious movements. One creak from the chair might alert Matthew. She wriggled her wrists beneath her bottom and behind her knees. She eased into the seat again. Now she concentrated on maneuvering the handcuffs to her ankles. Matthew wrapped two strips around each, ensuring they remained locked against the thick wooden chair legs. Dozens of muted groans later, she freed both ankles.

She stood up, listening for movement in the back bedroom, then traversed the dark room. The street lights threw shadows across furniture, forcing her to move in delicate, measured steps. Her hand touched soft fabric – the sofa – then grazed cool wood – the edge of the side table. She maneuvered to the dining table, squinted her eyes against the dimness to see a pile of neatly folded clothes stacked on top. Her clothes. She rifled the pile, hoping to find her phone. She found it between her blouse and jeans, powered it up.

The home screen illuminated the immediate area like a beacon. She pressed the bright screen to her chest with an irrational paranoia that the light might alert Matthew even around corners and through the walls. Savannah stepped to the kitchen to access the contact list. She scrolled until locating Christine Clark who was on shift that night. Christine picked up on the second ring. Savannah cupped her hand around her mouth, whispering into the phone, "Christine, it's Savannah. Matthew Carlisle abducted me and Dane and I don't know where we are. Track my phone's GPS."

"Will do. The cavalry will be there soon, just hang on and be careful."

Savannah clicked off the call but left the phone on. She tiptoed to the kitchen for a glass of water. She ran the tap quietly, filling the glass halfway then crept back into the living room. Kneeling by Dane, she gently peeled the tape from his mouth then touched his arm with a whisper, "Drink this water."

His eyelids parted to slits, saw the glass then closed again. She nudged him, "Dane, *drink.*" She held the glass to his mouth but he refused. She dipped her fingers into the water, pressed them to his dry lips. His mouth opened, accepting the moisture onto his tongue. She lifted the glass again, whispered in his ear to take a drink and followed it with, "If you want to marry Georgia, you have to drink."

She dribbled a few drops between his lips. He welcomed the water into his mouth but stopped with one swallow. She tilted the glass once more, "A little more, Dane, please."

The small amount of liquid trickled into his mouth. He tried to swallow but coughed instead, his body racked in violent throes. He heaved a groan, "I'm so sorry, Peach."

They both knew what he meant. The noise stirred Matthew awake. A bed squeaked. Two feet thumped to the floor. Matthew cleared his throat. Savannah stood, her mind racing, eyes searching in the darkness for a weapon. She raced to the kitchen, rummaged one drawer after another. Nothing. The glint of metal in the sink caught her attention. A knife. A six inch boning knife, the only one in the kitchen, had to suffice.

She rounded the corner to the living room and in the dim light, she saw Matthew – still fully dressed – standing and staring at her with pure hatred as he switched on the light. Panic rioted inside her. *This* Matthew was new to her. Without uttering a word, *this* Matthew Carlisle promised a swift demise, not a hard slap across the face and long lecture. *This* Matthew Carlisle held a large knife of his own – larger and more imposing than her puny boning knife. His sported a curved blade perfect for slicing a person's throat. And *this* Matthew Carlisle advanced on her the way Jeffrey Holland had – with a single-minded goal to end her life.

In the distance, she heard sirens wailing. If she could hold him off long enough, the cavalry would ride in to save the day, as Christine had said.

Matthew lunged at her, thrusting the knife at her belly.

She jumped back. Her bare back and bottom slammed against a closed door (the one leading to the garage, she assumed). She had no more room to maneuver around him. The small "shotgun" kitchen barely accommodated two people standing side by side, much less one normal size woman and a homicidal Goliath. Through him, not around him, was her only hope. She'd painted herself into one hell of a corner now, she thought.

She focused on Matthew's hands that remained rock steady while hers hopelessly trembled, her meager stand against the marine (with her six inch boning knife) verging on laughable and pathetic.

The sirens grew louder now. Police cars were driving down the street. Matthew's eyes narrowed, "How do they know? What did you do?"

The fearless woman from many years ago sprung forth with a vengeance. She straightened with unflinching defiance, "I called the cops, asshole. They're here now and they're taking your ass to jail where it belongs," she ended the statement with a swing of the boning knife. It sliced across his forearm, the wound bloomed with crimson, dripped down his forearm onto the floor.

Matthew cursed through clenched teeth. Savannah shoved past him, ran for the front door. He kicked the back of her knee, collapsing her leg and sending her to the floor. Matthew straddled her back, leaving her struggling against his weight. She lay defenseless and at his mercy – of which he promised none.

The sirens neared. Savannah clawed at the carpet, trying to crawl from beneath her former brother-in-law. She twisted under him, the muscles in her back pulling and straining. She channeled her strength into one solid swing of the knife, cleaving a gash in his calf. Savannah expected him to react to the pain, perhaps the way normal humans might. The attack only infuriated Matthew.

Fingers fisted in her hair, yanked her head back. A sharp blade nestled at her throat. This is it, she thought squeezing her eyes shut. *This is how it ends. I survived Jeffrey Holland twice and that crazy Irishman Troy Quinn only to be murdered by my half-baked ex-brother-in-law...*

The sirens stopped. They were close if not right outside. That hurt the worst. She came within a minute of saving Dane and herself. Now they were both toast. "The cops are here, Matthew," she fought to reach the common sense part of his brain – if he still possessed one. "They're gonna bust down the door and arrest you." She prayed for the door to do exactly that. Bust open and for half a dozen cops to charge into the house with guns drawn and just one, just *one,* to pull the damn trigger on Matthew.

She heard his heavy breathing. Felt the knife press a degree harder against her throat. Then the heaviness on her back lifted, the blade withdrew and pushed to his feet to make a mad dash to the bedroom. When he emerged, he carried a duffle bag and a small black case with a padlock.

Still wielding the boning knife, she scrambled to oppose him, putting herself between him and Dane.

He smirked at her supposed threat, "This isn't over, no matter what you think." Matthew raced out the back door with barely a limp to his stride.

Marines, she thought. Tough as nails but some had a few loose screws. Pulling the drapes aside, she saw him slip out the gate and turn down the alley.

The front door slammed open and two uniform cops barged in, guns aimed at her. Angry that Matthew got away, she threw the knife aside and wheeled, covering her nudity with both arms, "Carlisle went out the–"

"On your knees," an officer demanded. "Keep your hands where we can see them."

"Hey," she barked back, "I'm a cop–"

"I don't care who you are. On your knees now, hands behind your head."

She stood her ground with a parental tone, "Young man, my hands are staying exactly where the hell they are. Where do you think I can hide a weapon anyway? *I'm naked.*"

Behind the two uniforms she breathed a sigh of relief when Ennis pushed past the presumptuous officer. "That's my partner," he snapped in a way suggesting the officer was deficient. "Take your gun off her now."

The men lowered their weapons as Savannah said, "Matthew went out the back, turned right down the alley." She stared at the uniforms, nodded to the back door, "Go... find... him."

Ennis wrapped his arms around her, "Are you okay?"

"Past being knocked out a while, I'm fine. Dane needs a hospital quick though. He's severely dehydrated."

Paramedics poured in behind Christine Clark who retreated behind Savannah, out of the way. Savannah shooed the paramedics away, pointing to Dane instead, "Help him. He hasn't had fluids in two days."

Ennis wrapped his jacket around her shoulders as she kneeled beside Dane. She began stripping the tape from his ankles, "Dane, help is here. You have to hang on for us and for Georgia."

His eyes opened to see her and Ennis, the latter put a hand to his shoulder, "My brother's got vows to exchange and a honeymoon scheduled. He's not jumping ship, are you, bro?"

Dane tried to shake his head. Savannah patted his knee, "We'll see you at the hospital," she winked, "unless Georgia hogs you all to herself."

She turned, pulled the jacket tighter around her. She saw Christine staring at her back before Ennis draped his suit coat around her. For a brief second the old self-consciousness wormed its way in. After a while, she accepted the numerous scars crisscrossing her back and bottom for what they were. Not just a testament to suffering at the hands of brutal men but a visual reminder of the price of survival. Growing up, her father put marks on her but nothing compared to Jeffrey Holland's damage. Those scars went from her thighs to her shoulders.

Savannah stepped to the dining table, picked up her clothes. It was clear Christine felt uncomfortable with what she saw and frankly Savannah was tired of being on display. "Thanks for getting here so quick, Christine," she said. "Dane and I would have been dead if you hadn't arrived when you did."

Clark snapped out of her daze, "What? Oh, yeah, sure. I told them you were a cop but," she shrugged, not making eye contact, "I suppose they do things different on this side of town. I know it was embarrassing for you a while ago. I'm sorry for that."

Savannah ducked around the corner into the kitchen, slid on her panties and jeans. "Better to be embarrassed than dead."

Now Christine's dark eyes met her gaze, "Why are you dressing? The paramedics need to check you out and you need to be examined for sexual assault at the hospital."

Savannah chuckled now. She understood her colleague's concern however, "Matthew Carlisle would eat glass before violating me, Christine. He can't stand the sight me, the sound of me or the idea of me."

Clark clamped her hands to her hips, "He's lost his ever-loving mind. People who snap are capable of anything."

"She's right, babe," Ennis agreed. "You need to be checked."

Savannah continued dressing. She shed the jacket, handing it to Ennis with a thank you. She faced her colleague and husband to prevent Christine from viewing the scars again. After hooking her bra and slipping on her blouse, she said, "I know Matthew well enough to say he'd never rape me. The exam is a waste of time but I'll do it."

16

NOW

"If I ever see that bastard again, I'm stealing his clothes, covering him in honey and hanging him beneath a beehive," Savannah declared with finality. It hadn't been easy being in the company of a crazy man. Worrying about Dane's safety and her own since Matthew's choo choo jumped the tracks. Ennis and Christine demanded a rape kit which annoyed her to no end. Wasn't it enough Matthew subjected her to sitting in her birthday suit in front of him *and* Dane? Wasn't it enough that she nearly flashed herself to two uniform cops because they assumed she, a cop (a *naked* cop), might be a threat to them? Apparently not, considering her husband and colleague wanted her bare assed at the hospital too, getting poked and prodded in places no one except a husband should poke and prod. The rape kit returned negative, which she figured, because Matthew would rather French-kiss a barracuda than touch her in a sexual manner.

Even after a day and a half the search for Matthew turned up empty. The man ran like the wind, evidently, or took a header down his own private gopher hole. The idea of dodging more attacks or possibly another attempt on her life gave her a headache. Georgia spent most of her time with Dane either at the hospital or at home but found time to cook and bring supper over to her and Ennis which hadn't surprised Savannah at all. The woman was a human Energizer Bunny and during times of stress, she worked off tension in the kitchen which meant good eats for quite a while.

Now the Bunny sat on the sofa beside Savannah who held her sweet baby. Lily's reaction to seeing her mother warmed Savannah's heart. A toothless grin spread across the child's face accompanied by a giggle. Lily was happy and so was Savannah.

Ennis plopped beside her as well, put hand on her knee, patting it, "They'll find him, don't worry."

Savannah *did* worry. She worried Matthew might come after Lily or Ennis as a perverted form of payback. Until the marine resided not-so-comfortably behind bars, she'd worry sure as the sun rose in the mornings and Ennis serenaded her to sleep at night with his snoring.

Georgia pulled her sister close with arm around her shoulders. She'd arrived two hours earlier bearing gifts of a chicken enchilada casserole and German Chocolate Cake. A cake, she learned, that wasn't even technically German but named for a chocolate maker by that name and was originally called German's Chocolate Cake.

Georgia educated her sister on such details as she tidied the kitchen and living room, changed the bed sheets then made the bed with military fastidiousness. Savannah didn't have the heart to tell her she didn't really care if the recipe was developed on Mars by little green men. She just loved eating the cake. She listened dutifully, however, because her sister chatted like a magpie since walking through the door. Between stories on food, Georgia took over Lily's feeding and changing, and ran a load of laundry "for good measure" she told Savannah. The sheer amount of work exhausted Savannah so it was nice when her sister joined her on the sofa to visit. The only problem: Georgia switched from the history of food to apologizing for Matthew's behavior. It was as though she felt responsible for his fanatical spree.

"Maybe he left town knowing the police are searching for him. I'm just so sorry…"

"Georgia," she met her gaze, "you didn't abduct me so stop apologizing. The man's screws came loose a long time ago. You are not at fault."

Georgia kissed her cheek, "I'm grateful you're alive to say that. I never realized his anger about you verged on violence."

Savannah smoothed the brown wispy hair on Lily's head, "He blames me for ruining his time with you back then and for his dishonorable discharge now." Which still rang strange to her. She'd ask Seth about dishonorable discharges when she found time. If Matthew was given the worst kind of discharge known to military history, why was he out rousting and terrorizing good and decent people and not rotting behind bars?

The phone rang and Ennis picked it up. Savannah heard her father's boisterous voice loud and clear. He demanded to speak to "his baby". Ennis handed the phone to Savannah like it was ablaze, "Your daddy."

She greeted her father with a pleasant, "Hi Daddy."

"Hi, baby. How ya feelin'?"

"At least I'm alive. Could be worse."

"That cur been in contact?"

"No, he hasn't bothered me."

"That sonuvabitch calls or drops by, let me know. My shotgun's loaded an' I got plenty of shells."

The degree of protectiveness R.J. displayed surprised Savannah. It made her smile imagining her daddy running Matthew off with that old shotgun.

"I'll kill him if I ever see him again," he continued. "Ain't gonna mess with my girls and get away with it."

The smile faded. His steadfast vow caused a ripple of nausea to climb up her throat, "Daddy, no, please don't. He's long gone–"

"Damn well better be. Pump that bastard so full of lead he'll sink to the bottom of the river I throw 'im in." Evidently sensing her impending lecture, he finished, "I ain't arguing with ya 'bout it either. Put your sister on the horn. I wanna talk to her."

Savannah surrendered the phone to Georgia, whispering, "Your turn."

Georgia slanted her a guarded glance, took the phone. Savannah looked to Ennis who stated the obvious, "Gonna kill Matthew, right?"

She nodded. Her husband leaned closer, pecked a kiss on her lips, "He'll have to wait in line behind me, Georgia and Seth."

She returned the kiss, "I don't want my whole family in jail for murder. Don't get me wrong. It's a heartwarming gesture but I can't afford the bail for all of you."

Next to her she heard Georgia's repetitive answers. *Yes, Daddy.*
Yes, Daddy. Yes, Daddy. Then finally, "No, Daddy, we won't go out
alone. Dane's still in the hospital so maybe Seth will go with me... Yes,
Ennis is right here... I don't know if he's taking time off–"

"He damn well better!" R.J. yelled.

Georgia flinched, yanked the phone from her ear while R.J.
proceeded to shout, "My baby nearly died 'cause he was missing in
action! Tell him to protect his wife – *my baby* – or I'll be on him like
white on rice!"

Georgia squirmed, uncomfortable with the outburst and
unwilling to meet Ennis's gaze. She chanced bringing the phone to her
ear again, "I'm sure he knows, Daddy."

So does the whole neighborhood after that rowdy fit, Savannah
thought. She patted her husband's knee with a sympathetic smile. Ennis
tolerated her father better than she expected any man to. If anything it
told her how much Ennis loved her. Enough to be raked over the coals
for something that wasn't his fault.

"Daddy, I need to heat Savannah's supper and Lily looks restless.
She may need changing."

Liar, liar, pants on fire, Savannah's expression said. Lily's smile
and grabby hands told Mama that baby's mood was fine and rather
spunky. Georgia's talent for fibbing her way out of phone conversations
with their father bordered on masterful. Savannah sat in awe *and* envy.

Georgia pressed a finger to her lips as a sign to hush, "I'll see you
tomorrow. Love you." Georgia clicked off, blew out a breath, her
shoulders sagging. "He's so hot about this, I pray he never lays eyes on

Matthew."

"Or me," Ennis frowned.

"Ennis," she replied, "he may be angry at you right now but be glad you're not Matthew. I hope that man isn't stupid enough to show his face in Augusta. Daddy *will* murder him."

17

NOW

Head in hand, Ennis waited for the marine colonel to return to the phone call. And waited. And waited. He rolled his eyes, bemoaning the bureaucracy of a simple inquiry to the military. So far he learned why Matthew wasn't overseas defending his country. The marines considered him a deserter. Whatever Carlisle did, he chose to flee justice rather than face prison time and a dishonorable discharge. Ennis pressed the colonel for details and after hemming and hawing, the man stuck him on hold. Ten then fifteen minutes passed when Ennis began doodling on his notepad. First he drew a tree. Then he sketched a noose dangling from a branch. In the noose he drew a stick figure, its head lolled to the side, tongue hanging out and two "X's" for eyes.

Christine Clark leaned forward in her seat to view his artistry. A little smile crossed her face. She knew who swung from the branch. She too vowed revenge on the rogue marine if they came face to face. No one touched a cop, she said, but absolutely no one on creation screwed with her friends. She'd used a more colorful word than *screwed* which surprised Ennis but not as much as her steadfast loyalty to his wife. The two friends grew close the past few months and he was grateful Savannah had a devoted female colleague.

Finally the colonel clicked back on. The pause before he spoke forewarned Ennis to prepare himself. The colonel's words slammed him harder than a sucker punch. He hadn't seen that particular revelation coming. His body went slack in his chair, the pen tipping from his hand like a felled tree. Images of Savannah naked and vulnerable clawed at his brain, making him cringe. She'd been luckier than anyone imagined.

Seeing his reaction, Christine leaned even closer, gripping the arms of her chair until her knuckles blanched. Ennis recognized this aggressive stance. The tall, lanky, black-haired detective (his temporary partner until Savannah returned) looked ready to pounce. Just wait till she hears *this*, he thought. Ball-buster Christine Clark might have a chance to live up to her reputation if allowed within striking range of Mr. Carlisle.

Ennis gathered the courage to repeat Matthew's offense, the one that the marines booted him to the curb for. "Aggravated sexual assault? Who was the complainant?"

The colonel backtracked a bit but after Ennis reminded him one, that Matthew abducted Savannah and two, he'd practically dismantled his ex-wife's house – his ex-wife who happened to be Savannah's sister – the colonel coughed up the complainant's name. Ennis wrote it down, "Where does she live?"

In Atlanta, the colonel replied then excused himself from the phone call. Ennis dropped the receiver in the cradle and sighed, unable to extricate the image from his mind. The image of his wife lying in that rent house, unconscious and naked and at Matthew's mercy. The hospital checked her for signs of rape, he reminded. And the result of that exam was the only reason he hadn't hunted Carlisle down in the streets the last few nights.

"Ennis," Christine spoke uneasily. "What did he say?"

He recited the colonel's words, tapping his finger on the name he'd written, "Carlisle sexually assaulted this girl."

His colleague appeared queasy. The bombshell effectively deflated her rigid posture, leaving her to slump in the chair, "I've heard of soldiers having issues after being wounded but few go off the reservation to that degree. Was he always disconnected?"

"Georgia said he was wound tight but treated her like royalty. It was others he held grudges against, especially Savannah. He blamed her for interfering in his and Georgia's marriage, for living with Georgia, for dr–" he stopped before finishing the word *drinking*. He concluded, "He blamed her for a lot."

"So what's the victim's name?"

"Kelsey Townsend. Lives here in Atlanta." He swiveled to the computer, entered the name on a DMV search and waited. His jaw slackened. How could two people favor so much without being related? Turning the monitor to Christine, he asked, "That look anything like Georgia?"

Like Ennis, Christine's jaw plummeted, "That's spooky. He attacked that woman because he thought she was Georgia. You need to call her, Ennis. Warn her."

He reached for the phone, dialed Georgia by memory, "That's

what I'm doing. She was going to Augusta today but maybe I can catch her before she leaves."

18

NOW

No wonder parents felt brain damaged after the birth of their little one, Savannah lamented while removing Lily's stinky diaper. In her career she'd smelled plenty of putrid, ugly odors but a baby's muddy diaper held a special kind of stench that tested her guts each time. "Lord, child," wrinkled her nose, "I long for the days you can eat solid food. Until then may God bless me with a stronger stomach."

She'd changed babies before. She changed Lindsey and Dylan's diapers many times so at least she claimed some experience in that area. It was the twenty-four hour care, the midnight, two and four a.m. duties that wore thin. She'd let Ennis help the last few days considering the week's events and he reacted the way most new fathers did. Owl-eyed and more inclined to walk into a nuclear blast than touch a dirty diaper. Savannah walked him through the procedure at the hospital when Lily was born. Then Mama Rutherford reinforced the steps when she visited. After that quick refresher course, Ennis picked right up on it, especially after Savannah assured him, "If the child survived being locked inside me for nine months, she'll survive you changing her diaper occasionally."

A smile crossed her lips. Ennis truly wanted to help. When Mama visited after the baby's birth, he'd watched his mother with a keen eye, noting step by step how to clean the baby, how much powder she used to dust the baby's bottom, how to line up the diaper tabs, how tight to fasten them. Savannah enjoyed witnessing the lesson as her husband jotted down the details. He looked like a detective taking someone's statement, not a new father learning to diaper his baby.

Savannah cleaned the baby, powdered her and slipped a new diaper beneath her daughter and fastened it. After washing her hands, she tickled Lily, inspiring a toothless smile and giggle from the infant. Lily was such a beautiful child, she thought. The best thing besides Ennis to happen to her. "Let's see how long you keep this one dry," Savannah teased. "You made it quite a while last night. Are you growing up on me already, little one?"

Lily laughed, her tiny fingers clamping around Mama's thumb. The baby seemed pleased her mother noticed the stretch of time she'd lasted last night without a change.

The phone rang, splintering their mother/daughter time. Savannah kept grinning at her girl and vice versa, even as the former answered the phone. "This better be good," she singsonged to the caller, "because I'm busy." She made a goofy face at Lily who giggled again.

"You heard from Georgia this morning?" Ennis asked, ignoring his wife's happy mood.

She didn't let that deflate her joy. She continued in the same cheerful, singing voice, "No, I haven't. We haven't heard from Aunt Georgia today, have we, little one? Nope, Daddy, not even Lily has–"

"I've tried her home phone and cell number and get nothing. Do you know where she was headed once she got to Augusta?"

Hearing a trace of panic in his tone, she instantly sobered, "Besides the house, the only other places that I'd figure are the orchards or the store. Why?"

"She's in danger. The marines consider Matthew a deserter."

"A deserter?" She couldn't believe her ears, "I know he's a brick or two short but–"

"He sexually assaulted a woman who closely resembles Georgia – and I mean *closely* resembles her."

Okay, forget deserter, forget the supposed dishonorable discharge. Forget everything except finding Georgia. She held a hand to her stomach to settle the rising nausea, "I'll call around. Would you call Lindsey, see if she can babysit this afternoon in case I need to leave?"

"Soon as we hang up. Let me know if you get hold of Georgia."

Savannah ended the call with a gentle admonition to herself not to jump to conclusions. For safety's sake, Georgia refused to answer her cell phone while driving. If family called repeatedly she'd pull over to answer. It was that fact alone that had Savannah speed dialing her sister. The phone rang two, three, four times before transferring to voicemail. "Georgia, it's me. Keep a watch out for Matthew. He's more dangerous than any of us realized. If he finds you, do whatever you have to do to protect yourself. And call me the instant you get this." She clicked off, hearing Lily's tiny whimpers of discontent. She scooped the baby into her arms, shushing and soothing her and wishing someone could do the same for her. "You don't mind staying with Lindsey, do you? Mama's got to find Aunt Georgia and make sure she's okay."

Lily gurgled, closed her tiny fingers around Savannah's pinkie and squeezed as if to comfort her. Savannah dropped a kiss on her forehead, "My sweet girl. Mama won't leave you long, I promise."

She walked the baby to the crib, laid her down. Lily's legs kicked, her arms and fists flailing. She hated the idea of Savannah's placing her in the crib and her fussing grew in intensity. Mama uttered a few tender words to settle the baby.

Savannah dialed Georgia's house phone. When the message picked up, she left the same message and hung up. She dialed the house in Augusta. It rang and rang with no answer. No R.J., no Georgia so she tried the orchards. Ray Slocum, the longtime manager, was an elderly black man with more manners than the majority of male society. His gentle nature and friendly disposition made all who met him feel right at home. He held Southern tradition close to heart by treating women like ladies and had always referred to Savannah as "Miss Savannah". Even when she stood knee-high to him, she answered to Ray's unique pronunciation of her name – *Miss S'vannah*. In his thick Georgia dialect, her name sounded short a syllable and Georgia's name emerged simply as *Jawja*.

She let the phone ring, envisioning the willowy, hunchbacked man toddling to it as fast as his arthritis allowed.

Ray answered on the fifth ring, "Prince Orchards, Ray Slocum speaking."

"Ray, it's Savannah."

His voice lifted with surprise, "Why, Miss S'vannah, this is a treat. How you doin' these days? Been long ol' months since I heard from ya."

"I'm alright, Ray. And you?"

"Still a'kickin' so life cain't be too bad. Feel good enough to load the sprayer for the pee-can trees. You needin' somethin'?"

"Have you seen Georgia this morning? I can't get her on the phone."

Ray chuckled, "That girl always tryin' her hand at grafting a pee-can seedlin'. Got here early this mornin', jes' left a bit ago before I got here at the barn."

Her phone should be on, Savannah frowned. Once Georgia arrived in Augusta, she would have answered her cell. "Did she say where she was going once she left the orchards?"

"Said she's fryin' Mr. R.J. a big ol' mess of catfish tonight so she needed fixins for it. She was going to the store then home to cook. That's what she told me. Miss S'vannah, why you askin' these questions? You sound plumb anxious."

Might as well come clean, she decided. Ray loved Georgia like his own. "She's in danger. Her ex-husband is coming after her. Have you seen him around lately?"

Ray's prolonged silence worried her. A couple of seconds passed when he admitted, "Seen him this mornin', in fact. Miss S'vannah, I hate speakin' outta turn but your daddy done put a whuppin' on that boy and truth be told, he right deserved it."

A point she completely agreed with. Matthew needed a good beating but even so, Savannah's heart sank at the news. If R.J. got hold of Matthew, the former-marine-now-full-time-nutcase probably met St. Peter pretty damn quick. Still, as much as Matthew deserved a beating, her daddy didn't deserve jail time, "Were the police called?"

"I was the only one who saw it and I sure nuff didn't call no police." He hesitated a moment, "It happened right out front, where the sign is so I guess no one else seen the fight. Don't recollect seein' much traffic this mornin'."

All it took was one person driving down the highway to see an enraged man punching the stuffing out of another guy. R.J. looked far younger than his actual age and was built like a brick shithouse. A brawl outside an orchard might draw attention to a passerby so she figured at least half a dozen cars drove by, and probably two called the cops. Just the thought gave her a headache. She rubbed her temple, "Was Georgia there when Matthew showed up?"

"Yes ma'am, but I told him she wasn't. He said he didn't believe me 'cause he saw her car pull in. I tell you, that man had a look in his eye no man should ever have, 'specially when talkin' 'bout ladies."

"What did he say?"

"Now, Miss S'vannah, ain't no way I'm telling you that. My mama'd come back from the grave an' wash my mouth out with soap. I'll jes' say your daddy shut his mouth but good."

She sighed, "Then he probably needs bail money. Ray, if you see or hear from Georgia, tell her I'm on my way to Augusta."

His voice softened with a lilt, "Sure will. Drop by if you got time, ya hear? Ray'd love to see ya."

"I have a feeling I'll be seeing you soon, Ray." She hung up, thinking where else her sister might have stopped off and why her phone went to voicemail. She glanced at Lily who spied her mother's worried features and mimicked them with a frowny face. She reached for Savannah who let the little fingers wrap around her thumb. She kissed her baby, "You up for a trip, kiddo?"

Lily smiled and giggled, giving Savannah the impression the baby used Daddy's unique phrase *saddle up and let's go.*

She gathered items for the diaper bag. Diapers, wipes, hand sanitizer, towels, disposable bags, and bottles of formula. She tossed in a change of clothes for Lily in case of an accident. She zipped the bag shut when her cell phone rang. No Caller ID but she recognized the Augusta area code. She clicked on with a puzzled *hello.*

"Savannah," Georgia answered. She sounded distressed, edgy.

Savannah's first thought was Matthew Carlisle grabbed her sister and subjected her to unspeakable cruelties, "Are you okay? You're not with Matthew, are you?"

"No, but can you come to Augusta right now? It's important." Georgia teetered on tears.

Something had happened, Savannah thought. Something bad. "What's wrong?"

"Matthew showed up this morning. He came to the orchards and Ray tried running him off but he wouldn't leave. Before that he'd been to the house looking for me then later he and Daddy got into it at the orchards."

"Daddy in jail?"

"Yes. And Matthew's dead."

The words almost took the knees from under her. Between their daddy and Matthew, she put her money on R.J. winning a fight with anyone. But murder? The rumor *had* circulated – and not been denied – that R.J. killed his brother for trying to molest Savannah when she was a child. If Matthew disparaged R.J.'s daughters the way Ray suggested, those inflammatory, insulting remarks likely spurred their father into *trying* to kill him. R.J. might have hit his kids back when – and wasn't above doing it now – but one thing he was: loyal to them. He protected them with such vicious tenacity it petrified Charlene when he went to "right a wrong" done to his girls. So no, bandying about the word *kill* wasn't exactly unheard of in the Prince household. *He needs killin'*, R.J. would say, *and I'm the man for the job.*

"Savannah, did you hear me? Matthew's dead."

"I heard you," she replied. Then she blew out a breath, her shoulders slumping in defeat, "Did Daddy do it?" After the local judges got hold of their father, there wasn't a bank in town with enough money for the bail she'd need. He was renowned all over Augusta for his copious drinking and scorching temper. Maybe she and Georgia could pool their resources to bail him but first she needed answers.

Georgia's silence practically gave her hives. If he murdered Matthew, life as they all knew it was over. Between trying to raise a child, retain a job and keep R.J. out of prison, her time, patience and sanity would be stretched to its limits.

"They're questioning him right now. They've been questioning me for the last hour or so."

"*You?*" she shouted in disgust. What the hell went wrong with the Richmond County Sheriff's Department? Didn't their cousin Bobby Prince, the freakin' *sheriff*, know Georgia better than that? "Why are they talking to you?"

"Because I was at the orchards when Matthew was. And because I'm the reason he came back. *To reclaim his wife*, he said."

"Shee-yet," she groaned. "You didn't kill him, did you?" The idea of Georgia in handcuffs, being read her Miranda Rights threw Savannah into an honest to God panic. She wouldn't have asked however a few months prior Matthew broke down Georgia's front door and rampaged through the place. Savannah and other cops found Georgia crouched in a corner, .22 in hand and aimed directly at her ex-husband. It took minutes for Georgia to release the weapon to Savannah. The hate in her eyes, the determination in her grip told Savannah that her sister reached her breaking point. If Matthew cornered her at the orchards that morning – or anywhere else – all bets were off.

"For heaven's sake, *no*," Georgia answered back, incredulous at the question. Then backtracked, "But they don't believe either of us."

"Where the hell is Bobby? Can't he at least intervene until I get there?"

"They said he's not here. We need you, Savannah. Please come quick."

"I'm on my way and Georgia, don't let those cops railroad either one of you. I'll drop Lily off at Seth's and be there as soon as I can."

19

NOW

I-20 from Atlanta to Augusta ran virtually straight as an arrow. On a normal day, the trip took just over two hours. On a day where her family sat detained in a police station, each one enduring leading, invasive and sometimes insulting questions, the trip took one hour and thirty-four minutes.

Savannah imagined – no *knew* – what the Richmond County investigators were doing to R.J. and Georgia and she meant to shut it down. The redundancy, the meddling and haranguing nudged any even-tempered soul to the brink of exploding. It took a great deal for Georgia to unleash her mighty temper – but a cop's constant barrage could do it. They were trained to do it. And their father? Savannah shook her head. She'd be lucky if he hadn't already bounced the detective's jaw off the walls. If that happened, any cop worth their badge would slap cuffs on him and charge him with assaulting a police officer. That, in turn, kept him safely behind bars and available for more questioning on Matthew's demise. A win-win situation for the cops, not so much for R.J. or their family.

She pressed the accelerator harder. She needed to get there before all hell broke loose or she'd just be a mop up crew.

Her watch read 4:15 when she pulled into the parking lot across from the new Richmond County Sheriff's Department building. They spent untold millions for the project, hiring a designing firm to make the place appear pleasant, even innocuous, with the landscaped flower beds on either side of the entrance. Red leaves clung to saplings planted several feet apart along the side of the building. Flowers bloomed along the edge of the flower beds, making the place resemble a mall entrance, not a sheriff's department.

During the drive, Savannah talked herself into a rage. How dare they accuse her family without proof. How dare Bobby *let* them. She'd broach that subject with her cousin as soon as she checked on her father and sister. Then the Richmond County clan better step back and brace themselves because the hard-as-nails hell-raiser Savannah Prince had returned to Augusta and she spoiled for a fight. Only this time she possessed a shiny gold badge of her own...

She took a second to clip that badge to her belt for insurance. Sometimes the sight of another cop toned down the rhetoric of the others. And sometimes it made things worse.

The desk sergeant glanced up when she opened the front door. His vision centered on the badge at her waist. "To what do we owe the honor of the Atlanta Police stampeding into our humble station?"

Already the situation looked dismal. She withdrew her police ID from her purse, showed it to the sergeant whose brow rose, unimpressed, "Prince, huh? You related to the two brought in earlier for the marine's murder?"

He wanted to play hardball? Fine, "I'm also supposedly related to Bobby Prince, the Richmond County Sheriff, if he hasn't skipped town on me, that is. Has *my* family been charged?" She made sure to exclude Bobby from the term "family" because family didn't throw their kin to the wolves the way he had.

"Not yet but they ain't going home anytime soon."

She'd see about that. She stomped off to find someone in charge. She settled for the first office she came to, "I'm Detective Savannah Prince, Atlanta Police. I'm here to see my sister Georgia Prince and my father Robert Jefferson Prince."

The man, around forty with his dark hair in a crew cut, looked up from his computer, scrutinized her for a good five seconds before speaking, "Investigator Cleveland Parker. Your family is currently being interviewed so take a seat out front and I'll be sure to fetch you as soon as we're done."

"You've had them all afternoon," she argued. "You've asked every question that can be asked. I want to see them."

Parker removed his reading glasses, "I don't know how the Atlanta Police work, Detective, but here we have protocols. You will wait. Outside. Until we're done. A marine was murdered today. It's a tragic day for those of us who served our country."

Oh, that's the problem. He thinks Matthew was a hero. She stepped forward, braced her hands on his desk, "Before you pin too many medals and accolades on Matthew Carlisle, look at not only his military record but his record with the Atlanta Police."

"He was a marine, Prince. He deserves justice."

"Everyone deserves justice, Parker. Even my family. Do you have proof either one of them killed Carlisle?"

"Your sister's alibi is sketchy and your father's basically confessed to killing him."

Savannah seethed at the cocky, smart-alecky attitude. She put him on notice by using his own words against him, "*I don't know how the Richmond County Sheriff's Department works*, but in Atlanta we have to provide proof, which means evidence, before we arrest someone for murder. The word *basically* doesn't sound like proof. Do you have the murder weapon?" Bobby wouldn't cotton to her attitude toward his investigators but damn it, they oughta act human, not like dictatorial machines.

He shook his head, "But several witnesses saw your father with a shotgun at your house, arguing with Carlisle."

"So Matthew was shot?"

"No. He was stabbed."

The stupidity of the conversation chafed her, "My daddy is a lot of things but a magician he isn't. How'd he manage to fatally stab Matthew with a shotgun? Until you can figure that one out, I want them both released."

Parker rose to his feet, ready to counter her. She refused to back down, "I didn't come here to wag my big city badge in your face or whatever you people think. You've made this adversarial, not me, and I'm gonna have a chat with my cousin about his department's tactics. Now 'fetch' my family or I'll get Bobby on the horn."

His chest bowed in protest until an unsettling grin curved his mouth, "Good luck with that. He's on vacation. Won't be back for a week." Parker sidestepped her, heading for the door, calling, "Dunne, there's another Prince you forgot about. This monkey wrench is from Atlanta." Then he turned back to her, "By the way, your father stays. He took a swing at an officer when they brought him in."

Another man appeared at the door, this one shorter, fatter and younger than Parker. Savannah and Owen Dunne went to school together so when the redheaded, pleasant looking fellow locked vision with his old classmate, an easy smile crossed his lips, "Hey, Savannah. Georgia said you were on your way. How've you been?"

Savannah's expression implied he'd lost his faculties. *How've you been?* "Well, things were fine until someone decided to incarcerate my relatives."

"They shouldn't have killed a marine," Parker wisecracked.

Savannah wheeled toward Parker, determined to shut his mouth one way or another.

Owen caught her by the arm, tried to talk her down, "I heard you're a new mom. Congratulations."

She winced at his hold that seemed to tighten the longer she stared back at Cleveland, Cincinnati or whatever the hell the guy's name was. For a short guy with stubby fingers, Owen Dunne possessed the grip of a hawk. She followed him down a long dimly lit hall – as if she had a choice. "Thanks. How've you been?" she asked, volleying his question back at him.

"Pretty good. My wife had a boy last year so you and I are both new parents. You had a girl?"

Evidently sensing the danger of a brawl had passed, he released her. With that grasp, Owen made her feel like a petulant child which further annoyed her with the department's occupants, "Yes, and I dread raising her if she's anything like I was."

Owen agreed, "You were a terror at times. You can still hold your own even now, I see. I know you're concerned about your family. Georgia can go home but I'm afraid your dad has to stay. He threw a right cross at an officer. Nearly connected too."

In the past, Savannah never campaigned for her father when he acted out. When he drank he was mean. When he didn't drink he was mean but a bit more coherent at least. "Owen, come on. He lives here, he drinks here. Let him go home. Please."

Owen did a doubletake, "Hell just froze. You *want* your father released? You realize he's mad as hell already. He might take it out on you just because you're there."

Savannah decided to take that chance, "He didn't kill Matthew Carlisle. Owen, I'm not stupid. You're holding him on the attempted assault charge so you can investigate further with him conveniently behind bars."

He lowered his voice, "Listen, I'll release him as long as he stays at home. Can you swear y'all will keep him behind those walls and out of trouble?"

"We'll do our best," was the best she committed to.

He proceeded down the hall then opened an interview room door, "Georgia, Savannah's here. You can go home now."

Savannah heard her sister's businesslike tone, "And Daddy?"

"He can too but only if y'all watch him. Don't let him go out and carouse."

Georgia emerged from the room, her back straight as a board, her lips pursed in a thin line. The instant she saw Savannah, her shoulders slackened and she sighed with relief, "Thank God you're here." She threw her arms around Savannah who returned the tight embrace.

Georgia verged on tears which, Savannah assumed, meant the cops probably went at her hard for a confession. She held Georgia until she calmed down then asked, "What happened?"

"I don't know. After I saw Daddy at the house, I left for the orchards."

"If you were at the orchards, what's the problem? Chances are people driving down the highway saw your car there so you couldn't be two places at once."

"Matthew was found at the orchards, just outside the fence next to the sign."

Oh. That's the problem. "Did the police–"

"There's my baby all the way from Atlanta," R.J. advanced on Savannah, arms open wide for a hug. He wrapped them around her, squeezing hard enough to realign her spine, "My girl. Sweets said you were coming to bail us out."

"Mr. Prince," Owen Dunne interrupted. "Savannah is the only reason I'm letting you go home but you gotta stay out of trouble. Don't make her regret her efforts, okay?"

"Go to hell," R.J. snapped. He released Savannah, kept an arm around her shoulders, "This one's my baby an' she loves her daddy. She don't regret nothing, do you?"

I hope I won't, she thought. She gave her father the answer he expected then addressed Dunne, "Thanks, Owen."

"I hope you're still thanking me tonight." He pointed to his chin, "Remember. Duck."

o o o

Savannah dropped R.J. and Georgia at the house then went to pick up hamburgers for their supper. She stopped by the package store for a fresh bottle of scotch for R.J. so he could drink at home instead of the bars. Between trips, she called Ennis for him to pack a few changes of clothes for her then pick up Lily and come to Augusta for the night. She'd need the help, she said.

While she was gone, Georgia tidied up the kitchen. Dirty dishes went from cabinet to sink. She removed empty scotch bottles from the dining table, tossed them in the trash. By the time Savannah arrived with supper, Georgia restored the kitchen to respectable levels.

Georgia set out plates, silverware and napkins while Savannah poured drinks. Sweet tea for the sisters and scotch for their father. She twisted the lid off the scotch and poured her father a decent glass full. Her sister's jaw dropped at the sight of the Johnny Walker. Savannah frowned, "You'd rather he traipse to the bar for his fix? Yes, I picked up a bottle for him. So shoot me."

"You only bought scotch?"

The underlying meaning slapped Savannah in the face. Georgia not-so-subtly asked if she'd indulged in her own personal purchase. "Just scotch. I've got too many responsibilities to drink now. Lily, Ennis, and now trying to exonerate you and Daddy of murder."

"What's that?" R.J. asked, suddenly tuned to their conversation. "What's that about scotch?"

Savannah handed the glass to him, "I got you a whole new bottle today, Daddy. But you have to promise to stay in and drink tonight, okay? No going out."

The first sign of discontent registered in his expression. Savannah prepared to step back just in case. He scowled at her, "Tellin' me what to do like I'm some invalid?"

"No. I'm telling you what to do because if you leave this house, you go back to jail and I can't help you this time. Owen Dunne gave me my marching orders."

R.J. harrumphed, "Owen Dunne. That sniveling little shit. Never even had the guts to ask ya out even though he liked ya. Good thing ya never hooked up with him. Your kids would be redheaded, limp-wristed idiots."

She did a mental eye roll while doling out hamburgers onto the waiting plates. Georgia sat down to R.J.'s right and Savannah to his left. A sad reality sank in. The last meal the trio ate at that dining table was two days before Charlene died. Back then she and her sister nibbled on meatloaf sandwiches. R.J. opted for straight scotch for his meal.

She shook the painful déjà vu when Georgia bit into her hamburger and groaned with pleasure.

R.J. eased into the dining chair, lifted the top bun of his hamburger, complaining, "Onions. You know I hate onions."

Amazed at how juvenile he sounded over the subject, Savannah reached over, traded burgers with her father, "Take mine." She scraped the onions off her newly acquired supper and took a large bite. The tasty, juicy meat was just what the doctor ordered. She took a sip of tea and indulged in another bite.

Their father sank his teeth into his burger. He seemed satisfied, "Your husband bringing the baby?"

"Yes. We're staying the night."

"I guess he's not so bad. He got busy with ya and gave me a granddaughter."

Savannah heard the silent criticism of Georgia. She and Matthew hadn't had time to make babies, she wanted to say, not with him deployed all the time. She gave her sister an empathetic glance. Georgia seemed mostly unaffected by their father's indelicacy.

"What happened today, Daddy?" Savannah wanted to know.

"You mean with that bastard? He demanded to know where Georgia was. I grabbed my shotgun to show him it wasn't his bidness where the hell she was." He lifted the glass of scotch to his lips, taking a couple of swallows. Unequivocal bliss brightened his features when he sighed, "God bless you and Johnny Walker, girl. Ya both brought me back to life."

Savannah guessed her status as being blessed would soon change, "You didn't fire the gun?"

"No, I didn't fire it," he sat the glass down, aggravated. "Are ya gonna grill me or let me eat?"

"I'm trying to figure out why the cops think you killed Matthew."

"Probably because I swore to half the town I'd do it. After what he did to your sister? Ain't no daddy gonna tolerate that."

"Did Matthew leave after you pointed the gun at him?"

R.J. swallowed another gulp then proudly announced, "Damn right he left. I did my Sweets proud." He smiled at Georgia who responded with an uneasy smile.

He refilled the glass. At the rate he drank, she'd have to make another run to the package store. Before he got too smashed, she inquired, "Was he in a taxi or did he drive his own wheels?"

"Drove his own."

"Did you follow him after he left?"

He ceased eating. Swiveling to face her, his voice deepened to an ominous tone, "Why're you asking me that? You sound like those damn cops downtown."

Georgia discreetly waved her off. Hush or you'll be sorry, her expression warned. "Savannah," she hinted, "let's enjoy our meal."

"I'm trying to help, that's all."

"I know but Daddy's tired." She mouthed *I'll tell you later* to her sister.

R.J. fisted his hand, "If you're gonna ask questions all night, go home. I've had a long, disturbin' day an' you're making it worse."

"But I'm only trying to find out–"

He slammed the fist against the solid oak table, rattling glasses and her nerves. "Savannah," he warned, "shut up or I'll shut ya up. I ain't talkin' about it anymore."

She sat back, pressing against the chair, preparing for a sudden swing of his fist. She'd pushed too hard too fast, "I'm sorry, Daddy. I'll hush."

"Damn right you will." He threw back another swallow, "Ya nag like your mama used to. Keep hounding me until I can't take anymore and I walk out. If you're sorry, go buy me another bottle."

"I'll go after supper."

He pounded the table again, "You'll go now."

No, "I'm eating first." She'd endured a long day as well and hers was without the benefit of a full complement of sleep. She'd squeezed three measly hours out of the night. And between Charlene's birthday and the resulting depression, tending to Lily, keeping Ennis fed and happy then dealing with Matthew's off-the-rocker behavior, and *this* calamity, no, her week hadn't exactly been a trip to Disneyland.

R.J.'s fist trembled, his shoulders squared. Sensing an impending disaster, Georgia put a hand to his, "Daddy, let Savannah finish."

"She thinks 'cause she bailed me she's got the right to boss me."

"I don't either," Savannah defended. "I'm trying to get facts while keeping you out of prison." She leaned to take another bite of hamburger but her father launched to his feet, instinctively causing her to draw back from the table.

He stabbed his finger at her, "I ain't going to prison."

"Okay," she capitulated. "I'm shutting up and you're not going to prison. When I'm done eating, I'll buy you another Johnny Walker.

Deal?"

Her acquiescence slackened his shoulders, relaxed his hands. He reached toward her, this time slow and easy, to pat her shoulder, "There's my baby. Finish your supper first. I can wait."

o   o   o

Savannah pulled her Charger in behind Ennis's Dodge Ram and blew out a long, tired breath. Relaxing in the seat, she closed her eyes, imagined her husband and baby. Imagined a calm, peaceful life, the kind they had before Matthew blew into town. Matthew turned their lives upside down the way he had the day he traipsed into that bookstore and declared Georgia his future wife.

Savannah ached to see her husband and baby. She missed Ennis's gentle, assuring embrace, his sweet kisses and her daughter's gummy smile and charming little giggle that cured plenty of bad days and dark moods. Savannah loved them both so much that being away from either of them literally hurt.

A knock on the car window startled her. She spun to see Roy Carlson waving at her, wearing the same silly grin she remembered in high school. Holding her purse under her arm and R.J.'s refill in her hand, she piled out of the Charger.

"Hey, Kitten," his deep voice caressed then pecked a quick kiss to her lips.

She returned the sentiment, replying, "Hey, you big lug. How's it going?"

"Better than you. Word's out your daddy's been busy with sharp instruments. Either him or Georgia but I can't see her wielding a knife except to slice an apple."

Savannah leaned against the fender, rubbed her temple with the heel of her hand, "It's a complete mess as usual. I try to get information from him and he threatens to hit me. Only way I find anything out is from Georgia or maybe Owen Dunne. I hope he will be forthcoming."

Roy curled an unruly dark wave behind her ear, "He helped with my case, he probably will with this one."

His touch awakened a feeling in her she assumed went dormant for the last week. The brief, whisper touch inspired images of her and Ennis in bed together, an indulgence they hadn't indulged in for weeks. If her husband were the man standing in front of her, she'd have leaned into his touch, given in to such luxuries as a deep, passionate kiss. She could almost feel Ennis's hand slipping behind her neck, urging her lips to his.

"Savannah," Roy called. "You on Planet Earth?"

She snapped out of the daydream, "Sorry. I haven't had much sleep lately. Mama's birthday was this week and, well, you know."

He nodded, not furthering the subject. Instead he leaned against the car, stroked the hood with the tenderness of a lover.

Oh, for God's sake, she berated herself. I really need alone time with Ennis. *Serious* alone time.

"Nice wheels, babe," Roy said. "What happened to the trusty Camaro?"

"You really don't want to know." And he didn't. Admitting that she goaded an Irish mobster into torching her cherished Chevy held no appeal.

He did a doubletake at the interior, "Is that a baby seat? Did you…" His brow shot up while his jaw dropped. "Did Savannah Prince have a baby?"

His sarcasm brought a smile, "Yes, Roy, Ennis and I had a girl in April. Her name is Lily." She sat the scotch down to retrieve a picture of her girl from her purse. This was, without a doubt, the highlight of her day. Showing off her little girl's picture.

Roy took the offered wallet, opened to a small photo of their baby grinning at the photographer – her daddy. Roy chuckled, "She's beautiful, Savannah. I know you're proud."

"Yes, proud and very weary. I pray one day I get a whole night's sleep again. How are you?"

"Good. Got a girlfriend. We're actually talking marriage so things are looking up."

"I'm happy for you, Roy. You deserve a good woman."

He put his arm around her shoulders, gave her a squeeze, "I had one but I let her get away in high school." He hesitated a second before asking, "Hey, can you make time to meet Crystal tomorrow? It's her day off and she kinda wants to see you."

Now that was strange. No woman in her right mind really wanted to meet a guy's previous girlfriend, did they? One brow hiked higher as a dubious inquiry.

Roy smiled, "She works at the sheriff's department in administration. She can get a few answers for you so I'm told."

Now her brow sank. Detectives weren't usually that cozy with administration so what gave Roy's girlfriend access to the information?

"Stop frowning or you'll get wrinkles," Roy teased. "She and Owen are good friends. He talks to her about his cases sometimes. Maybe he'll be chatty about this one too."

"I was going to the orchards in the morning. That's where they found Matthew so could we meet there?"

"Absolutely. I'll tell her."

The front door opened and Ennis waved her in. He waved at Roy, said hi and went back inside. Savannah leaned down to grab the scotch, "I guess Daddy's out of hooch."

Roy blocked her way momentarily, "If you need any help, call me. I'm available any hour."

She thanked him, kissed his cheek, "Your lady friend is one lucky girl."

Roy winked, "And Ennis won the jackpot. See ya, Kitten."

Savannah wandered up the sidewalk, wondering why Ennis seemed so impatient. She opened the door to an empty living room. The grandfather clock in the entry wound up to play the Westminster chime, and dutifully announced the hour as eight. She always knew when Georgia visited because after saying hello, the second order of business was to pull the clock's weight chains to run. R.J. could have cared less about the "noisy damn thing". Savannah tended to agree with their father, at least since having Lily. Any strange sound woke the child and depending on her mood, Lily occasionally ripped into a convincing rendition of a screeching feline.

Past the deep resonant chime, Savannah heard R.J. talking with Georgia in the kitchen. The older sister used a soft tone to chat up Lily while their father let it all hang out volume-wise. Savannah could imagine her daughter's rounded blue eyes staring at Grandpa, wondering how in the hell he could be so loud.

She shook her head, sat her purse on the entry table next to Georgia's. She turned to see Ennis standing behind her and gasped. What was it with men that night? They all scared the bejesus out of her – and smiled about it. "Trying to finish me off, eh?" She teased, "Well, good luck raising our daughter by yourself, buddy. She's a handful."

Ennis chuckled, "Like her mama." His arm slipped around her waist to pull her close. His lips descended on hers in the very fantasy she entertained outside minutes earlier. She greedily responded to his advances as his arm curled around her waist, drawing her body snug against. He separated from the kiss, making her groan, "That's mean. Just when I was falling in love again."

"Oh," he beamed, "then allow me to proceed." He claimed her lips once again, his tongue enticing hers to join his in a deeper, steamier kiss than before. A take-no-prisoners kiss that weakened her knees and her resolve. If only they were home alone…

"Savannah back with my scotch yet?" R.J. called from the kitchen.

This time her moan meant something different as they parted. She cleared her throat, hoping to eliminate the lusty passion from her voice, "Yes, Daddy, I'm back." Trekking through the living room, she stopped at the kitchen door as if running into a brick wall. R.J. cradled

Lily in his arms, talking sweetly to her. Savannah's stomach clenched, panic rose in her brain. Why would Georgia or Ennis allow him to hold the baby?

She glanced at her sister, silently asking that very question. Georgia replied, "We've been taking turns keeping Lily company." Then mouthed *it's okay.*

Maybe to her it was. That wasn't *her* child in their drunken father's embrace. Savannah slid the bottle from the paper sack, "Daddy, your scotch."

R.J. surrendered Lily to Savannah's arms, more interested in downing another shot than bonding with his granddaughter. That was fine with her. She wheeled to the living room, cornered her husband, "What were you thinking, letting him hold her? He could have dropped her."

Ennis backtracked physically and verbally, "I, uh, well, he was steady enough. He insisted on holding her. What was I supposed to do?"

"Say no," she gathered Lily closer, placed a kiss on her forehead. "You're safe, baby. Mama's here." The last two words surfaced in a defensive tone, as if everyone around her were brainless idiots.

She walked with the baby, to feel her warmth, her softness, and hear her tiny breaths. With all the ruckus, the baby managed a sound restful sleep. Savannah calmed down in those couple of minutes, passing the child to her husband with a warning, "Don't ever do that again. Why do you think Seth wouldn't let him hold Dylan? Because he dropped Lindsey a few years earlier. Stone drunk and dropped her."

Shame crossed Ennis's features, "It won't happen again."

Savannah went to the entry, picked up the break-action shotgun leaning against the wall, opened it and unloaded the shot shells. If he'd shot Matthew, the marine would have been ventilated well enough with the birdshot to be a fountain. Shaking her head, she bemoaned the fact her father's answer to unruly men was his trusty double barrel with a touchy trigger. Unloading it served as a fruitless task but it made her feel better. Next time he looked at it, he'd just reload it and she didn't have a clue where he kept the shells. At least for the interim the world was safe.

"Savannah?" R.J. shouted from the kitchen.

Lily stirred, making small grunting whimpers that escalated into crying. Great, Savannah thought. Now he woke the baby. "Yes, Daddy?" she said, her jaw clenched.

"You got a girl that looks just like you," he slurred. "A beautiful baby."

"Thank you," she shook her head, trying to figure out his logic. He'd seen Lily numerous times since her birth. Maybe because Savannah bought him Johnny Walker, he felt sentimental toward her.

"Can you shut that kid up though?" he griped. "The noise is killing me."

And so much for sentimental…

20

NOW

Once R.J. retired for the night, Ennis took the baby upstairs. Savannah and Georgia stayed in the living room to review the day's events. Savannah sat on the sofa nursing a glass of sweet tea. Georgia opted for the wingback closest to the sofa. She brought a Sprite.

Exhaustion wore heavy in Georgia's features. The two hour trip to Augusta plus spending all day being raked over the coals by cops then being accused of killing her ex drained the vitality and color from her features. Savannah scoped out the booze cabinet much to her sister's mortification. No doubt Georgia assumed she rummaged for bourbon but exercised tact in not asking. No, Savannah wasn't searching for *her* drink of choice, she searched for Georgia's. Once she located the brandy, she poured some in a small glass, handed it to Georgia who visibly slackened in the chair.

The older sister wrapped both hands around the glass, heaved a grateful sigh, "Thank you. It's been a horrible day." She tipped the brandy to her mouth, almost draining every drop in one gulp.

Savannah's eyes saucered, "You planning on flying the sofa

tonight? You drink that fast and you'll pilot yourself right into a hangover. Believe me, you will crash and burn because furniture never stops spinning."

Georgia tried for a smile. She only halfway succeeded, "I'm worried. Daddy said he and Matthew fought outside the orchards then Daddy said he left for the bar. Owen said no one at the bar remembered seeing him at all this morning. Ray wasn't there when Matthew was killed, only when Daddy beat him up." She took another swallow, emptying the glass.

Savannah rose, refilled it with another caution to nurse the brandy, not knock it back.

Georgia nodded, cradled the glass in her hands again, "I'm scared, Savannah. Scared the police will railroad Daddy based on his history and his threats. He's not well liked around town and there are people who wouldn't mind seeing him in prison."

"That's why I'm here. To try and keep the cops honest."

Georgia snorted, "They were looking at *you* too, hon. After Matthew abducted you, you were their primary suspect besides Daddy."

Ah, more members of my fan club. "Nice to know I'm well thought of 'round here."

"I told them you took Lily for a checkup this morning and Owen verified with your doctor's office."

Right about then Savannah supported their daddy's description of Mr. Dunne. The gutless little shit. She could imagine what the doctor's office staff thought about the cryptic call from Augusta – a detective asking for confirmation of another detective's whereabouts.

Savannah shook her head, rolled her eyes.

Georgia sipped the brandy, her posture sagging further in the wingback, "They were relentless. I explained my morning over and over. After a point they began interrupting me, asked me questions like *could I have forgotten this or that, was I sure of the time,* and *since I was sure of the time, what made me check my watch so often?*"

Until then, Savannah never gave much thought to how detectives came across. Never considered her family being under that microscope. Now that they were, she was angry and ashamed of her fellow cops. Owen Dunne knew better – yes, his job entailed questioning suspects but Georgia fell far short of a cold blooded murderer. "Georgia, I'm so sorry they subjected you to that. I only lean on a person when I'm sure they're either hiding something or they're guilty."

"Don't apologize, hon. I did okay because I told the truth. The day just wore me out."

Savannah dreaded reminding her that she promised to recite those same details to her after their father went to bed. She let Georgia work on the brandy – and vise versa. In the meantime they chatted about less upsetting topics.

Georgia sat the empty glass aside. Savannah watched her finger lazily trace the rim.

"Well," the eldest heaved a sigh, "here goes. I left my house at 7:00 this morning. Came by here to see Daddy, to make sure he'd be home for catfish tonight. We'll have that or lasagna tomorrow. Anyway, when I arrived at the orchards, I visited with Ray a minute then went to the red barn to try grafting a couple of seedlings."

Everyone associated with the orchards always called the building at the back of the property the red barn. It looked like a small barn, had once been painted red (in the seventies) but in actuality was a storage and working area. Ray kept equipment, fertilizer, weed and pest management sprays and tools in the back and tools, worktables, and pruning and grafting equipment up front.

Georgia continued, "I stayed at the orchards until around 10:30 then left and went to Publix for groceries."

"Did you leave out the front or back gate?"

Georgia's brow furrowed, "The back. Why?"

"I'm sure the cops took the video footage from the front gate. Guess we should have installed a camera at the back too. Probably would've come in handy. Which Publix did you go to?"

Augusta had several Publix stores in the city and surrounding area, and all but one or two were within a few minutes of the orchards or on the way home. Savannah figured she shopped at the store on Washington Road. Washington was a main thoroughfare that paralleled Augusta National Golf Club and led straight to Walton Way where they lived.

Georgia's mouth screwed to the side, her expression asking if Savannah was serious, "The one I always go to. The one on Washington Road. I did my shopping, came out and got in the car. It was 11:45. I know because I planned to clean the house while the fish soaked in the brine. I had just enough time to clean the bathrooms and possibly dust."

Savannah indulged in a sip of tea, nodding for her to continue. Confusion wrinkled Georgia's brow, "You're not writing anything down."

"I can remember your day and the times, don't worry. Besides, you're innocent and Publix has cameras in the store and parking lot. There's proof you were there at that time. And there are traffic cameras that probably caught your Tahoe cruising by on the way to Publix."

The creases between her brows disappeared as Georgia broke into a giant grin, "I love that you know that."

Savannah raised the tea glass, "I aim to please."

Georgia continued, "When I got in my car, I noticed the woman next to me had a flat. She said she was in town visiting family and didn't know her way around so I offered her a ride to a garage. Poor thing had grime all over her hands from trying to change the tire herself. She promised not to dirty up my car and used a tissue on the door handles and to buckle up. I drove her to Al's shop two blocks away. She thanked me, offered to pay for my trouble but told her no, it was on my way home anyway. That took ten minutes. By noon, the police were knocking on our door, asking us as nicely as the Gestapo to come to the station for questioning. It took them forever to tell me Matthew'd been murdered."

"Did they say approximately when he was killed?"

"Between 10:30 and 11:30. According to Owen's bunch that leaves time for your homicidal sister to knife the old ex and still come home to play Susie Homemaker."

"Owen's an idiot if he thinks you killed him. That woman you helped. What was her name? Where was she headed in town? I'll try to contact her."

Georgia laughed and not in a nice way, "Her name? Claire. I never thought to ask a last name. Her family lives in Augusta, but she never said where."

Great. A dead end. Savannah moved on, "Did you see Matthew at all today?"

At the mention of Matthew, Georgia threw back the rest of the brandy in one big gulp, "No, and thank goodness I didn't, considering the outcome."

"Did you know about the fight between Daddy and Matthew when it happened?"

"Not when it happened, no. Ray called the barn sometime while I was there and checked in with me. I suppose he was making sure I was okay. At the time I thought it was odd. He usually leaves me to myself while I'm working."

The corners of Savannah's mouth turned up. That was Ray, alright. Looking out for Miss Georgia. During their childhood years, Ray gathered both girls with him when they visited the orchards. Kept them safe and sound while they helped pick the fruit for their mama's cobblers and pies. If it hadn't been for Ray Slocum, Matthew would have found his ex-wife and subjected her to unspeakable horrors, if Mr. Carlisle's history held true. Her smile broadened a bit. Thank God for Ray, she thought.

O   O   O

Sardines had more room in their little can than he and Savannah had in her bed, Ennis lamented to himself. Of course the sardines had the advantage of meeting their maker before being crammed into their tiny tin coffin too. He straightened his legs that reflexively encouraged him to stretch them. Then the pain began. The tightening started small but quickly escalated into a burning, gripping distress only a muscle cramp provided. The invisible fist clamped around his calf tighter than an eagle's talon. He immediately stopped all movement, including his breathing that barely allowed a shallow intake of air. He dared not actually *breathe* or a rowdy holler might burst from his lips, awakening the whole family, and perhaps the neighbors next door.

In his youth Ennis spent the nights in the top bunk of a bunk bed with Jake sleeping below. Small beds were okay as a kid, he further complained, but as a married adult, trying to sleep in a full size bed with his beautiful wife wasn't exactly pleasant.

Instead of attempting the impossible by turning over in the dinky bed, Savannah looked over her shoulder, asked what was wrong.

He whispered between clenched teeth, "Leg cramp." Husband and wife lay spooned together in her childhood bed with Ennis curious as to how his five foot nine wife ever fit in it.

Lily slept next to them in a crib, her tiny form still and peaceful. Ennis wished he could be too. The muscle relaxed a degree, giving him a chance to catch his breath. Savannah reached back, placed her hand on his hip. His whole body tensed again, this time in hopes of preventing Little Ennis from rousing.

"Do you need to sleep on the couch?" she asked.

How outrageous. He'd sleep in a teacup as long as he was with

Savannah. The cramp eased up so he tried flexing his foot, "I'll be fine. Used to our queen size at home, that's all."

Her hand reached back for his, held it, "Thanks for staying tonight."

Her sentiment dissolved the remnants of the cramp. After his shift he'd driven to Augusta with their daughter sound asleep in her carrier. He arrived in time to eat a sandwich and pilfer a beer from R.J. who preferred scotch over anything. Ennis needed that beer too. Traveling alone with an infant presented a challenge for a new father. He could care for his daughter just fine but if Lily needed serious help, Savannah was always there. For those two hours, the isolation of being Lily's only available parent made him feel one fish short of a full string (but not a sardine, at least). Every snort, sniffle or general noise from the child put him on edge.

He leaned to Savannah's ear, kissed it, "No thanks necessary. The vow said for better or worse and truthfully, *this bed is one of the worst.*" He chuckled which inspired one from her. He released her hand, let his fingers caress her thigh. They drifted upward to her warm soft belly then his fingertip teased her nipple through her pajama top. He waited for her arm to move, giving him better access to his goal but it remained motionless, blocking his way. Ennis supposed he should play nice but damn it, he was horny all the time. They hadn't indulged in sex in forever and he ran on empty.

He wormed his hand past her arm until palming her breast, caressing it. He tenderly squeezed, his lips dropping warm soft kisses along her nape and ear, "If I wasn't afraid your daddy would come in here and kill me, I'd ravish you right here, right now."

She moaned softly, "He'd kill us both, not just you."

Ennis nipped her earlobe, snuggled against her bottom so she felt his arousal and whispered, "Let's live dangerously."

She covered his hand with hers, "Let's don't. Ennis, we're flanked by Daddy on one side and Georgia on the other. Not to mention Lily's right beside us."

"So far I'm staying above the Mason-Dixon line," he teased, giving her nipple a little pinch. Her nickname for the area below her navel always amused him, kinda like the way she said *shee-yet* instead of shit. It was *uniquely* Savannah. And he was *uniquely* randy at the current time so he chanced slipping his hand down her belly and into her pajama bottoms. His touch glided to the apex of her thighs. He pressed a hot kiss beneath her ear while his fingers tried to burrow into her most private place.

This time she gripped his hand to dissuade him, "Not here, babe, okay?"

He sighed, withdrawing his hand. Shot down, he groaned to himself. What did it take to get nookie these days? Little Ennis, ready for action, hadn't received the message yet and Big Ennis doubted he would for a while. His arousal threatened to be the death of him. It reminded him of their dating days when it practically required presidential permission and a signed note from God to finally get her into bed. Hell, he'd probably forget *how* to have sex after this hellacious sabbatical. The baby took all their time and energy. Not that he complained, but damn, there wasn't any time left for them. How did people conceive more than one kid when the first one kept demanding every minute? Thankfully, Georgia had an idea. It was the only reason he kept his protests to a minimum. While Savannah fed Lily, he and Georgia conspired together, crafting a plan to break the couple's sexual dry spell. That was a blessing because during his trip to Augusta, he'd dreamed of a dozen places and ways to jump his wife. Making love in the backyard pool, doing it at the orchards under the apple trees, or simply taking her in her bed (before realizing the blasted thing measured the size of a postage stamp). Postage stamp or not, he wanted sex so he tried again, "I'm dying here, babe. Can't we squeeze in some time after your trip to the orchard?"

There was a smile in her voice, "As long as it's not in this house, it's a date."

He nuzzled her hair, kissed her neck. Her pulse throbbed beneath his lips. He nudged his luck a bit further, "You're as horny as I am. If we're quiet, no one will hear–"

"Ennis, the prospect of Daddy barging in here while we're in the throes of sex dampens my urge considerably." She ended it with a firm, "We can wait."

Despite her age, somehow entering the house brought out the younger version of his wife. The more judgmental Savannah with the quicker temper, the one who took no shit from anyone for any reason. She hardly ever spent the night in the house, she said, because of the memories. The last time she stayed overnight was before their marriage when Roy Carlson was accused of murder.

Ennis disliked that side of his wife. The hard woman who felt ganged up on. The one who emerged when she saw R.J. holding Lily. When she rounded on Ennis, he shrank back at the cross nature and livid glare. It reminded him of when she drank. The pure rage that built inside her, fighting to explode onto the nearest bystander. A shiver worked down his back at the remembrance.

Earlier, while Savannah and Georgia conversed downstairs, Ennis took the opportunity to look over Savannah's room. Nothing changed from the day she moved out from what he could tell. The room, suspended in time for over fifteen years, provided tremendous insight into her childhood and teenage years. The desk beneath the window had a banker-type lamp, a writing pad with a pen on top and a five by seven frame containing a picture of Charlene. Prints of landscapes hung on the walls. A set of shelves on one wall displayed eight various golfing trophies layered in a thin coat of dust. Using the year engraved on each, he calculated her age at those times to be from seven to eighteen. In that span of time Savannah devoted her whole life to golf. Her success garnered several scholarship offers and she chose Georgia Tech, not only for proximity to Georgia's house but for the program's success. The university canceled her scholarship once her grades and performance bottomed out. It pained her to talk about those days so he mined the details years ago from Georgia. Then he understood why all her trophies back home sat packed away in boxes. Her dream, along with her mother, slipped from her life. The harder she tried, the faster it all fell apart then she turned to bourbon to ease the hurt. Until recently, anything golf related reminded her of her mother's illness and death. After so many years, she finally resumed playing and without even intending to, proved that the Augusta Bomber was older but still an expert with the clubs.

Savannah's room caused an unease to sweep across him now. Seeing the relics from her past, he realized coming home meant pain and sorrow for her. It was as though old ghosts lingered in the dark corners, waiting to torment her once again.

He cuddled to her again, pressed a kiss to her temple, "I love you."

Her head turned enough they could kiss. She smiled the smile of the Savannah he fell in love with. The one that brightened her eyes with adoration when their gaze met, "I love you too, babe."

21

NOW

Savannah, Ennis and Georgia awoke at six. Savannah cleaned up, and dressed in a fresh change of clothes Ennis brought. She chose jeans and a burgundy blouse. When she descended the stairs, the smell of bacon frying permeated the air. Georgia was already hard at work so Savannah pitched in to help with breakfast while Ennis tended to Lily.

Soon the kitchen blossomed in mouthwatering aromas. Homemade biscuits, fried bacon, and scrambled eggs all mingled to stir a loud hunger pain from Savannah's stomach. For a minute she swore time slipped back to when she and Georgia joined their mother in the kitchen, when the same delicious smells filled the house. She closed her eyes, picturing her mother at the stove stirring the eggs, checking the biscuits as they baked and calling her girls to set the table. Being the oldest, Georgia handled the hot pans, transferring them from stove and oven to the table. Savannah took over distributing plates, silverware and drinks. Charlene was quick to quell Savannah's dejection over the simplistic responsibility. Setting the table symbolized family and love, she said then added, "And you set such a beautiful table."

Her mother the diplomatic liar, Savannah smiled. The woman could make mowing a lawn sound elegant.

"What are you thinking about?" Georgia asked, smirking at her goofy grin.

"How Mama sold me on my talent for table setting. She could do anything, even sell religion to the Pope."

"Or wood to a forest. She was good but she wasn't lying about the table settings."

"Not you too," Savannah groaned good-naturedly. "All the fuss over plates and forks." For whatever reason, her mood brightened that morning. Normally returning home brought back painful memories that, like bad relatives, refused to leave. The tick-tock of the grandfather clock in the entry. The sight of her mother's favorite chair with the worn wooden armrests where she spent untold evenings reading the Good Book. Savannah could almost hear the strains of Charlene humming "In the Sweet By and By" in her beautiful alto voice.

She turned to the doorway leading to the den and spied their mother's pencil marks on the door facing. Her impromptu yardstick for measuring the children's budding height was still there. Charlene took great pride in every measurement and shared the joy of every mark left behind. She drew a line then wrote the child's name and what age they were at the time.

Savannah ran her fingers along Seth's growth points, at five, at seven, ten, thirteen and sixteen. Was her brother really that tall at ten years old? Georgia's mark at seven far outshined her younger sibling's at the same age. Savannah's growth spurt hit at thirteen and by sixteen she'd shot past her sister to stand five feet nine to Georgia's five feet six. The memories lingered but strangely, she heard her mother laugh, saw her smile and realized that coming home shouldn't be a vault of ghosts that haunted her. Coming home should mean spending time with her mother, her memory, her love.

Savannah left the wall and the memories aside, focused on the day's task. Number one, find out the details of Matthew's murder, two, ask if they found the murder weapon and three, if Owen Dunne had any leads.

She dutifully placed the utensils and plates on the table, leaving Georgia to transfer the pots and pans. A sense of déjà vu struck her. How funny, she thought, that they fell into their old roles so easily. The three sat down and joined hands while Georgia said grace. Digging into the meal sent her appetite soaring. She grabbed two pieces of bacon, a spoonful of eggs and a biscuit. Her eyes rolled back upon tasting the bacon. Georgia cooked it to crispy perfection. Savannah's biscuits emerged golden and fluffy and according to Georgia, tasted comparable to their mother's efforts. Ennis concentrated on the scrambled eggs, dumping two large spoonfuls onto his plate along with two slices of bacon. Georgia opted for a more conservative approach with one each of everything.

Savannah swiped two more pieces of bacon then felt guilty for her gluttony. Amused, Georgia reached forward, added another slice. "For good measure," she winked. "You've got a long day ahead and need your strength."

Savannah returned the smile, adding a thank you. Times like

these reverted her back to a little girl when Georgia mothered her in a way she loved. All her life Georgia watched over her, fussed over her. Savannah was proud to have a big sister who protected her, made sure she had what she needed. Charlene and R.J. were good parents despite her father's temper but there was something about having her big sister's attention, approval and love that amounted to piles of gold.

Ennis scooped a forkful of eggs in his mouth, "You girls cook like Ma. No wonder I'm getting fat."

After a few minutes, Savannah sat back to enjoy her coffee and digest. Georgia dabbed her mouth with her napkin, "So what do you think Roy's girlfriend knows?"

"Question is, what is she willing to share with the enemy? Owen'll kill her if he finds out we're talking about the case and I don't see her jeopardizing her job." She shrugged, "Roy's always been a dreamer and an optimist. I'm just happy when life doesn't go totally backwards on me."

O O O

Depending on traffic, Prince Orchards were located about fifteen to twenty minutes northwest of Augusta. With the rush hour, Savannah wanted thirty to arrive and mentally settle down before meeting Roy's girlfriend. Roy said she drove a blue Nissan Altima. But what was her name again? It was... Oh shit, she thought, reaching in her pocket for her note. It was some weird name, she recalled. Like a stripper but no matter how she tried, she couldn't remember it.

She unfolded the note, "Crystal Rivers." Yep. Stripper. But hopefully easier to remember now.

Savannah climbed in the Charger, cranked the engine and backed out of the driveway onto Walton Way, made the turn onto Milledge Road then Washington Road. Because of morning traffic, ten minutes lapsed when she finally merged onto the highway toward Westside and twenty when she approached the exit for the orchards.

The orchards were built behind a shelterbelt of trees and the exit wasn't marked. Locals knew where the exit was but everyone else relied on the new sign to find the place. Seven years prior, she, Georgia, Vince and Royal invested in an updated sign for the property. They chose a Kelly green background with white script reading "Prince Orchards" and below that in smaller white script "Est. 1875". A two foot high masonry stone wall encircled the base, in it numerous bright, colorful flowers flourished, including Lily of the Valley, Lisianthus, and a few other varieties. Savannah let Georgia coordinate with Roy for the job since she owned the green thumb in the family.

Normally it was a beautiful sign and garden. Today instead of the sign or patchwork flower bed, crime scene tape attracted any passers-by attention. The tape cordoned off not only the sign but the entrance to the orchards, a flair of overkill if one asked Savannah. The whole city read the headlines about the "hero" slain outside their prized business. It also decided to mention the connection between Georgia and Matthew. The rag went so far as to allude to the police dragging Georgia and R.J. in for questioning. Savannah once respected the Chronicle but that morning, she wanted to burn it.

Pulling onto the entry road, she stopped short of the yellow tape stretched across the open gate then nudged the Charger's nose beneath it just for spite. Savannah sneered at the ugly tape, wishing Matthew had stayed away from Georgia like he was told, because now he was dead, their father and Georgia were suspects and their orchards were a crime scene.

She glanced up at the corner of the large iron gate that stood open. Their security camera gave a wide angle view of the drive and sign. Any vehicle driving onto the premises activated an audible alarm in three places – Ray and his son Marcus's houses (both on the property since Marcus helped his father) and the red barn. It also triggered the video system to begin recording. There would be video of Matthew's murder, courtesy of the cousins' safety-minded vigilance. Savannah felt sure one viewing would exonerate her family.

She killed the engine, climbed out to get an up close and personal view of the manicured flower bed's devastation. She cursed under her breath. The cops wrecked and ruined it, shredding beautiful petals from their heads, tearing whole plants asunder in their search for evidence. A smoldering dislike burned inside her. Owen Dunne and his ilk destroyed nine hundred dollars of blood, sweat and tears in mere minutes. She and the cousins would be forced to hire Roy for cleanup and replanting.

In the grass beside the botanical carnage sat a large, dark pool of dried blood. Matthew was stabbed, according to investigator and pinhead extraordinaire Cleveland Parker. Judging from the massive pool, Matthew bled out where he fell. She saw no blood trail indicating signs of movement or any attempt to crawl toward the highway and flag down help. Whoever killed him knew exactly how to expedite a person. In her limited knowledge of anatomy, she knew only a couple of ways to do it, including severing the descending artery.

"Miss S'vannah," a voice called from afar. "Miss S'vannah! Over here!"

Savannah glanced up the road to Ray's modest white clapboard house. When Grandpa Prince took over the orchards, he hired Ray and built the cozy two bedroom abode for his new orchard manager and his wife. Since then Ray maintained and even added on to the place over the years. He enlarged the kitchen for his wife then for himself he extended the porch until it spanned the front of the house. He slapped a coat of white paint on it and placed three rockers on his new addition. It was perfect for gathering in the evening with a glass of sweet tea or quiet time alone listening to the birds sing. The place was small yet quaint set against the orchard's deep green leaves and when the apples ripened to their brilliant red hue, it was literally breathtaking.

Ray Slocum stood on his prized front porch, hunched over his cane and waving at her. His posture slumped from arthritis and backbreaking work over the years. As long as Savannah could remember, he carried his cherry wood walking stick topped with a brass eagle's head. He used the cane as an extension of his arm – or mood. One gentle, fluid swing of the stick urged a person aside whereas a quick jab set them back a step when they riled him.

Savannah waved back, seeing him begin the arduous task of descending the porch steps. The man, in obvious discomfort, shouldn't have to traipse a hundred yards because the cops went nuts with the yellow tape. To hell with this tape, she thought, and ducked beneath it. She jogged up the road, telling him to stay put, that she'd come to him.

Ray's thin, frail arms managed a surprisingly strong hug, "You're a sight for sore eyes, girl. You look good. Don't go losing too much of that baby weight. You get scrawny too easy."

"I eat like a horse, Ray. No worries. How are you?"

"Fine, just fine. Ol' back givin' me fits but that's expected at my age. How's your sprout?"

The mention of Lily brought a beaming smile, "She's fine. Her personality is really showing now."

He slanted a mischievous wink, "Got that twinkle in her blue eyes. Gonna be a rascal like you."

"God, I hope not." But she saw it too. Lily Christine would test her the way Savannah tested her mama. Charlene spent most of her time praying for her daughter to grow up normal, or at least less spirited. She spent countless hours in parent/teacher meetings discussing her rowdy little girl's behavior and why she continually disrupted class or threw a punch at a boy who tried to kiss her. Savannah explained that it wasn't because he tried kissing her, it was the *wrong* boy that planted one on her. Oh Lord, Savannah thought with a pained wince. With her luck, Lily *would* be her mini-me.

She asked Ray, "How are you after yesterday?"

"I'm mad over that mess there," he poked his cane toward the sign and blizzard of flower petals. It looked like a Walt Disney tornado blew through. "They done tore up all your hard work. Flowers all shredded, footprints ever'where. You and Miss Georgia need to complain 'cause Miss Royal and Mr. Vincent are outta town. They wouldn't approve of this either."

"Don't worry," she chuckled. "If Georgia doesn't speak up, I will."

Ray gave a succinct nod, "I know you'll get it done. You got the badge, you got the power." His tone turned dark, shook his head, "The po-lice here, they said they're *lettin'* me stay on the grounds while they investigate."

"Letting you?" Oh, the nerve. She'd jerk a knot in Owen Dunne if that twit bothered Ray, much less tried to evict him from his own home. "Do I need to set them straight because–"

"Settle down, girl. I took care of it. I told 'em *you* wanted me here. That *I'm* in charge of this place."

"You're right, you are in charge. And if those cops give you any trouble, call me." She watched his chest broaden with her words of support. She continued, "This is your home and no one's kicking you out for any reason. They can work without disturbing you."

"I told them that. They didn't like it but I didn't care. I was already upset they askin' me about Mr. R.J. and all."

"What did you see, Ray?"

"I saw Miss Georgia's ex-husband drive up then Mr. R.J. park behind him. Miss Georgia's ex stormed up to my house wantin' to see her. I told him she wasn't here." Ray shivered, "Oh, he started rantin' like a madman. Mr. R.J. came up the drive while that boy sayin' terrible things about you and demandin' to see Miss Georgia. That set your daddy off. He started beatin' that fella an' I wasn't about to stop him, not with the meanness comin' outta that boy's mouth."

"What did Matthew say about me?"

Ray gave his head a vehement shake, "No, ma'am. I don't speak those words to ladies an' I don't repeat them. I jes' know the more he talked, the harder your daddy hit him. An' if I'd been twenty years younger, I'da joined him. Ain't nobody talks trash 'bout either of you girls, not 'round us."

Savannah knew he meant it too. She halfway expected him to say he'd grabbed his shotgun and toted it out to help their daddy teach Matthew a valuable lesson in manners. She asked, "Ray, did Daddy have a knife? Did you see him stab Matthew?"

Ray again shook his head, "No, Miss S'vannah, your daddy didn't need no knife, not with *his* fists. All I saw was the hurtin' Mr. R.J. put on him. Last I saw he was draggin' that boy down the drive by the collar. Once your daddy left, I went to the barn to load the sprayer."

She looked up at the camera aimed at the entry, "Did the police take the security footage?"

"Yes, ma'am, they did. I'm afraid your daddy's thumpin' is gonna get him into trouble."

"As long as he didn't kill Matthew, we can deal with anything else. Did you see the footage?"

"Naw. They jes' told me to get it and I jes' wanted 'em off the property." He stabbed a bony finger toward the sign, "They done enough damage."

That was true. It would take years for the flower beds to mature to their previous glory. "What about Georgia? She got here early and left at what time?"

"I'd say 'bout 10:30, 10:45, thereabouts. Can't rightly recall 'cause I was waitin' on Marcus to help me spray the trees. We jes' started when the po-lice came."

"What time was that?"

Ray squinted into the distance, thinking. Savannah knew he mentally walked through the steps of driving to the red barn, loading the spray, and the time it took to arrive to the pecan area of the massive orchards. "Oh," he said, "maybe 'bout twenty, thirty minutes. Marcus got a better sense of time than me. Might ask him when he gets back tomorrow from Valdosta. They went to visit Shanise's mama."

A horn honked from the entrance. With a scowl, Ray turned. A blue Nissan eased behind her Charger and stopped. The sight of a strange vehicle prickled Ray. Savannah guessed he pegged it for an interloper with a badge. To ease his concern, she said, "It's okay, Ray. It's Roy Carlson and his girlfriend. I'm expecting them." She waved at the two, acknowledging them.

Ray patted her back, "I'll leave you to your business. Give your little sprout a hug for me when you get home."

She hugged him, "I will, Ray. Take care and let me know if you need me."

Savannah strode toward the Nissan. The driver killed the engine, opened the door. A petite blonde about Georgia's height, climbed out in a wine colored pantsuit with a black blouse, the latter buttoned respectably to conceal the lion's share of her abundantly large breasts. Roy's girlfriend lived up to the stripper name with big boobs and stick thin waist. Savannah's mouth quirked with humor. *Roy Carlson's personal Playboy Bunny.* No wonder the man never stopped smiling. She figured the busty Ms. Crystal's popularity soared at the police station. Whether she carried a badge or not, women endured unwanted attention from the knuckle-dragging Neanderthals – and every station had a few. The remarks, grab-ass and *accidental* brushes with their hands... A woman required a backbone of steel to traverse the waters of law enforcement officers. She was lucky if she found one decent fella among them like Ennis.

Roy swallowed Savannah in a hug and pecked a kiss to her lips which raised the needle on the discomfort scale. No girlfriend wanted her betrothed to smother another woman in such blatant affection – especially if the woman was an ex. However, if Crystal knew Roy well, she realized he was a gregarious, affable teddy bear who loved unconditionally the way dogs did.

She'd assured herself that Crystal took the hug in stride until Roy addressed his ex-girlfriend as "Kitten". He uttered the normally intimate name in a casual manner. Still, she thought. *I wouldn't want Ennis to address Jenny Lee Crawford as "sweetheart" while in my presence, no matter the inflection.*

Savannah returned Roy's hug then extended her hand to Crystal, introducing herself. They exchanged how-do-you-do's with Savannah mentioning possible wedding bells for the two. Crystal grinned a languid grin, easing Savannah's anxiousness. "It's a serious possibility," Ms. Rivers admitted, winking at Roy.

"I hope you keep me and Ennis in mind for an invite," Savannah hinted. "We'd love to attend."

Roy slung a heavy, hairy arm across her shoulders, "Aw, Kitten. You know you're invited."

Savannah got down to business, "Roy said you might have information regarding the investigation."

The woman glanced at Roy – not a happy-go-lucky one either, Savannah noticed. An *oh shit* one. Indeed, Crystal began with an apology, "Owen's tight-lipped on this case with me. I guess he's afraid I'll tell Roy and he'll tell you."

Savannah sighed, rubbed her jaw hoping to release the tension. Owen wasn't stupid. She just hoped he'd cooperate. Hope was overrated sometimes and downright disappointing at others.

Guilt crossed Crystal's features, "I know Roy left the impression I could help and I would if I knew anything. Owen's protective of this case for some reason. I've never seen him like this."

Savannah had. Even in school getting the little twerp to share was harder than carving granite with a butter knife. Oh, he played nice, but when it came to trading his muffin for her Twinkie, he reminded her of an obsessed miser. He'd been sweet on her but the desire for his damn muffin outweighed his infatuation. She harrumphed, "Same old Owen, except it's my family's lives we're dealing with, not his stinkin' blueberry muffin."

Roy and Crystal looked at each other, puzzled. Savannah explained, "He was a horse trader in school too. I'm surprised he's not a banker or broker."

"Oh!" Crystal exclaimed.

Savannah leaned past her to see if Roy goosed her. No such luck.

"I did find out from the medical examiner," Crystal said without the same explosive exuberance, "that the descending artery was severed. He said death was basically instant, that Carlisle lived only a few seconds or so. Whoever killed him twisted the weapon when it went in."

"Have they found the murder weapon yet?"

"No. That's why they… um…" Crystal nodded to the orchard sign, "tore everything up. Looking for it."

"Inspector Miser better open his penny-pinching wallet. He and his department are getting a hefty bill for this mess. Tell him I said that."

Judging by the woman's pale complexion, Savannah doubted Crystal would tell Owen Dunne anything. Roy's girlfriend removed a piece of paper from her purse, "I overheard Owen say they located Carlisle's motel room at the Holiday Inn on Gordon Highway. "They're supposed to search the room in an hour."

22

NOW

Roy and Crystal pulled onto the highway from the orchard entrance. Savannah pocketed Crystal's note with the motel's name and room number. She trudged to her car, contemplating a trip to the sheriff's office. She had two choices. Go in and beat Owen into submission until he coughed up details regarding the case. Or two, go in and play nice. Her fist ached to choose Door Number One but reality said exonerating her family from behind bars was impossible so Door Number Two won out. She'd try her hand at diplomacy then head out to the motel to see what they found in Matthew's room.

She reached in her pocket for her car keys just as a car slowed on the highway, pulled to the side near the entrance. Georgia parked the Tahoe along the roadside, well shy of the entrance. She waved at Savannah who waved back, curious why her sister hadn't pulled in behind the Charger. She motioned for her to do so. With a crafty grin, Georgia shook her head. Ennis piled out of the passenger side, thanked Georgia then bid her farewell. As the Tahoe rolled by, Georgia winked at Savannah which confused the younger sister. Why had she winked and what was up with that smile?

Ennis stepped up to his wife, dangled his handcuffs, "Turn around, Mrs. Rutherford."

Shock registered, "Turn around?"

"I'm taking you into custody. Turn around or I'll use force," he challenged and sounded somewhat hopeful that she might refuse.

She stared at him, wordless. After the past twenty minutes the last thing she wanted was to joke around. She'd put too many eggs in Crystal's basket, believing she had information to share. Now she felt foolish. Worse, the setback cost valuable time. Time she could not spare horsing around.

A warm, strong grip encircled her wrist, his other hand urged her by the shoulder to turn. She followed the prompt, turning to face the Charger. Ennis flattened his hand on her back, gently bending her over the hood. Now she put up an argument, "Ennis, honestly. What the hell's gotten into you?" She heard cars passing behind them, wondering what went through the onlookers' minds. Crazy man, for one thing or maybe they assumed he arrested the person who bumped off the marine "hero". They'd be lucky if the local cops – probably Owen Dunne – weren't dispatched to the orchards again for this bizarre scene. The mere notion sucked the energy from her. Facing Owen was hard enough but to explain *this*? "Ennis, people see us."

Apparently, he felt okay about that. Of course he wasn't the one bent over the car, was he? She felt him snug against her bottom, his arousal more than evident as he locked a cuff loosely around one wrist then the other. He leaned to her ear, whispering, "You have the right to remain silent though cries of pleasure will not be held against you…" He continued with a customized version of the Miranda Rights while she prayed no one dialed 911 on them. Ennis never attempted role play in public and she certainly never wanted to for several reasons, modesty and potential witnesses being the biggest.

"Who are you and what have you done with my husband?" she wanted to know. Why now, was her next question. All hell broke loose in her life and he wanted to play around?

"Come quietly and I'll make you forget all your troubles for the next few hours."

How tempting it would be to forget the cops pegged her family as murderers. The last several weeks were stressful but the last twenty-four hours were a nightmare. He intended to help, and his answer was to remove her from the source of the stress. Besides the handcuffs and bad timing, it sounded wonderful.

"Ennis, I appreciate your efforts but I have work to do. The police took the security footage from the front gate and I need to see it."

He patted her pockets, found the note and confiscated it. He ran his palms down her left leg then her right in a typical pat-down, "Newsflash. You're not employed by Richmond County. They'll close ranks and deny your request."

"I wasn't going to request, I was going to *demand*."

His hands eased up her inner thighs in a slow, sensual, not at all typical pat-down, "They will deny your *demand*, Mrs. Rutherford."

She squirmed against him, "I don't have time for games, Ennis. I've got one hour before they search Matthew's motel room."

"And they won't allow you within a mile of it." His fingers eased around her waist, retrieved her phone, "You won't be needing this and stop squirming or I'll charge you with resisting."

She tried to straighten but his hand on her back prevented it. Her frustration escalated, "Daddy needs my help. So does Georgia. I can't do this right now. Unlock the cuffs. *Please...*"

"You owe me, Mrs. Rutherford. I specifically recall making a date last night. A date for hot steamy sex and the only stipulation was we don't have that date at the house. I've made other arrangements so," he stood her up and turned her to face him, "in the car."

Impatient and irritable, she grumbled her way toward passenger side when he stopped her. Savannah gasped when a black cloth slipped over her eyes and he tied it behind her head. Now this was a bit much. She turned to protest but a sharp swat on her behind stilled her. *Okay, this is way out of hand.* "Ennis, you'd best tighten these cuffs if you plan to spank me again. If I come out of them–" The metal squeezed down, locking her in snug. The action took her aback, jarring her from her surliness, "I thought I was joking."

Ennis didn't speak but. His hot beath caressed her ear, "Now I've got you." He retrieved the car keys from her hand. His hand clamped on her arm in a firm, no-nonsense hold, and guided her past the passenger door to the back seat. She decided not to argue. Whatever was happening, she knew Ennis wouldn't hurt her.

She heard the door open and he helped her inside. The door slammed. The car gently rocked when he sat in the driver's seat, closed the door. The engine roared to life. Ennis shifted into reverse, assuring,

"Before you ask, Georgia's taking care of Lily today and she's got strict orders to keep the baby from your daddy. Now you can relax."

O   O   O

Ennis drove down the highway, as per Georgia's instructions. No matter how many times he drove around Augusta, he'd never learn the place. At over one hundred ninety-three thousand, the city's population basically equaled Amarillo, Texas, the largest town closest to his hometown of Vega. He knew Amarillo like the back of his hand because he patrolled its streets and even earned his promotion to detective there. But Augusta? Feh. He'd get lost at the city limit sign every time. It took him months to learn the route to Savannah's house. The highway exit was simple – Walton Way. But to see Walton Way was to wonder what spaced-out idiot decided to have one extensive street stretch nearly halfway the length of the city. Walton Way sounded short, quaint and lined with cozy looking homes with kids playing in the front yards. In actuality it was a thoroughfare containing businesses at one end – including the Richmond County Sheriff's Department – and homes on the other – and some weren't very small either. Savannah's two-story childhood home encompassed approximately three to four thousand square feet. No small fry.

When Georgia helped him devise his plan to cart Savannah off and have alone time with her, he also employed the sister's map-making skills and so far she was spot-on.

He pulled into the motel parking lot. Savannah rode in veritable silence most of the way, probably questioning his sanity. She wasn't thrilled by his timing, he figured that out, however Georgia insisted they spend part of the day at the motel. If Savannah's stress level spiked, she said, no one could live with her, and Georgia noticed it soaring yesterday afternoon.

Ennis escorted his wife inside the motel, assuring her no one could see them, which he hoped no one had. He closed the door behind them. The only sound in the room was an air conditioner that really needed to ease up on its efficiency. He adjusted the thermostat and noticed Savannah hadn't moved an inch.

But she did venture to speak, "Wanna tell me what's going on?"

"You're stressed out, even Georgia mentioned that. She helped me plan this. We take time out for us then you can breach the fortress of the Richmond County Sheriff's office."

Her mouth dropped as she rattled the cuffs, "She helped you with this?"

"The idea is mine. She just tweaked some particulars and drew me a map to the motel. You know I need help getting around this place."

She nodded. Oh yes, she understood in graphic detail the depth of his confusion regarding Augusta's streets. Savannah shrugged one shoulder, "So have you had this fantasy a while?"

To his surprise, the question lacked the judgmental or horrified quality he feared. She presented it in a matter-of-fact manner.

Ennis, afraid she'd balk at the whole idea, stripped away the blindfold, "I've dreamed of this for years." His fingers buried in her hair,

"And you're not leaving this room until I say so." His lips descended on hers, his tongue pushing into her mouth and plundering to his heart's content.

Her resolve and rigid posture relaxed the longer he subjected her to the kiss. Drawing her against him, he heard her breathing quicken and felt her struggle to keep up with his movements. He smiled inside. She was actually enjoying herself. He sweated bullets the night before, worried she'd run screaming into the street when he cuffed her. She never approved of the idea of restraints and blindfolds. He took a huge chance listening to Georgia who assured they'd been married long enough Savannah trusted him and probably wouldn't argue too much. Sure enough, Savannah put up a mild fuss but now met him stroke for stroke with her tongue against his, twirling and dancing in silent acquiescence.

His problem: Things escalated way too fast and it was his fault. By holding her snug against him, Savannah's breasts pressed into his chest and his hand on her ass pushed her against his groin. Little Ennis answered the call to duty in quick, efficient fashion. He needed to slow down to avoid a jailbreak down south. He broke the kiss, their ragged breaths the only sound in the room.

Savannah nudged his crotch with her hips, teasing, "I hope there's more than that coming."

This was better than his fantasy. She wanted this, his inner rogue high-fived himself. She wanted this to happen, cuffs and all. But his excitement threatened to derail the whole plan. He forced himself to control the rampant thoughts racing through his brain that repeatedly flashed two words like blazing neon signs. *Sex now, sex now...* And Little Ennis gleefully joined the chorus. Stay on track, he told himself. "You'll be surprised at how much is coming and how often."

Savannah's smile nearly tipped him over the edge. He wanted his wife right then and there but he also wanted to satisfy this long-anticipated fantasy to its fullest capacity. Ennis dreamed of this moment for years, ever since laying eyes on the Southern beauty before him. Images taunted him of her straining against the cuffs as he buried himself inside her. In those dreams she begged for more until her cries of pleasure drove him to thrust faster and harder until finally surrendering to his own release.

Those images returned now as Ennis descended on her in the same forceful manner. His tongue commandeered her mouth once more, his tongue sliding against hers, chasing, stroking.

He noticed Savannah pulled at the cuffs, tried drawing back. She broke the kiss, breathing heavily. "My God, what happened to you?"

He slanted her a devious grin, "It's not what happened to me. It's what will be happening to you. Spread your feet. I'm searching you."

Her left brow lifted. He read it as resistance, maybe even an unspoken protest. Or was that a dare? Did he see a challenge in those beautiful blue eyes? Yes, he did. To show her he meant business, he placed his foot between hers, firmly pushed them apart, murmured against her ear, "When I tell you to do something, you do it. Understand?"

He slid his hands over her breasts. Her eyes closed on a sharp breath while nodding her answer.

"Good. Now stand still." He eased his hands from her breasts to her waist then gave her bottom a squeeze, "Are you hiding anything here?"

"No."

"I'm checking to be sure," he gave it a tender squeeze. He slid his hands around her front, unbuttoned her jeans, "Are you hiding anything here?"

"No."

Ennis heard the anticipation in her voice. He stroked just below her navel, felt the muscles tighten beneath his fingers. He eased his hand into her panties, cupped her warmth. "Your reaction is telling me otherwise, Mrs. Rutherford. I need to make sure you're not hiding something in here. Do you consent to being searched?"

"I consent, Detective."

Sex now, sex now, the randy teenager between his ears preached. *Now, now, now.* Ennis shoved the voice aside, vowing to take his time. He watched as she toed her shoes off then he slid her jeans down her legs and chanced unlocking her right wrist. "Don't move," he told her, his voice gaining a rough edge.

She stood perfectly still, only moving when he instructed, to expedite the task of stripping down. He drew the blouse down her arms then unclasped her bra, allowing her breasts to fall free. Bending down, he pressed a wet kiss to each taut nipple, coaxing a moan from her depths. *Sex right damn now, you idiot,* the teenager nagged, *or I promise you'll die with this hard-on...*

"Lie down," he pointed to the bed. The voice shrugged and waved him off as hopeless.

She obeyed his command except she held her cuffed wrist out to him, silently asking to be released. His arousal pounded in his jeans, straining for freedom as he shook his head at her. The next command was the hardest and he nearly hesitated. *Georgia said it would work.* The sister never steered him wrong before so he bulled into the lion's den with, "Hands above your head, Mrs. Rutherford."

Yep. The fantasy came to a screeching halt. "Ennis, if you're planning to do what I think–"

"*Hands above your head now*," he repeated with authority. Georgia was wrong, Little Ennis taunted. *Way to go, stupid,* the teenager chimed in. *I told you to jump her while you had the chance but no, you had to push it.*

Ennis stared, unblinking at his wife. Waiting for her compliance. He'd come too far to give in now, he told himself. She knew she could trust him but she hated relinquishing control. To tilt the odds in his favor, he added, "Don't make *me* do it."

Her eyes widened when he neared. He warned, "You're resisting a police officer. The penalty for that is far worse than simple compliance." He motioned to her hands, "Get 'em up there."

Savannah's cheeks darkened to a deep scarlet but she lifted her arms, squirming restlessly as he looped the loose cuffs around two sturdy wooden slats on the headboard.

He extended his hand palm up. By her expression she knew what he asked and plopped her free hand in his waiting one. She met his gaze while the cuff cinched around her wrist.

"Exactly how long have you had this fantasy?" she inquired.

The straightforward question turned the tables. He stopped, measured her features, then replied, "Since we met."

Savannah readjusted her shoulders for comfort then nodded with an easy, "Okay."

His brain stripped a gear with the laid-back answer. Okay, she said. Not *get me the hell out of these cuffs before I kill you.* Not another accusation of losing his marbles but simply *okay.* He could not believe it. Savannah Prince, his wife, finally mellowed out.

Sex now? The teenager was back, eager as ever.

Sex now, he replied with a smile.

O   O   O

Savannah's eyes drifted open. She swore her husband was on a rampage – or some quest where he served up enough pleasure a woman's body melted into a mindless heap. Well, either way it worked. She judged the time as mid-afternoon by the sun's position. The beige drapes filtered the rays to a temperate level preventing the need for extra lighting. The motel provided excellent air conditioning against the blistering heat outside, wherever the motel was. Ennis still refused to disclose their location.

Who cared anyway, she thought, allowing a languid smile to surface. They'd romped and played until they both gave out. Only thing was, Ennis really put her through her paces and as much as it galled her, she was no spring chicken anymore. She wasn't old but her body certainly reminded her of the miles she'd accumulated over the years, especially when her young buck had the staying power of a twenty year-old.

Her young buck flaked out before she had however, aligning against her back, his arm draped over her waist, his knuckles brushing her breast, and then he proceeded to snore. For the first time that day, every part of him was limp as a dishrag.

Somehow she doubted she was limp anywhere. After having Lily, she noticed the aches and stiffness setting in sooner. Probably the goings-on of caring for their firstborn, she figured. First babies put so much pressure on parents with worry and running back and forth. But that day she could only credit their cavorting for any sore, cranky muscles.

For their first romp he left her restrained to the headboard while he had his way with her. He moved inside her with such tormenting slowness she begged him for more, her hips arching into his, thrust for thrust. He carried her to the brink of climax then backed down only build her up again. When she came, it left her boneless, senseless and exhausted.

His next plan – swoop in with his mouth, teeth and tongue. His five o'clock shadow chafed her inner thighs (and more intimate places) repeatedly as though he aimed for a specific number of orgasms before letting her reclaim her breath or a shred of sanity. Between his long, skillful fingers and his hot, probing tongue, he'd given her so many orgasms she lost count, writhing in bliss until finally collapsing, sweaty, hoarse and barely able to draw breath or string two coherent words together.

She stretched her legs. The urge to groan floated close to the surface. God, she was sore all over. Sensitive and tender in others. She glanced down her body. Yep, she still had boobs but a bra would set her nerves on fire all over again. Ennis attacked them with such lustful hunger she smiled at the memory. Her hand slipped down her belly then further until she stopped on a gasp. Shee-yet, she winced. He'd worked her over until walking, along with thinking, would be a genuine challenge.

Savannah glanced at the end table where he laid his cuffs. She'd never look at those handcuffs the same way again. Her first impulse was to say no to him. Skydiving into a volcano sounded more appealing than restraints and sex. But the anticipation – and hope – in her husband's eyes had changed her mind. Now she was glad she had. She saw a whole new side to her husband that day. One that aroused her more than she expected. His aggressiveness and tone perplexed her at first since Ennis normally wasn't so forward and certainly not demanding. Replaying the day in her mind gave her a delightful shiver.

Ennis's knuckles stroked her breast. A kiss on her bare shoulder turned her in his embrace. They both smiled. Ennis curled a wayward lock of hair behind her ear, "Thank you for indulging me. I know how you feel about those things."

She saw the appreciation in his eyes. The pride of her trusting him. She pressed a kiss to his lips, "You know how I *used* to feel about those things." By the end of her statement, she felt his erection growing against her thigh.

"Used to?" his voice buoyed with hope.

Her fingers traced lazy circles in the thick, dark hair on his chest, "I trust you not to hurt me. But I do reserve the right to reverse roles sometimes."

His erection lengthened with every syllable and he smiled, "Anytime, Mrs. Rutherford. Just as soon as I feast on you again." In a flash, he rolled her onto her back with him lying atop her.

Her body protested his statement, imploring her for a respite from the intense passion. One more orgasm and she'd lose her mind. "Ennis, I need to be able to walk *and* think today."

"Who said?" His mouth closed on her right breast, his tongue raking the already sensitive nipple.

Savannah winced at the continued attention to the sore nub, held his head between her hands and lifted his vision to hers, "*I* said. I'm sure Georgia will babysit for us again."

He kissed her nipple with a pouty frown, "But my cuffs need breaking in and they have your name on them."

"I already look like a criminal," she said, showing him the marks on her wrists. It was her fault for pulling on them, unfortunately, but anyone who saw them would probably realize how the marks got there. "I really need to check my messages. Where'd you put my phone?"

Ennis sighed, levered off of her, "I'll get it. Geez, you're leaving me in a world of hurt here, babe."

"Ennis, you're always in a world of hurt when we romp. You have more stamina than Superman."

He went to the dresser where he placed her clothes and

belongings. He tossed the phone to her then plopped beside her on the bed.

She powered it up and while she waited, gently elbowed her husband with a smile, "You can arrest me anytime you want."

He waggled his brow, "Don't tempt me. Cause you're looking mighty guilty of a crime right now."

"What crime is that?"

His fingers traced her shoulder, eased down to her breast, "Escaping from custody. Those violations have long incarceration times. Real long," he drew the words out while his finger circled her nipple.

"I'd make a break for it now except I can barely stand, much less run." She kissed him, her lips parting, their tongues sliding and twirling together.   Ennis's warm hand closed over her breast just as her phone chimed with a message.

She tried to pull back but Ennis dove in for a deeper, more persuasive kiss while capturing her sensitive nipple between his thumb and index finger.

The phone chimed again. Then again and again. Savannah pulled away with a minor flinch when Ennis wouldn't release her nipple. It popped free leaving him to sigh, "I need a leash on those things. They keep getting away from me."

She thumbed a few buttons, noticed two messages from Georgia's cell, another from Owen Dunne and another from Seth. With Owen's name appearing, her anger mounted – until Ennis pushed his way beneath her arm to attack her breast with his mouth. His manipulations shattered her anger. Her brain chose to bask in the pleasure of the sensations instead of planning a redheaded runt's demise. She slid her fingers through his wavy hair, tried to gently nudge him away, "Ennis, let me check these."

He overpowered her, pushing against her, his teeth trapping the nipple hard enough she sucked in a sharp breath. "Your prisoner is asking for a five minute parole," she said, hoping it might work. It didn't. Ennis eased his hand between her thighs. He tried everything to derail her concentration and it began working until she pushed his hand away, saying, "Owen called."

Ennis grabbed for the phone and not nicely either. He wanted one more foray before returning to the real world. Before getting too worked up, Savannah announced, "Georgia and Seth called too. I need to call them back."

Crestfallen, her horny husband ceased the sexual blitz, his dark eyes staring into her blue ones, "Right now?"

"I'd better," she sighed with equal disappointment. "Damn it."

"You're still in custody, remember that."

A sly smile crossed her lips. One that brightened his glum features when she replied, "Yes, Detective Rutherford. I remember." She dialed Georgia's cell but it went to voicemail. Owen Dunne's did the same. She dialed Seth who picked up with a gruff, "Where've you been? Where are you?"

Frankly she didn't know since Ennis abducted her and she spent the entire trip blindfolded. How did she answer without sounding stupid? "You'll have to ask Ennis."

"What the hell was so important you skipped out on Georgia?"

Now *that* lit her temper. He wanted to know? Fine, "We were making love, Seth. It's been quite a while if you recall what it's like having an infant."

An awkward pause halted the conversation then, "Well, I asked, didn't I?"

"Yes, you did. Georgia offered to babysit so we accepted. We didn't skip out on her. Why are you so angry at me?"

"If you'd kept your phone on during your... *your activities*, you'd have realized two hours ago that they arrested Georgia for Matthew's murder."

"What?" She couldn't believe it. "Why? What evidence do they have, do you know?"

"No," he snapped, "because I'm not a cop. They won't tell me. Lindsey and I beat it down here so she could babysit Lily. That little troll Owen Dunne at least let us get here before he hauled Georgia away."

His accusatory tone set her off, "Seth, we didn't run off and leave Georgia with the baby. She *offered* to keep her while we had time alone."

"You and Ennis sure pick a crappy time to get horny."

She toyed with the idea of hanging up. Indignation stiffened her backbone, "Sorry we left our crystal ball at home. We had as much forewarning she'd get arrested as you did, big brother." Oh, the nerve. His sanctimonious attitude reared up at the worst times. As if she and Ennis could have predicted Georgia's arrest – or prevented it.

"Whatever."

She'd show him *whatever*. Right when she got in the car and drove from… from… from wherever the hell they were and arrived at the house. Her brother would then learn a thing or two about *whatever.*

A baby's wailing cry splintered her impending rebuttal. She heard Lindsey call her father. "What's wrong with Lily?" Savannah demanded.

"She's hungry. You and Ennis get to the police station as soon as you can. I'll stay with Lindsey and Lily."

She never got the satisfaction of hanging up on him because he beat her to it, leaving her with a zealous yearning to slap the shit out of him. Savannah gripped the phone in her fist, wanting ever-so-desperately to hurl it against the wall.

A soft kiss pressed to each shoulder then Ennis covered them with his hands, "He was pretty rough on you for something that wasn't your fault. I'll straighten him out, let him know this afternoon was mine and Georgia's idea."

"Don't bother," she sighed. "He forgets we have a life too. We need time alone, even when things are tense which they have been. Seth can take a flying leap." She eyed the handcuffs on the end table, picked them up, played with them. "Reckon these would fit around his neck?"

O   O   O

With Ennis following, she threw open the door to the Richmond County Sheriff's building. He stayed back a step for fear of exacerbating her rage. Judging by her stride and lethal expression, she meant more than business. She meant to maim.

They approached the sergeant's desk, Ennis opened his mouth to speak but Savannah beat him to it. She put hands to hips, "*Atlanta Police* to see Owen Dunne."

The spite in her tone held enough venom to kill off a continent. Between her brother's tantrum and the Richmond County investigators' ineptness, she toed a thin line on her temper.

Ennis saw the sergeant's eyes narrow. The man in his early forties stared back at her with a visual challenge. The sergeant had his gang of Richmond County cronies, it taunted, whereas Savannah just had Ennis. *If you're picking a fight, you chose the wrong department,* the expression said. *So go ahead. Step over this line. I dare you.*

The sergeant didn't realize Savannah Rutherford made it a point to step over lines of all kinds, especially to protect people she loved. She bent rules more than she broke them but cracking a few in half wasn't unheard of. She hadn't risen to detective by standing by and watching the boys do the heavy lifting.

Savannah nodded to the phone, "You paging him or should I personally yank him from under his rock?"

Someone behind them whistled low and slow then added a tsk-tsk. Savannah wheeled, ready to confront yet another antagonist with a badge. A man – not Owen Dunne – mimicked her hands-on-hips stance, foolishly goading her. He looked to be in his mid thirties and had decent features crowned by a thick crop of wavy dark hair. He buttoned his expensive looking gray suit jacket over his expensive looking burgundy tie, then proceeded to toss more fuel onto the fire, "Atlanta Police shaking their mighty fist again and Savannah Prince is leading the march."

Ennis watched his wife bow up, spoiling for a fight. He stepped closer, just in case. The constant badgering and prodding about Atlanta chafed her so raw, she scarcely held her tongue and probably her right hook. This guy gets the first swing, Ennis imagined her thinking. I'll practice on him before I clobber Owen Dunne...

"Do I know you?" she accused more than asked.

A grin splintered the guy's sternness though Ennis detected a hint of disbelief, "Geez, I hope so. We graduated the academy together and even dated for a while."

Still swimming in the red haze of fury, she maintained the hostile posture, ready for battle no matter who stepped in her way, friend, foe or academy classmate. So Ennis inquired, "What's your name?"

Without breaking eye contact with her, the guy replied as a question, "Adam Rafferty? Ring any bells?" He leaned closer but stayed a respectable distance from her temper, "You *do* remember me, right? We spent our time bemoaning our misfortunes about Deanna Bradley and Riley Murphy?" His vision swept her from head to toe, "When we weren't busy with other things, that is."

Ennis felt that one in his gut. When they weren't busy with other things, eh? Yeah. Mr. Slick. Now, along with the desk sergeant and Owen Dunne, he wanted to punch Rafferty's lights out too.

Savannah's breaths came hard and deep as if she'd run the whole way from the motel, her crimson face a testament to a soul pushed beyond reasonable human limitations and common decency. The Richmond County investigators stripped her patience bare when they hauled her sister away in handcuffs.

She gave Rafferty a curt nod, "I remember. Now where's my sister?"

Rafferty's mouth thinned, apparently unhappy that his reminder of their past meant so little, "At the detention center being processed. You can see her in another hour."

The term "detention center" tipped her anger. Ennis put a hand to her tensed arm, whispered for her to calm down which he realized sounded perfectly stupid. However leaping onto this Rafferty fella caused more problems than it fixed. Unless Savannah wanted adjoining cells with her sister, she'd heed his warning.

For years the old jail sat next door to the building they stood in. Before he and Savannah married, springing R.J. from lockup was a matter of traipsing down a hallway. The county built a massive detention center on Phinizy Road, in south Augusta. It was one of the few places Ennis could find by heart thanks to her father's regular visits there.

The Charles B. Webster Detention Center resembled a high security prison, with its towering fence topped with razor wire. The interior looked as quaint as a SuperMax prison. The image of Georgia being led to a cell wearing handcuffs and orange jumpsuit sent his blood pressure out the roof. And judging by Savannah's expression, hers already jumped the tracks.

She advanced on Adam Rafferty, backing him up a step until he held his ground, aware his colleagues witnessed their confrontation, "Savannah, stop. We're friends and I don't want this adversarial."

"Then show me your proof she killed her ex-husband. Otherwise I'm taking my sister home where she belongs."

Adam laughed then a short second later sobered at her scowl, "I can't do that."

Ennis watched Rafferty's vision sweep the length of her body once more. His hands itched to encircle Mr. Slick's throat and squeeze until his eyes popped.

Rafferty cocked his brow, "Unless you're willing to compromise, that is." His bold vision settled on her breasts then lifted to her narrowed eyes, "Surely the two of us can work something out."

Normally, Ennis felt obliged to step in. Today he chose to sit out because his wife teetered on the edge of violence. He'd intervene if she jumped Rafferty and commenced beating him. Otherwise, he'd let her handle it.

Savannah took Adam's arm, towed him to a corner with a tone that refused argument, "Yes, let's work something out between us. How about this? If you show me your evidence against Georgia, I promise not to wipe the floor with you. Deal?"

Her counterpart scanned the room that went silent over the last few minutes. Half a dozen uniforms and the desk sergeant listened, waited. Adam capitulated, "Save your mopping for home. I'll show you what I can." Then he sighed, "God, I'm such a sucker for those blue eyes even now." He shifted to Ennis, offered his hand, "Investigator Adam Rafferty, resident pushover and Spitfire's one-time boyfriend. And you are…"

Ennis shook his hand, "Detective Ennis Rutherford, Spitfire's husband."

Adam's dark eyes widened as they centered on her left hand. One decent glance at the diamond ring seated on her finger and he winced, "Ouch. Sorry for the earlier comments. Didn't know she got married."

"*She's* right here," Savannah emphasized, "and she'd like to see that evidence before my sister is loaded on a prison bus never to be heard from again."

Rafferty shook his head, "Still sharp as a knife, I see. I'll show you what we've got. And Savannah, keep in mind, I didn't arrest Georgia. Owen did. So if you exercise your throwing arm, do it on him."

23

NOW

Adam hustled them to the back of the building, right into an interview room. He opened the door, held it for them while scanning the gathering crowd of curious officers. Savannah felt his hand on her waist, urging her inside. Ennis muscled in, crowding Rafferty and forcing him aside as they approached the utilitarian metal table and matching chairs.

Ennis pulled out a chair, put his hand to her waist, "Sit down."

Adam quickly closed the door, sequestering the three in the small room. Savannah sensed his anxiety, figuring he shoved them in a nice quiet corner in case Owen Dunne happened by. It wasn't Owen he worried about, she finally realized, watching him volley his vision between Ennis and her. It was her temper. His worried expression seemed to ask Ennis to intercede or at least grab her if she should pounce.

Savannah struggled to calm down. She'd overreacted and lost any toehold she may have had with the Richmond County group. It isn't every day my sister is arrested so give me a break, she'd tell Adam if need be. But losing her cool meant other, more important, doors would close. She had to be careful around Adam for he might be her only semi-ally in the department.

"Sit down," Ennis repeated, moving his hand to her shoulder.

She declined his insistence, saying she was fine. Across the way, Adam stood with a hand on the doorknob for a quick escape. He cleared his throat, offering, "Coffee? Donuts? Valium?"

Cute, she thought, curling her lip. *Just what I need. Jokes.* "I want answers."

He opened the door, promising, "Hold on. I'll be back."

She used that time to concentrate on deep breaths. The tiny fireflies flitting across her vision disappeared, her throbbing temples eased. Her temper rarely inspired such extremes but again, it wasn't every day her sister got dragged away in cuffs.

Ennis massaged her shoulders, "You can't help Georgia if you're laid up in the hospital. Calm down before you keel over."

"I'm okay," she said though she really, really wasn't.

A few minutes passed when Rafferty entered the room holding a DVD. Savannah figured he'd watched through the one-way mirror to gauge her anger because unless he brought the DVD from across town, he sure took his sweet time.

"Sorry for the delay," he said. "I had to sneak past Owen to grab the video." He rolled a cart with a nineteen inch combination TV/DVD player to the table, loaded the DVD. "This is the footage from the orchards."

She stood, arms crossed, her blue eyes focused with laser intensity at the black and white security video. She expected to see her daddy pounding on Matthew but the footage began later, after R.J. left. She knew by the way Matthew cradled his gut and walked with a slight limp.

Savannah stared as a female figure in jeans, short sleeve blouse and baseball cap rounded the back of a Chevy Tahoe and charged toward Matthew.   Savannah admitted the woman favored Georgia in build, height and weight, even her dark hair pulled into a ponytail. But the detective struggled to see her face since the woman never looked at the camera.

Matthew grabbed the woman's arm, yanked her to him. His other hand clasped the woman's jaw much like he had Savannah's at the rental house. She rubbed along her jawbone, recalling pressure strong enough to make her teeth ache.

Adam watched from the corner of his eye, his vision settling at her wrist.

She glanced in his direction, suddenly self-conscious of her action then remembered the cuff marks on her wrists. Great, she did a mental eye roll. More humiliation…

He kept staring at her wrist then at her then Ennis. His cocked brow and semi-smile telegraphed the fact he suspected hubby and wifey indulged in a saucy tryst and that incensed her more.

Movement drew her attention to the screen. Matthew shoved the woman away, causing her to stumble back against the Tahoe. She reached in her pocket, removed what looked like a knife. To wield such a pathetic weapon at a marine, the woman either suffered a serious disconnect between the ears or had more training in knife fighting than Georgia. Just another thing that did not add up. Her sister believed in space. If a stream of pepper spray failed to dissuade an attacker, her .22

would. Georgia wanted room to run if things went wrong but this woman charged at Matthew, full on, with no fear.

Matthew's open hand swatted at her as if he shooed a pesky fly. He turned, trekking back to the closed gate. That's when the woman dashed behind him, arm extended with knife in hand, then swung it against his chest. Savannah assumed the blade hit its mark but the female onscreen wasn't finished. She swung again, driving the blade to the hilt from behind. Matthew fell to his knees, then flat on his face. He did not move.

Savannah blew out a breath. It took a moment to regroup after witnessing such brutality. Then she recalled the knife he held at her throat. She visibly shivered, realizing yet again how close she came to losing her own life. She pointed to the screen, "First of all, I can tell that's not Georgia. Second, Georgia knows about the security camera. She helped buy it. Only a nitwit would park her damn car in view and attack the bastard *on camera*. Third, she said she never saw Matthew so that couldn't be her – unless there's a twin Mama never told us about. Fourth, my sister would never wield a frog sticker at the likes of Matthew Carlisle, a marine trained in hand to hand combat and knife fighting. She is not foolish. And what was her motive for such a brutal attack anyway? They hadn't had contact since March."

Rafferty replied, "From what I understand she nearly shot him. That's according to her and the police report from Atlanta. There was bad blood between them but there usually is between divorced couples."

Except, "She's engaged to Ennis's brother Dane. The wedding is next month. Adam, it's not as though she sat around pining for the bastard to come sweep her off her feet. She's moved on with her life and is happy – or was until Owen and Cincinnati began their quest to jail her."

"Cleveland," he corrected, "and he's not investigating this case. Owen and I are. And Savannah, it's really not a quest, I promise. I don't know what Georgia's motive could have been. I believe what I see and what I see is Georgia," Adam pointed to the bottom of the screen, "stabbing her ex at 10:40 yesterday morning."

"You're wrong. And, FYI, Georgia left at 10:30," Savannah stated.

"Can you prove it?"

Of course she couldn't, her frown answered. "Explain your screwy logic, Inspector. You're saying that at 10:40 my sister knifed her ex-husband, left the orchards, scurried home to change clothes and/or wash up from the blood, then sped down to Publix for groceries. Raced home, put the groceries away and looked calm and April Fresh when Owen Dunne got there at noon?" She hoped he recognized the idiocy of his logic as expertly as he recognized her handcuff marks. If not, she added, "In that time she kills the man, runs home to clean up, change, go to the store, shop, then go home – all by noon. That's amazing efficiency even for Georgia because it takes fifteen to twenty minutes to drive from the orchards to the house. At least another twenty or more to clean up and ten to hit Publix. Add fifteen more to shop and check out. And the drive home between 11:30 and noon? Ridiculous, if you've seen traffic at that time." Yes, she admitted (to herself) that she could be wrong. If Georgia hadn't gone home to clean up, for example, which seemed rather stupid since there would have been *some* blood on her from the attack. Who in the hell roamed the produce aisle wearing *parfum de murder* on their blouse? Adam's timeline could have also worked if Georgia raced home to tidy up and caught a lull in traffic. That too seemed equally as laughable since traffic was always a nightmare before noon and *her sister, damn it, just wasn't a killer.*

Adam's mouth open to speak but she held a hand up to hush him, "Let's not forget the fact my sister is calm personified but she's not so serene she could off a person, pretty herself up then hit the Betty Crocker aisle without breaking a sweat. She'd show signs of shock and distress. Georgia is not a killer. She barely sleeps if she chases a rabbit from her flowers because she thinks it'll starve."

As for Adam, *he* showed signs of shell shock from the dissertation. Whether the lecture hit its mark she wasn't sure but he appeared tired now, if not deflated. "Savannah, I appreciate your efforts. I really do. I can't answer all your questions but before you waste another breath on this, you should know we found the murder weapon in Georgia's Tahoe. That's the reason Owen arrested her. It was a knife engraved with Prince Orchards on it."

The revelation deserved a hearty denial but her tongue abandoned her. Shit like this happened in bad dreams, she reasoned. She had to be thrashing and moaning in bed, waiting for Ennis to wake her, not sitting there listening to Adam wrap a bow on Owen's murder case against her sister. Savannah stared at her former boyfriend as if a third eye appeared on his forehead. Then shock drifted in, stealing her strength.

Ennis's embrace around her waist stopped her descent when her knees buckled. Dizziness followed by a high-pitched ringing in her ears forewarned of a fainting spell and she'd never fainted in her life. Her heart throbbed so hard and fast in her chest, she feared a heart attack might be imminent. I don't have time for a heart attack, she told herself. I have to help Georgia.

In the misty fog of confusion she saw Adam scramble past her. A second later he placed a metal folding chair beside her. Ennis eased her into it but braced her shoulders for support.

Rafferty left the room to fetch a glass of water. She needed a stiff drink, not water. *And make that a double, please...* Her trembling hand touched Ennis's at her shoulder, "Tell me I misunderstood. Tell me I did not hear my sister had the weapon in her car."

Ennis gave her a tender squeeze, "I wish I could, babe."

"None of this makes sense. Even if that was Georgia, why would she park her car in camera range? Why would she kill him on camera with a knife bearing our name on the handle? It's not her, Ennis. Mistaken identity, that's what it is, but how do I prove it..." her voice trailed off. She held a hand to her head when the room spun again.

"Sugar, settle down if you can. We'll get what information we can, go home and discuss it with Seth."

"Oh God," she groaned, cradling her head in her hands, "I'd rather be hit by a bus than tell Seth and Daddy."

As evidenced by his earlier reaming out, her brother possessed a knack for putting people in their places. He and Savannah exchanged plenty of words in her life but instead of leaping into the fray the last couple of years, she tried to dial down her quick temper and bite her tongue. His heated phone call tested her limitations. Her ears still burned from that conversation but she'd be damned if he bullied her, no matter how right he thought he was. Still, the impending confrontation coiled a rock hard knot in her stomach. She decided to let Seth tell their father. Let those two argue and shout at each other. She'd had enough for one day.

She pressed her shaking hands to her thighs, seeking stability somewhere, anywhere in life. The dizziness slowly subsided to a general malaise and numbness all over. She wondered if she appeared as devastated as she felt. "You can tell that's not her on the video, right?" she asked her husband.

Ennis crouched beside her, drew his hand down her cheek. His touch broke her gaze and she met his warm, empathetic brown eyes. "Babe, we know it's not Georgia but you gotta admit, whoever that is looks a lot like her and even drives a Tahoe like hers. We'll help Georgia past this, no matter how it turns out."

"I'll tell you how it turns out, Ennis," she replied defensively. "These assholes are railroading my sister into a life sentence or worse, the *death penalty*. *That's* how it turns–" she snapped her mouth shut when the door swung open.

Adam stepped in, sat a water glass on the table. If he heard her outburst, he didn't let on, "Savannah, I'm not sure what to say except I'm truly sorry."

She indulged in a tentative sip of water. When it stayed down, she ventured to ask, "Where in the car did you find the knife?"

"We found it wrapped in a hand towel under the passenger seat. Georgia's prints were on it. No one else's but hers."

Savannah sat the glass on the table, abandoning it. Her stomach warned of a volcanic eruption if she attempted one more swallow. No one's fingerprints but Georgia's. Great. Fantastic. Her sister was toast.

Adam pulled up a chair, sat down and leaned onto his knees, "Georgia's a kind, soft spoken lady. She was always nice to me when you and I were dating. But even the kindest people have a limit. I read the police report from Atlanta. When he broke into her house it scared her – as it would anyone – and it put her on edge. When he showed up here, maybe he pushed her over that edge. Our job shows everyone has that point of no return. Thankfully most of us never reach it."

But *she* had. When Jeffrey Holland came after her a second time – in her house. Yes, that limit could be reached if the right person pushed the wrong button. Survival instinct drove her to swing a golf club at Holland's screwed-up noggin after she'd shattered his leg. Only Ennis prevented the bastard's demise by stripping the club from her grasp. If Georgia felt her life threatened, it made sense she'd protect herself but stabbing Matthew until he dropped dead? Definitely *not* Georgia. And plus the fact, "My sister has more sense than to filet someone then keep the murder weapon. Adam, she writes books about this stuff. She'd get rid of the knife – if she killed Matthew which she didn't. I'm sure of it."

"I'm just telling you what we found and if Owen finds out I've told you anything, my ass is grass."

"*His* ass is grass if I lay eyes on him," she vowed, the strength returning to her voice. "You got the footage from the orchards so what about the security tapes from Publix?"

Adam shook his head, "Bad news on that front. Their security cameras were undergoing maintenance all morning until 1:30 in the afternoon."

"Is it against Owen's decree to provide me snapshots of this woman on the orchard video? I'd like to show them around, see if anyone remembers her or recognizes her. Because it is *not* Georgia, no matter what you people think."

His silence disheartened her. How was she supposed to exonerate her sister if Adam joined the Dark Side too? She added a desperate "please" to the request.

Adam contemplated her request for several seconds until, "If I do this favor for you, may I ask one in return?"

"Depends on what it is."

"Can we go to your house?"

Despite her best efforts, Savannah recoiled at the request. Why did he want to go there, she wondered, so he could troll for more evidence? Letting a cop loose in one's house invited nothing but trouble. She was about to ask if she looked stupid when he clarified, "So we can talk in private." He nodded to the mirror, "Away from potential prying ears."

"On one condition. If you cared anything about me when we dated, you'll keep my sister segregated from the other women. Please. Protect her by keeping her isolated."

He nodded, "I can do that. I'll leave instructions with the

detention center."

24

NOW

The aroma of cinnamon and apples caressed Ennis's senses when the front door opened. It mingled with a fainter hint of tomatoes, garlic and onion. The house smelled delicious, tempting him to seek out the source of the delectable goodies Georgia prepared before the damn cops hauled her away.

He left Savannah speaking with Adam to search out Lily, Seth and Lindsey. That's what he told his wife anyhow. He really meant to find the apple pie and see what Georgia made for supper.

He breezed into the kitchen innocent-like, throwing casual glances here and there until zeroing in on the Dutch apple pie complete with golden brown crumble topping. It sat on the counter just waiting for rampant and gratuitous consumption. His stomach pained him. After the sensational sex, he was starving. He couldn't resist bending closer for a long whiff. He smiled.

Beside the pie was a note in Georgia's handwriting. "Savannah – lasagna's in the fridge. Heat at 350 in the oven. Love you."

Ennis winced as his stomach voiced its opinion on the subject.

Georgia's lasagna verged on paradise. Savannah copied the recipe for future meals and he'd studied it on the sly. Mozzarella, Parmesan and ricotta cheeses, marinara sauce, Italian sausage and spinach (which he forgave Georgia for since the dish tasted scrumptious). He hoped Rafferty hit the road soon or Ennis would conveniently abscond to the kitchen to heat the meal himself.

Tearing himself away from the food, Ennis leaned out the back door to see Seth and Lindsey sitting at the patio table. Lindsey cradled Lily in her arms while her father gave someone the what-for on his cell phone. Ennis waved at them to let them know they were back.

In his usual abrupt manner, Seth signed off the call with a "gotta go" while Lindsey approached Ennis, "Is Aunt Georgia coming home soon?"

"We're trying to get her home, sweetheart. It may take a while but we're trying." He beamed at his baby, "How's my girl?"

Lindsey proudly announced, "She's okay. She pooped and I changed her."

With hands on hips Seth sneered, "You and Savannah done with your... business?"

Ennis refused to argue in front of Lindsey and the baby. He asked the girl to tote the baby to Savannah. Once Lindsey was out of hearing range, Ennis barely restrained his anger, "Listen. No one expected Georgia to be arrested. The motel thing was mine and Georgia's idea. Savannah's been under a lot of stress, you know, with Carlisle kidnapping her last week. Before that, your mother's birthday sent her into a deep depression. She needed this morning to happen and

Georgia insisted on it. She said she'd babysit while we were gone so don't blame Savannah for anything, got it?"

Ennis wasn't sure but Seth Prince actually looked taken aback by his candor. The older brother stared at him a moment then capitulated, "Got it. I didn't realize she was that depressed over Mama this year. I bet Lily's birth brought it on. Leah got in a powerful blue funk after Dylan." He changed the subject, "How'd it go at the station? Did you see Georgia?"

The two went inside while Ennis searched for a palatable way to explain the interloper in the house, "No, not yet. She was being processed at the detention center. They said we can see her in about twenty minutes."

He heard cooing, oohing and ahhing from the living room.

Glancing in, he saw Adam grinning at the baby in Savannah's arms. He made a goofy face that drew a giggle from Lily. Rafferty bothered him. His daddy taught him to read a person's body language, their facial expressions. Ever since Adam laid eyes on Savannah, the man swaggered – not in an overt way but one that perceptive, *married* men picked up on. Rafferty still had feelings for Savannah and that made him as welcome as a tornado on a trail drive. The fact Adam was a year divorced and his wife ended up with custody of their two year-old son perturbed Ennis in a mighty big way. The winks and flirty little looks he gave Savannah – when he thought Ennis wasn't watching really tweaked the urge to knock his teeth out. Adam was on the prowl for his former girlfriend (married or not), Ennis smelled it on him but he also trusted Savannah to slap some sense into him if the guy got too nervy *or* handsy with her. Cause if she didn't, he'd drag Mr. Horndog to the pound where he belonged.

Ennis's vision shifted to his wife. Rocking Lily in her arms, the gentle swaying motion eased the baby's fussing. Savannah's soothing voice quickly settled their daughter. Ennis saw the joy in his wife's expression, heard it in her voice when Lily giggled. She was happy being a mother and a wife. Ennis couldn't stop himself. He chuckled at the sight, remembering a time when she swore off marriage and kids, saying she'd be lousy at both.

Seth stepped around Ennis into the living room. The instant the brother spied the Richmond County badge clipped to Adam's belt, his back straightened, his jaw clenched. His ire shifted to his youngest sister, "What's *he* doing here? Haven't they destroyed enough lives today?"

Savannah shushed him, glanced at Lily then back at Seth as a warning. Ennis read her thoughts – *I've had enough of you today, big brother. Upset my baby and you upset me – and you do not want to upset me again.* Her voice remained deceptively calm, "Adam wanted to meet in private, away from the station."

Seth's brow dove between his eyes, "Yeah, so he can rummage for more evidence against Georgia. Get him out of here, Savannah. We've got all the cops we need with you and Ennis. Cops that don't railroad innocent women."

Lindsey backed away from her father. Seth's anger verged on terrifying at times, Ennis discovered a while back. Once in his crosshairs, the target either risked their safety by standing their ground or they ducked for cover.

Savannah chose the former. The baby squirmed, her tiny fists moving in a fitful way that seemed to beg for peace and quiet.

She tried cooing to Lily with soft words while gently rocking her in her arms. But once riled, Lily took after her mother. It took more than words to pacify her temper. The infant wound up to let the world hear her disgruntlement when Lindsey reached over to tickle her foot. The fussing unexpectedly quieted to burbles then to a tiny laugh. The sound melted the rising tension in Savannah's posture, smoothed the lines between her eyes.

Nice move, kiddo, Ennis nodded to Lindsey in thanks. Distract Savannah before giving her own temper a chance to light. Lindsey was a smart girl and not even a teenager yet. Ennis attributed not only her golden brown hair and cute smile to her mother Leah, but her smarts and patience as well.

Savannah snuggled the baby against her, spoke sweetly to her while offering Adam a refreshment. Ennis sensed she needed more time to tame her temper. The oldest and youngest Prince siblings knocked heads on occasion with uncomfortable results for the bystanders. Seth demanded compliance whereas Savannah fought tooth and nail against it.

After receiving a polite refusal from Adam, she answered her brother in a calm voice, "Seth, he's not rummaging for evidence. He wants to talk."

"So talk," Seth made a point of checking his watch, "and make it fast so we can spring my other sister from your jail before midnight."

Savannah gave her brother another warning glance then eased onto the sofa with Lily in her arms. When Adam occupied the wingback

Georgia usually chose, Seth huffed a loud, frustrated sigh, "He's got that much to say? Should we invite him for supper too?"

Savannah ignored her brother as Adam proceeded, "I wanted privacy to discuss Carlisle's motel room. We located it, collected his things. We also went through his rental car. Georgia may have a case for self defense."

"That *wasn't* Georgia," Savannah corrected. She addressed Lily in a nicer, sweeter voice, "Adam is assuming it was Aunt Georgia and we know what assuming does, don't we, little one?"

Unhappy with the mild scolding, Adam continued, "We found maps showing the routes to this house and the orchards. We also found a journal of Georgia's comings and goings for the last three weeks. He was also tracking Savannah up until last week. There were detailed drawings of your street, front and back yards and pictures of your house."

Seth's voice hardened, "He abducted her and Dane last week. He was planning to kill them. You should know this already." He tapped his watch at Savannah, "Let's go, sis."

Like Savannah, Adam ignored Seth, "We found a knife, rope, duct tape, restraints, women's clothes still with price tags. There was another map too, this one of Guadalupe, Mexico. In the journal he mentioned taking Georgia there. Since it's not a tourist location, I figure he was going to keep her there." He glanced at Savannah, "But there I go *assuming* again."

From her neck upward, Savannah turned a dark shade of red. Ennis called it plum. She called it pissed off. He figured images abounded of big brute Matthew manhandling her petite sister. Tying her up, slinging her over his shoulder caveman-style and hauling her off to some ramshackle hovel in a hot, miserable Mexican town where no one spoke English and she never learned Spanish. Probably with no running water, air conditioning, or phone either. Most importantly, there would be no family or friends.

Ennis sensed it took great effort not to speak her mind about Matthew's gruesome death being plenty late in coming. The only reason she held her tongue: Lily. Her voice, however, retained a dangerous edge, "I'm sure not shedding tears over his death. He was nuts."

Adam didn't deny that, "There was also a court martial scheduled but he disappeared before it began. I'm guessing that's when he arrived in Atlanta. According to the journal, he still considered Georgia his wife. Only thing is, he accused her of adultery with Dane. His writings were disjointed and delusional. That's why I said she may want to plead self defense."

Seth cursed under his breath then, "*She didn't kill him.*"

Savannah agreed but added a caution, "Seth, the woman on the orchard video looks similar to her and a Tahoe is parked just inside the camera's range. Adam said they found the murder weapon in Georgia's car. That's why they arrested her. It's not Georgia but we have to prove it's not."

Adam maintained, "Look, if it's her, self defense is her best bet. I read the police report from March when he broke into her house and the report from last week on Savannah and Dane's abduction. Those two instances and the traffic stop from two weeks ago give her a valid reason to plead self defense. Carlisle was obviously dangerous to anyone who had contact with him."

Seth glared at him. Ennis waited to see if he lunged at the cop. He didn't but Adam pressed back in the chair to be safe.

"What traffic stop?" Ennis and Savannah asked in unison.

"Atlanta pulled him over for running a red light. He told the cop he was late picking up his wife. He verged on rude with the uniform and nearly got arrested because of his aggressive and disrespectful behavior. The cop thought he was drunk or high. Had him do the sobriety tests but Carlisle passed. Searched the car but found no weapons or dope. If he had the kidnap kit, he must have kept it at his motel room or wherever he was staying. Savannah, I'm trying to help. Mention the self defense aspect to Georgia when you see her. Have her lawyer work on that."

"Gee, thanks for that heads-up, Inspector," Seth snapped. "You haven't proven Georgia killed that rotten bastard anyway. If you don't mind, I'll stick with the advice the cops in *my family* offer." His cell phone rang, and Ennis thanked God for the interruption. Savannah and Adam also appeared relieved.

Despite stepping away to answer the call, Seth's voice carried loud and clear, "No, she's not at the sheriff's department on Walton Way. They took her to the *detention center* on Phinizy Road."

They heard the emphasis on detention center. Seth aimed his scowl at Adam while continuing his conversation, "Exit onto Bobby Jones Expressway then turn onto Peach Orchard Road. Phinizy's on your left." There was a pause then, "No, our place is on the other end of Walton Way, south of Westover Cemetery. I'll give you directions when we meet at the *detention center.* Yeah, one of 'em's here trying to do your job for you." A nasty grin spread across Seth's features, "Oh, I'll tell him, don't worry."

The second he disconnected the call, Savannah gave him marching orders, "Whatever you intend to say to Adam, don't. He didn't have to tell us anything but chose to."

"That was the lawyer I hired," he replied, stalking closer to Adam's wingback chair. "You ever heard of Justin Davis, Mr. Rafferty?"

Ennis barely heard Adam say no. He was too busy watching Savannah's cheeks lose their color. She swallowed hard. Ennis leaned closer, asking if she was okay. Shaking her head, she replied, "This keeps getting worse."

"How's it getting worse?"

"Justin Davis and I hate each other."

25
NOW

Justin Davis became a part of their lives thanks to one of Seth's closest friends. The recommendation of Davis, a ruthless shark of a lawyer, sent Savannah into a tailspin of emotions. Mostly resentment. Years ago, she testified against one of his clients. The testimony she gave was sound, factual. Davis took the truth and twisted it, mangled it and managed to free his client on a technicality that neither she nor other law enforcement witnesses saw coming. Savannah hadn't taken the loss well, even though her personal testimony hadn't sprung the killer loose. After the trial fiasco, she'd called Justin Davis a plea peddler and a Philadelphia Lawyer, polishing the insult with, "You gotta be working on Satan's side of the fence, Counselor, because he rewards his little minions. Maybe you'll get the extra warm corner in Hell for that verdict."

Now fate rammed the arrogant Armani-wearing jerk down her throat. She pulled into the parking lot at the detention center and climbed out to the sound of trains in the distance. For a brief second she entertained throwing herself under one just to avoid Davis.

She wiped her brow, weary of the stress and the hot weather.

Combined with the heat, the humidity sank to the bone that late in the afternoon. A bit like Seth's vicious attitude the last hour. They'd driven in silence to the Charles B. Webster Detention Center, neither of them venturing a glance at the other. It rated as the longest twenty minutes of her life with her brother.

They started the hike to the front door while Adam parked his sedan in the lot. She asked, "You're sure your friend knows Justin Davis? Cause I've been in a courtroom with him. He's as pleasant as a Nazi root canal."

"You're jaded because you're on the prosecution's side. Did you win or lose the case?"

Her brow wrinkled. She still had her pride, after all. She shook her head, "Oh, forget it."

Seth took the hint, "That should tell you Davis is good, at least good for us right now. Funny thing though. He kept repeating our last name. Like he'd heard it but couldn't place it."

Oh boy, she grimaced, here it comes. She knew why the guy chanted their last name. Davis attempted to place where he'd encountered it before.

Seth continued, "Then he asked if my wife was a detective. I told him no but my sister was."

"Oh God," she rubbed her forehead to ward off the growing ominous pain. "This'll be a nightmare. What did he say?"

"Not much. Just mumbled something about Philadelphia lawyers. What did he mean?"

She tried to wave it off, "You wouldn't understand."

"Is Davis from Philly?" Seth asked.

Fed up with the inquisition, she blurted, "No, I called him a Philadelphia Lawyer years ago. That's an ultra-competent lawyer who knows the ins and outs of legal technicalities. Or..." She hesitated a moment, "an unscrupulous lawyer. Since I added that he'd get the hottest corner in Hell for getting a killer kicked loose, you can imagine which definition he figured I meant."

"Savannah," he groaned, "you didn't."

"I did. He made us look ridiculous. By the time the verdict came, every cop wanted his head on a pike."

"I hope he can overlook your past disparagement long enough to *Philadelphia* his way to Georgia's freedom. We're dealing with her future, Van, so behave around him."

As if she needed reminding, she wanted to say. Adam sprinted past them in the meantime, telling Savannah he'd bring Georgia to the visitor's area while they checked in.

"How damn sweet of the bastard," Seth mumbled.

"Take your own advice, big brother. I'm not happy about this either, but hassling our only semi-ally isn't helping. Adam's at least talking to us," she said, opening the entry door.

The building looked liked a maximum security prison's little brother. Imagining her sister spending a minute inside, much less years, tore Savannah apart. If Justin Davis couldn't schedule an arraignment hearing that afternoon, Georgia had to sleep behind bars. This was one time Savannah rooted for the gussied-up, pricey chiseler.

Seth groused, "Rafferty knows Georgia and the dumbass should know murder isn't in her vernacular except to write about it. I just want her home."

"So do I." They trudged into the building to the front desk and were met with a stern request for ID. She pulled her department ID and badge, while Seth presented his driver's license.

The rotund officer scanned both, his attention lingering on the Atlanta badge. He said nothing when their vision met. Adam appeared in a doorway across the room. He reluctantly made eye contact with Savannah. Something about his expression screamed *Houston, we have a problem* but mostly it was the cowering stance that triggered her question, "What happened?"

He waved the two to follow him, "She had her own cell like I promised..."

"But," Seth's mood soured further.

Savannah took a moment to realign her brother's temper, "Do anything to him and you'll end up in here too. None of us has enough bail money for that."

They turned into the large visitation room. Most of the tables and chairs remained empty. Searching the room, Savannah estimated ten inmates in orange jumpsuits gathered to chat with their families. A lone figure sat by herself at the back of the room. Georgia. She faced away from the door, her shoulders slumped in defeat.

Leaving Adam stumbling for words, Savannah rushed to her sister, "Georgia, we're here."

Georgia turned from the window and Savannah stopped cold at the sight, "What the hell happened?"

The room fell quiet. Inmates and their families suspended their conversations in favor of tuning into the drama across the way. Savannah rounded on Rafferty who retreated a step when she barked, "Adam, why does my sister's face look sideswiped by a wrecking ball?"

Seth grabbed his sister's arm. "Heed your own advice, Van," he seemed to taunt. "None of us has enough bail money for what you're thinking."

She slung his hand away. A plum sized knot bulged from Georgia's right cheek, the swelling so severe it narrowed her bruised eye into a slit. Someone would pay for this, Savannah vowed, and that someone was named Rafferty who stood flushed with shame. Her hit list formed in a flash. First Rafferty then Owen Dunne. When she finished with them, they'd look much, much worse than her sister. "You *promised*," she growled at him. "Explain this because you don't get a shiner in administrative segregation."

Adam surveyed his audience. Georgia gingerly wiped a tear, her silence and devastated expression pleading for answers. Seth united with his youngest sibling with a posture daring Rafferty to move or speak. He mustered the courage to say, "Savannah, I did have her separated. According to the officers, it happened just after transport. I wasn't responsible for that, was I?" He glanced to Georgia and apologized.

Whether it was the apology or the sight of her siblings, Georgia's carefully restrained façade dissolved into inconsolable tears. She threw her arms around Savannah, wrapping her so tight that drawing a simple breath became doubtful.

Savannah held her, her voice gentle to shush Georgia's crying.

She hadn't heard her sister cry so hard since their mother died.

"I didn't kill him," Georgia said between sobs. "I don't know where the knife came from, but I didn't kill Matthew."

Savannah leveled a molten glare at Adam, "I know you didn't, sweetie. We all know you didn't do it. Ennis and I are working to find evidence to help you and Seth's already got a good lawyer on his way from Atlanta."

Seth joined the hug, "He's one of the best in town, sis." He scowled at Rafferty, "I'm going to make sure he tears these clowns to shreds."

"Savannah, get me out of here," she cried harder, held tighter. "*Please...*"

The younger sister tilted her head at Adam, questioning what came next. He looked at Georgia then at Savannah whose expression still vowed grievous bodily harm. "She has to see the superior court judge first," he checked his watch. "I could make a call, see if there's time. If she makes bail, at least she could stay at the house." He walked away with cell phone in hand.

Georgia released her sister who drew a deep breath to expand her lungs and ribcage from the fierce hold. "We'll get you sprung as soon as we can, sweetie," Savannah reassured with a supportive squeeze on her hand. "Just try to calm down while I make one little phone call right quick." She retrieved her cell phone to call Owen Dunne. The phone rang once, then twice when Owen answered. Savannah let him have it, "Inspector Dunne? Detective Prince. Just what part of *administrative segregation* don't you understand?"

"What?" Owen asked, confused. "I understand it fine, Savannah. Why?"

"My sister looks like a Joe Frazier victim because you people can't control inmates during transport." She turned, lowered her voice, "Didn't she get enough beatings from our father, Owen? Did you think letting the whores and druggies work her over would get you a confession?"

"Hold on, Detective," he backtracked defensively. "I agreed to keep Georgia separated from the general population. I'm not there when they transport them to jail. I don't know what happened and I'm sorry she got hurt but it's not my fault."

"That's the refrain of your whole department. *It's not my fault.* Tell you what, Owen. Put it on a plaque and shove that plaque where the sun doesn't sh–"

"Satan's minion has arrived, Detective Prince," a voice crowed from behind her.

She hung up on Owen, turned to face Justin Davis, an average looking man in his early forties with strands of gray peppered throughout his short cropped hair. He still bedecked his stocky frame in Armani and still sported the usual shit-eating grin.

Davis tipped his chin back slightly to look down his nose at her, "Your brother hired the best Philadelphia Lawyer in Atlanta."

Her rage for Owen and Adam probably translated in her expression. She relaxed, trying for a neutral look as she extended her hand, "Counselor, I hope you can overlook our previous encounter and my unfavorable remarks."

He shook her hand with a haughty, "I find it rather ironic our paths cross again, except this time you're on *my* side." Justin glanced past her to her sister, "You must be Georgia. I'm Justin Davis, your new best friend."

She nodded, shook his hand while swiping tears with her other, "Good to meet you, Mr. Davis."

He chuckled easily, "Call me Justin. I'm not a stickler about formalities, just ask your sister. She calls me many interesting names."

Ouch, Savannah winced. Seth frowned at her. Look what you did, it seemed to say. She mouthed *I said I was sorry.* Maybe not in those words but that's as far as her dignity could allow.

"What happened to your cheek?" Davis asked his client.

"Police negligence if you ask me," Savannah growled. "According to the grapevine, it happened during transport."

Davis lifted a brow, "Interesting to hear one cop accuse another of negligence."

"Get used to it, Counselor," she replied. "Apparently, this department is rife with it."

Adam clicked off the phone, surprised, "She's already scheduled with the judge in an hour."

Davis smiled, "I called the judge earlier, asked him to fit her in." He winked at Savannah, "See, Detective? Even minions have a heart sometimes."

26

NOW

The house soon filled with the aroma of seasoned tomatoes, spicy meat and creamy melted cheese. Georgia's lasagna fit the bill for alleviating not only hunger but the stress of the day. The second the family arrived home, Savannah slid the foiled covered feast in the oven then grabbed a bag of peas from the freezer that Georgia earmarked for a casserole. She carried it to her sister who gingerly held it to her swollen cheek.

Savannah tended to Lily then headed back to serve supper. Justin Davis bowed out of the meal, choosing instead to prepare for his interview with Georgia.

Georgia joined him in declining supper, a move that ruffled Savannah into a mild irritation and a mandate that she *would* eat, whether lasagna, a sandwich or soup. The older sister capitulated, gifting Savannah with a heartfelt smile, "Yes, Mama."

The name warmed Savannah, remembering the many times she used the *Yes, Mama* with Georgia as a flattering sign of surrender. Now Georgia bestowed the same upon her. Strange as it sounded, Savannah felt like she'd graduated from the School of Little Sister to University of

Equal.

Once the brood was fed, they moved into the living room where Davis claimed the other wingback across from Georgia. Savannah and Ennis occupied the sofa with Seth serving as straggler at the far end. Lindsey busied herself with outdoor activities in the back yard and blocks away R.J. roosted at his usual bar, unaware that his oldest daughter had been dragged off in handcuffs and booked for murder.

With reading glasses perched on his nose, Davis sat his briefcase on the floor, his legal pad in his lap then switched on the tape recorder and got down to business. He listened to Georgia without interrupting, his pen scribbling notes along the way. Davis asked occasional but important questions and allowed Georgia to explain at her own pace.

Savannah was grateful Seth called Justin Davis. The Richmond County rubes needed an ass-kicking, she fumed. They deserved it for framing an innocent woman for murder and for allowing the masses of hookers and druggies to slug out their frustrations on her soft-spoken, kindhearted sister. Maybe she underestimated the guy, Savannah thought. He came through on Georgia's arraignment and being nearly evening, that took serious influence. Yes, the stubborn detective and Justin Davis crossed swords in the past but she'd damn well get along with him now.

Exhaustion seeped in all over, rolling the day's tension into a mass of muscle aches and throwing her brain on automatic. They could sleep comfortably that night knowing Georgia was safe. The task ahead, however, drove the fatigue to the bone. Proving her sister's innocence would test her patience and experience as a detective.

While Georgia relayed her story, Savannah noticed her sister's hands began trembling. She got up, poured Georgia a glass of brandy to calm her nerves. Georgia knocked back the entire glass in one swallow. Savannah refilled it with a caution, "Are you on a spree? Slow down."

Savannah positioned herself behind the wingback chair to knead the tension from her sister's shoulders. The muscles bunched hard as steel beneath her touch. She worked her fingers along the tightness in Georgia's shoulders and neck then lightened her touch when she heard her sister sigh.

Savannah checked the grandfather clock in the entry. In two hours, Dane would arrive at Bush Field on the connecting flight from Atlanta. His stay back home was cut short when Ennis called with the news of Georgia's arrest. Dane hopped on the next flight out of Amarillo. Calling with regular updates, Dane told of an excruciating three hour layover in Dallas due to storms. His last call came shortly after the family arrived home from the jail. A one hour layover in Atlanta and another hour flying to Augusta separated him from Georgia then his true love could seek refuge and comfort in the arms of her sweetheart.

Savannah tried easing into her own questions, "Besides you, who's been in your car lately?"

"You, Dane, the kids and that woman I took to the garage. Why?"

"Haven't left it unlocked for any reason, anywhere?"

"No, I'm very security conscious. You know that."

"And you're sure no one else has been in your Tahoe?"

"I'm sure."

"Okay, so that woman you helped. What did she look like?"

Georgia closed her eyes a moment, "Slender, about my height, maybe an inch or two shorter. Medium brown hair. She wore it just below her shoulders like me. Pleasant features. She wore jeans and a short sleeve pullover..."

Savannah continued kneading her sister's tense shoulders, "Like you."

"Yes, like me."

"What kind of car did she drive?"

"A green Tahoe."

"Like you."

Georgia paused then confirmed, "Like me. Why?"

Savannah retrieved the photo Adam gave her, handed it to Georgia, "This is from the video at the orchards."

The muscles beneath Savannah's fingertips tensed. She patted Georgia's shoulder, a sign to calm down.

Georgia sat silent, staring at the photo as if trying to accept what she saw. "That's a Tahoe and, and... That's Claire, the woman I drove to the garage. Only she's wearing jeans, a ponytail and ball cap in the photo. When I saw her she wore her hair down." She studied the photo, shrugging while sipping the brandy, "I guess I can see a resemblance to me. Maybe."

"But it's not you and we know it."

"The police are sure it is."

"Well, they're idiots," Savannah shot back. "One, you're not a killer. Two, you said you didn't do it. Three, I can tell that woman isn't you. Four, I doubt you'd go after Matthew with a frog sticker with *Prince Orchards* emblazoned on it. Five, because of where he was stabbed he lasted only seconds. How many people know where to stab a person for a speedy death?"

"Are you talking about the descending artery?" Georgia wondered aloud.

Savannah's mouth dropped open, "How'd you..." The she recalled Georgia penned a book where the victims suffered stab wounds to the descending artery, killing them instantly.

Georgia lifted a brow, "Remember 'Betrayal'? I wrote about a killer who tortured his victims then finished them off by severing the descending artery."

A headache pinged at Savannah's temple. Trying to exonerate Georgia was like trying to swim with bag of bricks tied around her waist. She rubbed the pain, exasperated, "Why couldn't you write romance? There's less controversy when your ex-husband gets bumped off."

"Detective," Davis called. "You said he was stabbed twice from behind. And the killer twisted the knife, am I right?"

Savannah nodded as Seth entered the conversation, "Stabbed from behind? And she ran behind him to do it?"

Davis kept writing, "Less blood spatter."

It was nice to know she and Davis were thinking alike. Savannah added, "Less mess for her and she can leave within a few minutes of Georgia's departure."

Georgia tipped the glass of brandy for an additional healthy slug, "Why would this woman frame me for murder?"

"That's what we have to figure out." Savannah stood behind her, rubbed Georgia's shoulders that tightened in that short time. "But it's obvious she's targeted you. I'll see what I can dig up tomorrow on security footage from other businesses. Surely someplace caught you both on camera. You said she used a tissue to close the car door and latch the seatbelt."

Georgia nodded, "Her hands were filthy from working with the tire and jack. She said she didn't want to get my car dirty."

"Or leave fingerprints behind. Close your eyes and replay those few minutes. At any time did she reach beneath the seat? Did she get in her purse for any reason besides the tissue?"

The room fell quiet while the group waited for her answer. With eyes closed, Georgia murmured each motion while mentally reenacting the time, "I climbed in, waited for her. She already had the tissue out so she got in, closed the door. We chatted as I started the car, locked my seatbelt. Shifted in Reverse, turned to check for traffic and..."

Savannah paused with the massage. A moment later Georgia's eyes opened, "I can't prove she reached under the seat. When I turned to look behind me there was a truck backing out so I waited. I heard her moving around so I turned to her. She leaned back, saying she put her purse in the floorboard then she buckled up. I thought it was strange she waited to buckle up."

Savannah was convinced, "That's when she planted the knife."

"And the Tahoe was a rental from Atlanta," Georgia blurted. "The emblem had an "A" with wings. That's A-1 Rental if I'm right. It'll be difficult to locate who rented it because there are several A-1

Rentals in town."

She kneaded a little harder at the stubborn muscles, "Difficult but not impossible." Trying to pry any information from the rental company would be the trick. They tended not to share without official paperwork but she'd try anyway.

After several more minutes of the massage, Georgia's hand slackened on the glass of brandy, prompting Savannah to set it aside and resume the neck rub.

The older sister's eyes drifted closed then lazily opened, "Hon," Georgia patted her hand, "I need to stay awake for Mr. Davis."

Justin rose to his feet, buttoned his suit coat, "I've got enough information for tonight. We'll get together tomorrow. Get some rest, take care of that shiner." He gathered his notes, placed them precisely in his briefcase, locked it, "Detective, you and I should talk. You said the security cameras at Publix underwent maintenance at the time Georgia was there?"

She knew where his statement led, "I'll drop by tomorrow to verify that since I can't seem to trust the cops."

He cut his eyes to her, "Glad to see you're thinking along my lines."

"That makes two of us. I'm planning to drive Georgia's route tomorrow. Hopefully there are other stores that caught her on camera with the mystery woman."

Davis nodded, "Good. We need solid proof of her alibi so anything you find, contact me."

"Counselor," she extended her hand which he easily shook, "tell me what you need and I'll work on it."

Over the last hour and a half, Davis loosened his stiff posture along with his tie, and the chill in his voice thawed in her presence. She tried to see him as Georgia's only real hope. Seth was right, she told herself. If Davis could win the tough cases, this one fell right in line.

Justin glanced at his watch, "Checking for other cameras is priority. If you get time perhaps you could visit Prince Orchards to talk to... Ray, is it?"

"Ray Slocum. His son Marcus helps him run the place. He said Marcus and his wife were out of town yesterday but would be back today."

"Try to talk with Marcus as well. While you're out, Georgia and I will discuss the woman she helped." He looked past her to the older sister, "Make sure she gets some sleep if you can. After her day, she's got to be bushed and I need her sharp tomorrow."

What once would have choked her now came naturally. She smiled at Justin Davis, "I will. And Mr. Davis, thank you for getting that arraignment tonight. Having her home means a lot to us."

His face eased into its own smile, "You're welcome, Detective. I never like to see innocent people behind bars and I have no doubt she is innocent."

O O O

After getting her sister settled in bed, she called Georgia's agent Avery Dean and her publicist Randolph Klein to forewarn them of the day's events. Savannah promised to have Georgia call them once her sister rested up.

Savannah spent the first three hours in bed not only hearing Seth raid the fridge for a midnight snack but wander the downstairs. She consumed herself with Georgia's situation and when she exhausted that subject, she was plagued with Ennis's impression of Adam. Mr. Rafferty's sly smile at Ennis, as if Adam stowed a salacious secret about his and Savannah's past grated on her. His merry grin suggested she and Adam romped like rabbits when they dated – which they had not.

The unspoken innuendo hit its mark, however. By the time they adjourned from the station, Ennis's rigid posture and reserved nature told the story. Adam's baited comments, his blatant, provocative stare at her boobs and his flirtatious wink stirred a storm in her husband.

On the way home, she'd explained that Rafferty embellished their relationship, probably to save face in front of his buddies. Nothing like being threatened by a woman to injure the male ego, she finished. Without making eye contact, Ennis nodded.

Savannah sensed his skepticism so she flat-out confessed, "Ennis, we had drinks, dinner and watched movies. That's all. I didn't want to get too involved that soon after Toby." This was the only lie that fell from her lips. She *had* wanted a permanent relationship with Adam. Admitting to Ennis that she loved Adam at one time was a surefire recipe for disaster. With his jealous streak, the tidbit stayed locked away forever.

They drove the rest of the way in silence. And once the day's chaos waned and the house fell as silent as the ride home, she fought the bed, her conscience and the fear Adam stirred a hornet's nest in her marriage.

She rolled out of bed at four-thirty groggy and tired. Ennis was already downstairs, probably drinking his coffee and waiting for her. She made a pit stop to the bathroom to freshen up then padded down the stairs to the kitchen to find her coffee already poured and doctored to her preference.

Ennis sat at the dining table, the Augusta Chronicle spread out on the table. "Mornin'," he yawned.

"Mornin'."

"You're getting as much sleep in that dinky bed as I am."

The "dinky bed" hadn't caused the insomnia. Old ghosts had. Those and visions of Georgia behind bars.

"What time did you drift off?" he asked.

"About two-fifteen, two thirty. You?"

"'Bout two." He nodded to her coffee cup, "I heard you up so I poured it."

She thanked him then indulged in a sip. The rich flavor promised consciousness soon when it slid past her palate. She'd heard of the pause that refreshes. This was the pause that restored her to a human being. She moaned with pleasure then sat across from him.

He turned the page, "Hey, the Rangers won last night." He lifted the paper, busied himself reading.

Savannah glanced at the front page and choked on the coffee. Coughing spasms shuddered through her until tears welled in her eyes.

Ennis laid the paper down again, "You okay?"

She shook her head, pointing to the front page, still battling back another racking cough.

"Oh yeah," Ennis grumbled. "That."

Her throat convulsed while she mentally digested what she'd seen. Georgia's photo splashed across the front page with a quaint, attention-grabbing headline "Author Arrested for Murder."

Savannah snatched the periodical and wadded the whole mess between her fists much to Ennis's dismay.

"My sports and crossword were in there," he protested.

She relented, tossed the mangled, semi-spherical mass to him with an apology, "Sorry. Just," she whispered, "get rid of the front page before she sees it."

"Too late," Georgia said from the kitchen doorway. Wearing a long, burnt red satin robe from years past, she shuffled into the kitchen. She looked terrible. Her hair, usually combed and styled now showed signs of a long, fitful battle with a pillow. A battle she clearly lost. She wore no makeup which brought out the deep purples and burgundy hues of her swollen cheek and eye, "I didn't get any sleep so Dane and I stayed up talking. He went to bed about an hour ago."

Ennis fired mad, "He kept you up? You needed rest."

Georgia's thoughtful smile came easy until she flinched, "I couldn't sleep anyway, Ennis. It's okay. I used that time to call Avery and Rand." She looked at Savannah, "Thanks for letting them know, by the way. They're working on a statement for the press this morning."

Savannah's jaw dropped, "This early in the morning? The rooster hasn't rolled outta bed yet."

"Neither one went to bed after your call." She retrieved a gallon of milk from the fridge, poured herself a glass. "Then I fetched the rag serving as our local paper. At least they used a nice publicity shot for me instead of that tacky thing they snapped at the jail." She eased into the chair across from Savannah, "I'll pay you both back for my bail, I promise."

Savannah clasped her hand, "Let's get you cleared of these ridiculous charges before you start fretting over money."

Georgia shook her head, maintaining, "No. You've got Lily, not to mention your own bills. Seth and Leah hired Justin and you and Ennis paid my bail. I am paying you all back."

Why couldn't her sister just accept the help? She'd always been quick to offer financial assistance, even when none was needed. Nothing wrong with returning the favor, if she'd only let them. Irritation crept into Savannah's voice, "We're not discussing it right now. If you insist, we'll talk about it later."

That seemed to satisfy Georgia. Then she leaned back with a surprising, devious grin, "You two have fun yesterday?"

Savannah's cheeks burned, "I saw a whole new side of my husband, that's certain." She noticed Georgia's green eyes focused on her wrist. The handcuff bruise still screamed the fact they indulged in kinky sex.

"May I suggest fur-lined cuffs next time?" Georgia winked.

For the love of God, she groaned to herself. It was like chatting with Dr. Ruth, or worse, Duke Shelton, a professional dominant who'd delight in sharing his two cents – and she'd commit hari-kari before considering *his* suggestions.

"You speaking from experience?" Savannah joked. Or she assumed until Georgia's face darkened to the color of her own. The older sister mimicked locking her lips and tossing away the key. For Savannah the moment soared past uncomfortable to outright unbearable. She rose from her seat, half afraid to finish her coffee for fear of choking to death from embarrassment, "I gotta go."

Raising one brow, Georgia pressed the issue – most likely to aggravate her, "I'm sure Duke would gladly offer advice on restraints – and give Ennis more ideas for the bedroom..."

"Georgia, don't make me puke. Ennis doesn't *need* help in the bedroom, particularly from Duke. Neither of us do."

27

NOW

The Texas Rangers may have won the night before but today Savannah's at-bats mattered more than theirs.   If she struck out, her sister went to prison. By mid-morning, the situation circled the drain.

Inquiries at A-1 Rentals in Atlanta came up empty. At all four locations. The surprisingly forthcoming managers checked the records only to say they hadn't rented a Chevy Tahoe to a female matching the woman's description in the last three weeks. Strike one.

Strike two came when Publix reiterated their security cameras were undergoing maintenance during the time Georgia arrived and left.

Savannah trudged out of Publix, disappointment draining not only her hopes but energy as well. She resorted to her long shot, trolling businesses near Publix for security video showing the grocery store's parking lot. National Plaza, the outdoor mini-mall where Publix was located, sat back from Washington Road about a hundred yards. The mall also contained a Chinese restaurant, pizza joint, a beauty supply store and nail salon. Savannah sat in the store's parking lot, surveying the surroundings, searching for places that might have security cameras.

Businesses within camera range of the road to Publix included exactly one. A tire store – but discovered they had no camera. All she needed was one decent shot of Georgia or her Tahoe at the store during Matthew's ugly demise but it was looking like strike three sped toward her, right between the eyes.

If her efforts came up short, she'd head to the sheriff's department to finagle a look-see at the knife they found in Georgia's car. If nothing came of it, she'd talk to Ray and Marcus then retrace Georgia's trek from the orchards to Publix in search of traffic and security camera footage that showed Georgia's car at specific times. She needed a timeline for her sister – and proof Claire followed her.

O   O   O

The security video wasn't exactly a home run, but it was a base hit. She'd spoken with the managers of the Chinese and pizza places first. Though she hadn't expected them to have cameras, she wanted to verify. Next came the nail salon. Nothing. It was the beauty supply that, after scrounging in the back, the manager emerged with a videotape. She was lucky, he said, because it was scheduled to be reused the following morning. The owner installed the security because of two break-ins in the last year. Without saying so, Savannah wondered who was desperate enough for hair-care products they felt the need to thieve a store. No, instead she asked to watch the video and what she saw lifted her spirits. The black and white camera's wide angle lens captured two rows of parking at Publix. The picture blurred out a bit considering the distance but one could see the cars and discern people climbing in and out of them but not actually identify individuals.

Savannah saw her sister's Tahoe pull into a slot nearest the camera. Georgia parked facing the camera so when Savannah saw a faint flash beneath the rearview mirror (an angel ornament), she knew the car belonged to her sister. Georgia climbed out, tucked her purse under her arm and went inside the store.

A minute later another Chevy SUV – a Tahoe – pulled in beside Georgia. She watched the video then drove it directly to the Richmond County Sheriff's Department.

"There it is," Savannah stabbed a finger at the TV screen with such vehemence Adam Rafferty frowned.

She replayed the video so he could, for a second time, witness a second dark colored Tahoe pull in next to Georgia. She held a finger to the time stamp, "Just like Georgia said. Another Tahoe. And if you'll note the time, it matches Georgia's story."

"It certainly verifies there were two Chevy Tahoes running loose in the city that day."

She assumed he meant to introduce humor into the conversation to diffuse the tension in her room. If he didn't remove the smile from his face, she'd do it for him while explaining that she was *trying* to save her sister's life and future.

He recoiled at Savannah's murderous scowl, "Okay, okay, but how do you know," he pointed to one vehicle, "that's Georgia? And how do you figure that *other* car is actually following the first Tahoe?"

She expected the questions – even an argument – but she had

rather present her evidence to Adam than to Owen whom she yearned to punch until her knuckles bled. She paused the video, pressed her finger to the Georgia's rearview mirror, "See that thing hanging on the mirror? The one glinting in the sun? That's her silver angel I bought her years ago. I bought one for each of us in remembrance of our mother. You've still got her car, check it. And incidentally, if I brought more footage of that other Tahoe following my sister, would it really matter to you? You're already discrediting this one."

He lifted his hands in surrender, "I'll watch it, Savannah. Calm down."

She hit the play button. People on the screen began their treks back and forth to their cars. Georgia's driver door opened. The tape showed a somewhat fuzzy but still recognizable image of Georgia climbing out and marching into the store. The second Tahoe rounded the back of Georgia's, parked beside it then a woman about Georgia's height, same hairstyle and length and dressed in jeans and a pullover, exited then crouched between the two cars.

"See what she's doing?" Savannah lilted. *The same thing Matthew did to my car, that's what. To lure and trap me and this woman's doing the same thing to Georgia.*

The woman removed an object from her purse then plunged it into her own vehicle's right front tire. Adam watched the front end sink, askew, as the tire deflated. His eyes cut to Savannah, "I admit it appears the woman sets up the meeting with Georgia but it's a far cry from planting a murder weapon."

"The towel with the knife in it. Was it pristine or did it have smudges on it, like someone with dirty hands touched it?" She let the video play while speaking, "Georgia said the woman's hands were filthy from handling the tire and jack. And have you checked the towel for hairs, fibers? I mean the *inside* of the towel where the knife was found, nothing that transferred from her carpet onto the *outside* of the towel because we all expect that to happen, don't we? Whether my sister touched the towel or not."

"We're not stupid, Savannah. Of course forensics is checking the towel and I'll personally note whether the outside appears soiled with, what was it again? Filth?"

Her jaw clenched at his smartass tone. He watched her bow up at his lecture and crossed his arms, "Despite what you believe, we're not trying to frame Georgia. All the evidence points to her."

"Then thoroughly investigate the case and don't be misled by the obvious. That's how innocent people end up in prison." She turned back to the video, fast forwarded to see Georgia talking to the mystery woman about her flat tire. The two got into Georgia's Tahoe, the video showing the shadow of the driver reaching to buckle up however, the passenger didn't move. Georgia started backing out then stopped. Savannah remembered her sister's words – *when I turned to look behind me there was a truck backing out so I waited. I heard her moving around so I turned to her. She leaned back, saying she put her purse in the floorboard...*

On screen, the passenger bent forward for a second then straightened in the seat. That's when she planted the knife, Savannah told herself.

Adam's impatience intensified. He rubbed his forehead, "This only proves the woman deflated her tire and that Georgia gave her a ride."

Ignoring his constant pessimistic viewpoint, she sighed, "I'm going to the orchards to talk to Ray and hopefully his son. In the meantime, could I see the knife?"

"I'll get it but Savannah, it won't help Georgia's situation." Opening the door, he offered a sympathetic frown, "Remember, we found only *her* fingerprints on it."

How could she forget? Inspector Sunshine wouldn't let her if she tried. It was the biggest obstacle in this whole disaster, the most concrete as far as evidence went.

Adam returned with a photo. Confused, Savannah asked, "Where's the knife?"

"Owen's here. He was already suspicious of me grabbing a photo of it." He handed her the glossy 8 X 10.

A white bloodstained towel lay open beside a red handled folding knife measuring 6 ½ inches (according to the ruler beside it), its blade open to reveal the blood smeared blade. Savannah's heart sank. One, because she couldn't see if the towel's exterior had been soiled with grime and two, because she recognized the well-worn wooden handled, hawkbill bladed knife. She and Georgia both grew up with those knives in the orchards, held one, used one. What made the grafting and budding knives at their orchards so unique – Ray Slocum engraved them all to read *Prince Orchards* for ID purposes. In the photo the photographer arranged the knife so that *Prince Orchards* shined for the world to see –

and to help convict the Prince Orchards heir whether she was guilty or not.

"That's a grafting knife, right?" Adam asked, already knowing the answer.

Duh, her sour expression said. "Yes, and I see how neatly our family name is presented in the photo. So the jury can pitch my sister to the farthest reaches of the prison."

Adam ignored the slam. "If you want me to believe that woman in the video killed Carlisle then you tell me how she got a grafting knife from Prince Orchards. Until we get that knife in the other woman's hand and explain how *her* prints aren't all over it, *and* find her motive for killing Carlisle, I'm afraid Georgia is still our suspect."

"Where on the knife did you find her prints?"

He pressed a finger near a rivet on the handle , "Here," then on the smooth wooden butt, "and here."

"But no prints in the blood?"

"Forensics couldn't recover any discernible prints, no."

"Just these two places," she pointed to the spots he had, "where there's no river of blood. There *is* the distinct image of a hand in Matthew's blood but *no* prints from that hand." Pardon me but, "Doesn't it look obvious someone wore gloves to handle this knife?"

The door to the interview room opened. Owen Dunne's complexion matched the color of his blazing red hair. Hands on hips, he zeroed in on Savannah, "What are you doing here, Detective?"

His stance verged on ludicrous. He may have outweighed her but she stood at least four inches taller than him, plus her notorious temper could whip his two-bit tantrum whimpering off into a corner. She refused to be bullied, especially by the likes of little Owen Dunne, "I think you know."

He stepped aside, pointed at the exit, "Get out, Savannah. You're interfering with my investigation and I'm not above tossing you in a cell just to keep you out of my business."

Savannah stalked toward him, hoping Dunne read the violence in her expression. Adam's hand went to her elbow but she slung it off, "Georgia is *my* business, Owen. You jail me for helping her and I'll dent your nose with my knuckles. Got it?"

For all his bluster, her threat hit home. He pushed his shoulders back to hold his ground but she saw the flicker of fear in his eyes when he replied, "I'll have you escorted out if you don't leave."

Adam captured her arm again, this time the fingers cinched securely around the tensed bicep. Her face contorted in an all-consuming anger at Mr. Dunne, "Daddy was *so* right about you," she accused without elaborating. "I'll leave but you try to railroad Georgia and I'll lay you out, you little twerp."

28

NOW

The Charger purred along the highway. That and the rhythmic feel of the car gliding over the road pacified the raging beast inside her, the one yearning to sock Owen Dunne in the schnoz. She'd like to see him *try* to lock her up. Honestly, he might give it a go and it would probably work since the sheriff was on vacation. She'd left messages with Bobby to call her but not heard a peep from her cousin, making her wonder if he'd jumped off this familial Titanic too.

She gave Adam Rafferty a shred of credit. Besides preventing Owen a busted nose and her a set of bruised knuckles, he decided to tempt fate and join her on her excursion to the orchards. Owen nearly had a stroke, Adam said, when he bailed out the door to catch Savannah before she sped away.

At first she refused his request to accompany her to the orchards. Hurt feelings and a smarting ego combined with good old fashioned rage kept her from unlocking the passenger door for Adam. He'd basically said she was grasping at straws before Owen the redheaded idiot bounded into the room. One sentence changed her mind. Adam's beguiling

James Garner features stared at her through the driver's window and four heartfelt words fell from his lips. *Let me help you.*

In that brief instant he reminded her of the Adam Rafferty she dated years ago. She pressed the unlock button, seeing Adam race for the passenger side before she changed her mind.

"Thanks for coming with me," she told Adam. "I figure about now Owen's campaigning to sever your employment status."

"As thanks you can pay my rent and child support until I find another job," he joked. "Know any malls hiring security guards?" He waved off her comment, "Owen's upset that you don't trust him."

A plethora of scathing words filled her brain to describe her feelings regarding Owen. She settled for a generic, "He's surprised I don't?"

Driving down the highway to the orchards, she noticed Adam faced front without a hint of glancing at her. She eased off the accelerator, "Are you afraid of me too?"

Adam chuckled, "In the sense Owen's afraid of you? No. I remember how you work. Unless something's changed, you bluster until push comes to shove." Then he winked at her, "Though I did wonder if Owen had a plastic surgeon handy. A dent in *that* nose would be catastrophic."

An unexpected smile broke through. Adam's knack for humor rated in Ennis's neighborhood, to her at least. She retrieved her phone, thumbed through a few names then dialed Ray to open the front gate.

She disconnected the call, challenging Adam with a good-natured, "So you think you know me that well, do you?"

Rafferty leaned back in the seat, confident of his reply, "You're still the same headstrong woman that outshot the whole class in the academy. You don't look a day over twenty-two and you're as beautiful as ever. You sink your teeth into any assignment you get and don't let go until you get results. You haven't changed a bit."

She was pretty sure she had. A lot happened since their relationship ended. No one stayed the same, no matter how quixotic it sounded. And *not a day over twenty-two?* Yeah, right. She just laughed.

"Okay, laugh, but to prove my point, you're stranded on a deserted island and you could only have one thing. What is it?"

She shrugged one shoulder, "Easy. A boat."

"A-ha!" he exclaimed with a deliberate nod. "Of anything on creation you choose a boat."

It sounded like a compliment so she accepted it as much. "What would you choose?"

"You – and your boat."

"Technically, that's two things."

"But," he answered, "with you comes your boat so really it's one."

Savannah's grin broadened. Same old Adam. If police work fizzled, hustling or becoming a lawyer would serve him well. Of course in the grand scheme of things, there wasn't any difference in the last two anyway, she thought. She glanced at him and her smile faded a degree as Adam reached over, his fingers lightly stroking her hand on the gearshift, "I'd choose you with or without a boat."

O   O   O

Savannah swallowed the lump in her throat. His whisper-soft touch and suggestive gaze inspired a sudden shiver and sent a healthy ripple of guilt through her brain. Once the guilt subsided, she questioned why Adam made the bold move. He knew she was happily married or assumed he did but there was no mistaking the intention of his tender caress.

Her left hand gripped the steering wheel in a death grip. Anger replaced surprise as Adam's knuckles stroked her forearm. She leaned away, "Don't." Mr. Rafferty better lose that come-hither expression or else, her demeanor warned. Her marriage was perfectly fine, thank you very much, and Ennis was her one and only. No amount of sweet-talk, innuendo, or touchy-feely crap would change it.

Savannah cut her vision to him again. Adam's intense gaze caused her to squirm. She hadn't felt this uneasy since meeting Duke Shelton for the first time. The dominant intended to set her emotionally ajar and she had a feeling Adam Rafferty meant to also. *His* wife may have divorced him but Ennis's wife meant to stay married – and faithful. She didn't have time for this, she'd tell him and certainly no want for it either. The day's stress piled on anyway but dousing an old flame's intentions about broke the last strand of her civility so she changed the subject, "We're nearly there."

Savannah slowed the car, turned onto the entry road and drove through the open gate. Hopefully with Ray present, she doubted Adam would say or do anything out of place. The drive back to town, however, she dreaded like a back alley beating.

She parked in front of Ray's house. Adam bounded out, opened her door. Savannah took it in stride. After all, he'd always been courteous. She thanked him, and climbed out.

In the span of a second, Adam Rafferty braced her against the car, framed her face in his palms. His lips met hers in a firm, urgent kiss that shattered her already fragile composure. In that same span of time, her emotions flip-flopped from utter shock to utter outrage. She shoved him by the shoulders hard enough he stumbled three steps backward. "What the hell is wrong with you?" she demanded, swiping the back of her hand across her mouth, ridding herself of the kiss and his taste.

He grimaced while reclaiming his footing. He reached back, gingerly plucking the seat of his slacks from a yellow rose bush. She couldn't care less that he nearly tumbled into Ray's rose garden. It might have done him good, she thought.

Adam rubbed his backside then dared to approach her. She stabbed a finger at him, holding him at bay, "Don't come near me right now. Whatever you're thinking about me and Ennis, you're wrong. We are happily married *and we're staying that way.*"

Rafferty lifted hands to shoulders, a sign of admitted defeat, "I apologize. I got caught up in the past. It won't happen again." His wounded ego emerged in his tone. He eased by her, keeping distance between them, "I promise, Savannah. I got the message."

"That's good because I'd hate to remind you. You might lose teeth next time." She glanced at Ray's door. The curtain in the *open* front window fell into place. Oh great, she pursed her lips. Ray saw and heard it all.

The door swung open. Ray tottered onto the porch with cane in hand. He focused on Adam then her. No smile. No hello. He stood there the way R.J. would if he'd seen the kiss moments earlier, except Ray let his eyes do the talking, not his fists.

The painfully bright sun baked her to the bone in those few seconds, with perspiration forming on her brow and her complexion already burning from guilt, anger and embarrassment.

Savannah shielded her eyes while climbing the stairs to the cooler shaded porch. She shored up her courage, waved half-heartedly, "Hey, Ray."

"Hello, young lady." He braced his back with his hand, approached the porch's edge, zeroed in on Adam. "Everything okay?" The question indicated everything was certainly not okay, at least with him.

She and Adam both realized who he spoke to so she replied, "Everything's fine. How about you?"

"This ol' back says it's gonna rain," Ray said, his posture and expression losing their stiffness. His brow sank with displeasure when Adam joined Savannah on the porch.

Savannah moved aside a step, claiming space between them. Ray's disapproving frown focused solely on Adam, not her, but the shame delved straight to her heart because he'd witnessed the blatant, unwelcome kiss.

Ray poked his cane at Adam with a strict, "Give her some room, boy."

Adam's brow shot up, startled at the dressing down but he stepped back as ordered. Ray's eyes tightened and she sensed pain was not the reason. He leaned onto his cane, "Never crowd a lady else she might take offense. Cause I guarantee her husband will." His heavily lined face broke into a smile at Savannah, "Now what can I do for you, young lady?"

Unless Adam developed a terminal case of the stupids, he'd behave around Ray Slocum. She motioned to the old wooden rocking chair behind him, "Sit down, Ray. Rest your back then we'll talk."

The rocking chair groaned as his weight settled into it. He used his cane to point to a white wicker chair across the way, "Pull that chair closer, girl. Sit a spell."

Savannah shook her head, "I would but I can't stay long. Ray, this is Richmond County Investigator Adam Rafferty. Adam, Ray Slocum, manager of Prince Orchards."

Adam extended his hand to him then quickly retracted it once the title Richmond County Investigator registered with Ray. The older man looked Adam up and down as if he suffered a flea infestation then turned his frustration on her, "Now why you bring him here?"

She began wondering the same thing after Adam subjected her to his outrageous and inappropriate behavior. Why indeed had she made such a foolish decision?

Ray continued, "Those folks done ripped up the property and arrested sweet little Miss Georgia." Disgruntled, he snorted at Rafferty, "Her picture on the front page of the paper thanks to you. No account skunks."

Savannah tried to feel bad for Adam but put little effort into it, considering that scene at the car minutes earlier. "Ray, calm down. I'm trying to find evidence to clear Georgia of the murder charges. Adam said he'd help me."

Ray shook his head, preaching, "Girl, you're smarter than that. They ain't out for no one but themselves." Ray's vision flicked to Adam with a skeptical, "So you working with Miss S'vannah to clear her sister's name, are you?"

Ray's accent deepened with stress, much like Georgia's did. *Clear* emerged *clee-ah*, and *sister* as *sista*.

The nickname provoked a smile from Rafferty, "Miss Savannah?"

She chose not to acknowledge his show of humor. Instead, she asked if Marcus returned from Valdosta yet. Ray shook his head, "It'll be this afternoon 'fore they get back. Shanise's mama needed work done on her washer so they'll be late getting home. I'll have him call ya when he gets in town."

She handed Ray the security photo from the front gate. It showed the unknown female gesturing to Matthew – a most unladylike gesture involving her middle finger. "This is a photo from the front gate just before Matthew was murdered," she told him.

Revulsion passed over his features, "Her daddy needed to whup her as a young 'un. Ain't no call for that behavior. She didn't act that nasty 'round me."

Around him? He'd met the woman?

Adam asked the question, "Around you?"

"I thought Miss S'vannah was askin' the questions," Ray snapped.

Rafferty waved his hand to her in a grand *if you please* gesture.

She took the hint, "When did you talk to this woman, Ray?"

"Last week it was. She came in the back entrance, sayin' her dog ran into the orchards. She wanted to look for him so Marcus and me helped her. Never did find that rascal."

She cut her eyes to Adam, "She came in the back entrance where the red barn is?"

Ray nodded, "Yes, ma'am. She even searched inside the barn for her dog."

Now she turned to her colleague, "There's *opportunity* for grabbing the murder weapon. Ray, where do we keep all the grafting knives?"

"In the red barn. We'd lose those little devils all the time if we didn't keep 'em there."

She asked, "You saw the woman exit the red barn?"

He tapped a bony finger to his temple, "With my own eyes I saw her. These old peepers ain't what they used to be but they saw *her* comin' outta that barn holdin' her purse and no dog." His eyes narrowed at Adam, "How do you like *that*, Mr. Po-liceman? Or are you gonna call me old, blind and feeble?"

Adam took it in stride, "I wouldn't dare to, Mr. Slocum."

The older man gave a stern nod, "Cause I remember thinkin' how that girl resembled Miss Georgia from a distance. She was close but ain't no lady as pretty as Miss Georgia," he winked at Savannah, "'cept for her sister here."

Savannah's face heated with a blush. Ray could charm the birds from the trees.

"I completely agree with you, sir," Rafferty slanted her a sly smile that put her on edge.

 Ray's lip curled, "Who asked you to?"

 Savannah interrupted their spat, "Ray, Owen Dunne thinks this woman *is* Georgia."

 Ray's mouth dropped open in disbelief, "Good Lawd, how ridiculous. Miss Georgia's got class. She'd cut off her own hand 'fore tossing that hateful hand gesture to anyone." He gave another snort, "Po-lice got it all wrong *again*." He tapped the photo, challenging her colleague, "If that's Miss Georgia, I'm Hank Aaron."

 "The murder weapon was a wooden handled grafting knife from the barn," she continued. "They said they found Georgia's fingerprints on it."

 "'Course they found 'em. She's handled every grafting knife in there. Her favorite is that trusty grafting knife I've had for fifty years. That's a quality tool. Made with a wood handle, not this plastic they have now."

 "Where was the knife when you saw it last?"

 "On the bench where Miss Georgia left it. It was odd, though. I noticed it gone after that woman came looking for her dog."

O O O

Savannah wished exonerating her sister was the only subject on her mind. A growing undercurrent of anger mixed with confusion overrode that goal. Adam sat beside her, stone quiet. He'd done so all afternoon. After leaving Ray, she and Adam spent the remainder of the afternoon scouting more witnesses to corroborate Georgia's story. They dropped by Vallarta's Mexican Restaurant across the lot from Publix then Starbucks and three other places. Everywhere they stopped turned up empty on witnesses or leads. The lack of progress and the uneasiness between the detectives extended an already arduous day.

The two called it a day at five forty-five. She was tired, hungry and wearing off the whole lousy day of fighting off cops trying to railroad Georgia and one trying to test the bed springs with *her.*

For the last couple of nights she practically worried herself into a rash about Ennis's impression of hers and Adam's past. Rafferty stoked a dangerous fire by over-exaggerating their relationship and building it into a sweaty, horizontal one. Savannah thanked God they hadn't considering Adam found Amy What's-Her-Name and married her instead.

She stopped for traffic before turning onto Walton Way, took a moment to stretch her back. Once she settled in at home, she'd call Justin Davis and give him the trifling bit of information she'd gathered that day. She planned on speaking with Marcus when he called then retiring early for an equally early morning. She'd travel Georgia's route from the orchards to look for business and traffic cameras. Tonight she was just too tired and disheartened.

"I'm sorry for this afternoon," Adam apologized. "I swear I'm not trying to cause trouble in your marriage."

Funny, it kinda felt that way at the time. Traffic cleared and she made solid eye contact before venturing onto the thoroughfare, "Ennis and I love and trust each other too much for that to happen."

"The second I saw you, all those memories flooded back. We did have some good times together back then."

"Yes, back then we did," Savannah made sure to stress the *back then* part. She pushed the speed limit on Walton upon seeing the sheriff's office come into view. *I want to go home. I want to kiss my husband and hold my baby. I want this day to end.* Before facing Ennis, she needed to collect herself and erase Adam's unwelcome, unsolicited attention from her already chaotic mind.

Adam spoke again, "Please don't let my stupidity make it awkward between us. I'd hate to lose you as a friend."

"Then do right by Georgia. Work harder to find this woman that's framing her." She pulled to the building's entrance, stared straight ahead.

He climbed out, rounded the front of the car to the driver's side. She checked the car's clock. Five fifty-one. She needed to call Ennis and see how their day fared. She hoped it was better than hers.

Adam bent toward her, she retreated from the open window sill as a sign to back off. He didn't, "I'll do what I can to help Georgia, I promise." He hesitated a second before speaking again, "May I kiss you just as a friend?"

She considered his request. Judging by his demeanor, he regretted his actions so she capitulated, offered him her cheek.

His eyes closed, his lips lingering a moment with the kiss. *Even this simple platonic kiss feels like I'm betraying Ennis,* she berated herself. Her hands remained on the steering wheel, fighting not to grip it hard enough it broke. *Ennis could never find out.* She would not tell him and hoped Ray kept it to himself. She didn't have the energy to visit

Georgia *and* Ennis in jail.

Adam lingered a moment and when he separated, he whispered in her ear, "I wish I'd married you."

O O O

She checked in with Ennis, pleased that the situation at home seemed serene. No fights, arguments or anymore surprise arrests. They'd ordered pizza for supper so she decided to head to the nearest burger place to decompress from the day's disappointments and the Adam Rafferty fiasco.

Located on Walton Way (and a short mile from home), Olde Time Burgers sat in the middle of a mini-mall. The parking lot consisted of two rows stretching the mall's length, one row facing the business fronts, the other facing the street. Savannah pulled into one of two available spaces near the restaurant. The place was small and quaint but served ideal food that rewarded a person for surviving crappy days. A thick meat patty cooked to perfection and tucked between toasted buns and a compliment of lettuce, tomato, mustard and pickles. That and a large Coke were just what the doctor ordered.

A rush of cool air washed over her when she walked in, along with the delicious smell of burgers, fries and onion rings. The ambiance rivaled an afterthought with scant pictures on the basic white walls and to top it all off, none of the dining tables and chairs matched. She was used to the hodgepodge atmosphere but overlooked it because the food more than compensated for the weirdness. It was approaching closing time for the business so she hustled to the counter for her order, glanced at her watch and figured she'd have just enough time to scarf down the meal. The place already began emptying of customers by the time she brought her supper to the table. She was grateful for the peace.

She savored the delicious juicy burger – her first morsel of food since morning. The ice cold Coke tasted sweet and divine. Another bite quieted her hunger pains, slackened the tension in her shoulders. Halfway through her meal she decided she'd probably live instead of expire of starvation. She glanced out the door to see the sun sliding toward the horizon. She grabbed a sip of Coke, checked her watch. She wanted to be home before seven to spend quality time with her family.

"Excuse me. You're a detective, aren't you?" a woman asked.

Curbing a groan of discontent, Savannah placed the burger back on the open wrapper, leaned back to acknowledge the fact that yes, she was indeed a detective. Not a very good one, apparently, or her sister would be cleared of an erroneous murder charge.

In her late thirties, the woman stood around five six in height, had average features (but way too much makeup) and shoulder length raven black hair. She wore a pressed navy blue pantsuit, white blouse and dark blue flats. She folded her designer sunglasses, placed them in the small, stylish shoulder bag, "I hate to bother you but I noticed you and another detective asking questions at Starbucks about twenty minutes ago. I overheard you mention the murder at Prince Orchards."

The woman's initiative should have brightened her, given her hope. Maybe, just maybe she saw something to help prove Georgia's innocence. Adam's half-hearted promise to help and overall apathy, however, drained every ounce of hope from her.

Opting to reserve a modicum of energy for the drive home, Savannah sighed, dabbed the corners of her mouth with the napkin, "Do you have information about that case?"

"I was driving down the highway and saw something from a distance."

"Exactly what did you see from a distance?"   Probably nothing, the pessimist in her said.   This represented the cherry on top of her crappy day, another dead end.   But she'd listen to the woman's account anyway.   After all she'd tracked the detective down for some reason regarding the case.

Uncertainty crept into the stranger's expression as if questioning why she approached the gruff sounding detective.   Savannah observed a subtle change in her features.   The bold stranger admitted with a blunt, "I witnessed the murder."

Finally.   Something tangible.   Savannah sat straighter, squared her shoulders.   The detective offered her the seat across from her, "What's your name?"

The woman folded her slim frame into the ladderback wooden chair, "Alexis Lloyd.   I truly hate to disturb your dinner, Detective..." The statement trailed to a baited silence.

Savannah wiped her hands on her napkin, extended her right one to shake Ms. Lloyd's offered one, "Savannah Prince."

Lines trenched deep between Alexis's brows, "Prince?   Are you related to the woman arrested for the murder?"

Savannah did a mental eye roll.   Oh great.   Another roadblock.

Her gaze remained steady, unblinking, "I'm her sister."

Alexis drew back in a manner implying murder ran in the Prince DNA and she expected to be the next victim. "Actually, I should go." She rose with an apology, "I'm sorry for bothering you."

Yep, Savannah's brain taunted, another dead end and all because of your name. Well, as Seth so eloquently put it – whatever. Savannah's weariness trumped Ms. Lloyd's brusque behavior. Her back ached, and her head bullied her with a doozy of a headache if she didn't relax soon. Her patience level flat-lined, "If you're uncomfortable talking with me, try Inspector Adam Rafferty tomorrow at the sheriff's office." Yeah, she snorted. As if he'd care. His lack of enthusiasm spelled out the truth. The police had an easy suspect, and the perfect one. The ex-wife who'd already pulled a gun on Matthew months earlier. They had the murder weapon – from the ex-wife's orchards – complete with her fingerprints on it. They had video with a woman matching her description knifing Matthew to death. The woman who drove a green Chevy Tahoe. A gift wrapped case. No, the police didn't *want* to disprove their case.

Savannah returned to her meal but a nettling feeling stopped her in mid-chew. Alexis was staring at her. The piercing emerald gaze depleted the last of Savannah's composure. The detective swallowed, wiped her mouth again this time harder, "Is there something else you need, Ms. Lloyd?"

Alexis's aloof nature yielded to a more soft-spoken one, "Your name surprised me is all. If you don't mind," she motioned to the chair.

Savannah nodded, "Knock yourself out."

The woman eased back down, placing her purse in her lap, "I

promise to make it brief."

Savannah hoped so because the desire to go home far outweighed this bizarre dance.

"I don't know how this works," Alexis mentioned. "Do you take notes while I explain what I saw?"

Ah, nice. A subtle reminder. "I can do that, yes." She reached beside her for her purse. It took a moment to find her notepad and pen. She turned back, making sure Ms. Lloyd saw she was ready to transcribe the details, "Okay, shoot."

"I was driving down the highway, approaching Prince Orchards – that's your orchard?"

Savannah tried not to sigh. She opted for another healthy sip of Coke then replied as pleasantly as possible, "Our orchards, yes."

"I was driving along and saw a dark green SUV parked at the side of the road."

"Did you happen to see the license plate?"

"Only a D and M and a 4. I remember the letters because my first husband's initials were DM."

The mention of those simple letters and singular number stunned her. Her hand refused to write them down. This was definitely not a dead end. No, it was much, much worse. The tag on Georgia's Tahoe began with DLM and ended with 4. She rubbed her forehead to ease the pinging ache, "You're sure about the plate?" She grabbed her Coke, took a few swallows just to force down the acid rising in her throat.

"Yes. When I passed by, I tried to memorize the whole plate but could only remember that much. I approached the turn for the orchards and saw a man and woman arguing. I saw him push her and she stumbled backward toward the highway so I slowed down. I didn't want to hit anyone."

The grueling day gradually took its toll. Savannah rubbed her forehead again, her mind growing fuzzy from the long, stressful hours. Her muscles joined the chorus and she stretched her back, releasing a pent-up sigh. She focused on taking notes, not that they'd help. All Alexis did was pound the final nail in Georgia's coffin. "What else?" she asked to speed things up.

"By that time, I was drifting off the road so I corrected but when I looked back I saw the man lying on the ground."

The day reached such abysmal depths, she failed to see how much further it could sink. Savannah threw back another swallow of Coke. The evening swirled the drain and now a small wave of dizziness disoriented her. She took a bite of burger, figuring lack of a decent meal prompted the sudden downturn. Georgia always warned her of low blood sugar. Not eating regularly wreaked havoc on the body, she said. Boy, was she right. "Could you..." she stopped, closed her eyes a second to concentrate on her words. "Could you... repeat the partial... license plate again..."

"Detective, are you okay?" Alexis asked.

Savannah glanced up and her head spun as if she'd ridden the Tilt-A-Whirl at Six Flags. The sounds around her softened then abruptly sharpened, going to and fro like a ship tossed in a storm. "I need to go home," she mumbled, groping to stuff the notepad and pen into her purse. When she rose to her feet, she swayed, grasping at the small wooden table.

Alexis jumped from her seat, steadied Savannah, "Let me help you outside. Maybe you need fresh air."

"I... should call my husband. I can't... drive like this."

She reached for her phone but Alexis suggested, "Let's get outside and see if you feel better first."

Her mind clouded and through the fog she halfway remembered the feeling from when she drank. The heaviness of her legs and arms, the wooziness, the complexity of putting one foot in front of the other... But this felt different. She didn't experience the warm, mellow relaxation from when she drank. Nope, she felt flat-out, flying stoned.

Alexis retrieved Savannah's purse, slid her arm around her waist, "Hold on to me."

Savannah slung a limp arm around Alexis's shoulders. The woman's strength surprised her. For such a petite woman, she supported and helped her out of the restaurant without a grimace. Savannah tried again, "I really need my husband to pick me up. Can you call him for me? The number is—"

"I can take you home if you want." She nodded across the lot, "My car is over there."

They started down the sidewalk, passersby stopped, staring at the two. Savannah recognized the expressions from when she drank. A curled lip, scornful scowl, whispers passed among the onlookers. I'm not drunk, she wanted to declare. No, her brain said, but you're certainly not right either. Savannah's stability vacated her, her eyes refused to focus, her legs grew steadily weaker and liquid beneath her.

"I'm a nurse," Alexis said. "Did I tell you that?"

"No," Savannah muttered, not giving a crap if the woman was a nurse, a hot dog vendor or a trapeze artist. She just wanted to go home and go to bed.

"I work at Mercy Hospital in Charleston."

Charleston, Shmarlston, just get me home, lady. The vague image of her Charger wavered into view. She veered toward it but Alexis tightened her grasp, tugged her in the opposite direction, "No, my car is this way."

Savannah's knees threatened to buckle. Her brain spun into a hippie fantasyland where colors brightened to soft vivid hues. Whatever was happening, it was all new to her.

She held harder to Alexis who leaned in with a secretive whisper, "I have a confession. A couple, actually. While you were looking in your purse, I slipped a little GHB into your soda. Colorless, odorless and virtually tasteless. You'll be tipsy a while but it'll wear off. My *big* surprise is this. My name is not Alexis but I *am* a nurse at Mercy. Before that I was a nurse stationed in Iraq. My name is Rachel Gordon, but you always call me Florence Nightingale, at least according to Matthew."

Florence Nightingale. Matthew's fling. The bit of information twinkled like a star far, far away in the black velvet sky. It was there but she couldn't reach it. The fact she'd been doped registered a minuscule blip on her brain's seismograph. No big deal, it seemed to say. The drug wrapped her brain in a cloak of complacency, assuring her nothing mattered anymore, that she should relax and enjoy the ride – if she didn't throw up first.

Rachel led her to a black Highlander where she fished in her pocket for the keys, "I drugged you to get you out of the way a while. You're really screwing things up for me." She jabbed the key in the lock and twisted, "I'll explain the situation. You have two choices. One, you can let Georgia go to prison for killing Matthew or two, I kill her."

That hit home. In a clumsy, uncoordinated motion, she reached for her gun. She imagined the drug shaking its head at her as her trusty snub nose slid from the holster. The normally lightweight weapon weighed a ton in her hand. The sudden movement caused an uprising in her failing equilibrium, making her stumble sideways. *I told you so*, the drug taunted. *You better not do that again. FYI, you're not in control anymore. I am.*

Rachel confiscated the .38 from Savannah's loose grasp, jammed the gun back in the holster with a parental sounding reprimand, "Don't test me, Savannah. I've worked too hard for this." Rachel opened the passenger door, "Believe it or not I like you. You were the one person I could count on to push Matthew away from Georgia. He told me what happened in March, how you and your friend ran him out of town. I appreciated that."

"I did it for Georgia, not you," she slurred.

"I know but I got the benefit of it too – or hoped I would – but that bastard left me anyway," she sighed. "Now, it's decision time. Are you backing off the investigation or not? Before you answer, ask yourself this question. Would you rather visit Georgia in prison or put flowers on her grave?" She leaned to Savannah's ear, "Because I'll kill her the same way I killed Matthew. Seconds to live, no chance of survival."

The familiar tune "A Little Less Conversation" cranked up, the music and lyrics sounding like a distant AM radio station fading in and out. Finally, Savannah thought. Elvis to the rescue. Her hand moved to her belt to answer the phone but Rachel's got there first, "*Be still.*" She looked at Caller ID, "It's Inspector Rafferty." She thumbed the *off* button, placed the phone back on Savannah's belt, "Now he won't bother you."

Savannah heard traffic pick up along Walton Way. The local baseball team, the Augusta Greenjackets, had a game that night at Lake Olmstead Stadium and Walton Way was a thoroughfare to the ballpark. The usual sharp blare of car horns softened as if she buried her head under a pillow. She needed to flag down help, her mind advised in a moment of semi-clarity. She needed to call Adam and tell him about Rachel – and ask him to please get his ass there quick before this crazy woman did something worse to her.

Rachel cast a nervous glance around them, her bravado evolving to anxiety, "Get in the car."

"I can't."

"Yes, you can. Get in. I'm taking you somewhere you can sleep it off."

"Then take me home." *Please take me home.*

"You'll warn Georgia and I can't allow that. Get in." She strengthened her hold around Savannah's waist, "Lift your left leg."

Lift it? She could barely *feel* it. "I *can't*," she emphasized.

Rachel yanked the .38, gave it a covert push into her gut, "Can you *now?*"

Go ahead, shoot me. It's not like I'll feel it. She pulled at her leaden foot but the motion pitched her sideways and buckled her right knee. Her surroundings whirled and tumbled. *You're falling*, the drug sang in her system, *but don't worry, everything will be fine and dandy.*

Savannah collapsed to the asphalt, grateful for something solid to lie against. She still struggled to find balance, her fingers clawing at the pavement to get a better grip and stop the world from spinning.

A hand clamped on her arm to pull her up. Rachel pushed the .38 back in the holster, her eyes wide with fright as a couple of people turned, appraising the scene beside the black Toyota.

"Savannah!" a voice yelled from across the lot. "Is that you?"

Savannah recognized the voice and practically broke into tears. Not Elvis but Ray's son Marcus came to her rescue. She attempted to turn onto her side, saw the hefty black man in his mid-fifties sprint toward them. She reached out to him, "Marcus, help me."

Two strong hands hooked beneath her arms, lifted her effortlessly to her feet. Savannah wobbled while facing the round, friendly features of Marcus Slocum. Then she grabbed for his arm before she toppled once more.

Marcus brought her into his embrace. He looked worried and personally so was she. Things weren't right anywhere above her toes.

She was in the process of constructing a short sentence (which took enormous effort) when Marcus glanced from her to Rachel, "What happened?"

"She began feeling bad in the restaurant. I was going to drive her home."

Liar, Savannah said – or thought she said. *Liar, liar, pants on fire, you were kidnapping me, you mean, crazy lady.*

Marcus turned his attention to the woozy female in his arms. He leaned closer, whispering, "You drinking again?"

"No," Savannah swiveled her head side to side for emphasis. She instantly regretted it. *You know that's not a good idea*, the drug shook a finger at her. No shit, she answered back. She held tighter to Marcus, "Not a drop. Marcus, call the cops. She drugged me, she killed Matthew and now she's after Georgia."

"What?" He asked in a way suggesting she not only lost the ability to speak clearly but let her common sense get away from her too.

She lifted a feeble pointing finger to Rachel, "She drugged me with GHB." There, she thought. That was crystal and coherent.

Marcus glanced at Rachel who shrugged, "She wasn't acting sober inside the place. That's all I know."

He gathered Savannah closer, turned, and waved to someone in his car.

"Are you calling the cops or not?" Savannah worked hard to enunciate this time and it seemed to work. More strength drained from her body, leaving Marcus to lift her into his arms with a gentle, "No ma'am, I'm not callin' no po-lice. I'm gettin' you home." He nodded to Rachel, "You mind reachin' in her pocket for her car keys?"

Rachel handed Savannah's purse to Marcus then slipped her fingers in the front pocket of the detective's jeans, withdrew an angel key ring with several keys on it. The subtle smirk on Rachel's face angered Savannah – she knew the woman fooled Marcus into believing she was drunk.

A black woman with soft, amiable features and several gray streaks in her hair rushed to Marcus's side. One peek at Savannah and her eyes rounded, "My lands, what happened to her?"

"Shanise," Savannah formed the name carefully, "tell Marcus to call the cops. I know they're idiots but they're all we've got here."

Marcus's wife referred to her spouse for answers. He shook his head, "I'll tell you in a minute. I'll drive her home. Follow me in the truck." He hurried away from Rachel, readjusting his hold on the load he carried. "Savannah, you still awake?"

Her brain continued pinging S.O.S. signals for her friend to dial the police. The words never reached her lips. She barely nodded, feeling consciousness slide away faster.

"I know you're not drunk but I didn't want to spook that lady. Soon as I get you in the car, I'll call the po-lice."

Shanise leaned nearer, "Marcus, what's going on?"

"I recognize that woman from the orchard. Claimed she lost her dog. Daddy and me spoke how she looked like Georgia, even drove the same kinda Chevy she does. She changed the car she drives, her hair color and has tons of makeup on but that's her, no question. Now Georgia's arrested for murder and her baby sister's babbling nonsense. That woman did something to Savannah and boy, do I dread Mr. R.J.'s reaction. He'll hunt that woman down and kill her. Ain't nobody messes with his girls and she done messed with both."

Savannah curled her hand in his shirt to compensate for Marcus's loping gait.

He unlocked the Charger's back door, eased her inside, "Lie down now, girl. I'll drive slow so I don't rattle your stomach."

Savannah did as he said. He climbed behind the wheel then pulled his phone from his pocket. He dialed the police and just as she floated into LaLaLand, she heard him explain the previous several minutes and the fact they could find the mystery woman at Olde Time Burgers if they hurried.

"Rachel Gordon, Marcus. That's her name. It's Matthew's fling, the slut he slept with behind Georgia's back."

By his tone, her boisterous, slurring outburst embarrassed him, "Yessir, it's Rachel Gordon. Accordin' to Savannah that's the woman Mr. Carlisle had an affair with while he was married to Georgia."

"She's planning to kill Georgia," she announced, pleased with the surprising clarity. *Ha! Take that, you obnoxious drug...* "Tell your lousy police department to protect my sister!"

Marcus's tone sharpened, "Hush now, girl. You're makin' a spectacle." He returned to his call, "She says Rachel Gordon is out to kill Georgia. Said she told her that, yessir."

Her next statement melded words together so smoothly it sounded reminiscent of her drinking days, "Ican'tprotect*everyone*, youknow." She wrinkled her nose, "Someone *else*hastodoit." Then she remembered Rachel taking her .38, "Marcuswhere'smygun?"

"Your gun is on your hip," he replied.

"Areyousure?"

"*Leave that gun alone, girl.* You're in no condition to handle one." Marcus shook his head, said into the phone, "No, she's trippin' on the dope that woman gave her."

"YoutalkingtoRomanHandsRafferty? Tellhim–"

"Hush up, Savannah. You're outta your mind right now."

She heard him convey more information over the phone and after a few more exchanges, he clicked off, cranked the Charger's engine. The throb vibrated through her. She hadn't noticed the intense arousing thrum before. How had she missed it? The powerful engine's throaty rumble sounded aggressive, carnal. Sexual.

Oh God, she blushed. Heat flooded her face, traveling in a fiery wave past her navel. In the rational recesses of her mind, she questioned how a person experienced drowsiness, dizziness, nausea and a ravenous libido all at the same time. "Marcus," she called, "I'm horny. I need Ennis quick." Then giggled, "And often."

"*Oh Lawd*," he emphasized. "That girl musta given you a big dose of crazy potion."

Savannah closed her eyes, noticing how her body pounded in time with her heartbeat. The throbbing went to her toes and her fingertips which mesmerized her. Her body pulsed with the heavy concussions and sent salacious thoughts racing through her brain.

Her muscles went limp while her mind partied with colors and shapes. Meanwhile, south of the border, things awakened with profound sensitivity. The rumbling and vibration of the engine, the dips and bumps in the road all intensified the sensation, "This thing'll go faster than that, Marcus. Hit the gas. I need Ennis *now*." Memories of their motel tryst trickled in. A sensual moan poured from her lips, remembering Ennis's touch, his mouth, his...

"What're you doing back there?" Mortification laced Marcus's voice as he twisted to see her. "Whatever it is, stop it."

"Okay," she sighed, letting the visions retreat to her favorite corner in her mind. An overwhelming urge to sleep closed her eyes again. She laid back, feeling her heart gradually surrender its furious battle on her ribs. "Marcus, thank you for saving me," she mumbled.

"You're welcome, girl. We're just about home so you can rest and wear off that potion."

Consciousness toyed with her, slipping in and out. Her eyes rolled back, her brain succumbing to the drug's relaxing effects.

29

NOW

Ennis seethed over Ray Slocum's call. The orchard manager hemmed and hawed, going so far as to question his decision about dialing Ennis's number. In the end he confessed to what he witnessed, following it with a proud declaration that Miss Savannah cleaned Rafferty's clock by shoving him into a thicket of rose bushes. The cop deserved more than thorns in his heinie, Ennis fumed then turned his attention to R.J.'s shotgun leaning in the entry corner. He see-sawed between plugging Adam or perhaps beating him to death with the long barrel gun.

Instead he dialed Savannah's cell. She called earlier saying she dropped by Olde Time Burgers for supper. By his watch she should have been on her way home by now.

His brow furrowed when the call went to voicemail. She'd turned off her phone but why?

A jarring collision thrust Ennis forward. He stumbled as R.J. muscled past him mumbling, "Out of my way."

Georgia trailed behind her father, begging him to stay home.
The same argument raged for the past thirty minutes.   R.J. insisted on
leaving the house for his favorite haunt, a bar several blocks away. With
Rafferty after his wife and R.J. depleting his patience, Ennis rounded on
the older man, "R.J., the cop's will haul you in the second they see you
drunk. Stay here."

R.J. bristled, "You gonna make me, boy? I need peace and quiet.
This house – *my* house – has been a circus since ya *all* loaded in here. I'll
come back when you're gone." He searched the entry table drawers for
his truck keys. He'd done it twice now which made Ennis think of the
definition of insanity. R.J. would keep doing the same thing over and
over expecting different results. The location of the keys was a mystery to
everyone because Savannah secreted them away where no one could find
them, not even Georgia. The lack of transportation failed to quell the
man's desire to leave, however. He'd walk to the damn bar, he'd said.
Anything to get peace.

Georgia about-faced to the kitchen with a frustrated sigh and
mumbling about her father's pigheadedness.

Ennis followed R.J. to the front door, volunteering, "I'll go get
your scotch."

R.J.'s eyes narrowed, "Y'know, I don't know how Savannah puts
up with ya. You nag like a woman." He threw open the door, and
practically ran into Marcus Slocum.   His stocky frame cradled an
unconscious Savannah against his chest.

"What the hell," R.J.'s voice trailed off.

Normally Ennis appreciated their father's silence but witnessing the surreal sight he too found himself speechless. Staring at his wife lying limp in the man's arms sent him reeling.

Marcus transferred her to R.J.'s waiting arms while explaining the events in detail. He handed the purse and car keys to Ennis, "I drove her home. Shanise is waiting for me in our truck. I'm meeting with an Inspector Dunne shortly. I'm gonna tell him everything. Rachel Gordon gonna pay for what she done."

"What happened?" Georgia rushed to her father's side with Leah, Seth and Dane right behind her.

"Rachel Gordon?" Seth asked.

Georgia answered without the vehemence Ennis expected, "Matthew's fling. What did she do?"

Marcus swiped a hand across his forehead, pointed to Savannah, "She drugged your sister. Savannah said it was RBG, GRB, or whatever it's called."

Leah's eyes widened, "GHB? Why would she use a date rape drug on Savannah?"

Marcus shrugged, "She used something mighty potent on her cause she been acting crazy the whole way home. Acting plumb ridiculous. But she said Rachel Gordon admitted to killing Georgia's ex-husband and is coming after Georgia next. That part didn't sound crazy."

R.J.'s back straightened, his jaw set, "She comes near my kids again, I'll plug her. Boy," he called Seth, "get my shotgun."

"Pops, let's get Savannah help," Seth suggested. "She doesn't look very good."

R.J. stepped past the group, started for the stairway, "Marcus, you tell that detective everything Savannah said then you tell him he'd better protect both my girls." He hugged his daughter closer, "My poor baby. I'll get you to bed."

Dane watched their father walk away. He turned to Seth, incredulous, "By the looks of her, she needs a hospital."

Seth lowered his voice, "Probably but it'll take us all to get her there. Pops won't let her go. He believes anyone who goes to the hospital will die there. I'll get Leah to look her over first."

"Mr. R.J.," Marcus called. "I'd like to know how Savannah does."

Georgia answered for her father, "I'll let you know, Marcus. Thank you for your help."

Marcus nodded then leveled a piteous frown on Ennis, "Boy, you're in for it when she wakes up."

Ennis measured everyone's reaction. What, exactly, did that mean? Marcus didn't offer an explanation so Ennis asked him.

Marcus pulled a hanky from his back pocket, mopped his face and neck, "You better have more stamina than a jackrabbit on the Blue Pill."

Oh... *That's* what he meant. Well, at the current time sex appeared rather unlikely considering her unconscious state. He just hoped she was okay and if it took a squad of SWAT officers to drag her from R.J.'s arms to the hospital, so be it.

Ennis watched as R.J. ascended the stairs, his stride strong and steady as if completely sober, his voice soft and tender while he spoke to his youngest daughter.

The change in R.J. Prince astounded him as completely as seeing Savannah passed out in Marcus's arms. R.J.'s strength and stability never wavered as he climbed the staircase with smooth, fluid steps. Ennis knew the man was strong as an ox and could beat a man into submission or a coma within minutes. The gentleness he used with Savannah was unreal.

Everyone followed him upstairs. By the time R.J. reached the top of the stairs, Savannah stirred, her voice meek as a child's, "Daddy?" The words dripped like thick molasses, "What're you doing here?"

The question produced a rare whimsical smile from R.J., "I live here, remember?" Then he assured, "Marcus told us what happened. Don't worry, baby. Daddy will make it right." He stood beside her bed, motioned for Georgia to pull back the covers.

"Where's Mama?" Savannah asked. "Is she here?"

R.J. eased her onto the bed, "Mama's not here but the rest of us are."

"She's not making sense," Dane hinted. "Isn't that something to worry about?"

He posed the question to Leah who examined her incoherent sister-in-law, "Confusion and hallucinations are common on GHB. At least she's awake. That's encouraging."

Savannah's eyes open to slits, "Tell Georgia that Rachel Gordon killed Matthew. And tell her to stay safe. Rachel's out to kill her." Then her eyes drifted shut.

R.J. smoothed her hair back, placed a gentle kiss on her forehead, "I'll tell her. Rest now, baby."

Ennis leaned down, plucked the .38 and holster from her belt, followed by the cell phone. He unbuckled her belt to remove it when her eyes opened. The azure pools sparkled at the sight of him. "Ennis," she breathed, wrapping a hand in his shirt, the other in his hair. She pulled his lips to hers in a deep passionate kiss.

"Whoa," Dane blurted. "Keep it G-rated, Peach. There are children in the house."

Surprised by Savannah's boldness and embarrassed that all except Lindsey witnessed the fiery French kiss, Ennis tried to separate and after several moments of trying, finally succeeded. His wife wasn't happy and frankly neither was his situation below his belt. Little Ennis wanted the action she promised. Big Ennis displayed a sheepish expression, "That was unexpected."

"For us all, bro," Dane released a long sigh. "Do we need to leave the room?"

"That's not funny," Ennis warned his brother.

"I'm not laughing either." Flustered, he pointed at her, "Look at her."

"Make love to me," Savannah moaned, grabbing at him, this time for his zipper.

Ennis's owl-eyed vision skipped to each person in a silent plea for help. He captured his wife's hand, held it in a gentle manner, "Not now, sweetheart." He turned to Georgia, "Why is she so adamant?"

Leah answered with an amused smile, "GHB heightens the sex drive."

Every part of him deflated – except Little Ennis. "So Marcus was right. I'm in for it."

Savannah fisted her hand in Ennis's shirt, tugged him to her until they were nose to nose, "Ennis Daniel Rutherford, do you love me?"

"Of course I do," he replied, hearing Leah and Georgia giggle like schoolgirls.

Savannah's free hand attacked his fly, unbuttoning the top button so fast it left him dumbstruck. "Then show me how much," she dared.

"Please don't show her in front of us," Dane deadpanned.

Ennis hurled a glare at him, "Do I look stupid?" He fought her greedy pawing, trying to remove her grabby hands from his zipper.

"What the hell's gotten into her?" R.J.'s lip curled with disgust. "Stop that, Savannah. Behave yourself."

For once Ennis agreed with their father. Before she embarrassed them both, he wanted to press the pause button, at least until he gained control of the situation – and his growing erection – but the feel of her hand brushing his crotch reinforced the futility of his efforts. He wasn't losing the battle, he was losing the whole damn war.

Frustrated, Dane scrubbed a hand through his hair, grumbling, "I can't take anymore unless Georgia'll join me in *her* bedroom for our own episode of this pay-per-view show."

Ennis's jaw clenched at his brother's smartass attitude. Like he actually *desired* to have sex in front of his wife's family, he wanted to argue. He halfway expected Seth to speak up but Savannah's brother stood in mute shock at his sibling's sudden wanton behavior.

Savannah smiled a dreamy, heavy-lidded smile. With her wandering touch and faraway expression, he wondered if her eyes focused. The density of her Georgia accent deepened, the clarity of the words drawled like thick syrup. Until, "Come on, Ennis. Bring your handcuffs." With a lusty grin, she bobbed her brow, "You can arrest me again."

Yep, he flinched. Clear as a church bell on Sunday morning.

"*Savannah Charlene...*" Her father warned, his temper shortening fast.

"Detective Rutherford," Savannah drawled seductively, "you need to strip search me again. This time I promise to resist so you can–"

Ennis covered her mouth, mercifully muffling the explicit description of her desires. Little Ennis wasn't so little anymore because as muted as her words were, *he* distinguished the gist of them. Beneath his palm she uttered words and phrases so foreign to her nature he questioned if that was his wife. Thankfully no one else deciphered her babbling – he knew this because no one fainted from outright shock.

His face felt alive with heat with what she requested, no, *demanded*, he do to her. He couldn't bear to meet anyone's gaze, "The cuffs aren't a bad idea. It'd keep her hands subdued at least."

"What'd you arrest Aunt Vanna for?"

Ennis froze at the sound of Lindsey's voice. He swallowed hard. Somehow the youngster snuck in while no one noticed.

Everyone looked to him for an answer. Georgia and Leah still appeared plenty tickled by his wife's antics. Seth, on the other hand, threw him a glare defining the term "pain and suffering" if Ennis breathed a word resembling the truth. Ennis stumbled for an acceptable answer and settled on, "Illegal use of hands."

Ennis's hand clamped tighter across Savannah's mouth to ensure their young niece didn't receive a crash course on sex education from her aunt's sudden risqué language.

He gracefully countered another attack on his zipper by seizing the offending appendage. The night would last forever at this rate.

Georgia barely curbed her laughter upon seeing R.J.'s simmering aggravation, "Daddy, it's the drug talking, not Savannah."

Leah tried in vain to hide her own smile, "She probably won't even remember any of this."

Ennis finally removed his wife's brash grasp from his waistband, "I think we'll all remember it just fine for her."

Hands on hips, Seth shook his head, "I don't know who the hell that is but it's not my sister." He ushered his daughter downstairs before she posed more questions.

R.J. stared at Savannah. "I knew your mama's crazy side of the family would show up in one a' ya. Now it's happened. My baby's gone nuts," he grumbled his way back down the stairs.

With the exception of the "crazy family" comment, Ennis wholeheartedly agreed with their father which, as anyone knew, landed in the vicinity of blue moons and lightning striking twice. Savannah *had* temporarily lost her mind or at least her modesty and inhibitions.

In those brief moments the color drained from Savannah's cheeks. Her hand flopped to the bed, limp. The lusty grin vanished. Her eyes, once semi-focused, threatened to roll back in her head.

"Leah," Ennis frantically waved her over, "something's wrong. She acted drunk before, now she looks real sick."

Leah checked Savannah's pulse, asking her, "How are you feeling? Any nausea? Dizziness?"

Savannah blinked, forced herself to meet Leah's gaze, "Yes." She tried to prop on her elbows, "I think I'm gonna be sick."

Leah rolled her onto her side, "Stay on your side and don't move."

But the instant Leah removed her hand, Savannah lolled back on the bed. Leah waved Georgia and Ennis closer, "Brace her or she'll aspirate when she throws up. Seth!"

Feet pounded up the stairs. Ennis swore only two seconds passed when Seth spanned the doorway, "What's wrong?" He glanced at his sister, "What the hell happened? She was fine, well, not *fine*, but… Hell, you know what I mean."

His wife assigned orders like a drill sergeant, "You and Dane handle R.J. in case we need an ambulance. Ennis will help if need be. I need Georgia with me." Leah switched on the desk lamp, directed the light toward her patient then bent to eye level with her, "Savannah, open your eyes."

Savannah struggled to keep them open. Ennis glimpsed at them. The pupils encompassed most of his wife's beautiful blue eyes. Holy shit, he thought, wanting to step back. "That can't be healthy," was all he felt qualified to say.

Leah didn't answer. She watched Savannah's chest laboring to rise and fall with each breath, "I don't care what R.J. says. The drug is peaking and she's safer at a hospital."

Savannah's eyes closed. She lifted a shaky hand to wipe the

growing perspiration from her face, mumbling, "Don't feel good."

"It'll be okay, honey," Leah assured in a calm voice while grabbing the phone. "We're calling an ambulance for you."

Ennis prayed Leah meant it, that she'd be okay. He'd track Rachel Gordon to the moon if Savannah suffered serious harm – or worse – from the GHB.

Punching in 911, Leah instructed, "Keep her awake if you can and leave her on her side. At this rate she won't even know if she throws up."

"What's going on?" R.J. barked. He, like his son, spanned the doorway with hands on hips, "What's she doing now? Stripping?"

The urge to belt their father escalated. Ennis's eyes narrowed while he balanced his options. Either way a fight brewed among the family – R.J. just hadn't realized it yet.

Georgia's concern dialed down Ennis's anger, "Savannah's in trouble, Daddy. Leah's calling an ambulance."

He moved to the foot of the bed, assessed his daughter's condition then, "Ain't nobody taking her to the hospital. She's sleeping it off."

"R.J.," Leah tried to reason, "GHB is a central nervous system suppressant. A person can quickly drop into a coma, have seizures or die. We don't know how much she ingested. *She* doesn't even know that. Plenty of people die when left to *sleep it off.*" She stopped long enough to confirm the address to 911 then whimpered when R.J. forcibly wrenched the phone from her hand.

He disconnected the call, met each person's vision to put them on notice, "She ain't leaving this house."

Leah argued, "She's short of breath, her pulse is slow. She's showing signs of an overdose. She belongs in a hospital."

"Daddy," Georgia pleaded, "she needs help. Think of Lily. If anything happened to Savannah, she wouldn't have her mother. We know how devastating that is."

R.J. shot her such a scathing glare, she recoiled. Ennis read it as a warning to shut up, whether about hospitals or Charlene, he wasn't sure.

The phone rang. R.J. gripped it tight, daring anyone to reach for it.

Ennis told him, "That's 911 calling back because you hung up on them. Answer it."

He squared his shoulders, "Make me, boy."

Dane appeared at the bedroom door as R.J. reminded Leah, "You're a nurse, ain't ya? Why drag her to a hospital when we got what we need here?"

Normally a placid soul, Leah's patience dissolved with the asinine squabbling, "Because she might die, R.J., that's why. Do you want that? There's a chance she'll die because you denied her emergency care."

R.J. fisted his hands, stepped closer only for Seth to step between them. R.J.'s voice honed to a razor sharp edge, "Tell your wife to shut up, boy. I ain't sending my baby to no damn hospital. My wife never came home from one so I ain't sacrificing my child, not for anyone." He leaned around his son's shoulder, met Leah eye to eye, "You're the expert. Take care of her."

"Savannah's been to a hospital before and come out fine," Ennis snatched his wife's cell phone from the desk.   He dialed 911 but before

he engaged the call, R.J.'s free hand wrapped so hard in his shirt, he

ripped out a good amount of chest hair with it. The older man's features

evolved to one he'd never seen.   One that transformed from not-quite-

right to full-blown-crazy. Ennis finally grasped the depth of Savannah's

fear of her father when the older man warned, "You make that call and

Savannah'll wake up a widow. You understand me?"

Ennis predicted bloodshed before midnight at this rate.   R.J.

stepped over the line when he dictated Savannah's treatment – and lack

thereof. Ennis yearned to serve R.J. a generous dose of the treatment he

doled out to his "baby" years ago.   Before retiring each night, he was

reminded of her father's brutality with the marks on her backside and

lower back. R.J. Prince, the same man who came down on a person like

the right hand of God if they mistreated "his girls", also beat the hell out

of them as children. For years, Ennis dreamed of paying R.J. back with

interest. Tonight was the night. "My wife will be in an ambulance in

less than twenty minutes. You can either step aside while it happens or

be their next patient."

R.J. wheeled and headed down the stairs. Ennis tossed Georgia

the phone, "Call." His primary concern as he descended the stairs: the

shotgun. He wouldn't put it past R.J. to use it as furious as he was. He

remembered Savannah unloaded it earlier but had R.J. noticed and

loaded the shells back? And was her father hellbent on killing him simply

because he wanted Savannah checked by a doctor?

Dane and Seth both raced down the stairs along with Ennis,

apparently fearing the same thing. Seth rushed to grab the weapon. R.J.

jerked it out of reach, "Get the hell out of my way, boy. I'm ending this thing once and for all."

"Ending what, Pops?" Seth asked.

Ennis gulped. *Not my life, I hope.* Dane stepped in front of his brother, fists clenched, ready for battle in case R.J. tried shouldering the shotgun.

R.J.'s murderous stare intensified at Ennis while he held the double-barrel shotgun. To Ennis he seemed to weigh his options before taking action. Was repainting the walls worth blasting him away in the living room or should he haul Ennis to the boondocks to kill him?

R.J.'s hand gripped the weapon until his knuckles blanched. Seth blocked his father's path to Ennis, "Pops, give me the gun. We've had enough trouble for one week."

R.J. snapped around when Lindsey appeared at the kitchen entry. Dane waved her back with Seth instructing her to take care of Lily. The ruckus disturbed the baby and her wailing would, without a doubt, magnify R.J.'s temper.

Lindsey darted toward the dining room. The fear on her face reminded him of Savannah's on rare occasion. R.J. was a fierce man to face when enraged, he learned – and now the man wielded a shotgun...

Any other day R.J.'s death warrant in disguise might have given Ennis pause. Even as their father eyed him, he felt like a man about to draw his last breath. But today his wife needed help and he intended to get it for her no matter the cost. He set his jaw, prepared to defend himself to the best of his abilities. *Well, now's the time to test that "till death do us part" clause in the contract.*

R.J. lit up the room with a blistering string of obscenities hotter than brimstone.   He could cuss the paint off the walls and probably had once or twice.   He finished with, "You heard Marcus.   That woman who's framin' Georgia and drugged Savannah is still loose.   I aim to stop her."

"Then you're aiming to spend your life in jail.   Pops, put the gun down."

R.J. ignored the order, marched to the door and before opening it, told Ennis, "If ya haul my baby out of this house," he lifted the shotgun in one meaty hand, "I'll put some holes in ya."   He jerked the door open.

Adam Rafferty stared back at him, "Evening, Mr. Prince."   The inspector sounded rather cheery, "Where are you taking that shotgun?"

"None of your business."   He sidestepped Adam only for Rafferty to block his exit.

Adam extended his hand, "Give me the gun, Mr. Prince.   Don't make me call backup.   You will go to jail."

"That's all you people do – jail me and my family.   Ain't ya got better things to do," he shook the twelve gauge at Adam, "like find the woman who's trying to destroy my family?   Hell, Savannah even got the killer's name.   She's doing all your work for ya."

Adam pointed in the house, his tolerance exhausted, "Hand me that gun and get back inside now."

Only when Adam's hand moved to his holstered Glock did R.J. surrender the gun.   The inspector opened the break action shotgun.   His brow shot up, surprised and a little confused, "Empty."

Meanwhile Ennis released a long breath. For a moment, he'd feared R.J. meant to blast *him* to the moon, not Rachel Gordon. He took the offered shotgun from Rafferty, held it with full intention of hiding it in Savannah's closet, under her bed, or simply chuck it out a window.

"911 received a call from here," Adam told Ennis. "Operator said she heard arguing before someone hung up. I recognized the address so I dropped by."

"Seth's wife called an ambulance for Savannah. R.J. hung up on the 911 operator," Ennis replied, halfway grateful to see Rafferty. If R.J. got out of hand, Savannah's admirer could take the punch in the jaw instead of him. "Georgia called them back. They're on the way."

"Owen is speaking with Marcus Slocum. He told Owen what happened at the restaurant and the GHB. Can Savannah wait for the ambulance? We can run her to the hospital in my car."

R.J. rounded on Adam, "You gonna make me fight you too?"

"No, Mr. Prince," was the sighed reply, "there will be no fighting because this is happening whether you approve or not." He pointed upstairs, "Let's go get her."

On the way up the stairs, Adam furthered his conversation with Ennis, "Slocum said the killer's name is Rachel Gordon?" When he received a nod, he continued, "And this is the woman Carlisle had an affair with while he was married to Georgia."

Ennis nodded again, hating that it took his wife being Rufied before Rafferty believed Georgia was framed for murder. He kept his eyes straight ahead, not trusting himself to speak to Rafferty beyond simple answers. His brain flashed images of Adam planting a steamy kiss on Savannah's very married lips. The only thing keeping him civil – the fact Savannah shoved Rafferty into a rose bush for his trouble.

"I need Savannah's statement when she's feeling better," Adam mentioned. "I tried calling her cell earlier but it went to voicemail."

Ennis hesitated during his ascent. Call her for what, he wondered. The old urge to exercise his right hook kicked up until Rafferty expounded, "We found a green Tahoe two miles outside of town at an abandoned house. It had blood-spattered clothes and latex gloves in the center console. We're having the inside of the gloves analyzed for prints and I'm guessing they'll be this Rachel Gordon's. Also the car rental was from ATL Rentals, not A-1. Owen was on the phone with them when I left."

At the top of the stairs, Adam stepped aside to let Ennis lead the way. They walked into Savannah's bedroom to see Georgia sitting on the bedside holding her sister's hand. Leah checked the pulse and judging by her reaction, she wasn't happy.

"Evening, ladies," Rafferty greeted.

Both turned, their expressions evolving from concern to outright rancor at the interloper. Adam swallowed hard, "I see she's still sleeping. Let me call for backup and we'll get this in motion."

Georgia lashed out, "Get what in motion?"

"I'm transporting her to the hospital. I need backup in case your father gives us trouble."

She rose from the bed, her eyes narrowed, "And if he does – which he will – what is your plan, Inspector? Arrest him?"

Adam put hands to hips, "Calm down, Georgia. No one's being arrested. Not unless he pushes the issue with a weapon."

She crossed her arms, "I find it difficult to believe you, Adam. You were a nice guy when you dated Savannah. Hard to believe you're the same person."

He finally gave up, "Maybe I can redeem myself with you some day."

"Before she passed out, Savannah managed to tell me that Rachel Gordon framed me for Matthew's murder and she intends to kill me too."

According to his flinch, Adam felt every barb, "Georgia, I was in the process of assigning protection to you before the 911 call came in a while ago. Please give me a chance *and* a break right now. I'm worried about Savannah." He addressed Leah, "How is she?"

She shook her head, "Labored breathing, slow pulse, shaking. I don't know if it's an overdose or not but I'm not willing to risk her life with an incorrect diagnosis."

Ennis slid his arms beneath Savannah's shoulders and knees, lifted her limp form into his embrace. He thought of Lily and the chilling possibility of Georgia's earlier statement. He couldn't bear the thought of their daughter growing up without Savannah. It sent a shiver down his spine thinking about it. Visions haunted him of a young child in his arms asking where Mama was. Of her never personally knowing how much her mother loved her, not realizing that Savannah had a deadly serious side but a fun-loving, carefree one to offset it.

"I love you, Ennis," Savannah declared.

Her words emerging sluggish and viscous but he heard them all the same. Emotion rose in a tide, forcing him to push it away. He pressed a kiss to her hair, told her he loved her too, "Hang on, babe. We're getting you help."

30

NOW

Judging by the symptoms, the doctors diagnosed it as a medium dose of GHB. Nothing to worry about, nothing that time and hydration wouldn't heal. After thanking God for such good news, Ennis toyed with laughing. A medium dose, the doc said. Nothing to worry about. Well, Ennis wanted to say, tell that to his crotch. That doctor hadn't witnessed the results of a "medium, nothing-to-worry-about" dose. It turned her into a raving nymphomaniac. A very determined nymphomaniac. He hadn't recognized the sex freak that materialized out of his normally stable, straight-laced spouse. Ennis considered buying himself a chastity belt in the meantime, just in case the drug rebounded on her.

The doctor planned to monitor her for the night then release her by early morning. Ennis applauded the decision and not due to the change in her demeanor. It was the quick, drastic downward spiral in her condition. One minute, nympho. A minute later, passed out.

He wiped his brow, pausing when he heard her moan then smile. *Medium dose, my eye. She's loaded to the gills with that stuff.*

"Wonder what she's dreaming about," Georgia thought out loud as Dane took a seat beside her. He gave her a quick kiss, slid his arm across her shoulders.

What's she dreaming about? Probably sex, Ennis considered saying. Instead he toned it down, "Whatever it is, let's hope it doesn't include handcuffs."

"Ennis," Dane admonished, "don't paint me pictures I can't unsee."

Georgia chuckled at her fiancé's awkwardness, "Apparently, Ennis made quite an impression with her at the motel."

Ennis blushed, rolled his eyes, "And now the whole family knows."

"We're all human," she assured. "Daddy and Seth are the two that get touchy about sex talk."

"Don't forget me," Dane huffed. "I was there and I was touchy."

Georgia slanted him a wily grin, "You're in for a rude awakening when we get married. I'm the one that tweaked Ennis's plan."

Dane withdrew a bit, appraised her with shock – and a tad of awe, "You?"

"Yeah," Ennis replied, "so strap in tight because you got a wild ride ahead of you."

Dane pulled her closer, "Long as she's not nutty like her daddy, I can deal with anything."

The memory of R.J. Prince retrieving his trusty shotgun flashed in his mind. The prospect of his bloody demise still lingered like a bad omen. He rubbed the back of his neck, blew out a breath, "Man, your daddy is ferocious. He nearly followed through on that threat of making

Savannah a widow."

Georgia didn't dispute the fact. Her face told him how lucky he'd been that Seth was there to run interference. "He holds the hospital responsible for Mama's death. It about drove him crazy when Savannah had breast cancer surgery. You remember how drunk he was when he arrived at the hospital. That's the only way he can walk into one. So when we all ganged up on him – and that's what he considered it – we all walked away luckier than we could have."

Ennis figured he should have been a cat since he needed nine lives being around R.J. Prince. When he and Savannah partnered up, she never warned him about her screwy father. No, he plunged into the abyss by accident when her former partner, Terence LaVeau, sent her on a wild goose chase around the city, with his ultimate goal to throw Savannah off the tallest building in Atlanta. Savannah didn't always find trouble but it sure found her. Only an idiot would get involved with such a magnet for turmoil, he told his mama. But he'd done more than that. He fell head over heels in love with that magnet.

When Captain Josh Hunter informed him who his new partner was, Ennis flinched. Not *her*, he wanted to say. In his brief time in Atlanta, Ennis gathered copious amounts of information about the residents of his new precinct house in Zone 2, the Buckhead area of the city. A detective recently transferred to Zone 5 so that left two homicide detectives – John Mathis – forties, fat, brash and grouchy and Savannah Prince – thirty, ball-buster, "zero to bitch in 2 seconds". This was not looking good. Before meeting her, he prepared himself by imagining what that personality merged with that name, Savannah Prince, might result in. The name Savannah aroused thoughts of beauty. A trim, shapely figure and, he blushed to say, naked centerfolds. The ball-buster thing, well, not so much. She was probably ugly, short and fat with butch-cropped hair and a voice that carried to Canada.

The instant he laid eyes on his new partner, he nearly fell to his knees thanking God. The naked centerfold won out. Savannah Prince, no matter how bitchy, was a beauty and every cell in his body wanted her. When she spoke in that sultry bedroom voice, the space in his slacks vanished. When her soft, warm hand shook his, the firm grasp conveyed confidence and the smile she displayed only worsened his situation below the belt. Police work? Sure, he'd do police work. He'd clear her desk, strip search her, investigate every part of her in painstaking detail then bend her over her desk and have his way with her.

His first week, he waited for the bitchy part to rear up. She got cantankerous, but only with incompetent cops or stubborn suspects. To him, she displayed no symptoms of crazy-mad that the rumors warned of. She seemed normal enough, he told his brother Dane, and not insane at all.

He eased into trying to wrangle a date out of her. He offered to buy her a drink at the nearby bar. She refused. He suggested a walk in the park. Unless he was running the mile with her, she said, no thanks. Because after shift she changed into her running gear and drove to Piedmont Park for her evening run. Ennis did not run. He hated running so how about dinner or a movie? Maybe later, she semi-committed.

Ennis finally resorted to calling her sister Georgia. Savannah always spoke highly of her sister and respected her in all ways. Though he'd only known his partner a month, once he met her sister Georgia the two acted as if they'd known each other since childhood. She was easy to converse with, open about subjects and eager to pair him and her sister together. If his brothers were as forthcoming about him as she was about Savannah, they'd lose a few teeth.

What he needed, Georgia said, was a hook. Being from Texas, his first thought was a fish hook. He knew *that* was wrong. "What kind of hook?"

"She loves lavender and lilac. Maybe a few roses, chrysanthemums, things like that. A small bouquet can make a difference."

"No offense, but she doesn't act like the flower type to me." Hell, she was atypical from the word go. Why would a headstrong tomboy enjoy a bundle of stems and petals?

Georgia laughed, "Ennis, she's a woman. She loves flowers, especially from the right man."

She'd been right. Savannah gushed over the flowers – after she recovered from the shock of receiving them. He'd put a card with it reading "Dance beneath the stars with me." She'd agreed to a date that evening. No running, no delays, just driving home after work to shower and change and wait for him to pick her up – the latter he insisted on. He never underestimated Georgia again.

After he and Savannah finished their dinner out, they dropped by her place. She invited him in but forewarned him the only refreshments she had were coffee, juice, soft drinks and Yoo-Hoo. No problem, he said. He purposely avoided stating he wanted no drink but wanted *her*, as much as she was willing to give. If she gifted him with a kiss, fine. A tongue kiss, better. A naked romp, perfect. But his plans for Savannah went beyond a sweaty one night stand. He wanted Savannah for his wife which meant patience, as difficult as it was. She inspired lascivious thoughts of skin against skin, deep kisses and cries of pleasure.

The first thing he noticed upon stepping inside her small house: the subtle hint of lavender and Savannah. He drew in a deep breath and smiled.

"You can come past the entry," she joked. "I don't booby trap the place."

Ennis stepped into the living room. She kept the place nice and neat though not manically so. To his left sat a recliner and couch that faced a thirty-seven inch TV and DVD player sitting atop a glass stand.

The dining room was rather tiny with just enough room for the dark wood pedestal table and four ladder back chairs. The centerpiece: an arrangement of purple and white carnations. Boy, he thought, Georgia truly knew her well. He watched his partner replace the existing arrangement with his bouquet. She smiled, thanked him again.

The immaculate kitchen had an Italian flair to it. Maple wood cabinets, hardwood flooring, and small black granite countertops gave the room a rich, warm feeling that invited guests to come in and stay a while. She had an ivy in the corner that thrived from sun shining through the nearby kitchen window.

"Make yourself at home," she continued. "Remote's on the table beside the recliner if you want to catch up on the game."

"I'd rather spend my time with you," he replied scanning the side table she spoke of. Beside the TV remote was an issue of Southern Lady along with Georgia's latest book, already half-read. He picked that up, thumbed through it.

"I'll be right there after I put water in the flowers," she said.

He heard the water running and took that time to admire the landscape prints adorning the walls – all except the one with her computer desk against it. That nook was her personal space, where she hung family photos and drawings from her niece. He commented on how nice her place was while sneaking a peek at the current branches of the Prince family tree. In one picture, he recognized her and Georgia as teenagers. Another photo, this one of a family of four. A girl of four or five sat in her daddy's arms while the mother held a toddler in hers. He guessed the people were Seth and his family.

"The picture in the middle is of Mama and Daddy." Savannah's voice caressed him when she spoke. Since supper, the tone eased into a laidback velvety softness. A perfect sex voice.

She'd sidled up behind him until he felt her breasts lightly brush against his back. As she verbally labeled pictures, she leaned closer. Ennis stayed put, forcing her to crowd against him, her hand on his waist for balance. He pointed to another, "That you as a kid?"

She nodded, "I was gangly and had more than one awkward year as you can see."

"You were gorgeous then and now." And all legs then and now, he thought. Dancer's legs. Legs that he fantasized wrapping over his hips while they… Down boy, he berated himself and refocused on the photo.

He noticed both girls favored their mother, Georgia more so than Savannah but the resemblance was undeniable. "You look like your mother."

He felt her stiffen. Her hand withdrew from his waist, and she retreated a step. He knew he'd screwed up but he meant it as a compliment. Her mother resembled Rita Hayworth, the film star from long ago. Why wouldn't a woman consider that a compliment? "Did I say something wrong?"

Savannah turned from him and he noticed her dabbing a tear. He touched her shoulder, "Hey, I'm sorry. I only stated the obvious."

She refused to meet his gaze. In that short time, she steadied her voice, straightened her face, "She passed away years ago but I still miss her. Thank you for the compliment, Ennis. It really meant a lot."

He gathered her in his arms, held her snug. He expected an instant retreat but she returned his embrace, her curves molding to the contours of his body. It broke his heart to see her sad. He wanted to soothe the pain and sorrow from her face, and shift her mind to another subject.

He eased his lips to hers, still halfway expecting a shove backwards. One gentle brush and her eyes closed. No shove. Another tentative sweep. His tongue traced the fullness of her lips. Still no shove. Ennis dove in for what he planned to be a tender, slow, persuasive kiss. The instant their lips met, all reason abandoned him, as he kissed her with the devouring hunger of a long lost lover united with his soul mate. She relaxed in his embrace and in the recesses of his brain he high-fived his inner rogue.

Savannah buried her fingers in his hair, inviting more, not only surrendering to his forceful lip-lock but sliding and twirling her tongue in an intimate dance with his. Ennis met her stroke for stroke, his mind reeling with visions of them in bed, their bodies matching thrust for thrust, in the throes of boundless ecstasy. Oh Lord, he thought. If she made love with half the passion she put into her kisses...

Ennis slipped his hand from her waist to her breast, stroking the soft, plump flesh with his thumb. She rewarded him with a faint, low moan.

Savannah parted from the kiss, her breathing heavy, her cheeks flushed. She put a hand to his chest, "We'd better stop. I don't want you getting the wrong idea about me."

He found that funny, "Sugar, there is no wrong idea about you because you told me a million times how you'll never get involved with your partner. And you know what? I'll change that stubborn mind of yours. You and I are destined to be together."

Then *she* laughed, "We've only known each other a month. You can't possibly feel–"

He swooped down in another passionate kiss. long and demanding to show her *precisely* how he felt...

With one arm around her waist, he brought her close, surprising her. His mama would have shook her finger at him for the semi-rough treatment but Ennis fought for his future. He never felt so sure of anything except this. Savannah was his one and only, the one true love of his life.

Her house phone rang. Ennis figured fate really hated him.

Between Savannah's pigheadedness and all the interruptions, he'd be lucky to ever score another date, much less marriage.

She pulled back, forcing him to hold her to the kiss. He wanted to make a point with her, to convince her they belonged together. But when her hands gave a gentle push on his shoulders, he broke the kiss, suggesting she let the answering machine take a message. Besides, he thought, they both panted like dogs so answering a phone in that condition would certainly raise eyebrows.

She apologized for the interruption, but it tickled him that she remained in his embrace.

Her voice emerged on the machine's message. She greeted the caller then finished *you know the drill.* The beep sounded then a man's irritated voice blasted from the speaker, "Change that damn message. Sounds like your brother's machine and I hate *it* too." The caller sounded plastered, Ennis noticed. So drunk the words melded into scarcely intelligible sentences. "Are ya there? Where the hell are ya?"

Savannah wrenched from his arms and raced to the phone.

Meanwhile the caller leveled a threat, "If you're avoidin' my calls, I'll knock the shit outta ya–"

She answered the phone panicked and breathless, "I'm here, Daddy."

Daddy? That was her *father?* The man, or *Daddy*, had her scrambling for the phone without regard for her own safety. She'd missed bashing her foot on a dining chair by an inch.

Ennis shook his head. If anyone wondered whether Savannah Prince ever expressed fear, they hadn't heard – or seen – her react to her father's voice. And what was the man's problem? Ennis's father never spoke disrespectfully to him or his brothers and he certainly never used vulgar language with them.

While she spoke to her father in hushed tones, Ennis stood, rooted to the spot, unable to prevent himself from eavesdropping. She tried skirting the subject her father harped on, using carefully cultivated words to avoid Ennis from discovering the nature of the call. Except Ennis heard the gist of it, thanks to her father's powerful set of lungs. Mr. Prince got arrested for drunk driving.

He glanced at the small picture gallery again, this time with new perspective. He centered on the man with his hand on his young daughter's shoulder, a pretty girl who resembled both mother and older sister. In his quest for Savannah's heart – and her hand in marriage – Ennis prepared himself to one day brace this man and teach him some respect.

Savannah ended the conversation with, "I'll be there in two hours."

Ennis scowled at the man in the picture then turned, "What's wrong?"

She returned to the entry, re-equipped the holster, cell phone and badge, "Daddy needs me."

"Need help? I'm free."

She shook her head, grabbed her purse, "Thanks but he's particular about who shows up. Ennis, I hate cutting our evening short but I have to." She went to him, cupped his face in her soft, warm palms and kissed him. "I'm sorry about this."

When it came to Savannah, his brain worked overtime finding ways to spend time together. The perfect solution materialized, "How sorry are you? Sorry enough to have a drink with me tomorrow?"

She smiled, "Sorry enough to skip the drinks and dance beneath the stars with you..."

Ennis chuckled as he emerged from the memory from long ago. Peering up from his wife's face, he saw Dane's arm around Georgia. His brother had laughed when he told him his plans to marry Savannah. Accused him of not having *any* sense and her of having *too much* to visit the alter with him. Then Dane met Georgia. Ennis entertained resorting to hysterics just to pay his brother back. Problem was, like him and Savannah, Dane and Georgia made a perfect pair.

"Penny for your thoughts," Georgia said, snuggling into her beloved's embrace, held his hand.

Ennis stroked Savannah's hand then held it, "Thinking about our first date."

"Tell us about it," she encouraged.

Dane warned, "But make it G-rated, bro. My lady and me don't require the intimate details, if you get my drift."

Georgia elbowed him good-naturedly, "Leave your brother alone. It's his first date, let him tell it."

Ennis assumed, "I figured Savannah told you about it."

"Honey, my sister is a vault. She only told me certain details that revolved around how attractive, sweet and thoughtful you were. She left out the juicy parts and I want to hear *everything...*"

31

NOW

Her husband sounded a thousand miles away. Savannah floated in an almost magical haze where her body felt both leaden and weightless. The spinning kaleidoscope of vibrant colors behind her eyelids faded and her brain finally settled down.

She concentrated on pulling herself toward Ennis's voice, swimming her way from the depths of blackness to the sparkling surface above. To be with him again.

He told of a memory they both shared – their first date. His inflection rose and fell for emphasis when he spoke, the way a person did when they read aloud from a book. Except she *knew* the ending of that chapter. She drifted on the soft waves of his voice, rocking on the gentle tide, and remembered back…

Ennis Rutherford made it difficult to say no. For weeks she fended off his requests for a date, not that she really wanted to fend them off. Fate struck a cruel blow when Josh Hunter assigned the big handsome Texan as her partner. A whopping six feet two inches of brawny male stood before her every day, smelling of Irish Spring and exuding pure temptation. It certainly hadn't helped when he spoke either. That light drawl mixed with the sexy baritone resonated in her fantasies but also a part of her that she'd hung a "Closed For Business" sign on long ago.

The biggest drawback to getting involved with a colleague: it spelled disaster with a capital D. She'd heard the horror stories. No way, she promised herself, would that happen to her. Then Ennis Daniel Rutherford arrived straight from the Lone Star State, determined to break – no, demolish – that personal vow.

In the end she sold out for a flower bouquet and refused to feel one bit bad about it. After shift, she went home to shower and pretty up, secretly hoping the date led to a kiss or two. Nothing raunchy or too steamy, especially not on the first date. That might give Mr. Texan the wrong idea about this Georgia girl.

Ennis suggested an Italian restaurant for supper. Not one of those inexpensive quickie places that popped up around town lately, he said. No, he demanded a proper sit-down, full length meal, complete with stuffy waiters and real menus.

He picked her up in his Acura and once at the restaurant, opened the car and restaurant doors for her, pulled her chair out and seated her at the table. His gallantry got her thinking of Ennis on a horse. Not the white knight kind of fantasy but the cowboy who rode hundreds of miles through blizzards, rainstorms and marauding Indians just to reunite with his true love. How romantic, she shivered. Maybe just *one* ever-so-slightly steamy kiss, she decided. That wouldn't be so bad, would it?

She shook out her napkin, placed it in her lap, "People will talk," she said referring to their extracurricular time together. "You know that, right?"

"Let 'em. They have no idea how long and hard I worked for this date."

Savannah cocked a brow, teasing, "You still calling this an official date?"

Ennis winked, "Tonight is only the beginning. I predict one day we will get married and have three kids."

She had the glass of water in her hand and promptly sat it down before spilling it from utter shock. The cowboy strutted with confidence bordering on arrogance at times, didn't he? "I can say one thing about you. You're one hell of an optimist. Married with *three* kids? You plan on staying busy."

His eyes raked boldly over her, "Bet on it, sugar."

A delicious shudder heated her from head to toe, made her blush. This enigma of the male species confused, delighted, charmed *and* scared her. She'd fallen for sweet talk before. Let her guard down for a tender touch and passionate kisses. She'd believed the man's convincing words, earnest promises. In the end she regretted it all when her heart shattered with broken promises, lies and sometimes bruises or worse.

Ennis Rutherford seemed different. When she wasn't salivating over his good looks and muscular physique, his presence comforted her, made her feel safe. His warm brown eyes had a kindness about them, an honesty she'd not seen before in a man. Hmm, she thought. Perhaps two semi-steamy kisses were in order that evening – with the option of more at a later date. The Georgia girl wanted to impress the Texan, not come across as a tramp.

When they arrived at her place, she felt compelled to explain she leased the house and hoped to own it someday. She also felt compelled to do numerous things when in the company of Mr. Rutherford. Plenty revolved around plowing her fingers through that thick, wavy mass of hair he had. It begged her to, tempting her with its dark chocolate color and silky soft texture. At night she caught herself thinking about doing exactly that – and more – with her new partner.

For a month her dreams taunted her with lustful images of them naked, of Ennis atop her, inside her, driving her to the edge then...

"You cold?" Ennis asked. "You shivered."

No, she certainly wasn't cold. It was exactly the opposite. "I'm fine," she assured, embarrassed he caught her daydreaming.

He held the flower bouquet while she unlocked the front door, telling him, "I have coffee, sodas, juice or Yoo-Hoo. No beer or alcohol, sorry."

"Damn," he joked, following her inside. "I'd planned on drinking my Boilermaker from your belly button." He waggled his brow, "But juice will do."

A spontaneous grin brightened her features. She loved his sense of humor. His reaction to her "no liquor" statement relieved her concern. She'd never tell him about her battle with booze. Her past was humiliating enough without disclosing it to a man she fancied.

She sat her purse on the entry table, followed by her badge, holster and cell phone, "Make yourself at home. Remote's on the table beside the recliner if you want to catch up on the game."

Savannah veered off to the dining table, cleared away the vase of lavender and white carnations. Ennis handed off the bouquet and blushed at the kiss she placed on his cheek. "These are beautiful. Thank you again," she said.

She sat the wicker basket arrangement squarely in the table's middle. She could have presumed her partner's detective skills honed in on her preference for purples. On the color scale, purple outnumbered all other colors in her wardrobe. Logically, however, she guessed Ennis recruited Georgia for Cliff Notes on her. Since meeting Ennis, Georgia gushed at how much she liked him and what a fine gentleman he was, as if hinting to her sister that this guy deserved a wife named Savannah. Ennis commented on how thoughtful, smart and friendly Georgia was. Savannah nearly laughed. Of course Georgia was thoughtful. That was her nature. And smart? Absolutely. People learned quick that Georgia Prince wasn't all beauty. She possessed true intelligence and common sense and a heart full of love despite her wacky efforts to fix up little sister on blind dates and yes, Georgia's gentle disposition remained firmly ingrained unless someone threatened her or her family. Then the offender discovered a whole new, perilous side of the Steel Magnolia.

Ennis wandered to the back wall with her computer desk. He studied the pictures surrounding the central picture of R.J. and Charlene and their children. Savannah was ten in the picture. Ringing the middle photo was a picture of Georgia and Matthew, another of Seth and Leah and their two children Lindsey and Dylan, and other various photos of the family on special occasions.

She eased behind Ennis, put a hand to his waist as she leaned, pointed to the middle picture, "That's a picture of Mama and Daddy." She noticed his eyes drifted closed then opened again to focus on the photo.

"That you as a kid?" he asked.

She nodded self-consciously. Georgia inherited the looks in the family. Savannah considered herself okay, she supposed, but nothing as beautiful as her sister. "I was gangly and had more than one awkward year as you can see."

Ennis, ever the gentleman, commented that she was gorgeous even as a child and finished with, "You look like your mother."

The observation stunned her. After a lifetime of hearing how beautiful Georgia was, to be compared to her mother brought tears to Savannah's eyes. She turned away, refusing to let Ennis see her emotion.

His hand covered her shoulder, gave it a soft squeeze, "Hey, I only stated the obvious. I sure didn't intend to upset you."

She struggled to face him, assuring, "You didn't upset me, Ennis. I get very emotional about my mother. She passed away years ago but I still miss her dearly. Your compliment meant a lot. Thank you."

His arms enfolded her. She returned the embrace that felt so perfect she wanted it to last forever. His fingers massaged ever-so-gently along her lower spine. Besides his good looks and personality, Ennis's hands counted as a valuable asset. She could imagine those hands skimming up her bare thighs until they…

His lips feather-touched hers, bringing her from the dream. His lips swept hers again as if testing her mood. He probably feared a shove in the chest for his efforts.

She responded, lingering, savoring the moment and movement of his mouth on hers.

Without a word he seduced her, assaulting every sense, with a simple but powerful kiss. Savannah felt her inner barriers crumbling in this persuasive man's hold. The barriers she erected after enduring Toby Jackson, the ones warning her how disastrous, how devastating falling too fast for a guy could be.

A light brush of his hand on her breast penetrated the haze of carnal desire. It proved a challenge but she forced herself to reclaim her self-control. Sure, she wanted to proceed. She wanted him to sweep her in his arms and continue their evening in a horizontal position. But things moved so fast, she needed to apply the brakes and hunt down her morals again. After all, she reminded herself, this Georgia girl wanted to impress the Texan, not come across as a tramp.

She broke the kiss, her breathing heavy and ragged, "Ennis, we'd better stop. I don't want you getting the wrong idea about me."

He frowned like the idea was preposterous. He told her not to worry, that he remembered her vow never to get involved with her partner. But he announced a vow of his own, "I'll change that stubborn mind of yours. You and I are destined to be together."

Now look who was preposterous, she wanted to say. "We've only known each other a month. You can't possibly feel–" her declaration was cut short when Ennis descended on her with a soul-reaching kiss that weakened her knees and had her clinging to him for stability.

Ennis was a dangerous man, she warned the stupid-happy side of her brain. The one that begged her to thread those fingers through his soft brown hair, kiss him and plead with him to lift her in his arms, rush to the bedroom and make love to her.

As he plundered her mouth, she considered surrendering to Stupid-Happy – or pulling away. Stupid-Happy won. Her hands glided down his strong shoulders and arms. Every inch of the man's body spelled power but in his embrace she felt safe, protected and, well, cherished.

The phone rang, startling her back to reality. Inadvertently she'd fallen further under Ennis's charming spell, a willing victim to his seductive skills. She tried separating but Ennis snaked his fingers in her hair, held her firmly.

Another ring then another. Savannah's hands went to his shoulders, pushing gently as a sign to break the passionate kiss.

Ennis did. On a somewhat frustrated sigh, he reminded, "You have a machine. Let it pick up."

It was too late anyway. She kept her message short and sweet with a general greeting and *you know the drill*.

After the beep, a familiar voice blasted from the machine, "Change that damn message. Sounds like your brother's machine and I hate *it* too. Are ya there? Where the hell are ya?"

Stark fear flooded her. Adrenaline shot through her veins, as she broke free from Ennis's comforting embrace and bolted to answer the phone before her father said anything worse. She dared not guess what Ennis thought of her tearing away and scrambling like a mad woman just to answer the phone.

It was just as well, she tried telling herself. Things got

complicated the longer they kissed so the phone call served as both a curse and a blessing.

She grabbed the phone as R.J. warned, "If you're avoidin' my calls, I'll knock the shit outta ya–"

"I'm here, Daddy."

"Took ya long enough." He waited for the requisite apology.

Savannah turned her back to Ennis, lowered her voice to a near whisper, "Sorry. I was out of the room."

"Yeah, well, the damn cops brung me in again," he slurred. "When can you bail me?"

She rolled her fist, wanting to hit something so hard she broke it or her hand, she didn't care which. Of all the nights to be arrested. "Were you driving?" Say no, she closed her eyes begging fate not to be so damn hateful. *Say no,* please *say no…* Of course R.J.'s demeanor told her the unvarnished truth. Her night with Ennis was screwed to China. Her only consolation: memories of his persuasive kisses and the way his touch made her tingle in all the right places.

"What do *you* think?" R.J. snapped.

She rubbed her temple, "Daddy, drunk driving *again?*"

"Hey," he yelled so loud Savannah knew Ennis heard him, "are ya judgin' or bailin' me, girl? Get down here now or I'll call Georgia. She loves me."

He hurled the last three words as an accusation. He never called Georgia to bail him because of her propensity to lecture. No, good old Savannah always got the call. The daughter who showed up, shelled out bail money and kept her mouth shut… She yearned to shoot back at her daddy with that gold nugget of truth but this Georgia girl wanted to impress the Texan standing in her living room – the one trying hard not to appear obvious about his eavesdropping.

"*I* love you too, Daddy," she replied without the sarcasm. "I just don't understand why you..." She stopped, realizing her voice grew louder to counter her father's. She side-glanced at Ennis who had the good sense to pretend he hadn't heard anything. "I don't understand why you insist on driving home. You can afford a cab–"

"I don't want no damn cab," he yelled again, and she cringed covering the receiver tight with her hand. She heard her father's muted rant beneath her palm, praying Ennis didn't think her family was an inbred tribe from the hills of Tennessee – or Mars.

Without uncovering the earpiece, she told R.J., "I'll be there in two hours. Bye, Daddy."

The phone dropped in the cradle, leaving her debating over ripping the whole thing from the wall or just outright shooting it. In that brief time, her body went from energized to exhausted. Instead of spending an enjoyable evening with her handsome partner, she'd spend it alone on the road to bail her cranky, inebriated father.

She went to the entry table, shoulders dropped in defeat, and clipped her badge to her belt, then added her holster and phone.

Ennis turned from the picture gallery, "What's wrong?"

What isn't wrong is more like it. "Daddy needs me."

Ennis offered to help and for a fanciful, almost insane moment, she entertained letting him. Then her rational mind reminded her she wanted Ennis to like her, not run away like his feet were on fire and his ass was catching.

She grabbed her purse, made what she thought was a reasonable excuse then apologized for cutting their night short. She went to him, wanting another pleasurable memory to accompany her on the trip to Augusta. Her hands framed his face, relishing the five o'clock shadow scratching against her palms. She let herself imagine how that scratchy beard might feel in other places as she pressed her lips to his. "I'm sorry about this," she said.

Ennis closed his eyes, let her dictate the length and depth of the kiss. When she parted, he wanted to know, "How sorry are you? Sorry enough to have a drink with me tomorrow?"

She smiled, "Sorry enough to skip the drinks and dance beneath the stars with you."

32

NOW

A lot changed when a person slept off a Rufie. Once Savannah regained enough faculties to think straight, she learned Adam Rafferty tracked down the Tahoe rental at ATL Rentals – a Tahoe registered to Rachel Gordon of Charleston. The same Rachel Gordon who also happened to work at Mercy Hospital and before that, was a nurse in Iraq.

The police found the abandoned Tahoe with bloody clothes, different colored wigs and a pair of bloody gloves. Forensics found fingerprints inside the clear latex gloves matching Rachel's. During that time, Owen Dunne contacted Rachel's coworkers who described her as overly obsessed with Georgia ever since Matthew broke up with her.

Inside Rachel's apartment police found a journal on her computer that mentioned killing Matthew and a reference to how handy it would be to pin the murder on Georgia. For all their progress, they still hadn't located the elusive homicidal nurse but issued an APB for her in Augusta, Atlanta and the surrounding states.

Yes, a lot changed when a person slept off a Rufie. Even her family. Savannah meandered the living room, surprised that she felt among the living so quickly. She had no recollection of the GHB, at least not in detail. The last thing she clearly recalled was dropping Adam off at the station and feeling hopeless about Georgia's situation. After that, all hell must have broken loose because Adam, Marcus and Ray called to check on her when she arrived at the house. It was later, after being released from the hospital that her family filled in her memory. Under the influence, she apparently was conscious enough to warn Georgia that Rachel planned to kill her. She vaguely recalled Ennis standing beside her at one point but that was all. According to Georgia, a vicious disagreement broke out among the family in regards to Savannah's physical condition and nearly ended with her father shoving his double barrel shotgun down Ennis's throat and pulling the trigger. Between Seth and Dane, they managed to avoid bloodshed between the two.

The residual headache faded from the pounding monster it once was. The fatigue took longer but her strength slowly returned with the passing hours. None of this bothered her more than the looks. Her daddy maintained a safe distance from her as if she'd wielded the shotgun at *him* – or had contracted a rare, incurable disease – then he kept asking if she was normal yet, whatever that meant. Georgia and Leah sported sheepish, almost humorous smirks around her. Seth just ignored her and stayed out of her sight. It was Ennis who confused her most. The instant he saw her, he blushed as his hand raced to his zipper, covering it until he moved at least five feet away from her. Why was everyone acting so *weird* around her?

Ennis walked in the kitchen, spied his wife and immediately his hand went to his fly.

"Ennis, what the," she lowered her voice to a whisper in case kids were nearby, "*hell* is wrong with you?" She motioned to his crotch, "Have you developed a nervous habit about your zipper?"

Wide-eyed, Ennis referred to Georgia and Leah who sat at the dining table with their coffee cups. He shrugged like *what do I do?*

Georgia accepted the task of broaching the subject. She cleared her throat uneasily, "Hon, you know the effects of GHB."

Savannah nodded, "It causes unconsciousness, amnesia, nausea, and so on. What happened, did I puke on his pants?"

Leah added, "It can also increase sex drive and considerably reduce inhibitions."

"You can say that again," Savannah heard her husband mumble. From the corner of her eye, Savannah watched his grasp on his zipper tighten. She ignored it, "What, was I horny or something?"

"Or something," Georgia fought back a giggle.

R.J. stepped in the kitchen, stood behind Savannah, "You normal yet?"

She spun on her heel, demanding, "What does *that* mean?"

His vision passed across the others, "You ain't told her?" He shook his head, "Ya brought pure shame on yourself. Began to wonder if you was even my child."

Even as her mouth dropped in shock, she searched her brain for any hint to what disgraceful actions prompted her daddy to say such a terrible thing. She drew a blank. Instead she grabbed Ennis's arm, "You're gonna tell me what happened and *get your hand off your pants already..."*

Twenty minutes later she appeared at the kitchen door, crimson-faced, and utterly unable to meet anyone's gaze.

"You normal yet?" R.J. inquired again, downing a swallow of scotch.

She hung her head, mortified and humiliated at her behavior the night before, "Yes, Daddy, I'm normal."

Georgia rose from the dining chair, put an arm around her waist, "Hon, it was the GHB. There's no reason to feel ashamed. You weren't in control, the drug was."

"Tell that to Ennis. He's using his hand as a chastity belt – against his own wife. He acts like I came after him with a knife, not my libido."

"*Savannah Charlene...*" R.J. scolded. "You said you was *normal.*"

She defended her statement, "Well, you never ran from Mama when she–"

"Shut up until ya find your mind." He rose, gathered the scotch bottle and glass to abscond to the living room, "No more sex talk in this house."

Her shoulders slumped and she sighed. A familial leper, that's how she felt. The worst part: she hadn't one vague memory of her behavior. At least Georgia still loved her, annoying as she was when she laughed at her kid sister's misfortune.

Leah salved her hurt feelings when she too joined her and Georgia. She wrapped Savannah in a hug, "We're just glad you're okay."

R.J. sank into the wingback facing the kitchen. His frowning features settled on his youngest. After several moments, he turned his attention to Ennis sitting on the couch then poured himself another glass of scotch.

Dane entered the kitchen, "Hey, group hug. Count me in." He stretched his arms around the three women as far as they could go. When he pulled away he winked at Savannah, "Lookee here. We got our bride *and* our matron of honor back in action. Now if I could get my best man to disassociate his hand from his crotch long enough, I'd be ready for marriage tomorrow."

"God bless, boy," R.J. exclaimed rather disgustedly from the living room. This time the reprimand went to Ennis, "Let go of yourself. Neither you or my daughter are right in the head anymore."

33

NOW

Georgia and Savannah climbed in the Tahoe to go for the final fit on Georgia's wedding dress. The sweet smell of their towering magnolia wafted in the open windows as they backed down the driveway. For Savannah it inspired thoughts of relaxing on the porch with her sister, both indulging in a glass of sweet tea and listening to the birds sing. She'd mention it to Georgia when they got back home.

Until then, Savannah volunteered to accompany Georgia on her travels, not just for companionship but for protection. The police's search for Rachel Gordon garnered dismal results. No one could find her. No matter how invisible Rachel wanted to be, she was still out there, hunting Georgia down and Savannah intended to stop her. But right now she needed to know why her sister stared at her, "What is it?"

Georgia gave her a once over, "You've lost more weight since the last fitting. We can still get alterations on your dress."

She waved it off, "I'm fine. I won't drop much more weight anyway. The stress of this family keeps me from it."

According to Georgia's expression, that decision was

unequivocally unacceptable.

"Okay," Savannah capitulated, "we'll check the fit today."

Georgia slanted her a grin, turned left off Walton Way onto Highland Avenue, "I can't believe the wedding is next month."

"And you're not crazy yet. Congratulations. I was bonkers a month before my wedding and I had the least amount to do. Thanks to you, Mama and Bobbi, I just had to show up and say *I do*. Give those two the reins to anything and they'll drive it like a herd of cattle, like you do." Truth was, all Mama Rutherford and Ennis's sister-in-law required was a hint of a wedding and they diagramed, graphed, mapped and strategized the entire event down to the last second. Throw Georgia in the mix and nothing dared fail or had the audacity to try.

"Now I'm a trail boss? I thought I was General Georgia," she winked at her sister whose mouth dropped open in shock. Georgia found it funny, "I always knew about the nickname. I don't mind it."

Savannah turned away, her cheeks rosy, "It *is* a compliment, no matter how I meant it back then."

Georgia stopped at a four-way stop, "I need to pick up more Thank You notes too."

"Getting too many toasters?"

"Actually just one. I got a cast iron skillet from Dane's cousin though."

"Uh-oh. Is it for cooking a side of bacon or for keeping your new hubby in line?"

Georgia smiled, "Funny you should say that. She included a note calling it the *Attitude Adjuster.*"

Savannah raised a brow, "Say what you will but the Rutherfords know each other well."

The two shared a laugh until a voice at the window startled them, "Hello, ladies."

Shee-yet, Savannah winced. I recognize that voice... For all their searching, the cops never found Rachel Gordon. Well, they should have tailed Georgia's Tahoe, kinda like Rachel had. Then they could slap cuffs on the bitch.

Savannah and Georgia turned to face her. Since Savannah last saw her, Ms. Gordon's appearance digressed from runway chic to something the cat dragged in. Dark circles ringed her eyes from lack of sleep, her wardrobe scaled down to old worn jeans and an olive green t-shirt with "Marines" stamped in black across the front. The t-shirt, once obviously Matthew's, swallowed her. What held Savannah's attention, however, was the .38 pointed at Georgia and the unsteady grasp holding it. Rachel's finger rested precariously on the trigger, "Unlock the door."

The last time they met, Ms. Gordon resembled none other than Ted Bundy with her composure. Not only had she risked being caught slipping GHB in Savannah's drink, she recovered flawlessly when Marcus Slocum arrived and threw a glitch in her plan. Today though, her cool, unflustered nature flew the little coop between her ears. The woman verged on squeezing that trigger right there in public with possible witnesses. And, unlike the other day, she didn't seem to care.

Rachel pressed the barrel to Georgia's temple, "Unlock the door *now.*"

"Better unlock it," Savannah said.

With obvious disdain, Georgia mashed the button. All four doors unlocked in unison. Rachel climbed in the back. As she did so, Savannah casually slipped her .38 from its holster, hoping their new guest didn't notice. From the corner of her eye, she watched Rachel reach for the door to close it and lifted her .38 just as the woman pushed her weapon against the back of Georgia's head, "Bad idea, Savannah. Hand me your gun."

In a split-second, she weighed her options – not that there were any viable ones. She refused to sacrifice her sister to some maniac bent on unwarranted revenge but she also hated parting with their only means of protection.

Georgia cut her vision to her sister. Without a word, she pleaded with her to do as she was told. Savannah lowered the gun, slowly advanced it forward until Rachel snatched it from her grasp. "Thank you," Georgia whispered.

Don't thank me yet, she wanted to say. We just handed over our only insurance policy.

Rachel stabbed Savannah's .38 at her, "I want both your phones. Give me yours first. Do it slowly."

Savannah's hand moved to her left hip, her right hand in plain sight. She slid the phone free from her belt, handed it over.

"Now Georgia's. And keep your hands where I can see them."

Hands at shoulder height, Savannah pointed to the center console between the front seats, "Her phone's in there." The large console opened to hold items as big as a laptop so it accommodated Georgia's purse with ease. The fact it was a closed compartment seemed to agitate

Rachel who changed her mind, "Leave it. Georgia, we're going to the orchards. Drive."

They drove down Washington Road in silence. Georgia veered onto the highway toward Westside but kept the speed slower than the speed limit. She cut her eyes to Savannah on occasion. They exchanged looks, silently asking if the other had any ideas on how to escape the psycho. Problem was, nothing came to mind short of leaping from the moving vehicle.

"What are you trying to prove, Rachel?" Savannah inquired. "You've already murdered Matthew and for what?"

"Because he refused to give Georgia up. He still loved her – or what he called love – until his last breath. I wanted him to love me, not her." She reinforced the confession by jabbing the gun at Georgia's neck.

"I thought he did," Savannah continued. "After all, he broke his wedding vows to be with you."

"According to him, I was a stand-in for his wife. But during his rehabilitation, he said he loved me. I asked if he loved me enough to divorce Georgia. The liar said yes."

"He just agreed out of the blue?" Something sounded hinky about that. Remembering back, Matthew prided himself on Georgia. He may have treated Savannah like the dog that peed on his shoes, but he put Georgia on a pedestal. For him to up and decide to ditch the love of his life rang a sour note and always had.

Rachel scooted across the seat, positioning herself between the two but kept the gun solidly against the back of Georgia's head. Neither sister turned but Savannah noticed Georgia checking the rearview mirror.

Rachel's smartass side sprang forth, "Well, he did have a little help with that decision considering the levels of morphine in his system. He signed those papers the moment they arrived."

Georgia's self-control splintered. She spun to face Rachel, "You forced those papers on him?"

Savannah reached for the steering wheel to steady it. Geez, if some nutcase nurse didn't finish them off, Georgia's temper would. Rachel laughed, goading Georgia. Savannah suspected Rachel wanted Georgia to lose control, to justify killing her, at least to herself.

"Georgia," Savannah warned, "drive the damn car. I don't feel like being scraped off the pavement today."

For an instant, Georgia's lethal scowl transferred to Savannah then she gripped the wheel until her knuckles blanched.

"I didn't force anything on him," Rachel assured. "He contacted the lawyer, not me. He signed the papers, I didn't."

"Then what exactly is your problem with Georgia? Matthew left *her*." Savannah recoiled against the seat with a flinch, realizing how that sounded to her sister. But, she'd argue, she only tried to set the crazy lady straight.

Tears glistened in Georgia's eyes. Savannah whispered an apology. Her sister still cared for Matthew no matter how they parted, no matter how dead he was.

A sudden pressure in her side refocused Savannah's attention. Rachel pressed the gun against her ribs, "Because the bastard kept throwing her into me. That I didn't measure up, that Georgia did this and Georgia did that. " She scowled at the driver, "She's terribly difficult to live up to."

"And throwing her into you. I'll bet this came after the morphine cleared his system, am I correct?" Savannah winced when the gun shoved deep beneath her ribs.

Georgia offered her two cents, "Don't provoke her. She probably *will* shoot you. She *did* drug you, after all."

And that sparked her ire, "Yeah, thanks for that. I've never had a lovelier trip to the hospital."

Rachel seemed insulted, "I promise your next trip will be permanent – and it won't be to a hospital."

"No regard for human life," Savannah said to no one in particular. "That's certainly not in the nurse's handbook. Our sister-in-law would gnaw off her own hand before hurting any–"

Rachel's reply came in the form of a solid, meaningful jab of the gun. It not only cut off Savannah's thought but shut down her mouth as well.

Georgia shrugged with a reminder, "I told you to shut up."

They drove in silence along the highway for the next several minutes. Savannah used the time to scour her brain for a solution. Rachel intended to kill them both. In a symbolic gesture she chose the orchards for the act. Savannah bet the woman planned to do the deed right in front of the sign where they found Matthew.

With no weapons at their disposal, she saw no real alternatives other than ambush Rachel if they could. She saw one huge flaw in that plan. The unstable nurse retained custody of all the firepower and didn't seem reluctant to use them either.

Savannah wished Adam had maintained a police presence for Georgia's safety but he believed Rachel fled Augusta once her name and face were distributed to law enforcement and the media.

Cars in the distance shimmered in the heat rising from the asphalt. Mirages of water stretched across the road. What a miserable day to be held captive by an idiot and the worst kind of day to die. Temperatures the last week reminded Savannah of summer in Vega, Texas. Only fools and tourists presumed the Texas Panhandle never roasted in hundred degree heat. Nothing except experience taught the unwitting newcomer that the same place that sweated blood in July could also receive *feet* of snow in December. It was the most unstable place she'd ever visited. The Rutherfords' favorite saying: *if you don't like the weather, wait five minutes.* With absolute shock and chagrin, Savannah attested it was no joke. When Georgia and Dane set the wedding for August, she bit her tongue against calling them nuts. August was July's twin in that inhospitable oven of a place. They'd be lucky to feel a whisper of a breeze. The wind blew harder there than on Neptune, she said, *except* in the dead of summer.

They neared the turn off to the orchard entrance, leaving Savannah questioning whether there would be a wedding at all. Then a seed of an idea sprouted into an actual plan. It would take luck but hopefully not much. All she needed was her sister to be on the same mental channel with her.

Georgia slowed and activated the blinker, signaling her intent to turn. The car wheeled onto the narrow road and stopped directly inside the highway exit. Savannah knew why. To let passers-by see them.

Good idea but she had a better one. Savannah gave a subtle nod toward the gate. *Pull forward. Closer to the gate.*

Her sister let off the brake, eased the Tahoe forward until Savannah cleared her throat, "What now, Rachel?"

The woman lifted the .38, "Open the gate."

"I can't," she lied. She continued before Georgia contradicted her, "The manager is the only one who can."

The gun's barrel jammed against her temple. Rachel's finger tightened on the trigger, "Don't treat me like an idiot, Savannah. I know you can open that gate. You *own* the place."

She fought to keep her cool despite the raging panic. Rachel's composure wavered into dangerous territory and Savannah cautioned herself to pick her words with care. She closed her eyes, focusing on her reply, "But the manager lives here. Today the place is closed and he's locked the gate. We gave him the right to lock it down when the orchards are closed."

If Georgia doubted her plan, she displayed a perfect poker face, "It's true. Ray deserves privacy since this is his residence."

The news upset Rachel. Georgia sat, foot on the brake, not daring to meet her sister's gaze. She directed her vision to the mirror, measuring Rachel's mood.

"This'll have to do." The woman motioned with the gun, "Both of you get out."

Savannah waited for Georgia to shift into Park, shut off the engine. The two exchanged a brief glance before opening their doors.

Rachel waved Savannah aside, "Sit in front of the sign." Then swung the weapon between sisters, "Georgia, you stand by the gate."

Savannah took her time nearing the sign. Her mind raced with ways to distract the unpredictable woman. She prayed Ray heard the alarm announcing a car on the premises and prayed he checked the monitor. Her plan depended on her reliable old friend.

She lifted her hands in surrender to Rachel – and in full view of the camera – as a clue for Ray to call for help. Rachel stood close enough Ray could clearly see the gun in her hand.

Rachel approached her, held the .38 at arm's length while aiming at Savannah's head, "Turn around and kneel at the sign. Keep your hands flat on top of the bricks."

Paving stones, Savannah silently corrected for some unknown reason. It didn't matter what surrounded the destroyed flower garden. What did matter was the idea of dying, particularly at the hands of Matthew Carlisle's screwy mistress. The mob-ish command sounded almost comical if the woman hadn't brandished a gun. Savannah had been bullied by more imposing criminals than a rogue nurse and let her know it, "I've encountered formidable foes in my life and most of them had the decency to face me before they tried to kill me. If you're gonna shoot me, have the guts to look me in the eyes when you pull that trigger." She saw Georgia shake her head, heard her groan a plea not to provoke Rachel. Well, someone had to rile the bitch, she answered back with a frown. If she stirred her up, Georgia might be able to save herself at least.

Savannah unexpectedly stumbled sideways when Rachel shoved her. She tripped over a petrified plant that the cops had mined days earlier from the flower bed. She fought to retain her footing but her right leg buckled, slamming the knee straight into the paving stone wall. She landed on her backside with a cringe. *Shee-yet, that hurt.* The old golf injury pinged with a memory of ice packs and ibuprofen (and a slug or two of bourbon). None of which looked viable in the foreseeable future if she didn't disarm Rachel. One violent shove from a morally corrupt lunatic aggravated the previous injury that had, until then, lay dormant for years. That alone fired Savannah mad. She'd give that crazy bitch what she deserved then thrust her head so far into the flower bed only her feet stuck out.

C'mon, Ray, where the hell are you? I'm about to buy the farm and Georgia's next. She resisted glancing at the camera or crying out for Ray's help. Surely he'd seen them. Surely so…

She levered herself up, testing the knee with her weight but fell back, her hand trying to rub the pain out. Well, so much for dispensing justice…

Rachel advanced, the gun firmly in both hands, "Turn. Around."

But she still had her rage – and her dignity. Rachel would not shoot her in the back of the head. "No," she replied in her most defiant tone.

The hammer clicked back. "I said turn around."

Savannah pushed herself upright to sit atop the stone wall, flinched at the ache in her knee, rubbed it, "Lady, you'll have to kill me looking me in the eyes. I don't give in that easily."

In that time, Georgia had been easing toward the Tahoe, hopefully to access her phone so   Savannah wanted to buy her more time.

Rachel sneered at Savannah, "Matthew said you were impossible."

"Matthew was right."

"I wanted to spare you, despite his feelings for you. I didn't want to kill you. I only wanted Georgia but now I understand why he hated you so much. I'll shoot you whether you turn around or not."

How about a commercial break here, Ray? Before the finale of this show ends wrong. Savannah kept her cool while tracking her sister's progress from the corner of her eye. The door opened soundlessly. Georgia reached inside.

Savannah leaned back, propped her hands on the edge of the stone wall. She let her left hand sink into the dirt, scooped up a handful, "It takes a particularly cold-blooded person to pull that trigger while looking the victim in the eyes, Rachel." She saw Georgia open the console, reach in for her purse. Savannah continued with her thought, "You've spent your adult life helping and healing. Saving people's lives. One pull of that trigger and you've destroyed more than one life. Yours, mine, my family's, especially my baby daughter's life. And why?"

The lecture fueled Rachel's ire, the gun trembled in her grasp, "Because you won't stay out of my business. I loved Matthew. I wanted him to love me."

"Tell me how I interfered with that."

Her frustration mounted at Savannah's supposed ignorance, "You interfered with the investigation. If you'd left well enough alone, I could have had my revenge sooner and gone home."

"Personally, I'm not too keen on revenge," Savannah stated with absolute calm. "I just sit back and let karma take over. Like now," she flung the handful of dirt into Rachel's eyes.

Rachel's free hand furiously wiped at her eyes, aimed the .38 wherever she thought Savannah might be. Then she fired a shot. A shot that missed Savannah's hip by two feet but the next one promised to nail her squarely in the chest.

Somehow the pain of her knee diminished compared with the idea of being aerated by Smith & Wesson. She launched herself at the gun. Her fingers were within inches of subduing the weapon when Rachel tightened her hold and jabbed it directly against the detective's heart. "Step back, Savannah," she warned.

Savannah instantly froze at the murderous glint in Rachel's eyes. She'd seen that glint a few times in her professional life, usually with desperate people. Trapped, desperate people who had nothing left to live for. So she took that step backward, lifted her hands shoulder high, "Take it easy, Rachel."

"Don't," Rachel stabbed the gun toward her, "tell me to take it easy. Just shut up. Georgia," she called, not looking back, "get away from the car and come over here." She pointed in front of the sign.

Georgia had her purse in hand. She hadn't had enough time to get her phone. She dropped the purse in the seat, slammed the door hard.

Rachel turned, zeroed in on Georgia, lifted the .38. She wasn't waiting for Georgia to comply. She was going to shoot her right then, right there. Savannah lunged again, her fist coming down hard on Rachel's wrist. The gun fired into the ground but the woman never loosened her grip on it.

"Drop that gun or I'll shoot you like the polecat you are," a new voice commanded.

Georgia immediately sprung a flood of tears. Savannah nearly collapsed with relief. Ray Slocum stood with cane leaned against his thigh, his twelve gauge Winchester braced against his shoulder. He yanked the slide and aimed straight at Rachel. A chill ran down Savannah's back at his expression. If she were Rachel, one look would have convinced her to surrender the piddling .38.

Ray ordered, "You girls open that gate, come on in. I'll handle this one."

Except Rachel refused to drop the weapon. Instead, she swung the gun, aiming straight at Ray. He jerked the trigger on the shotgun. The ear-shattering blast sent both sisters ducking for safety as the recoil sent him back a step. He shouldered the gun once more, "That was the only warnin' you're gettin'. Drop the gun," he pulled the slide for a fresh shot, "or I drop you."

Georgia threw open the gate and Savannah raced to Ray, relieving him of the shotgun. She braced it against her shoulder, "I won't let my friend go to jail for killing you but rest assured, my intentions are just as decisive as his. Drop that gun."

"I called the po-lice," Ray spoke with pride. "They'll be here soon."

Georgia wrapped him in a hug, "Thank you, Ray."

"You parked in the right spot, Miss Georgia. That security system you installed, it alerted me lickety-split someone was here. Then I saw that despicable woman and what she was doin' to you girls. Took me a minute to load my shotgun or I'da been out here sooner."

The longest minute of our lives... Savannah blew out a breath, grateful he arrived when he had. "You were just in time, Ray." She stalked around the gate to Rachel, the shotgun aimed within five feet of her nose, "You don't drop that gun and get on your knees in two seconds, I'll show you what it takes to kill someone while looking them in the eyes."

With a blistering expletive, Rachel tossed the .38 into the flower bed, descended to her knees.

Savannah heard the distinct whine of sirens and saw tiny strobes of red and blue appear in the distance. For that speedy response, Ray evidently read the riot act to 911, telling them to step on it. Until Richmond County arrived, however, she'd keep the twelve gauge pointed between Rachel's perfectly arched eyebrows.

An army of police cars raced down the highway, clogging both lanes, and sending motorists veering to the sides of the road. Four patrol units and a detective's sedan came to a screeching stop. Adam Rafferty and Owen Dunne led the pack in their unmarked Ford, the former exiting the vehicle as if it were ablaze. By the time Owen extricated his doughy frame from the car, Adam already had Rachel handcuffed.

Adam's red face glistened with sweat, his words flew out of his mouth as fast as the car raced down the highway, "We were on the other side of town when Ray's call came in. I drove a hundred down the highway."

In contrast, Owen's complexion drained to an ashen gray, telling

Savannah that Mr. Dunne disliked his partner's driving style. Owen braced himself against the fender, held his hand to his mouth. Oh yes, she smiled at him. She'd been green around the gills too when Ennis drove a little supersonic Acura. He drove foot to the floor, heading straight for Warp Nine.

Owen slanted Rafferty a nauseous scowl, "A hundred? I clocked nearly *one-twenty* at one point. I hate riding with you."

Savannah handed the shotgun off to Ray who, along with Georgia, had ventured from behind the gate to join the crowd. Adam wiped a hand down his face, finally calming down, "Is everyone alright? No bloodshed?"

"No bloodshed," Savannah confirmed, still passing a concerned glance at Owen. He digressed from bracing against the car to leaning onto his knees. She dredged scant sympathy for him after the nightmare they'd been through because of him. She addressed Adam, "You'll find Rachel's gun in the back seat of the Tahoe and my .38 is in what's left of the flower bed." She approached Rachel, bent down and stuck her hand in the woman's back pocket for her phone. She slipped it back on her belt with great ceremony then pointed to the wrecked out flower bed, "We're sending the department a bill for that mess. Those were nice flowers."

"And," Georgia added with a snooty, "certainly not cheap."

Adam shrugged, "Go ahead and send it. I can't guarantee anything but you can try. Maybe Bobby will approve the funds."

"Our cousin better own up to something," Savannah snapped. "Going MIA on us and not returning my calls. Where'd he go, the moon?"

Rafferty elected not to say. Instead he replied, "I have a feeling that's the only safe place for him, at least from you."

A groan drew Savannah's attention to Owen who'd chanced standing without the assistance of propping or leaning. The worst of the nausea passed, she assumed, but not for long when she firmly suggested, "If the department doesn't pay, Owen will. Won't you?"

The meager color that had returned to his cheeks now sank back to his toes, forcing his hands to his knees again, "Rafferty should pay too. Don't heap all the cost on me."

"Why not?" she asked. "You heaped all the blame on my family for Carlisle's demise. Better pray Richmond County isn't miserly with their budget."

He looked at her, challenging, "How much could a bunch of petunias cost anyway?" His ignorance and unwarranted confidence nearly made her laugh. He forgot: Georgia selected the arrangement with Roy Carlson's help and when Georgia chose flowers she went gold and platinum, not run-of-the-mill petunias and daisies.

Savannah choked back a laugh. Georgia, on the other hand, scoffed at the question, "I'll have you know, Mr. Owen Dunne, that those flowers were *not* petunias. We planted Lilies of the Valley, purple Lisianthus, Hydrangeas and more. I'll compose a list for you but the cost was, at the time, nine hundred dollars."

Owen wilted against the car once more, muttering a curse under his breath. This time he looked down for the count, "Rafferty..."

Adam shook his head with vehemence, "No way. You're the one

who told 'em to search the flowers, not me."

Ray chuckled, "Miss Georgia and Miss S'vannah stirrin' up a hornet's nest. Nice to see *them* sweat for a change."

Both sisters shared a glance and a smile, agreeing with their friend. Ray shooed the two sisters behind the gate, "Let's go inside. It's too hot out here. We'll celebrate that polecat's arrest with some tea."

Adam called Savannah, "Before you go, I need yours and Georgia's statements."

Ray poked his cane at Rafferty with a vehement shake of his head, "You ain't doin' no business on this property, young man. You done caused enough trouble already."

Savannah smirked at the older man's declaration, "Adam, we'll come by the station before two."

She joined her sister and their protective, very vocal orchard manager on the trek to his house. She'd done this many times in her life, from toddler to adult. The gate creaked shut behind them, closing them off from the chatter and chaos from the other side. She was with family now, and her family was whole again. No more accusations, aggravations, or police interruptions. Just one happy family waiting for a summer wedding in Texas.

34

NOW

The Rutherford Ranch came alive with purple and lilac. Arrangements of roses and hydrangeas lined the bridal path that ended at a wisteria covered arbor.

Guests occupied all eighty white folding chairs lined in neat rows, forty on the bride's side, and the same on the groom's. Georgia's side accommodated more friends than relatives, the latter including Royal and Vincent Prince and their families – plus one straggler no one expected. Richmond County Sheriff Bobby Prince. He arrived bearing a gift and an apology both of which Georgia graciously accepted but her sister wasn't so quick to forgive. Yes, yes, she understood he was on vacation at the time, she told Georgia, but the bum coulda interceded somehow from beneath his beach umbrella in Hilton Head. A mere one hundred thirty-four miles separated Hilton Head and Augusta. A short trip if you asked her, even shorter by phone. Did a sheepish apology and a Mr. Coffee rate forgiveness for everything Georgia suffered? Apparently so. It was Georgia's day and Georgia said play nice so she did.

Friends packed the remainder of her side of the aisle, including

Avery Dean and Randolph Klein, her agent and publicist. For Dane's side, extended family and friends arrived in droves. In all, Savannah guesstimated half the population of Vega witnessed the nuptials.

Georgia was a vision of stunning splendor when she walked down the aisle. Her violet colored dress reminded Savannah of Southern Belles gussied up for a debutant ball, every one of them sashaying to their male companions saying "I do declare…" Savannah stood in awe of her sister. Movie stars and runway models had nothing on Georgia. She was walking magnificence and a vision of pure beauty on her special day.

While Seth escorted Georgia down the bridal path, Savannah battled her own tears. Her sister would finally have a truly loving, devoted husband (that wasn't crazy). She saw profound love in Georgia's eyes when hers and Dane's gazes met, reminding her of her own trip down the aisle to marry Ennis.

Now, with the vows exchanged and the toasts made, relief set in with such a satisfied tiredness, Savannah eyed one of those white folding chairs for a breather. She allowed herself a moment to recall the morning and how blissful the newlyweds looked while dancing to Elvis Presley's "I Can't Help Falling in Love With You".

The crowd settled in for the reception supper of tangy barbecue and spicy fried chicken (with plenty of side dishes) then dispersed in various directions. Some to the bar for drinks, others to the makeshift dance floor consisting of a large, finely manicured area of grass.

Savannah, however, really wanted to sit down. She gathered her wisteria colored dress, stifled a groan as she eased into the seat and toed her shoes off. She heaved a contented sigh. Georgia and Dane were officially hitched. She let her mind wander to visions of the future when her sister's kids spent weekends with Lily and her siblings and vise versa. She'd bet a hundred bucks Georgia got pregnant in the next two months. Rutherford men were spirited souls, and their energy never flagged. Considering their strength and vitality, it was clear Mama Rutherford ate her Wheaties when carrying her boys.

Savannah leaned back, taking in the sights and sounds around her. Laughter, music, dancing. Seth's kids mingled with Cal's rugrats. Rutherfords of all ages carried on, told stories or kicked up their heels with a dance or two. Georgia's publicist Rand Klein, in his navy three piece suit and Ivy League haircut, flitted around like a butterfly on uppers. Savannah always compared him to a hyperactive Halston, the clothes designer, with his angular jaw and downturned eyes. He was nice looking and friendly but impossible to keep up with. He made the most of the occasion, pointing and directing the photographer here and there for shots of every guest and dozens more of the bride and groom. The man exhausted Savannah, buzzing around like a bee at a hive. Six times he crooked his finger at her, beckoning her for yet another photo with someone or another. She and Ennis barely had five minutes to speak together. They were always being instructed where to stand and with whom and don't forget – *give us your best smile.* Her best smile vacated the premises about thirty minutes ago, she wanted to say, massaging her jaw muscles.

Rand's enthusiasm peaked lately since Georgia's arrest sent her book sales off the charts then skyrocketed again after the police cleared her name. Apparently the old saying was correct. There was no bad publicity. She understood his eagerness to capitalize on the sales spike but a person's face could take only so much smiling…

Savannah glanced at the newlyweds. Dane kept his arm around his bride, held her close while conversing with guests. Georgia reveled in the embrace, and Savannah spied that teenage excitement in her features once more, the look that erased years from her already youthful face.

She marveled at Georgia's resilience. She dealt with plenty in her life. At the tender age of six she welcomed a bratty little sister into her life and approached the situation with a rare maturity. She'd coped with their mother's illness, shouldering responsibilities for all three of Charlene's children and later tackled her death with grit and faith. She married a man who vowed to love and cherish her until death, a man who broke those vows by sleeping with another woman. Georgia hit bottom, regrouped her strength and pride to claw her way back to living and smiling again – with Dane Rutherford's help.

Watching her sister banter back and forth with her newly minted husband, Savannah smiled. She'd predicted disaster with the marriage to Matthew. This time a serene peace cloaked the younger sister from head to toe. This marriage would last. It would stand the test of time and trials. Dane wanted to share his life and love with Georgia. It wasn't a look Savannah detected nor the words he expressed about her sister. She just knew. Dane was Georgia's true love and of anyone, Georgia deserved true happiness *and* the Stupid-Happy feeling Savannah felt with Ennis.

"Hey, Wallflower." A man asked from behind her, "How 'bout a dance?"

She automatically grinned without looking back, "I'll have to clear that with my husband. He's the jealous sort and he's a deadeye with a firearm."

Soft lips pressed a kiss to her cheek, "He won't mind." A hand eased down her arm to her hand, grasping it, "C'mon, gorgeous. Let's go behind the barn – and don't forget those heels."

Her eyes shifted to the mid-heels she'd abandoned moments earlier. Georgia chose them instead of high heels for two reasons. One, she didn't want her matron of honor's heels sinking into the Texas Panhandle ground (a highly unlikely possibility) on her trek down the aisle and two, she realized how self-conscious Savannah was about her height anyway. But the fella behind her seemed enchanted with the idea of her wearing the modest mid-heels.

She curbed a smile, exaggerated her Georgia accent, "Sir, you're terribly forward for a stranger. You are a persuasive man to be sure but I fear your intentions might sully my reputation."

With a hand to her elbow, he urged her to her feet. Ennis stepped around the chair to face her, grinning from ear to ear, "I'll show you sullied, woman. I'll sully you from here to Dallas and back. Now," he tugged her along, "let's go have a private dance – and don't forget the heels."

"Let's go, Casanova," she pecked a kiss to his lips, slipped on the shoes and gathered her dress at the hem for a fast getaway, "Let's get outta here before anyone notices."

They made their way around dancing couples, ducked past Rand who seemed to be on the prowl for more victims. Savannah felt like a teenager skipping class to meet her boyfriend on the sly. She giggled as Ennis led her by the hand, headed straight – as he said – behind the barn.

She drew up short when someone tapped her on the shoulder, cleared her throat. "Uh-oh," Savannah winced. "Busted." She and Ennis wheeled to face Georgia's amused expression. One that said she read her sister and brother-in-law's minds.

Georgia arched one brow – but scarcely held a smile, "Like to tell me why you choose now to escape?"

"Not exactly escaping," was Savannah's roundabout, awkward reply. "Just taking an intermission of sorts."

"Behind a barn." Georgia hinted for additional details.

"We saw a horse," she blurted, trying her best to concoct a decent, believable story. Or sort of believable. "A horse got loose, it's running around," she pointed, "back there." Savannah nudged Ennis with her elbow for confirmation.

Georgia didn't buy a word of it, the gleam in her eye said. Not. One. Word. She crossed her arms, reiterating, "A horse?"

"Yep," Ennis lied with unsettling ease, "can't have that. I'm gonna tie that mare up and teach her a lesson."

Somehow that came out wrong, Savannah thought. Or perhaps he intended for it to. Either way his effortless ability to fib surprised her so much she blushed the color of a fire engine. Then she stared in wide-eyed incredulity at him. *Tie that mare up and teach her lesson?*

Meanwhile Georgia chuckled, "Before you two get too creative with the lassoes in the hay loft, Rand wants Savannah for another picture. After that, you can have your private rodeo."

Oh God, she fanned herself. She'd heard of spontaneous human combustion but never expected to try it. "Georgia..." she admonished. Her sister knew precisely what their plans were – minus the *tying up* part, at least. She was adventurous to a point, but not with lassoes and not in a hay loft – ever.

Her frustration waned when she watched her sister whisper in Ennis's ear.

Ennis bent at the waist, bowing, and swept his arm out in a chivalrous manner, "Let's make Mr. Klein happy so I can tend to that unruly mare."

She and Georgia meandered toward the publicist with Georgia waving him down. She leaned closer to Savannah, "I know Rand is wearing thin with you but if you can tolerate him for another fifteen minutes, we're home free."

She broke into a real smile, "Georgia, I'm fine. This is your day and I'll pose for a million pictures if he wants it. You made the most beautiful bride. Good thing Ennis brought an extra hanky. I stole it from him because I kept tearing up."

"Ladies," a man's voice lilted. The illustrious Rand returned. "Stay right where you are. Don't move."

Savannah watched Rand position the photographer in front of the two, adjusted the man's stance a tad then said, "I want two shots of them just like that." He addressed the sisters, "Best smile, girls. Best smile."

Well, that was easy. With her big sis beside her, joy beamed from Savannah. It was a wonderful day that nearly didn't happen thanks to

Rachel and Matthew. The photographer snapped the photos and Rand turned, scouting the crowd for his next shot.

"Rand," Savannah called.

He wheeled back, giving her his undivided attention. She put her arm around her sister, pulled her close, "One more."

Rand brightened as if it was the finest idea he'd heard, "One more it is."

Georgia's hand at her waist tugged her closer, the two grinned ear to ear at the lens. In that time, Savannah reflected how perfect this moment was. She and her sister embracing on this warm summer evening of new beginnings. Georgia and Dane would fly to Maui for their honeymoon shortly. Ennis and Savannah decided to stay at the ranch until mid-week then head back to Atlanta. Besides her own wedding, this day ranked as the most splendid ever.

The shutter snapped on the camera and the photographer went on his way. Savannah and Georgia surveyed the crowd of friends and family. Seth and Leah stood by the sturdy wooden arbor decorated with white and purple roses. They watched the photographer take the picture then waved at the bride and her matron of honor. Seth had given both sisters away at their weddings and seemed mighty pleased with the fact.

A loud whistle silenced the crowd. Dane waved at his new wife, motioning her to join him. Both women took off in the same direction since Ennis had already migrated to his brother's side. A congregation of family and friends amassed around them as Dane cheerfully inquired, "You ready to do this, bro?"

Savannah looked to her husband, puzzled, "Do what?" She

sincerely prayed it had nothing to do with unruly mares and lassoes. At least not yet…

Georgia took her sister and Ennis by the hand and joined the two together, "There." She stepped back, winked at Ennis, "Go ahead."

Savannah volleyed her vision between Georgia, Dane and Ennis, "What's going on?" She wasn't too keen on surprises and judging by those three, this one was a lulu. Ennis gently tightened his grasp on her hand, addressing her in a most gallant voice, "Mrs. Rutherford."

Despite the confusion, a tiny smile curled the corners of her mouth. Whatever the surprise was, she'd roll with it, "Yes, Mr. Rutherford?"

"A few years ago I made your acquaintance, and after a hundred requests for a date, you finally accepted. Do you remember that day?"

The crowd leaned closer to hear the exchange, most notably Seth and his family, the Prince cousins and every Rutherford from Mama down to third cousins thirty-six times removed. According to their faces, they were as clueless as she was regarding this mysterious conversation.

Savannah couldn't help but smile at the memory of her first date with Ennis, "I remember it well. You sent a beautiful arrangement of lavender roses and chrysanthemums."

"Indeed," her husband replied. "I attached a card with one request written on it."

Intrigued now, the eavesdropping group volleyed their vision to Savannah who now beamed, knowing exactly what he asked, "I'd love to dance beneath the stars with you."

A collective, wistful sigh rose from the ladies while the men cheered and whistled their approval. The group parted like a Red Sea of dresses and suits, giving the couple room to pass through to the dance floor.

She glanced back at Georgia who signaled the deejay for a new song. "Are you and my sister conspiring again?" Savannah asked her husband.

Ennis drew her close, waiting for the music to start. "Maybe a little. Georgia wanted to give you a special gift today. After everything you went through, she planned this for you."

She looked at Georgia who now nestled into her new husband's embrace. Savannah shook her head, still perplexed by the sudden spotlight, "But it's *her* wedding. This day is about her, not me–"

Ennis touched a finger to her lips, shushing her, "She said without you, today wouldn't have happened. Let her do this for you, sugar. Just enjoy."

The song began and within two notes Savannah recognized it. Ennis led into the dance, their bodies aligned so close she felt his heat, smelled the scent of his aftershave. Their steps moved in harmony, and the longer the song played the more she retreated a few years back when she and her new partner danced to the same song a day after their first date – when she promised to dance beneath the stars with him. Barry White's deep, melodious voice sang the refrain of "You're the First, the Last, My Everything". She held to her husband, grateful she surrendered to the Stupid-Happy side of her brain and fell in love with her partner.

Savannah met her sister's gaze, smiled and mouthed *thank you.* Georgia winked and nodded.

I pray that you grow closer as time passes, their mother told Savannah a month before she died. *I pray that someday you're as close as you were as children.*

Savannah's smile widened with a silent reply: *We're more than that now, Mama. We're best friends.*

Savannah relaxed in her husband's embrace, enjoying the feel of being loved by so many people, and thankful to have every one of them in her life.

J.L. Lemon lives in Texas surrounded by a loving and supportive family, two adorable and devoted puppies, and hordes of garden gnomes.

Before 2002, J.L. Lemon wrote opinions and product reviews for an online consumer guide. When fellow reviewers cited the author's knack for humor, she decided to return to writing fiction. Along with the standalone title Second Chances, she's published 11 books in the Savannah Stories Series.

www.ingramcontent.com/pod-product-compliance
Lightning Source LLC
Chambersburg PA
CBHW020922020726
47495CB00002B/309